Boatswain's Mate

By

Pat Johnston

AmErica House
Baltimore

© 2001 by Patrick Johnston.

First printing

ISBN: 1-58851-489-7
PUBLISHED BY AMERICA HOUSE BOOK PUBLISHERS
www.publishamerica.com
Baltimore
Printed in the United States of America

Dedicated to my daughter Venice and my son Charles, who supported
and humored me through all my impractical schemes.

And to my friends who read the first draft and gave me a "thumbs up"!
Jean, Leta, Jim, Graeme & Jennie, Dick, Pam,
Art, Mick, Noelene & Ken, Sue, Don.

Finally, to my sister Henrietta for her encouragement
and to my Swedish grandfather who inspired my
unending love for the sea.

Chapter One

I was a three-month-old embryo when my folks were married back in April 1928 in Hodskins, Oklahoma. When it was known I would be a guest at the wedding, not too people showed up. My Ma's folks were pretty rough and ready; her mother was a Cherokee Indian, so a few cousins and uncles from the reservation showed up for the free beer. None of my Pa's people were there, or so I heard, except for my Grandpa.

I learned to love my Grandpa the short time I knew him. He told me stories about fighting Indians and going places before there were places to go. I had no reason to doubt his tales; to a ten-year-old he was Kit Carson, General Custer and Daniel Boone all rolled up into one. He could whip anybody's ass, even though he was in his sixties, at least that was the challenge I threw out to all my friends and acquaintances. Poor old Grandpa wouldn't have been too happy with all the fights I put him up for. Fortunately, he never had to prove himself on my account.

He passed away the winter of my tenth year. How I cried. I damn near took his old long-barreled pistol and shot myself. Can we ever go back just one more day and make things different? I wished it so, but wishing ain't getting.

The next couple of years passed by quickly. It had been tough in Oklahoma and the dust bowl had driven most everybody out west to California. I sure missed my Grandpa; I found myself talking to him out loud sometimes when I was alone. I could hear him say "John Calhoun Rickmeyer. That's a mite too much name for one boy. Let's jist call ya Jake!" Seems my dad was from the South and one of his heroes was John C. Calhoun, a loud-mouthed Senator from South Carolina. Some folks said the old Senator was responsible for the South seceding and thereby starting the Civil War.

Life was hard in those days, in that part of the country anyway. It was a struggle just to get through the day and get enough gravy on the plate to at least wet the bread.

Then my dad was killed in a farm accident. He was helping some down-on-his-luck friend try to get a grain hopper working. The damn thing started just the one time it wasn't supposed to and tore my Dad's arm almost off. He didn't have a chance. By the time they ran for help, found an old truck, and drove him into town, he was dead. That was just after my thirteenth birthday, it happened January 10, 1942. I remember the day so clearly. The Japanese

5

had just attacked Pearl Harbor the month before and the United States was at war. My Dad was dead, and I only had my Grandpa to talk to through that first lonely day. Relatives and neighbors were coming and going at the house all day, but I needed to be alone, to think things through. The funny thing about it was my Dad's death never hurt me has much as Grandpa's had -- the reason being I had Grandpa to "talk" to; someone I knew cared about me and knew how I felt. I usually climbed up on One-Tree-Hill to talk with Grandpa; but on this nasty, cold winter's day I had to settle for a dusty, mouse-infested pile of old seed bags in a corner of the barn. I was lonely and lost, wondering what would happen to my Mom and me now.

I kept going to school and working around the place over the next couple of years, at least enough to keep the goddamn bankers from foreclosing. My Mom had to take in laundry for a few extra dollars.

Then she found another man. I was fifteen at the time, tall, strong and lifting hundred-pound hay bales like they were feather-filled pillows. That was the summer I was feeling my oats. Lionel Shanks, my best friend, and I got Cecelia Summers to come down the river bottom with us. It started with, "You show me yours and I'll show you mine." After a couple of weeks she was showing old Lionel and me every trick in the book. She must have been doing something with somebody else, because she had something new to show us every Saturday.

That summer was the best I can remember in my life. Never did talk to Grandpa much. I guess I was growing up. Then that fall, the new man in my Mom's life started beating the shit out of her and then he turned on me. As big as I was, he was bigger and one mean son-of-a-bitch. I could take a whipping, but I couldn't take seeing my Mom with bruises and black eyes.

The war had been going for some time; the Japs were being beaten all over the Pacific, or so we heard. Hodskins, Oklahoma was never the center of the world, so we just knew what we saw on the newsreels at the local movies or heard on the radio. We kids never talked about it much. Hodskins was a town of 250 people and didn't even have enough kids for a scrap metal drive.

We did have one veteran come home though. He had been shot landing on Tarawa or some other island. One of those million-dollar-wounds, he explained -- not life threatening, but it made him limp. And a "Marine with a limp can't run up the beaches, just get some other motherfucker killed!" so he explained to us a dozen times. Not that we ever got tired of it. We all were talking about signing up and getting in the war when we turned seventeen.

The trouble with the boyfriend came to a head later that fall. I came home from the movies one Saturday night and found my Mom lying naked on the bed; he was drunk and she was barely conscious.

He grabbed me and tried to push my face between his legs. I clamped my mouth shut and fought with all my strength. I got one hand free and grabbed his balls and squeezed. He yelled and threw me clear across the room. I hit the wall scrabbling to keep my feet, jumped back across the bed, and ran out the door.

I ran to the barn shouting, "Grandpa, where the hell are you? I can't leave my Mom in there…but he'll kill me if I go back in."

Whether Grandpa placed it there, or I just picked it up without thinking, the next thing I knew I had a long-handled shovel in my hand.

With piss running down my legs I ran back to the house. I was determined to hit that son-of-a-bitch across the head. When I got to the bedroom he was spread-eagled across the bed passed out and my Mom was trying to cover herself up with the floor mat.

Mom was crying; I was crying. "Jake!" she sobbed, "Ya got to go someplace else, anywhere…just get away from here!"

"What about you?" I replied, looking at that creep on the bed, with my anger blinding me. "Let's just kill the bastard and bury him out back, no one will know."

"They'll know, they'll find out," she whimpered, "I'll be Okay…I'll hide his booze. It's you he wants to hurt anyway. That's why he's so mean to me, he's jealous of you."

"Where can I go?" I asked desperately. I struggled to keep from driving that shovel through his skull, and half hoped he'd wake up and come at me. That would be all the reason I needed, but Mom was pushing me out of the room. "I'm not leaving you here!" I yelled.

"Please…please, for my sake Jake," she pleaded. "Just go…I promise I'll go to Uncle Joe's tomorrow. He won't come over there. He means to hurt you and I know he will."

"Damn, don't do this to me," I sobbed. She was right, of course. I had to get out of there. Mom and me had never been close; Grandpa was the only one who'd ever shown any real interest in me. Dad was just somebody who lived at the house, and my Mom was just somebody who fixed our meals.

It was true what she said, though. The drunken jerk would never follow her over to Uncle Joe's. Old Uncle Joe would put a shotgun up his ass just as soon as pick peas.

I took what clothes I could fit into a pillowcase and ran over to Lionel's place. It was late and I had to tap on his window.

"What the hell?" Lionel said through closed lips as he opened the window, "You crazy son-of-a...what the?"

"Let me in, it's freezing out here!" I said through chattering teeth.

We talked through most of the night in whispers; by dawn we had decided I should join the Navy. I had only just had my sixteenth birthday October 4th, but we'd heard some guys were getting in underage. The recruiters in Lawton weren't too fussy. I was big for my age and I could talk a good yarn. I made Lionel promise he'd check on my Mom, and then we must have dozed off.

The next thing Lionel's mom was shaking us awake. She was a good woman, never had been farther than her own backyard fence, but understood better than Lionel or me what was going on.

She made me get cleaned up, and then gave me a breakfast of ham and eggs and a big glass of fresh milk. She laughed, and said that was probably the last good breakfast I'd get for a while. Lionel, along with his dad, drove me into Lawton. I was shaking in my boots when they dropped me off at the recruiting office.

"I wish you were coming with me," I said to Lionel as he got out of the old Ford pickup and walked with me to the doorway.

"Oh, I got to help the folks...besides, you'd just get me in trouble with them gals out in California, or wherever else they send y'all!" Lionel grinned.

"Oh, oh, goddamn it Lionel!" I exclaimed. "I forgot to get my Grandpa's pistol. It's on top of the third rafter in from the barn doors, stuck in the elbow joint." In desperation I pleaded, "Will you promise you'll get it for me? It don't work a damn, but it's mine. I'll get it from you when this war's over and I get back."

"I'll get it for ya, don't worry...just as soon as that asshole at your place moves out," Lionel said, with a slight break in his voice, "You just take care of yourself. Remember the stories that veteran told us about seeing guys with their heads blown off."

"I will buddy, you take care too," I said, shaking his hand, "I guess I better go in before I crap myself standing out here."

Watching Lionel get back in the truck, and seeing him and his dad drive away was the loneliest feeling I'd ever experienced. I had the strongest urge to run after them and climb back in the cab. The truck was warm, they were my friends, and I was lost without direction.

"Hey lad, you comin' in?" An old guy in the uniform of a chief petty officer called out through the door.

I took a deep breath, stuck my one free hand in my pocket so he wouldn't see how much I was shaking, and went in.

"Ya got somethin' to show your age boy?" the Chief said as he took down my name and particulars, filling in a form.

"I lost most of my stuff coming over here. Don't think I'd have time to get a new birth certificate before the war would be over!" I said, as I tried to sound like I'd seen it all before and this was just another chore I needed to do.

"Yeah, you're probably right. If you swear you're seventeen, and your birthdate is October 4, 1927…well, that's good enough for me," he said, without looking up from his forms. "We have two more young fellas signed up for a medical tomorrow morning. If ya like, I'll put your name on the list; only thing is, if ya get a clean bill of health, we'd want y'all sworn in straight away."

"That's okay with me, Sir. Then what?" I said, without any idea of what was in store for me.

"Then y'all will be in the Navy. We're gonna get you and them other two fellas on a bus to San Diego; comes through just before five o'clock from Oklahoma City," he stated, looking at me as if I should already know this. "Like ya said, this war's gonna be over before y'all get skivvies issued," he added.

"That's fine with me, Sir. I want to get in this war just as fast as I can," I said with bravado. Just so goddamn glad I didn't have to wait a week; I didn't have a dime in my pockets.

"Okay, there it is…sign here. If ya pass that medical tomorrow, y'all will be in the United States Navy," he said proudly. "Be here at 0800 sharp!" he snapped after I'd signed on the dotted line.

I walked out of the office, relieved that it had been that easy. But where was I going to spend the night? What was I going to eat? Should I hightail it back home and see how Mom was doing? Should I just hop a freight train and keep going? "Goddamn it Grandpa, I'm not sure what I'm doing here," I whispered to myself.

I was at the office at 0700 hours next morning, standing outside the door shivering; I had curled up in an alley doorway all night and hadn't slept a wink. I was so damn hungry I could have eaten the crotch out of Cecelia Summers' panties right then and there! It was about seven-thirty when the old chief showed up.

"Well I'll be jiggered! Y'all gonna go far in this man's Navy if ya show up this early for duty," he laughed, somehow implying a joke I didn't quite get. He unlocked the door, stomped his boots on the mat, and went in. I did the same, half-a-step behind him, glad to get in out of the cold.

"Ya know how to make coffee?" he asked.

9

"Yes, Sir!" I replied, perking up as the warmth thawed the numbness in my hands.

"Good, then make us some. The fixings are in the kitchen, pot's on the stove," the old man said with a grin. "Make it Navy style, good an' strong and hotta than a turret barrel!" By the time I'd made the coffee and gulped down half a cup, washing down the dozen cookies I'd found in the kitchen, I heard voices in the outer office. Taking a full cup out to the Chief, I saw two guys standing in front of his desk.

"This here's John Rickmeyer," the Chief said, jerking a thumb in my direction. "John, this here's Edward Morrow and Tyler Dicks. They'll be with you on the trip," he nodded towards the other two.

The one called Edward Morrow grinned and offered me his hand. I knew I was going to like him. The other guy was a skinny, weasel-faced kid a little older than me. He offered me his hand, but his grip was soft and his hand felt slimy. I shook both guys hands firmly, feeling the strength in Ed Morrow's grip. Yeah, I knew I was going to like Ed. The other guy, Rabbit as I already thought I'd call the weasel-faced one, had the worst buckteeth I'd ever seen.

When the doctor arrived around nine I had already drank plenty of the Chief's "Navy Special" coffee. The medical examination was over in less than an hour for all three of us and with all the coffee I drank I had no trouble peeing in the cup. No such luck for Rabbit; he spent damn near thirty minutes without results. Finally the doctor said he was satisfied we were all A1 specimens, and he signed the documents the Chief had spread out for him.

The doctor left and another old navy type entered. He looked to be about seventy, but the Chief gave him a smart salute, and then raising his voice stated, "Men, this is Captain Reynolds, United States Navy retired. The Captain will administer the oath and swear y'all in proper!"

The ceremony was over faster than the medical exam. The old navy captain thanked us for our patriotism, and then left after returning the Chief's salute.

"Men...you are now sailors in the United States Navy," the old chief said proudly, handing each of us a pile of coupons. "These are your bus vouchers to San Diego, and these are your meal vouchers. You will not leave the bus except to eat or change buses." He continued, giving us each a large brown envelope, "And these are your orders. When y'all get to San Diego, there is a Navy information booth in the terminal. Go straight to them. Report in there, they'll take care of y'all...any questions?" he paused. "Good, be at the terminal in time to catch the evening bus at 1630, on this day November 1, 1944. Got all that? You miss it, you're AWOL; boys, it's been a pleasure," he shook each of our hands and ushered us out the door.

"What are you fellas gonna do until…what time was it…sixteen what?" Rabbit said in his irritatingly high voice.

"Sixteen thirty, that's four-thirty to a landlubber like you," Ed laughed, tapping Rabbit on the head. "What are you doing John?" he said, turning towards me.

"First of all, it's Jake, and second of all, I'm gonna use up one of these meal thing-a-ma-bobs!" I said, heading for the nearest restaurant.

Chapter Two

The countryside from the window passed by in a blur. I'd slept most of the way through the night after we'd left Lawton on the bus. We'd changed buses in Lubbock, Texas, sometime in the early morning; I'd hardly woke up. It was later on that morning, we had just stopped for breakfast someplace, and I felt relaxed. I began to talk to Ed. He'd taken the seat beside me, both of us wanting to avoid sitting next to Rabbit.

"Why'd you join, Ed?" I asked through my scrabbled eggs.

"I needed to get in the service before the war's over," he replied, after he'd swallowed a mouthful of hash browns. "I had two more years of college, but I was advised the war might not last that much longer."

"You were in college?" I uttered in disbelief. "What the hell did you need to join for?"

"Jake, my boy, I aim to enter politics as a career," he spoke in a deep, contrived voice. "Without some ribbons on my chest and a good service record I won't make it past city dogcatcher."

"It beats me, I ain't never been out much past Lawton," I said. "But I know fellows like me need to join, not college guys."

"You'll know a little more about what makes the world turn after we get back home again," he laughed. "Believe me, Jake!" he added.

We changed buses again in Alamogordo, New Mexico; I was starting to notice the country changing. It was still damn cold, but the country was starting to look more like old western movies I had seen. By the time we got to Tucson, Arizona, my face was glued to the window. All that cactus and desert, I kept looking for Hopalong Cassidy every town we passed through. It was getting warmer, too. I was glad to get my old overcoat off. The rattletrap bus we were on felt like an icebox and the old coat I had was worn pretty thin.

After a couple of days of sitting together on the bus, Ed managed to squeeze my story out of me. He now knew I was underage and the reason why I'd left in such a hurry. I got some things out of him, too. I now knew that his dad was a State Senator running for the United States Congress, and by this time we both knew Rabbit was the weirdest asshole we'd ever run into.

We stopped in Yuma to gas up and the driver told us to stretch our legs, but to be back on the bus in half-an-hour.

"Let's go and get some action fellas!" Rabbit said excitedly. "A buddy of mine came through here coupla months ago. He said you could get a blow job from the Mexican whores for only fifty cents."

"No thanks, Rabbit," Ed grinned. "You'll get your dick bitten off if you get an ornery one. They don't like Gringos in this town I hear."

"Bullshit!" Rabbit grunted. "You know nothin'! What about you Jake?"

Rabbit didn't seem to mind us calling him that, and his invitation sounded like something I might like to try. "I'll go along with you, but I may not try it," I said.

Two blocks from the bus station was the San Carlos Hotel. Rabbit started talking to a fat Mexican woman standing outside the side entrance to the place as we walked up.

"This is it Jake," he said, as he came over to me his voice husky with excitement, "She'll take us around the back alley."

"Maybe I better wait for you here Rabbit," I said, suddenly apprehensive, "I'll wait for you here."

"Suit yourself," Rabbit replied, as he let the woman take his hand and lead him around the corner.

I was starting to get nervous after five minutes, then I heard yelling coming from the back alley. I ran around the corner and saw two Mexicans holding Rabbit; one of them had a knife to his throat.

"Hey! Hey!" I yelled. "Let him go!"

The one with the knife turned towards me. I rushed him and swung my fist at him "haymaker" style. The sound of my punch connecting with the side of his head made a slapping noise as it echoed off the alley wall. The other guy let go of Rabbit and he bolted past me like the lanky, streak of nothing he was, as if a pack of hounds was after him.

"Come on!" he yelled, as he raced up the side of the building.

Without thinking about it, I turned and ran for my life after him. We didn't stop until we jumped back on the bus, gasping for air. Then Rabbit looked over at me and we both started to laugh, almost choking while we struggled to catch our breath and stop our legs from shaking.

"Okay, what happened?" Ed asked, looking at us wondering what the hell was going on. "What did you two knuckleheads get up to?"

The bus pulled out of Yuma with Rabbit and me still laughing, coughing, gasping, and doubled over with relief. The shock of coming close to getting caught up in a knife fight was just staring to hit home.

14

Chapter Three

We finally pulled into the bus terminal in San Diego. The place was a huge bustling city in itself -- restaurants, ice-cream stands, guys selling newspapers, servicemen in uniform everywhere. We pulled up alongside a seemingly endless row of buses. The world was getting bigger every day through my eyes.

The folks back home in Hodskins could never imagine all this. I could hardly believe it myself.

"Good luck boys!" the driver said as we got off the bus.

Ed took control of our little group and asked some sailors standing around, swinging billy clubs against their legs, where the Navy information booth was. They smirked as they pointed the way with their clubs across the busy lobby. The young officer at the booth looked briefly at the envelopes we gave him, then told us to go back out and wait on the Navy bus at Gate Ten. Struggling through the crowd of sailors, soldiers and Marines, we finally found Gate Ten and got on the bus.

It must have been almost an hour before anyone showed up, and then about forty guys got on. They had been coming down the west coast by train from as far away as Seattle, Washington, picking up a few here and there as they passed through Oregon and northern California.

A chief in winter blues got on and a driver in dungarees and watch cap. The driver slid behind the wheel and immediately started to back the bus out of the gate. The chief had six long stripes on his sleeve, and it didn't take long for it to be whispered around that he was an old salt, with maybe twenty-five years of service in the Navy.

It was a noisy trip to the training base. It was our last brief moment of freedom; the chief knew it, the driver knew it, but we poor, miserable dickheads were too damn dumb to know it. The bus was waved through the guardhouse gate and pulled up outside a large, brightly lit building. Then all hell broke loose.

"All right you pimple-faced, wanna-be sailors, get your fuckin' asses off this bus and line up!" the chief shrieked at us.

There was a mad scrabble to do as we were told. Guys tripping over each other, dropping their suitcases. We stared at each other and struggled to form a line outside the bus.

"Put out that fuckin' cigarette!" the chief screamed at one poor kid. "You're in the fuckin' United States Navy now."

15

The kid with the cigarette didn't know whether to swallow the butt or throw it over his shoulder; he quickly dropped it on the ground and crushed it into the pavement with his shoe.

"Now pick that cigarette up, you litter-bugging prick and find a trash can!" the chief ordered. Then added, "While you're at it, pick up every piece of trash, real or imagined, from here to the Main Gate…Move it!"

So began our introduction into Boot Camp. Our "Boot-Pusher" was a gunner's mate chief petty officer who had been injured on the *USS Princeton* when that ship had been sunk. He didn't cut us any slack, but wasn't as mean and nasty as some of the others.

It was six weeks of adjusting to ill-fitting uniforms, learning how to march, salute, clean toilets, or heads as they were called in the Navy, and heaven help you if there was a lapse in memory. We got used to lining up for chow, inoculations, showers, dentists, the PX…and yes, the head.

Our six weeks of Boot Camp finished just before Christmas. We were not to be issued any home leave, but we all got an eight-hour pass to go into town. With the war on, Rabbit, Ed and me were going to gunnery training the day after Christmas. A lot of guys from our division were being assigned to radar school, something the war had developed and all the new ships had been fitted with. Ed had said if we wanted action, then to get into gunnery school, as that would get us to sea faster than anything else. He would be proven correct in that.

We had no sooner learned the dos and don'ts and found out the difference between a 5-inch turret and 20MM bofors, when word came through that we were getting a billet on a destroyer. The ship had just arrived from an East Coast shipyard.

The *USS Roe* was a Fletcher Class destroyer, and had only just finished her shakedown cruise in the Caribbean, and then the destroyer transitted the Panama Canal to the Pacific. The *Roe* was tied up with a string of other destroyers, or tin cans as they called them, and was loading stores making ready to sail.

Our orders were cut and we cleaned out our lookers and reported aboard three weeks into the New Year. It was January 1945.

Reporting aboard the *USS Roe* was totally different to arriving that first day at Boot Camp in San Diego. We were shown our racks in the after crew's quarters, taken on a quick tour of the ship, and made to feel like we were at least human beings. Those friendly gestures had been something lacking in the rush, push, and impersonal world of Boot Camp, where any sense of being an individual was knocked out of you. Ed and I were assigned to the same watch; Rabbit got to go on another watch with the one other guy that had come aboard with us. His name was Billy Smith.

I loved looking over our ship; it was so new, so modern. The smell of her was a mixture of oil fumes, grease and new paint. The *Roe's* first movement was to the destroyer fueling station on Coronado Island to take on oil before we left San Diego. Ed, me and a couple of the "salts" who'd sailed the *Roe* around from the East Coast were having a mug of coffee standing at the railing. When the first guy finished his coffee he dropped his empty mug over the side, then the others did the same.

"Good luck before ya sail," said one, when he noticed me staring inquiringly at him.

Ed looked at me and we both shrugged our shoulders and dropped our mugs over the side.

The trip to Pearl Harbor in the Hawaiian Islands was one of endless drills. Gunnery practice with live rounds was a pain; it was chaos until we started to jell as a team. Fletcher Class destroyers had five 5-inch single barrel gun mounts, two forward and three aft. They were crewed by nine men, each with a different specific job. I was the "powderman"; my job was to place cordite charges behind the shell when it was dropped on the tray. The shell and powder were then rammed into the breech. The gun was now ready to be fired manually from within the mount, or automatically from a fire control station. The gun could hurl a fifty-four pound shell ten miles.

Rabbit and I had been assigned to number five mount aft as our General Quarter's station. Ed was on the number four mount.

When we weren't on the guns, we checked the small boats every ship carried. The 26-foot whaleboat on the port side was my baby; I checked her out as part of my other daily duties. We were referred to as "deck apes" and we worked wherever on the open decks we were needed, from repairing anchor chains to painting and scrapping.

The day we arrived in Hawaii I thought I would cum in my pants. It was so exciting seeing the palm trees as we approached the entrance to Pearl Harbor. So these were the Pacific islands, I had never in my life thought about them, yet here I was. You could smell the sweet, rich aroma from the tropical vegetation; the balmy late afternoon air almost made me swoon. The ship slowed while the net-tender pulled aside the submarine net that ran the length of the entrance. The *Roe* slowly steamed through and as we rounded Ford Island our sense of pleasure faded.

My duty station for entering and leaving harbor was bridge lookout; from there I had one of the best views from the ship. Ford Island still had piles of blackened wreckage piled up on one end. The reminders of the attack on December 7, 1941 were everywhere.

The tank farm still had blackened and unrepaired sections; docks and buildings showed signs of recent repair. Then we saw her, or what was still visible of the *USS Arizona*, lying where she had been sunk that day, the ship still containing the bodies of hundreds of her crew below decks.

After a moment of sober reflections, I soon resumed my excitement at being here in Pearl Harbor. Small boats darted everywhere, planes were taking off and landing and ships were tied up anyplace there was a space for them.

Captain Abe Poser shouted orders for docking the *Roe*. "Talkers" repeated his orders to the engine room and the docking parties fore and aft.

Bringing nearly 400 feet of steel alongside a dock with hardly a bump was an act of magic to me. I could see Ed and Rabbit on the bow preparing to throw lines to the dockside mooring party. Rabbit could throw a line farther than I could throw a baseball, but that was about the only thing that snot-nosed, buck-toothed shithead was good for.

Once the ship had tied up, all available hands were ordered to report to the gangway. The gangway party then started loading stores, everything we could find space for. Work crews came on board to carry out any necessary last-minute repairs. No shore leave was being granted, as we were leaving just as soon as we had the stores aboard, filled our ammunition magazines, and topped off our fuel-oil bunkers.

"I hear there's a big push on to take the islands close to Japan," whispered a skinny kid handing me a carton of canned meat, "maybe even Japan itself. We're gonna be part of it," he added.

You never knew when the scuttlebutt was true or just someone's over-active imagination, so everything had to be taken seriously.

"I heard the skipper and XO talking on the bridge," joined in the guy next in the line as I handed the carton to him. "We're escorting some tankers to the Philippines, then we'll be joining up with Admiral Spruance's fleet," he said, as he continued to pass the carton down the line.

The next morning, after fueling, we cast off and moved slowly out of the great harbor. After clearing the entrance, we closed up with two other destroyers, then about an hour out to sea we formed an escort around five large oil tankers.

The scuttlebutt had been right about the tankers. Were we really going to join the fleet about to invade Japan? I wondered as I finished my watch on the bridge.

"Goddamn you Rabbit!" a seaman named Bulow was saying as I joined the chowline for lunch. "I'll kick your fucking ass so hard your nose will bleed if I catch you in my locker again," he shouted, poking his finger into Rabbit's chest.

"I never been in your locker asshole," taunted Rabbit, a silly smirk on his face. "What the hell you got in there anyway?"

Rabbit had a nasty habit of spraying spittle when he talked. He was the most repulsive son-of-a-bitch I'd ever met, but I'd joined up with him so felt some obligation to him.

"I'll wring your scrawny neck you fuckhead!" Bulow grunted, as he lifted Rabbit up by his collar.

"Hold it!" I said, as I stepped in between them. "You ain't gonna wring anybody's neck Bulow."

"Break it up!" someone shouted. "You'll all be doing time in the brig."

"I'll see you, Rickmeyer!" Bulow threatened. "You and your long-streak-of-nothin' buddy...Yeah, I'll see you!" He walked off slapping the bulkhead with his hand as he ducked through the hatch.

The trip across the Pacific was uneventful except for refueling from one of the tankers. We almost collided as we came alongside the other ship. I'd never seen the Skipper so mad. The Chief Quartermaster was at the helm and we all kept tight-mouthed as Captain Poser tore him a new asshole. That was the only time we needed to refuel underway.

About two weeks out of Pearl we had a false submarine contact, all hands went to General Quarters. After zigzagging across our convoy's path for an hour without any further contact, we got the word to stand down.

The scuttlebutt was right. The Skipper came on the intercom one evening when we were at chow and told us we'd be arriving at Subic Bay in the Philippines the next morning. It was late February and we'd already heard about the Marines landing on Iwo Jima, and that General Douglas MacArthur had retaken Leyte and most of Luzon Island in the Philippines.

The old Navy base at Subic Bay was a hive of activity when we arrived. The tankers we had escorted went directly to the tank farm area to unload, and we docked alongside the two other destroyers that had been part of our convoy.

19

Chapter Four

We were allowed to go ashore and stretch our legs, but not much else while we were tied up at Subic. The dress of the day was clean dungarees. Manila and any place outside a five-mile radius of the base were off limits, so Ed, Rabbit, Billy Smith and I decided to go for a walk and strolled out through the base gate. The sentries were not too particular. They had another post a couple of hundred yards down the road, and that one required written orders to get through.

Outside the gate there were some makeshift roadside food joints, some even sold hot dogs. We had been warned not to eat anything off the carts; someone said cat and even human meat had been found in the hotdogs and on the sate sticks, which were a local delicacy.

Strolling down the nearby beach, a little Filipina girl about ten or eleven came up and started begging. Ed gave her a candy bar he had and I gave her the twenty-five cents I'd been carrying in my dungarees since the last peeknuckle game aboard ship.

Ed and I ambled on, throwing rocks out into the water. Rabbit and Billy had fallen behind and we could hear them laughing.

"What do you think about this big push on Japan?" Ed said, as he skipped a rock across the water. "I hear the Japs are crashing their planes directly into ships, committing suicide," he continued, picking up another rock. "Kamikazes they call them…damn crazy pilots just fly straight at our ships!"

"Don't know Ed," I replied, trying to get one extra skip out of my rock. "All I know is we got the best skipper in the fleet."

The next thing we knew Billy came running up yelling, "He's trying to fuck her, that crazy bastard is trying to fuck that little girl!"

Ed and I ran back to where we heard the girl sobbing. Rabbit had her legs apart and was pushing himself into her as hard as he could.

"You son-of-a-bitch!" I screamed, as I grabbed Rabbit around the neck and pulled him off.

I swung him around and punched him square on the nose three times in rapid succession. Billy and Ed quickly grabbed me before I could hit him again.

"No Jake, you'll kill him!" Ed hollered, as Rabbit slipped out of my grip and started running down the beach.

"Goddamn bastard!" I said through gritted teeth.

21

I turned back to the little girl and tried to help her up. She screamed and scrambled to her feet and ran awkwardly away crying.

"Let's get out of here," Ed said, grabbing my arm. "Come on Billy, let's go!" The three of us half ran, half walked back to the gate. We tried to look relaxed, without a care in the world, as we walked past the guards. Billy actually whistled, doing his best to look normal.

"I'm going to turn him in," I said to Ed after we were inside the gate and out of earshot of the guards. "I'm not letting him get away with it."

"Wait a minute!" Ed grabbed me and turned me towards him. "All you'll do is get us all in one big mess of trouble. Do you think they'll believe us? Four lowlife swabbies on the beach, one little Filipina, we'll all go down with Rabbit."

"How can you let him go, she was only a baby," I said, jerking myself free of Ed's grip. "You say nothing about this and we're through Ed."

"Listen Jake…I know how these things work. We'll get ten years in Portsmouth Naval Prison and we didn't have a thing to do with it," Ed pleaded.

"He's right Jake," added Billy. "I heard of guys going away for life for rape."

"Okay, but that don't mean I won't forget this. Anyhow, what's to stop the girl from going to the cops or the Shore Patrol?" I said, suddenly thinking of where she might have run off to.

"We were four sailors in dungarees. There are thousands walking around here. We all look the same," Ed said, now more at ease. "Let's get back aboard ship, forget it happened."

I never spoke a word to Rabbit that night at chow, but I was still boiling inside. I couldn't help seeing that look of terror on the little girl's face when I reached down to help her up. Ed was right, to her we were all the same, just big, mean American sailors.

Rabbit was sporting two nasty black eyes from the punches I'd laid on him. Billy Smith had spread the word we had been throwing a baseball around on the beach and Rabbit had failed to catch a fastball.

I was glad when we left Subic Bay. Our orders according to Captain Poser were to proceed to some point on the map and take up picket duty. Ships on picket duty were like sentries out ahead of an army. The *Roe's* job was to detect any enemy movements and then report them to the fleet. We were now officially part of Vice Admiral Marc Mitscher's Task Force 58.

For a week we saw very little action. Planes from the Task Force's carriers flew over us every day and we were on high stage alert most of the time. Then one morning as I rolled out of my rack following a couple of hours sleep, I heard a commotion on the deck above.

Sailors were running around as I came out of the after hatch from the crew's quarters. I felt the ship surge and vibrate has she picked up speed.

"What the hell's up?" I yelled at Boatswain's Mate Yates as he ran by.

"Rickmeyer, get your ass over to the whaleboat," he shouted at me. "We got a pilot in the water. We gotta get him before the sharks do!"

"Holy shit!" I thought as I ran down the port side. As I got there, the boatswain had grabbed Ed as well. We started to swing out the davits and rig the painter, getting the whaleboat ready to lower. We had drilled this many times, so we were ready to launch the boat and standing by in a matter of minutes. It was another thirty minutes, though, before the ship slowed.

"They've spotted him!" someone shouted.

We couldn't see a damn thing, but the ensign who'd taken control of the boat launch ordered the men standing by the davits to lower away. Yates, Ed and I were already in the whaleboat and we felt the ship shudder has she made a sharp starboard turn, slowing to barely a walk.

"Let her go!" shouted the ensign.

"Unshackle...haul in the painter," hollered Yates, as we hit the water with a thud. It was all done in one quick series of motions. Ed and I unshackled, Yates had the motor started, and we were crossing the *Roe's* stern.

An officer on the bridge wing pointed toward something ahead of us, off the ship's starboard bow. I was standing on the whaleboat's prow and spotted the yellow lifejacket almost immediately.

"Do ya see him Rickmeyer?" Yates yelled over the noise of the motor.

"Yeah, dead ahead," I yelled back, "I see him!"

We hauled up alongside the pilot, his head was barely out of the water and I felt sure he must be dead.

"Get a line to him," Yates shouted.

Ed was beside me, getting ready to throw a line to the man in the water.

"He don't look barely alive," I said, adrenaline pumping through me. "I'm going in, tie that line around me."

I jumped in and swam to the man in the water, grabbing him by the hair just as his head slumped forward. "I got ya!" I gulped, my own mouth half full of water. I grabbed him and kicked my way back to the boat.

"Up, push him up," Ed grunted, as he hauled the dead weight of the pilot into the whaleboat.

The pilot lay face down in the boat coughing as Ed and me pulled his lifejacket off and tried to get him out of his shoulder holster and other gear.

"Goddamn, it's good to see you fellas," the pilot gasped between coughs.

Yates had turned the boat around and we were racing back to the ship. We had covered about half the distance when unbelievably the *Roe* started sailing away at top speed, the water churning at her stern as the screws bit deep.

"What the fuck is she doing?" cried Ed, as we all stared in disbelief. The answer came a short time later. We heard the distant buzz of planes.

"Everybody get under the canopy. If they don't see anyone, they may think she's abandoned," yelled Yates, as he cut the motor and scrabbled forward. Ed and I dragged the pilot with us as we crawled under the canopy out of sight. There's not too much room on a 26-foot whaleboat at the best of times; now we had four guys trying desperately to make themselves invisible.

The buzz got louder as one of the planes came in low for a look. He must have seen something because he turned and came around again. We all tried to crawl into a space that wouldn't take something a fourth of our size. We were sitting ducks and we knew it.

"Jesus Christ!" Yates shouted. "If we have to we'll all go over the side, have a better chance than waiting for him to shoot the shit out of this tub."

The plane came in lower than before, the noise from his engine becoming a roar. Suddenly a hole tore in the canvas of the canopy and a piece of the boat's gunwale went flying, the bullets making a zip sound as they flew by. Before we could react and jump over the side, he was flying off. He must have thought we weren't worth wasting ammunition on. We waited for maybe fifteen minutes, then gingerly climbed out from under the canopy and looked around. The hole in the canvas and the big piece of wood missing out of the gunwale were the only damage. Thankfully they were above the waterline. We also saw something else, the *Roe* coming back to get us.

That evening I was standing on the fantail, looking off at the sunset. We had been relieved from picket duty and were sailing towards Ulithi, the fleet's present anchorage. I'd never heard of the place, but the scuttlebutt was there was going to be a big operation and hundreds of ships were gathering there. I turned when I heard approaching footsteps.

"Evening," said a tall, good-looking young officer in fresh khakis. It was the pilot we'd pulled from the water earlier that day. "I never got to thank you properly. My name's Sullivan Rooks," he said, holding out his hand.

I took his hand and shook it, feeling a little uncomfortable. I'd never talked much with officers, except to report to them, take orders, or answer their questions.

"What's your name seaman?" he said, with a grin as wide as the Mississippi.

"Seaman Apprentice Rickmeyer, Sir," I replied.

"What's your first name, I mean," he laughed.

"Jake, Sir," I replied feeling more relaxed.

"Well, Jake, I want to thank you for what you did today," he spoke softly, with genuine humility. "I had just about given up thinking I was going to make it. I'll probably get transferred onto the first carrier we meet up with and I won't get a chance to see you after that."

He put his hand on my shoulder. "I won't forget this. It was the day my life was over and then you gave it back to me," he said. With a tear in his eye, he looked at me and once more took my hand and shook it.

"I was only doing what needed to be done, Sir," I said, starting to choke up a little myself.

"Call me Sully, Jake, and good luck for the rest of this war," he smiled, and then walked away.

Looking after him I thought, "Well I guess all officers ain't assholes. Sully, eh? Well, good luck to you too, Sully."

Chapter Five

The fleet assembled for the invasion of Okinawa was like nothing you could ever imagine. There were ships as far as the eye could see.

The *Roe* looked pretty darn small as we passed by those huge fleet carriers and battleships. Destroyers were everywhere, most of them Fletcher Class like the *Roe*, and dozens of transport ships carrying thousands of Marines.

What was this Okinawa we were heading for? Was this going to be it? The real war? Being on picket duty since we had joined the Task Force hadn't prepared us for what we were now seeing.

The attack on the whaleboat by the Jap plane was about the only action anyone on the *Roe* had seen so far, and that was over before you could think much about it. Of course, the Skipper and the old hands had been in action on other ships, but for most of us greenhorns, this was the first time we felt we were really part of this war.

The night before the invasion was to start, Captain Poser came over the ship's intercom. "Men, this is the Captain," he began. "Tomorrow, April 1, 1945, we are going to be part of the greatest amphibious landing so far in this war. It is code named *Iceberg*. The Fleet will be landing almost 200,000 soldiers and Marines. Over a thousand ships of all types will be involved, and the *Roe* will be just one of two hundred destroyers." He continued, "And every one of them will play their part, just as I know all of you will play yours. It won't be easy, but we will prevail. Good Luck! And God Bless!"

It was also going to be Easter Sunday. I was not religious, but decided to join in a prayer lead by the Executive Officer, or XO as he was called on the ship. He had asked that anybody interested should assemble in the forward mess deck at 1800 hours.

The battleships had been bombarding the landing beaches and inland defenses for a week, and our first look that morning showed a blackened landscape. We were called to General Quarters and I ran to the #5 mount. Many of the destroyers were escorting the landing craft in as close as they could, and then standing by to give fire support. Next to me in the mount was the "shellman", Lou Demaris. His job was to drop the shell on the tray after I'd dropped down the cordite bundle. Rabbit stood behind us to make sure all the empty shell casings went through the hole at the rear of the mount after they were ejected from the breech.

You didn't do much else while the mount was firing except your job. Everybody was tense; the noise could be deafening and leave you feeling completely numb. There was very little resistance on the beaches at first, and troops were landing in large numbers, along with their stores and equipment. It was the same every day for three or four days. The landings were going off without a hitch and our people were pouring onto Okinawa.

Landing operations stopped each day when the light started to fade, and the *Roe* pulled back out to sea and we had a chance to eat a hot meal, grab a quick shower, and take a break on deck in the cool night air.

It must have been near the end of that first week when the Kamikazes started to appear, arriving in droves. The last thing I remember as I crawled through the hatch of the mount was looking over my shoulder, the sky filled with anti-aircraft bursts as every ship in the Fleet opened up.

We had loaded and fired dozens of rounds; then it happened. The mount felt as if it had been hit by a freight train and the jarring I felt through my whole body made me momentarily paralyzed.

Strangely, I don't remember hearing any sound. Lou was lying on top of me and we both started struggling to get up. The breech of the gun had twisted completely around, which must have been what saved us. Rabbit was jammed against the rear of the mount, his arm twisted behind him, and Lou and me were on the mount deck. We could see sky all around us; the mount had been almost completely blown apart.

"Give me a hand," I remember saying to Lou. "Give me a hand to get Rabbit loose."

Lou stumbled forward and grabbed Rabbit, who screamed in pain as he was pulled free. Our faces were blackened, our hair singed, and our clothes in tatters, but the three of us were in one piece, apart from Rabbit's arm.

We tumbled out of the rear hatch. I don't know why; there was nothing left of the rest of the mount and we could have just jumped off either side. My legs were jelly and they collapsed under me as I hit the deck. By this time men were rigging hoses and starting to spray water on the fires still burning on the surrounding deck, and at the front of the mount. I felt hands grab me and pull me aside.

"Take it easy," someone said, "you're okay!"

My eyes were still unfocused, my head was thumping, but I had enough presence of mind to check myself over. My arms and legs worked and I had no serious bleeding. I felt a small cut on my forehead, but nothing else as far as I could tell. I got up and staggered to the front section of the mount; it was gone! About all that was intact and resembling anything at all was the rear section where Lou, Rabbit and I had been.

Hands grabbed me again and a voice said, "Let's get you down to sick bay." Lou was already there and Rabbit was lying on a table, doped up with something they'd shot into his ass. A pharmacist's mate was working on his arm. It was then that I learned the other men in the mount had been killed, including Billy Smith.

I was standing on the deck amidships as we steamed back to Ulithi. The *Roe* was acting as escort to a seriously damaged cruiser. The cruiser, in turn, had another victim of the Kamikazes in tow, a badly mauled destroyer. At Ulithi the damaged ships would be repaired and sent back into action, or sailed back to the States for major repairs.

"You feeling okay?" Ed said has he appeared by my side.

"I'll be fine. Can't help thinking about Billy though," I whispered. "That fucker Rabbit gets a broken arm and a good kid like Billy gets blown apart."

"I know," Ed said, half to himself. "This has sure made things real for me. For the first time I'm damn scared."

When we arrived at the anchorage at Ulithi, a Landing Craft Vehicle Personnel (LCVP) came alongside to offload a team of shipfitters and welders. They'd be making what repairs were necessary to get us back off Okinawa where we were needed.

Ulithi was alive with LCVPs and Landing Craft Mechanized (LCM). These were small landing craft and all-around workhorses. They sailed from ship to ship, ship to shore, and back again taking off wounded, bringing out replacements and repair personnel, even delivering mail and ice cream.

Rabbit and Lou were taken aboard one LCVP and sent to ashore for further treatment. It turned out Lou may have some tiny metal fragments in one eye, so they wanted a surgeon to look at him. The Navy had huge hospital ships that were as large and well equipped as any big city hospital. I had noticed one when the *Roe* had first entered the anchorage, the *USS Repose*. It looked as magnificent as an ocean liner, something you might want to take a cruise on. Unfortunately, her decks and berths were full of horribly wounded and dying men.

The dead sailors from the Kamikaze attack had been buried at sea in canvas shrouds, at least what little they found and identified of them.

"Fucking Rabbit," I said to myself as I watched him being helped aboard the LCVP by a crewman, "I hope I never have to see your ugly face again."

Ulithi was a top-secret staging area. We found out later nobody ever knew about it until well after the war was over. It was really four islands; the native inhabitants had been all moved to one and the Navy used the rest. Mog Mog was the island designated for recreation. It had what were called "beer bars", where you could buy a lukewarm can of beer. We played ball and swam. The beach was a long strip of white sand and the water in the lagoon was straight off a South Seas picture postcard.

The temporary repairs completed, we sailed back to Okinawa, minus the #5 gun mount, which left me needing a new General Quarter's station. I was assigned to the bridge lookout position and there I had a first class ticket to what remained of the sea action off Okinawa. The battle for Okinawa would not be over until late June, three months after the bombardment by the battleships had first started it all.

During the battle for Okinawa, ship losses from Kamikazes amounted to thirty-four sunk and another three hundred and sixty-eight damaged, of which the *Roe* had been one. Okinawa cost us dearly; tens of thousands of men had been killed or wounded.

We resumed our duties again as a picket ship somewhere between Japan and Okinawa during the month of July, after we'd had another short R and R on Ulithi. We got the word on August 15th that Japan had surrendered. They had used some top-secret weapon, a bomb that used power never seen before. It was still all hush-hush and top secret.

"Look at that baby!" exclaimed Ed, after we'd dropped anchor just off the starboard bow of the *USS Missouri* and had secured from entering port stations. The *Roe* had arrived that morning along with dozens of other ships.

"Here we are, goddamn it! Tokyo Bay!" Ed kept yelling in my ear.

He slapped me on the back and threw his arms around me, then started shaking hands with everyone else lined up at the rails. The future politician, I thought. "Yeah Ed, you got your battle ribbons now," I said to myself, as I looked over at the battleship they called "Mighty Mo".

The Japanese surrender was signed aboard the *USS Missouri* on September 2, 1945. I'd been in the Navy ten months, not yet seventeen, but somehow I knew I hadn't seen the last of war.

Chapter Six

After the surrender ceremonies in Tokyo Bay ended, The *USS Roe* was ordered to Shanghai to show the flag and allow us to let off some steam I guess.

Sailing up the Pearl River, with its thousands of junks carrying goods and contraband from all over the Orient was a fantasy for a boy from Oklahoma. The Japanese during the war had occupied the city and there was still damage to be seen everywhere. The hatred for the Japanese by the Chinese was still running high, but Americans were welcome everywhere in China. We had been allies, and the inhabitants of Shanghai made us feel completely welcome.

"Hey Johnny!" a rickshaw driver cried out to us, "You want girlie?"

The sights, sounds, and smells were heightening our senses as Ed Morrow, Bugeye Millington and I walked along the ancient bung.

"I feel like some Chinese tail," whooped Bugeye. "Let's go with this guy."

"How the hell can he haul all three of us in that thing?" I said, with disbelief.

"Com-ee in, Com-ee in," squawked the old guy. He was as skinny as a split-rail fence, but he got the three of us in and started trotting down the road.

"Here good place, velly clean girlie!" the rickshaw driver smiled pulling up outside a bar, he was hardly out of breath.

"Here I go guys…Chinese tail…whoopee," laughed Bugeye. "Hey, ya think it's true what they say about it goin' sideways?"

"You can find out, then tell me all about it," Ed said, adding, "I'll sit at the bar and have a cold beer."

The place was like so many others, a bar downstairs and rooms with girls upstairs. There was one large room with dozens of girls sitting against the wall on display. You paid the mama-san, picked your girl, and then found yourself an empty room.

"Suit yourself, I'm on my way," shouted Bugeye as he took the stairs two at a time.

"Hold up!" I yelled, just two steps behind him. "How much should we pay?"

"Whatever the mama-san asks…give her half," Bugeye said, old salt that he was at 22-years-old.

31

I fell head-over-heels for the prettiest little Chinese girl. She was like a doll, her face pale as alabaster, with her cheeks and lips highlighted a rich red color. The mama-san said, "Two Yankee dollar, short time." I forgot Bugeye's advice and just gave her the money.

My only real experience had been with Cecelia Summers, and that was more teenage excitement then substance. This tiny girl made me take my time, she washed my dick with a warm cloth that made me even hornier, and then she climbed on the bed and motioned me to follow. After gently guiding me into her, she started to rhythmically move against me. When I came, it was as if all my nerve endings had come alive at that one moment in time. I was in love!

I was reluctant to leave the room, but the girl ushered me out after I got my pants back on. I was still confused about the feelings I felt, but went downstairs to have a beer with Ed.

"How was it?" Ed asked. "Bugeye must be doing all right, he's still up there." After looking at my confused expression he inquired, "What's up with you, Jake?"

"I don't know," I stammered, "I think I'm in love with that girl. How do I see her again?"

Ed threw his head back and laughed, "No you're not. Just come down from the clouds and have a beer."

I was still sitting there dreamily holding a beer when Bugeye came down.

"Man, oh man!" Bugeye grinned. "That was the best piece of tail this side of San Diego!"

"Don't bother Jake," Ed said to Bug. "He's in love with his little slant-eyed whore."

We were drunk when we left the bar. I was still drooling over the girl and demanding to be left there. I intended to jump ship, marry the Chinese girl, and stay in Shanghai. Ed and Bugeye wisely lifted me up under the arms and carried me out with them when they left.

We staggered, laughing, down the alley looking for a rickshaw. From out of nowhere Bulow and a couple of his friends suddenly blocked our way.

"I told you, Rickmeyer, I was gonna bust your chops," Bulow said menacingly. In my less-than-sober state he was a head taller than I was.

"Come on fellas, were all shipmates," Ed tried to reason. "Let's all go back and have a beer."

Bulow was having none of that; he struck me a blow in the stomach that dropped me, retching, to the ground.

"You asshole!" yelled Bugeye, as he swung a blow at Bulow.

Bulow sidestepped and walloped Bugeye across the ear, which dropped poor old Bug to the ground beside me.

"That's enough Bulow," Ed said, as he bent down to help me up. "You've had your fun."

"Come on pal, leave these pussies," said one of Bulow's buddies. "Let's go get some action." He grabbed Bulow's arm and they wandered off toward the main road.

"Where's that motherfucker?" shouted Bugeye, as he got to his feet, staggering around looking for Bulow through his bulging eyes. Bug's eyes seemed to double in size when he was drunk. "I'll kill the bastard!" he mumbled.

After Shanghai, we sailed to the Philippines, stopping at Subic Bay to refuel and take on stores, send off and pick up mail, and get members of the crew to dentists or doctors. There had been a large number of venereal disease cases after China; thank God I wasn't one of them.

On the way back across the Pacific the *Roe* developed shaft problems; temporary repairs were needed and we were ordered to Pearl Harbor. We were all looking forward to going home, so a forced stopover in Hawaii was not popular. It was Christmas and a shipboard celebration was about all we were going to get this year.

The New Year found us still at Pearl Harbor. The weather was great, the food was better than most folks were eating at home, liberty was available for those not on watch, but sailors will bitch no matter what the circumstances.

The occasional fight broke out on the mess deck. Everyone felt like we deserved to be home -- the war was over. The fights were quickly broken up, everyone was a little edgy, but nobody wanted to be brought up on charges and spend time in the brig. Funny thing about men,you may have a falling out, fight each other till you're black and blue, then when it's all over somehow you become the best of friends.

That was the case with Bulow. He was always asking me to go ashore with him, ever since that time in Shanghai he had gone out of his way to be civil to me. One night I was feeling restless and talked Ed into going into Honolulu with Bulow and one of his buddies.

Most of the officers hung out at the Royal Hawaiian on Wakiki Beach; the common old swabbies like us headed for Hotel Street.

The beers flowed, then the next thing I knew Bulow had me in a pool game with two Marine Corps jarheads, the losers to buy "shots" of whisky.

Bulow was one hell-of-a-player; I did nothing except chalk the cue occasionally and scatter the balls. The end result, however, was I drank an endless supply of whisky, washed down with Primo Beer.

Then Ed, deep in conversation with the bartender, mistakenly picked up one of the jarhead's shot glasses and emptied it in one gulp. The jarhead grabbed Ed, Bulow grabbed the jarhead, and a fight was only avoided when the bartender shouted he was buying a round for everyone.

"Goddamn it! I'm having the time of my life," Bulow slapped me on the back as he swallowed another glass of beer. "We'll take these jarheads to the cleaners, then kick their asses!" he whispered in my ear as he headed back to the table.

We were all well and truly hammered; Ed was as drunk and as talkative as I'd ever seen him.

"Jake, I got something to tell you," Ed said quietly, his arm around my shoulder. "I really like you man!" he started to get teary. "As a matter of fact, I want to head you Jake."

"What the...!" I couldn't believe my ears. "What the..." I stuttered, as I shook his arm off my shoulder.

"Jake, Jake, wait!" Ed replied in a panic. "No man, forget it, I'm sorry."

He looked so pathetic I couldn't even hit him. "No way, don't say no more Ed," I said, still in shock.

So that's why he never went into any brothels with us I thought, or talked about girls when the whole ship was boasting about the women they'd balled in Asian ports.

"I'd better leave. I'm so sorry Jake, it just came out," he sobbed, as he threw five dollars on the bar and left.

"Hey, where's Ed going Jake?" yelled Bulow. "Jake, where the fuck's Ed going?"

"Back to the ship, let him be," I said, throwing down a shot of whisky and grabbing my beer glass. I was strung so tight I could hardly breathe. The only thing I wanted to do right then was hit somebody. I swung around off the bar stool and hit the closest jarhead with a right cross.

"Holly shit!" shouted Terry Jones, Bulow's buddy, "Let's get the hell outta here!" The bartender picked up the whistle that they blew to alert the Shore Patrol. Terry grabbed me and headed for the door, while Bulow let the other jarhead have it with an uppercut.

"Goddamn!" he whooped as he dropped the man to the floor with the jaw-crunching blow, and then started running after us.

We managed to get around the corner and race up an alley. We could hear the whistles of the Shore Patrol somewhere behind us on Hotel Street.

34

"That's enough for one night," laughed Bulow. "Let's go home Jake," he said, as he helped Terry lift me under the arms. I was in no condition to walk; the whisky and beer hit me all at once, and my legs had turned to jelly.

The *Roe* was finally repaired and we set sail for the Mainland; our stay in the Hawaiian Islands had been memorable in many ways. Ed and I no longer met on the fantail of an evening to shoot the breeze. He'd made several attempts to talk to me since that night, but neither of us was ready.

One night I was leaning on the railing, with one foot on the lower strand in good old Navy style, swapping the news of the day with Bugeye.

"I tell you Jake, I talked to Chief Hoffman and he said we can make qualification for Boatswain's Mate Striker if we want it," Bugeye said. "You want to stay in the Navy just like me and that's our best chance."

"Did the Chief also tell you most of these ships are being laid up," I replied. "And that they'll be discharging thousands of guys."

"That's just it," he said knowingly. "The Chief told me they'll be mothballing these ships and they'll be needing deck apes like us to get the work done."

Bugeye not only had bulging eyes, but I was just noticing that the man never blinked. "Christ Bug!" I said, drawn to his unblinking stare. "I've got no place else to go, I have to stay in!"

Just then Ed walked up and said, "Can I talk to you for a minute Jake?"

I had missed Ed, despite what I now knew about him; he was still my oldest friend in the Navy. We'd joined up together and been through a lot of good times and bad.

"Sure!" I said, relieved that he'd finally decided to break the ice. Turning to Bugeye, I asked, "This is personal Bug, will you give us a minute?"

"I've got to go study my knots anyway," Bug said as he walked off. "Remember what I told ya Jake, let's go talk to the Chief tomorrow."

"Jake, I don't know what to say, except I'm so sorry for what happened," Ed said, taking a deep breath. "I apologize, that's all I can say."

"Forget it Ed, let's just forget it," I said. I had never even known such people as homosexuals existed until I joined the Navy; Hodskins, Oklahoma had never prepared me. After we got to Boot Camp though, it was "Watch out for the fags!" or "That cocksucker is a fag!" I don't think I even knew then what it was all about; I had no idea. Until one day, when we were at sea, Rabbit had told me what it was all about; that sorry-excuse-for-a-man had spared me none of the nasty details.

"I really appreciate you keeping your mouth shut about it," Ed continued. "You know I'm being mustered out as soon as we reach San Francisco?"

"Yeah, you and most everybody else," I said matter of factly. "You going back to Oklahoma?"

"Yes I am. I heard you say to Bugeye that you wanted to remain in the Navy," Ed replied. "That's great Jake, Boatswain's Mate eh? You always did love the small boats."

"Yeah, that's what I want to be," I continued. "I ain't going back to Oklahoma, that's for sure, nothin' for me there."

"Well, I just wanted to say I'm sorry Jake," he held out his hand.

"Sure," I said, taking his hand and shaking it firmly. "No harm done."

"Okay then, I'll see you before I leave," he said.

"Okay!" I replied, happy to be talking with Ed again. I didn't think we could ever do the things we used to do together any more, but I was glad we hadn't parted hating each other's guts.

Next morning Bug and I showed up at Chief Boatswain's Mate Bart Hoffman's office. Everyone called him "Black Bart" behind his back; to his face you called him Chief Hoffman.

"Come in!" he bellowed, when we knocked and stuck our heads in through the door. "You two want to stay in the service, I hear."

"Yes, Chief," I said, nervously twisting my white cap in a knot. "Bug...eh...Seaman Millington and I," I stuttered, "heard...heard they may not discharge everybody; that they'll keep some guys they might be needin'.'"

"That's right; you two know your way around a ship's deck pretty good, and that's what they're lookin' for," the Chief growled, looking us over. "I'll run you through some tests before we reach Frisco and get you qualified as Boatswain's Mate Strikers. Then I'll get the yeoman to cut the necessary paperwork, get you signed up for a regular hitch."

The rest of the way between Pearl Harbor and San Francisco I did double duty; standing regular watches and doing deck work, plus studying with Chief Hoffman to pass his Boatswain's Mate tests.

I was on morning watch the day we entered San Francisco Bay. From my station as bridge lookout, I had a million-dollar-view when we got our first sight of the Golden Gate Bridge. There was a slight fog that morning, so the huge span appeared ghostlike as we got to within three hundred yards, and then one after another the sights of San Francisco Bay came into view. The downtown skyline, Alcatraz Island with its formidable prison, and then Alameda with its massive naval facilities.

We tied up at Pier 2, alongside dozens of other tin cans; six tied together, five rows of them. Each ship distinct in its own way to a sailor's eye; they all had been modified in some small way during the course of the war. The *Roe* for example, still had her rear 5-inch gun mount missing.

Orders for most of the crew were to pack their seabags and move into barracks ashore, there to await their mustering-out paperwork. A skeleton crew, including Bug and me, were to remain aboard until further orders came through.

"Bye Jake; see ya Bug!" Bulow said, as he and several others shook our hands. Bugeye and I stood by the quarterdeck gangway seeing everyone off. "If you're ever in Kansas City, look me up."

"Yeah, you bet," we laughed, knowing we'd probably never see any of them again.

Ed took my hand and gave it a firm shake as he stepped off. "I mean it Jake, look me up when you come home to Oklahoma. I'll be easy to find, my father's now a US Senator, so don't forget."

"I will," I said, knowing a wall had gone up somehow between us, not fully understanding.

"You too, Bug," Ed continued his goodbyes, shaking Bug's hand and slapping him on the back.

"I wouldn't miss it for the fuckin' world," laughed Bug, his unblinking eyes starting to tear up.

"Let's go get our Boatswain's Mate patches sewn on our blues and go into town for a beer," I said to Bug, turning away so he wouldn't see my own tears. We had qualified before we reached Frisco, and wanted our crossed anchor patches sewn on as soon as possible. It was a chilly February day in 1946 -- and there's no place chillier than San Francisco Bay on a chilly February day.

Chapter Seven

Alameda was an island, the western third of which had been taken over by the Navy in 1936. It was the geographic center of San Francisco Bay and had deep water port facilities where the big carriers tied up. There were also repair facilities for ships and planes, an airfield, recreational areas, as well as housing for sailors and their families.

Black Bart Hoffman had been assigned to the group mothballing surplus ships. He liked Bug and me and took us under his wing, and when he found out I hadn't finished high school, he arranged for me to take the courses I needed to graduate. I was enjoying life in the Navy; our daily duties were soft, checking ships' mooring lines, making sure bilge pumps worked, and general checking over of ships that were tied up for long periods of time.

I was doing well with my schoolwork and had even started to study for my Petty Officer exams, which I intended to sit for after I got my high school diploma.

Bug and I had become inseparable and he asked me to double date one night with him and a girl he'd met in Oakland.

"Barbara-Jean, this is Jake," said Bug, pushing the young lady closer, "Jake, this is Barbara-Jean."

"Glad to meet you," Barbara-Jean said.

"Me too," I stammered. She was cute with blond hair, only a little over five feet tall. I fell for her immediately.

"Where shall we go?" Dory asked. Dory was Bug's date.

"Let's go to that new hamburger joint, then the movies," volunteered Barbara-Jean. I hardly tasted the hamburger or paid too much attention to the movie. Barbara-Jean had my hand on her breast as soon as the lights went down in the theater.

"Let's do this again!" Barbara-Jean yelped, as she jumped up and quickly removed my hand as the lights came back on. "When do you get liberty again Jake?" We put the girls on the bus and then hitched a ride back to Alameda. I was in love; never spoke a word to Bug on the ride home, or said hardly anything over the next two days.

I really took to being in charge of the range of small landing craft we used on a daily basis. The Landing Craft Vehicle Personnel (LCVP) and the Landing Craft Mechanized (LCM), as well as the whaleboats and cutters, were all familiar to me now. I had been home on leave just after we got back from the Pacific and found a world there I no longer belonged to. I had changed, the world had changed, Hodskins hadn't!

My 18th birthday was coming up October 4th, but the Navy records listed me as eighteen already, so I didn't make a big deal out of it. Bug got wind of it though, and organized a party at Dory's place.

Her dad was a World War I Gunner's Mate, so he was glad to let us take over his home for the evening.

The party was quiet, a few guys from the base and several of Dory and Barbara-Jean's friends. After the party broke up and I was alone with Barbara-Jean, she broke the news to me.

"I'm pregnant Jake!" she sobbed, "About two months."

"Jesus Christ!" I said in shock. "You're kidding me!"

"No, I'm not. I wish I were," she cried. "What are we going to do?"

"Only one thing to do, we got to get married," I said, remembering my upbringing in Oklahoma. A man takes responsibility for his actions, my dad always told me. It looked like my own life's beginnings all over again, my child would be present at our nuptials, just as I was present at my own parent's wedding.

Bug and Dory stood up for us; Chief Hoffman and a few other people attended the ceremony. Barbara-Jean only had her mother, she was an only child; her father had been killed in Europe at the Battle of the Bulge. I had written my mother in Hodskins telling her the news, and told her if she wanted to come out I'd send her a bus ticket, but she never replied.

I couldn't get housing on the base; lowly Boatswain's Mate Seaman were only one-step up from bilge scum. I'd passed my high school exams and the Navy exams for Petty Officer, and figured I'd be promoted to Petty Officer Third Class in a month or two. Then I could apply for base housing, married status.

Then one night, about four months after our wedding, Barbara-Jean started to have cramps. I was out at sea aboard a Landing Ship Tank (LST); we were taking the ship to Bremerton Navy Base up the coast near Seattle, in Washington State. I never heard what had happened until word got to me after we'd tied up. Bug telephoned and gave me the bad news.

Barbara-Jean had called him that night when she started having pains, and they'd tried to get her to a doctor. But it was too late, they couldn't do anything, she miscarried. We had lost our baby!

By the time I could get back from Seattle, it was all over. Barbara-Jean was home in our little two-room apartment, and the remains of our baby had been disposed of by the hospital. "What can I do?" I asked, as I threw my gear down. "How are you?" I added awkwardly.

"How the fuck do you think I am?" screamed Barbara-Jean. "Where were you when I needed you?" she added accusingly. She had been drinking and her face was swollen with tears and grief. I poured myself a good swig from the open bottle of bourbon on the table. We sat there, drinking together, saying nothing until she passed out drunk and exhausted. I put her to bed and then went back to the base, not knowing what else to do.

The next evening I went back to the apartment. Bug and Dory were there; Barbara-Jean was still in her bathrobe, sitting in a chair crying. Dory had her arm around her trying to get her calmed down.

"Jake, glad you came home," Bug said, looking at the floor, feeling embarrassed. "You've got to straighten this out man."

I walked over to Barbara-Jean and gently lifted her to her feet. "I'm sorry honey. We can get over this, I know it," I said softly.

"Maybe we should leave you two alone?" Dory said, as upbeat as she could sound. Then taking Bug by the hand she said, "Come on Desmond."

"Christ!" I started to laugh, not at the situation, but I just realized that was the first time I'd heard Bug's real name.

They left, and I sat down with Barb and held her in my arms. "I'm sorry honey, it must have been rough."

"I've got to get over this Jake, I can't stand myself right now," she cried.

"It's not your fault," I tried to sound positive.

"Then whose fault is it?" she cried, slipping out of my arms and running into the bedroom sobbing. That's the way it was from then on, Barb drinking, sleeping, and crying.

Both Bug and I had made Petty Officer Third Class and I'd applied for base housing. When it was available, Barb and I moved into a two-bedroom four-plex on Alameda. Times were good and Bug and Dory planned to marry soon. The two of them were everything Barb and I weren't; they were happy, we were miserable; they made plans for the future, we couldn't see a future.

At Bug and Dory's wedding, Barb got so drunk she fell on her ass on the dance floor and couldn't get up. I wasn't even embarrassed any more; I simply picked her up and took her home to bed.

Crews continued to take ships up to Bremerton in Washington State. Some ships were headed for the scrap heap, some were being held in the Pacific Reserve Fleet, while others were being handed over to other countries. The trip up, plus hand-over time and the bus trip back, sometimes took three weeks. If we had to tow the ship it took even longer; big ships or small, a couple of half hitches around a towing bollard were the same to old timers like myself and Bug.

As the end of 1948 approached, I looked forward to my first Good Conduct Medal for four years service in the Navy, or keeping your ass out of cracks as it was called. The long service stripe I would sew on my arm would be the first of many.

I began to hear whispers about Barb going out on the town with men -- sometimes into Oakland, sometimes even bringing some half-drunk sailor home to our house. How dead inside must I be? I didn't even give a damn when guys told me about what was going on.

I received my medal that November in a brief ceremony in the Unit Commanding Officer's office. Old Chief Hoffman was there and he said as he gave me a knowing wink, "You're in for life Jake, just like me."

Later, Bug, Dory, Barb and me decided to go out to dinner and celebrate. That Saturday when I'd come in from the boat pool, Barb had pressed my best blues and had sewn on my service stripe, as well as a new Petty Officer Third Class Boatswain's Mate patch. She had also pinned on all my campaign ribbons: World War II Victory, American Campaign, Asiatic/Pacific Campaign with a battle star for Okinawa, and a brand new Good Conduct ribbon. For the first time in ages, I felt like hugging and kissing Barb all night.

"You're the handsomest sailor in the place," teased Barb as we danced at the restaurant after dinner.

"If I weren't married to this slob, I'd go for you myself," joked Dory as she and Bug swept by and Bug laughed. He and Dory were the happiest people we knew. I have to admit though, I did look good in my dress blues; prettied up with stripes and ribbons.

That night Barb and I made love like we had done in the early days. I was content. This is going to work out I kept telling myself as we lay in each other's arms all night.

For the next few months Barb and I were like two young married people anywhere. We talked about family, having kids, getting a house with a white picket fence, and then Dory announced she was going to have a baby. Bug was more excited than I had ever seen him. Dory, a little square-shaped woman with a smile as big as the Atlantic Ocean, was going to be the ideal little mother.

The problem was Barb; I guess this brought the tragedy of her own miscarriage back. She started drinking again and as Dory got closer to the day, I heard the old whispers start up whenever I was away for a few weeks; men were seen coming to the house.

We were scheduled to leave with an LST that morning for Bremerton. We'd spent all day working on her, but the engines were giving us problems. They finally located a fuel line blockage by seven that evening. It was decided the job would require a couple of days, so we were told to stand down. The trip to Bremerton was postponed, so Bug and me grabbed our gear and we headed home.

"Let's give those gals a treat tonight." Bug was enthusiastic; he hated to be away now with Dory so close to having her baby. "We'll go over to The Fish Shack and have us some crab."

"I may take a rain check Bug, Barb hasn't been feeling well lately," I lied. "It'll only spoil your surprise. You go ahead and have a good time."

"I understand buddy," Bug said. He knew what was going on. He put his hand on my shoulder for a minute, then he trotted off.

When I got to my place, there was a strange car parked outside. Dropping my bag, I unlocked the front door and stormed in. There they were, in the bedroom. I stood with my mouth open, trying to catch my breath, opening and closing it like a stranded fish.

The guy jumped up when he saw me and headed for the door; I grabbed out at him and we both tumbled to the floor. I started to hit him wherever I could get in a punch. He was naked and slipped out of my hold, crawling away towards the kitchen.

"You son-of-a-bitch!" I yelled. "I'll kill ya!"

By then Barb had climbed on my back and was pulling my hair.

"Leave him alone you bastard!" she screamed, tearing my hair out.

I had struggled to my feet and dived at the fleeing figure, dragging Barb, still on my back, with me. I managed to get on him again and started to pound his head into the floor. Barb, still cursing at me, stuck her nails into the flesh of my cheeks and racked them upward towards my eyes.

"Jesus Christ!" I yelled in pain. I let go the half-conscious man on the floor and tore Barb off my back. I stood up and could feel the blood trickling down my face.

"You lousy, fucking asshole!" Barb screamed at me, with a look of absolute hatred on her face. "Get the fuck outta here you bastard!"

I hated Barb cursing; it just showed the dark side of her I despised. I pulled back my open hand and slapped her so hard she flew clean across the kitchen, falling against the wall, a stunned look on her face.

I looked down at the whimpering prick on the floor, then looked across at Barb, and realized I didn't want to be part of this life any more. I grabbed a dish towel from the sink, wiped my face, threw the towel back on the countertop and walked out, slamming the door behind me.

I stayed out most of the night drinking. When I came back to the apartment, she'd left. The place was in a shambles; all her things were gone.

"Hey Bug!" I joked, "Ever since you found out what it was for, you can't stop doing it."

"Well, Dory thought we had better get a little sister for Roy," Bug grinned as he swung out the whaleboat.

Baby Roy had been born soon after Barb had run off, and as they'd intended for Barb and me to be Godparents, they still offered the job to me. Another old school friend of Dory's stood in as Godmother. Little Roy had been named after Roy Rogers. Dory loved Westerns and every time a new Roy Rogers movie came out she'd have to go see it. Bug, who was from Wyoming, said most of his family were cowboys at one time or another, but he sure as hell couldn't remember any of them riding around all day singing.

Little Dale, named after Dale Evans, was born in May 1950. Dory and Bug couldn't have been happier. The event just reminded me of my own fouled up marriage; that month I was served with divorce papers. "Fuck it!" I mumbled as I signed them. "I hope that asshole she's marrying gives her a dose of clap!"

The scuttlebutt had been getting stronger every day. Korea was heating up and we could find ourselves in another war.

The United States Navy had started to overhaul and make ready submarines, destroyers, carriers; everything needed to fight a war on the other side of the world. Alameda, along with every other base where ships had been held in reserve, was working twenty-four hours a day.

I got my orders to report aboard the destroyer *USS Warhol* docked in Long Beach, down the coast near Los Angeles. I had moved out of the married accommodations months ago, so I was ready to catch the bus within a day of my orders coming through. I packed what I didn't need and left the suitcases with Bug and Dory.

With a teary goodbye, I tried to pull little Roy off my neck; he was determined he was coming with me. Dory had to pry him loose, as he was kicking and screaming.

"I'll be there soon enough," Bug said solemnly. "Save some of it for me," he added, with false bravado.

"Oh, Desmond, I hope you won't have to go," Dory sobbed, still struggling with little Roy. "Look after yourself Jake, we'll all be here waiting for you."

As I climbed in the taxi waiting to take me to the bus station, I heard Dory shout after me, "Write…please write Jake!"

Chapter Eight

The *USS Warhol* stood sleek and proud and I walked the length of her before reporting aboard. She was a Fletcher Class, just like the *Roe*. I swaggered up the gangway, saluted the ship's pennant at the bow and the Stars and Stripes billowing from the flagstaff at her stern.

"Boatswain's Mate Third Rickmeyer reporting for duty; permission to come aboard, Sir?" I saluted the officer-of-the-deck as I stopped at the head of the gangway.

"Permission granted!" replied the young officer, returning my salute. "Log the Boatswain aboard Humpteller," he ordered the duty Petty Officer on gangway watch. "Then get someone to take Petty Officer Rickmeyer below and get him squared away."

"Aye, aye Sir," replied the Petty Officer.

It was good to be back aboard your own ship. I could smell the mixed aromas; the galley, with the cooks busy baking tomorrow's bread, the comforting smell of cigarette smoke and coffee as we went below to the enlisted mess; the smells of men, machinery, fuel oil, grease and paint in every pore of her.

Our orders, as much as we were told, were that we were heading for Korean waters. Beyond that we were like mushrooms.

I spent the last few days before we sailed checking the *Warhol's* boats and gear. Most of the guys called me "Boats", which was the common nickname for Boatswain's Mates. Ben Humpteller, the Gunner's Mate who'd shown me aboard that first day, and I became friendly.

There were a few old salts aboard; none of whom I'd met before, and the skipper was a full commander named Lucas Everrude, a veteran from World War II. The first thing that made me feel at ease about a ship, was knowing the skipper was experienced and knew his way around. I'd seen panicky officers on my frequent trips from Alameda to Bremerton, and they didn't have someone shooting at them.

By the time we were two weeks out at sea, we heard the North Koreans had crossed the 38th parallel and invaded South Korea on June 25, 1950. Within days, in rapid succession, President Truman had announced US forces would aid South Korea, Seoul had fallen to the North Koreans, and the President had ordered a blockade.

As soon as we arrived off Korea, the *Warhol* immediately joined the blockading force of destroyers and cruisers. The news was the South Koreans were retreating all along the Peninsular and the U.S. Army's 2nd Infantry Division had left the States and was on its way. And General Douglas MacArthur was taking over and preparing plans for an offensive.

September 19th, the amphibious landing at Inchon, found the *Warhol* steaming alongside the *USS Missouri*. That great battleship was once again in the forefront of America's presence in the trouble spots of the world.

I never felt more proud to be an American than when I watched her cut through the water heading into harm's way. We had joined the *Missouri*, the carrier *USS Hornet* and six destroyers just south of the Korea Strait. Then had steamed north with them through the Yellow Sea to join the invasion fleet off Inchon.

The *Warhol's* role in the landings was identical to what the *Roe* did off Okinawa. We escorted ships as far into the beachhead areas as was safe and then pushed it a little farther. I was stationed on the bridge assisting with signals to the Amtraks all around us; these amphibious vehicles were being used by the Marines due to the lack of good landing spots for LCVPs. I also had charge of the 26-foot whaleboat should it be needed for rescue or recovery operations. The landings at Inchon had none of the ship-to-air and ship-to-shore action that Okinawa had, but it was just as dangerous and deadly for the soldiers and Marines in the assault. Where we had the whirlwind of the Kamikaze attacks on Okinawa, at Inchon it was large tidal changes, mud flats at low tide and stone walls at high tide, as well there was the unpredictable weather.

By September 26th Seoul had been recaptured, MacArthur was being hailed as a genius, and we were headed back around through the Korea Strait and north into the Sea of Japan. We were to steam up the East Coast of the Peninsular, escorting aircraft carriers of Task Force 77, which was carrying out air raids on enemy positions.

The air raids were constant; the planes flew off and returned in groups all day long. The *Warhol* was positioned off the launching carrier's stern to quickly recover any pilots who had to ditch coming in for a landing. During takeoffs we stood by to recover pilots in the water if their launch went badly. Helicopters were now being carried on the flattops and they did most of the rescue work, but a reliable old whaleboat was still a thing of beauty to a half-drowned or injured pilot. These waters were cold and a man needed to be picked up quickly.

"Now hear this…whaleboat party…standby to launch," the PA system squawked.

"Swing her out!" I ordered the seamen standing by the davits. "Jennings, you and Clifton climb aboard as soon as I give the word," I ordered my two crewmen.

The adrenaline started to flow as I felt my heart quicken. We could now see the damaged plane coming in, smoke trailing from its undercarriage. Whether it was going to make it aboard the carrier or not we had no way of knowing. My crew would be ready if he didn't and we had to go rescue him.

The skipper turned the *Warhol* in a wide circle, ready to change course and head in any direction should the pilot have to ditch. By now the pilot had been signaled by the carrier to make his approach. Just as the plane was about to touch down, it was waved off. The pilot started to fly his aircraft safely away from the carrier, crossing far to our stern.

The *Warhol* churned the water with her twin propellers as she went to flank speed. The plane was ahead of us, and the pilot banked to bring the plane in on a parallel course, flying in the opposite direction to our heading. The pilot came down to wave top level and hit the water; hitting water at that speed is like hitting a brick wall. As big and heavy as the fighter was, the plane just stood straight up on its nose.

"Launch whaleboat!" the order was given as the ship reduced her speed and her engines responded to "All stop!"

The drill went off like clockwork, the crew and I were in the boat, hitting the water, lines released, and on the way while the *Warhol* was still in motion.

The pilot was still in his seat as we approached; he had the canopy off and was struggling with his harness straps. The plane was slowly sinking and could go down nose first at any moment.

"Take the helm Jennings!" I yelled at the crew member closest to me. "Clifton get a line around me, I'm swimming over, give me your knife!" I ordered the other member of the crew.

I hastily checked Clifton's bowline knot by tugging on the rope, all the time watching the pilot continue to struggle. "Jennings…get in close, drop me off and then back off in case she goes down," I hollowed over the engine noise. I jumped in and swam the few strokes I needed to get a hold on the wing; from there I crawled up and shinnied along to the cockpit.

The pilot was struggling with his seat harness release; it was obvious his right arm was useless. It must have been broken when he hit the water.

"Hold on," I said as I reached in and cut the straps. It was the quickest way to get him out. The plane shook, and I felt a sensation I can only describe as when an elevator starts to descend. I helped the pilot out of the seat and pushed him into the water, then jumped in after him.

I grabbed at his flight suit as he floundered, the aircraft started going down, and I kicked with everything I had to get clear, dragging the pilot with me. There was a noise like an emptying bathtub behind me, loud enough to block out all other sound.

I was exhausted as Jennings steered the whaleboat in close, half swamping the craft as the plane momentarily caused a vacuum that filled with rushing water.

"Damn it Boats! I didn't think you were gonna make it," Jennings yelled, as he left the helm and ran forward to help Clifton pull the pilot and me aboard.

"Good job Bud," I spluttered, spitting water into the bilge. I went aft and took the helm, steering back to the destroyer; she was lying dead in the water a hundred yards away.

There were cheers from the hands lining the rail as we hoisted up the whaleboat. Once on deck, a pharmacist mate helped the pilot below to sickbay.

The pilot, whoever he was, hadn't said a word from the moment I cut him free until he was aboard the *Warhol*. That was war. He was in shock and I doubt he even knew where the hell he was at that particular moment.

"Boat's Crew to the Bridge," the PA squawked. I checked with a quick glance that the deck crew was securing the whaleboat properly. I then ushered Clifton and Jennings towards the forward ship's ladder, heading up to the bridge.

"Men...I want to commend your actions out there," the Skipper said. "No finer example of good seamanship and dedication to duty can be found anywhere than when men risk their own lives to save a shipmate." He continued, "Petty Officer Rickmeyer, I want to particularly single you out for your actions."

"Thank you, Sir," I responded.

"Well done!" he said, "Now go below and get out of those wet clothes."

The three of us gave a smart salute, did an about turn and left the bridge feeling pretty damn cocky.

That evening after we'd transferred the pilot back aboard his carrier, I was ordered to report to the Chief Boatswain.

"What's up Chief?" I asked, as I removed my cap upon entering his little cubbyhole of an office.

"I have a copy of a message passed down from the Captain," he said, matter-of-factly looking over a message clipped to a board. "A Commander Sullivan P. Rooks, commanding officer of that pilot you pulled out of the water today, seems to know you." He read from the message, "To Commander L. Everrude, Captain *USS Warhol*…stop…Many thanks for first class action on returning wayward pilot to mother…stop…Tell Petty Officer Jake Rickmeyer I now owe him twice."

"I'll be goddamned!" I half-whispered, as the name came back to me after all these years. I remembered those last words of mine to Sully, "And good luck to you, too." It was a long time ago, but the image of the two of us on the fantail of the *USS Roe* was just as clear as if it were yesterday.

"You're gonna get put in for a Bronze Star for your actions today," the Chief said. "I hate to lose ya."

"Lose me?" I queried. "What do you mean, Chief?"

"You're being transferred to an LST. They need boatswain's mates with time driving LCVPs," he answered. "Your records show both LCVP and LCM experience; sorry to see ya go."

"Damn!" I groaned, "You just settle in, then the Navy moves you!"

I shook the Chief's hand and went aft to tell Ben Humpteller and the other guys whom I had made friends with the news of my departure.

We met up with four Landing Ships Tank (LST) farther up the coast; I was being transferred to *LST-298*. The skies were clear and mild for an October day off the coast of North Korea. The Navy had been bombarding the coastal areas of North Korea and was now concentrating efforts around Wonsan. I didn't know whether they had a plan to send an invasion force ashore there or not, that was need-to-know stuff. The *LST-298's* cargo was trucks and jeeps, which gave me no real indication of what her mission might be. They could have been just going to dump them over the side to make a breakwater somewhere, which had been done many times in the Pacific during World War II.

The *Missouri* was one of the bombarding ships off Wonsan, and if you have ever seen the power of an Iowa Class battleship's 16-inch guns in action, you'll know the impression they can make on those ashore and afloat. You can actually see the shells going over, and they make a whirring sound as the giant projectile spins.

It was not until a boat came alongside from one of the other ships that I realized Bugeye was in the LST steaming alongside us. He was standing in the bow, about to throw a line across to our deck crew.

"Bug!" I shouted, waving down at him. "What the fuck are you doin' here?"

Looking up in surprise, Bug almost lost his balance. "Jesus, Jake..." he yelled, "I'm in Korea two weeks and I see your ugly mug again!"

I helped the deck apes tie the boat to our starboard side and watched as they lowered the ladder. A smart young lieutenant came aboard, and after saluting him, I slid down and threw my arms around Bug.

"Oh man, how the blue blazes did you finish up on an LST off North Korea?" I asked in a rush. "The last I seen of you, you were holding a couple of snotty nosed kids back at Alameda."

"I was on my way six weeks after you left," Bug laughed. "We've been nursing these army trucks for a month; no one knows where to put them."

"What's with the officer you dropped off?" I questioned.

"You know scuttlebutt Jake," Bug said, scratching his head. "Some kind of special operation, maybe with Marine commandos."

It was great to look into those unblinking eyes of the best friend I had. "Damn Bug, it's so good to see ya!" I grabbed his hand again.

"Boats!" a crewman called down from my ship. "You're to get back aboard."

"Okay!" I yelled back. Shaking Bug's hand once more I grabbed the ladder and climbed back up the ship's side. "See ya, sailor!" I yelled down to Bug.

The lieutenant came forward from the aft deck, still talking with our Captain. They saluted each other and the lieutenant went back down the ladder to the waiting LCVP. As they shoved off, I waved and yelled, "See you if we make Japan together!"

"Yeah buddy!" hollered back Bug, as he curled the bowline neatly on the boat's deck. "Beer and peanuts at a geisha house!"

The bay surrounding Wonsan was heavily mined and on October 12th two minesweepers, The *USS Pirate* and *USS Pledge*, were sunk after hitting mines, the surrounding waters were full of them.

The scuttlebutt that Bug had passed on to me had some truth to it. A day later two dozen Marines transferred from an Attack Transport Ship (APA) and came aboard loaded down with about a ton of equipment.

All those involved in the upcoming operation were gathered on the tank deck, wherever we could find space amongst the trucks and other vehicles stowed down there. "This is not going to be easy," the Captain spoke loud enough to reach those of us at the back. "Lieutenant Cummings here will map out the details of the landing party; this ship's role will be to get them there and bring them back. Our LCVPs will be involved in landing the party and recovery of the party when the mission is completed." The Captain continued, after pausing a moment, "The crews on the LCVPs will be given the details from Cummings on your roles in this mission during his briefing to the Marine raiding party. That is all…Good luck!" He gave us all a nod as he went aft to the tank deck ladder.

"Okay, listen up!" Lieutenant Cummings said as he took charge of the briefing. "We have to get onto the beach, make our way inland five miles, blow a communications station that is causing the Navy problems big-time, then get back out again." He continued as he pointed out locations on a map unfolded on the windshield of a jeep. "Our force will be divided between two landing craft, twelve men to each boat. I'll be in one and Gunnery Sergeant Malone will take the other team. We'll approach the target from two directions, giving maximum chance of success to the mission. The boat crews will handle the landing craft, and they'll wait off the beach after they've landed us. Both raiding parties will work independently, but must be back at the beachhead by 0400. If anyone is not on the beach by then, we'll have to pull out for the safety of the ships. They will be too close in to be caught by daylight…any questions?"

The lieutenant sounded like he knew his business, and the Marines he commanded all looked tough and lean.

"Gunny Malone will go over the explosives details with the men involved," the Lieutenant continued. "Everyone check every piece of your gear. The boat crews will be given landing details when we go, depending on conditions. We go over the side at 2200 hours."

He returned the Gunny's salute and walked away through the parked vehicles.

"Jesus Christ!" I whispered to Boatswain's Mate Henley, who would drive the other LCVP. "This could get hot, a night landing on a strange beach. We don't know where the fuck the Gooks are, then we have to sit offshore until they get back."

"If they get back," replied Henley. "We're off North Korea, that's enemy territory, Rickmeyer, in case you haven't heard."

"Oh, I know that goddamn much Bud," I said, as I swung up the ladder. "Let's get these boats checked out and go over what we do know about the mission."

That night was as black as the ace of spades, it wasn't a coincidence that they'd planned for a moonless night. My crew and I were standing by our boat at 2130. We'd had a big meal of steak, potatoes, gravy, and lots of hot chocolate; it was going to be a long night. I'd tried to rest in the afternoon, but all I did was toss and turn in my rack.

Lieutenant Cummings came by the boat about fifteen minutes before the time set to go and asked me if I was ready.

"We're checked out," I replied, with a mixture of pride and apprehension. "We're ready to get this show on the road."

"Good!" he nodded approvingly. "It's time to saddle up!"

The twelve Marines in our group were assembled and climbed down to the boat once we'd lowered it into the water. The Lieutenant was last aboard.

"Synchronize your watches…it's now 2200 hours," he spoke in a whisper.

The signals were all pre-arranged, the deck crew released the lines holding the boat to the ship's side; the motors had been checked out a dozen times, and now they purred smoothly to life. We had the mufflers on the exhausts to keep the noise down to a minimum.

After circling around the stern of the LST, we joined up with the other boat. The plans included an LCVP from the accompanying LST to follow us in, and then stand-by in case we damaged or lost a craft on the beach. The other LCVP signaled once with an infrared lamp telling us that he was on station. The operation had begun. We headed slowly towards the beach.

"Torpedo!" a Marine yelled from the bow.

"Shut the fuck up!" I yelled back in a hoarse whisper. "It's only phosphorus in the water. Lieutenant, shut that moron up!"

"Wilco Boats," the Lieutenant whispered back.

I could just see well enough to make out Cummings hitting the Marine across the helmet with his hand, and saying something I couldn't hear. My focus was on the beach and my bowman, who would signal with a lamp any changes as we went in.

We glided onto the beach; so far everything had been perfect. The bow ramp was lowered and the Marines ran off into the darkness. I raised my arm for the bowman to raise the ramp, and we backed off the beach. Our orders were to wait until we saw a light flash three times from the shore, which was the pickup signal, or 0400 whichever came first.

The other boat backed off about the same time and we waited about a hundred yards from the beach. A signal from the stand-by boat, fifty yards farther out, gave us the assurance that we had help if we needed it.

Time dragged, it seemed every minute was ten, every hour twelve. We thought we heard muffled explosions inland, and got ready for what we knew was coming. Then the signal, three long flashes from the beach. "Let's go!" I said to the crew, as quietly as I could.

The run in was smooth, the ramp was lowered, and then the hill above the beach erupted with gunfire. "The bastards have been waiting for us to hit the beach!" I yelled. "Get those guys aboard, move your asses!"

Thump…thump…thump, bullets hit the sides of the boat as the Marines climbed over the half-raised ramp. I counted two, then five, finally eight; two of them wounded. "Where are the others?" I hollered.

"Right behind us," gasped one jarhead, as he laid his wounded teammate on the deck.

"Come on…come on…" I was getting nervous. Finally the Lieutenant and two more Marines came over the top of the ramp carrying the body of a third man, the body looked lifeless.

"Raise 'er up!" I shouted to the sailor at the bow. "Get that ramp up!"

I started to back the boat off the beach, allowing lots of sea room before I started to turn her. Over my shoulder I made out the other boat starting her run back to the ship; I hoped all their team was accounted for.

The bullets kept hitting the sides of the craft and plopped into the water all around us. I was exposed in my helmsman position and could only crouch down, pulling my head into my shoulders. Whatever makes us think pulling our heads between our shoulder blades can protect us from flying bullets?

Wham! The water rose up in a cloud in front of us. "Mortars!" yelled Lieutenant Cummings, "They're laying mortars down on us, get going Boats!"

Wham! Wham! All of a sudden the entire front end of the boat lifted clean out of the water. The world erupted into shouting men, pieces of boat, cold water, blinding flashes, and a life and death struggle to stay afloat and get away from the beach.

"Here…over here," someone was yelling. "Help me, help!" someone else was crying. I found one Marine and slipped out of my life jacket and struggled to put it on him.

"Thanks," he groaned. He was badly wounded and couldn't have stayed up much longer.

Then the sound of the standby LCVP as it was coming in to rescue us. "Goddamn!" I shouted. "Over here!"

Hands lifted the wounded man onto the lowered bow ramp and then other hands helped me crawl on. I got up off my hands and knees and ran aft to lend a hand with the helm. "Bugs!" I yelled with excitement. "You goddamn motherfucker! I could kiss ya!"

Bugeye was driving the relief boat, and he was turning in closer to the beach, where a group of men were flaying about in the water.

"Hold her steady Jake," he said, handing over the helm. He was hollering over the noise of exploding mortars and rifle fire, "I'm going to yank the muffler off. They know we're here now and we'll get more speed without it!"

I started to reverse as the six or so men in the water were pulled aboard.

I felt a blow to my shoulder and fell back against Bug. "Jesus, I'm hit!" I gasped. Bug grabbed me, and then went limp as he too was hit.

"Fuck!" he groaned, as he slipped though my arms. I grabbed him as best as I could with my one good arm, then both of us dropped to the deck.

Bug's face was pale in the dark. "Bug! Bug!" I kept shouting, "Hold on you miserable bastard!"

The boat was spinning around in circles, until one of the other sailors grabbed the helm and gunned the boat out to sea. Bug looked at me with those unblinking eyes. Never had I felt so completely helpless, knowing there was nothing I could do. I sensed him fading away, he opened his mouth as if to say something, sighed, and then he was gone.

As we pulled up to the lowered ramp of *LST-298,* willing hands started lifting men aboard. The bow doors of the bigger ship had been opened, at some risk to the ship should she have to get underway at short notice. But it was the fastest way to recover us from the damaged landing craft. Men break the rules to help their shipmates in such situations.

I don't know how long it took them to get Bug's body loose from the grip I had on him. I only remember fighting them to hang onto my friend; his pale face had the appearance of only being peacefully asleep. His body felt as light as a child's in my arms.

"God, what about Dory and the kids?" I sobbed, and then I must have drifted into unconsciousness.

Chapter Nine

The days following the raiding party's mission in North Korea had been mixed. My shoulder wound had been serious and to prevent me from moving it and causing more damage, they had kept me doped up.

I had been transferred, along with some of the others, to a hospital ship. The few moments of clarity I'd had were when they lowered me into a small boat, then again when I was lifted onto a table. I remember some bright lights and then a feeling of being completely bound; like a mummy, unable to move my legs, arms, or head.

As I started to get my senses back and my health improved, I learned I was on the *USS Repose* -- that same hospital ship I'd seen and been so much impressed by when I saw her in Ulithi in 1945.

"Boatswain's Mate Rickmeyer?" a chief pharmacist's mate asked. He was all decked out in dress whites.

"That's me Chief," I answered.

"Good!" he said, a serious look on his face. "Congratulations son, you're being decorated with a Bronze Star this afternoon. I'll make sure the nurse gets you shaved and cleaned up. The ceremony is at 1400."

"I ain't going anywhere Chief," I joked.

At precisely 1400 hours, a Navy photographer appeared at my bedside, then behind him a full commander in dress whites. It took me a moment to get my fuzzy brain coordinated and recognize the face.

"Hello Jake," Sully Rooks said, a grin splitting his face. "I have the honor to present you with this Medal."

He then read out the citation, pinned the medal onto my pajamas, stood back and saluted, all the time the photographer was popping off photos. The photos would appear somewhere in the Navy News or some other military publication.

It was great public relations for the Navy and would get Commander Rooks some good press too. Just looking at him told me he was headed to the top; he was tall, straight, every inch a Naval Officer in his crisply starched and pressed white uniform.

"Okay Petty Officer," he said to the photographer. "That will be all, thank you."

"So how are you Jake?" he turned his attention back to me. "I…I… mean apart from the wound of course?"

"Getting better, Sir," I smiled. "With the Purple Heart I got for the bullet in the shoulder, I'm starting to feel like a hero."

"You are a hero Jake," he laughed, "and I give you permission to call me Sully whenever we're not in the presence of senior officers."

"I'll remember that, Sir," I replied. It was hard to break a habit. "I mean…Sully…thanks."

"It's great to see you again Jake," he said, continuing with a big grin on his face. "You're still taking it on the chin for the good ol' U.S. Navy, eh?"

I felt a little embarrassed by all this attention. I could see the doctor and nurse standing in the background with proud looks on their faces.

"I can't stay," Sully said, his face suddenly losing the smile. "I've got to get back aboard the carrier. I pulled a few strings to get here and present this medal to you personally. It's for the pilot you pulled out of the drink that day and for pulling me out back in 1945."

"I appreciate that…er…Sully," I mumbled, proud that this man counted me as a friend.

"Well, I've got to shove off," he said, looking at his watch. Sully then shook my hand and laughed, "We'll see each again, and then we'll get shitfaced!"

I laughed until my shoulder hurt so bad I had to force myself to stop. "It's a date Sully…maybe Tokyo when this is over."

"You're on," he smiled. Standing back he saluted once more, and then turned and walked smartly down the row of bunks.

I watched him walk away, remembering our last meeting. "Good luck to you too, Sully," I whispered those same words again.

The *USS Repose* docked in Yokosuka, Japan and transferred hundreds of wounded to the base hospital. I was now one of the walking wounded; my shoulder had healed nicely and I'd started to exercise it with the help of a therapist. I packed up what few things I had been transferred to the *Repose* with, not forgetting my two new medals, and took up residency in the hospital.

One morning, a week after I'd moved to the hospital, the doctor stopped by my bed during his early rounds.

"Petty Officer Rickmeyer," he said, "I'd like to transfer you back to duty. You're taking up a badly needed bed here and I'll arrange that you be given light duties." The doctor looked worn out. "What do you think of that Rickmeyer?"

"That would suit me fine, Sir," I replied.

"You'll get your orders to report to the base administration office," he continued. "They'll get you settled with some desk job, nice and easy, but it will get you back doing something."

"Sir, I couldn't be happier," I grinned. "I'm starting to get antsy layin' around in here."

"Good!" he stated, as he wrote notes on his clipboard. "Of course, I'll set up weekly sessions with the therapist to make sure your shoulder is getting the right exercise."

"When can I get out of here, Sir?" I was half out of the bed and packed already.

"This afternoon will be fine," he said, nodding his approval at my enthusiasm. As the doctor and his accompanying nurse walked on to the next bed, I lay back on the pillow and took a deep breath.

I reported in that afternoon to the base Administration Office, dressed in fresh dungarees that had been issued to me at the hospital. The striker at the front desk showed me into one of the nearby offices after he looked at my orders; "*Master at Arms*" was written in large letters on the door. The chief within, sitting behind a cluttered desk, told me to sit down.

"I'm Chief Master-at-Arms Van der Broeke," he said, nodding at me. "You'll be working for me, just filing papers and generally taking it easy. I've read the note on your medical report, and anyone with a Purple Heart ain't gonna get any grief from me."

"I don't expect to lay around Chief," I smiled. "To tell you the truth, I'll be glad to get back to sea."

"You'll have lots of time for that," he said. "Meanwhile, I want you issued with some new uniforms, and seeing as how it's almost Christmas, take a coupla days off."

"Thanks Chief." I was starting to warm to this guy. "I can use the clothes; don't know when anything from my last ship will catch up with me."

"Sims!" Chief Van der Broeke called through the open door. "Get your ass in here!" he continued in a booming voice. "Take Rickmeyer here to stores, draw dress and work clothes for him and anything he needs; get him a rack, then list him on the day duty roster...er...starting December 28th."

"Aye, aye Chief!" replied Yeoman Striker Sims.

"Aye, Chief!" I stuttered, getting up from my chair and following Sims as he gestured towards the office door.

"That old salt is the meanest son-of-a-bitch in the Navy," Sims confided in me as we hurried over to stores. "Dutch they call him, but that's only if you're on friendly first name terms and he's accepted you as a shipmate."

"Oh, I've seen meaner assholes than him around," I said, with an air of salty pride. "Where's the chow hall and what time's supper?"

I spent the couple of days liberty Van der Broeke gave me getting my new gear organized. I did go into town a few times. I was expecting the Japanese to be resentful of us being in their country, but they weren't. I was treated with respect in the streets, or whenever I stopped to eat at a local restaurant.

I liked to spruce up with my full chest of ribbons, including those from World War II. The ribbons were available at the base PK. I'd done that to show off for all the greenhorns around the base; the war in Korea had called up thousands of young men. But it was the Purple Heart that really opened their eyes. I was a veteran who had seen combat action and had the scars to prove it. In fact, even old salty Van de Broeke looked at me admiringly when I reported for duty that first morning. I had seen action in two wars, and wore my four-year good conduct stripe with pride. He nodded his approval as I walked into his office that morning, ready to go to work.

"Mornin' Rickmeyer," he said approvingly. "I like a sailor who takes pride in his uniform; just sit at that empty desk outside the door. Sims will refer any business for me through to you. Got that?"

"Aye, Chief," I said, thinking this job won't be so bad, at least till I get another ship. I sat down at the desk, and waited for something to do. "Sims!" I shouted, trying out my new authority, "Bring me some coffee will ya?"

"Let me tell what we did last night Boats," grinned Sims, as he brought the coffee over to my desk. "We went into some place called *Yokohama Mamma's*, and damn it Boats, I tell ya, they had women on stage that showed us everything they had! Then get this…they had some kind of lottery and the winner got to go up on the stage and do the woman," he was getting excited just telling me about it.

"Sims!" a voice boomed from Chief Van de Broeke's office. "We don't give a damn about your perverted liberties, and if I hear one more yarn about *Yokohama Mamma's* I'll place it off limits!"

"Aye Chief," answered Sims, his balloon busted.

"Now get back to what you're supposed to be doin'!" Van de Broeke's voice could raise the dead. "And you Rickmeyer, don't listen to these apes, they've been here too long. Maybe a little sea time is what they need, maybe that would curtail their permanent hard-ons."

"I hear ya Chief," I replied. Then winking at Sims, "You won't find me in any of those joints." Sims went back to the front desk mumbling under his breath; a perfectly good morning ruined for him.

Two days later the Chief called me into his office. "Sorry Rickmeyer, but I need a Petty Officer to take charge of a four-man Shore Patrol detail New Year's Eve."

"Chief, I'm on light duty…if some drunken swabbie takes me on I could injure my shoulder," I said looking for sympathy. I wasn't worried so much about the shoulder, just the detail; every sailor in the Navy hated the Shore Patrol, including me.

"I understand that Rickmeyer," he went on, "but you're the only one available, and I need you tomorrow night. There are several ships in port and New Year's Eve is gonna be hell." I knew I could have gone to the hospital and reported the Chief to the doctor. But then, I also knew being on Chief Van de Broeke's shitlist could haunt me for the rest of my days in the Navy.

"Don't worry, you can wear a sidearm and I'll give you four of the biggest sons-of-bitches I can round up to take with ya," the Chief continued. "I'll write a notation in your records for helping out over and above your normal duties, that won't go astray when your next promotion is due."

Van de Broeke had been around long enough to know what countered in the Navy. Notations and recommendations on your records went a long way to where the Navy put you, and how they looked on your promotions.

The next night after I'd eaten a big supper, it had been a pretty good meal being New Year's Eve and all, I went to the armory and drew a belt, holster and 45-caliber pistol. After that I reported to Van de Broeke's office where my four-man squad was waiting. All had their SP armbands on and were holding nightsticks, and all were big, husky farm boys from the South judging by their drawls.

"Okay, Petty Officer Rickmeyer," the Chief began, "let's hope this don't get too messy. There's a van outside, with a driver who knows his way around the hot spots."

"What should we do if we collar somebody?" I asked.

"If they're just drunk and rowdy, take 'em back to their ships and let their officers take care of the problem. We don't want to be holding any key personnel when a ship sails," he explained. "That just brings the shit down on our heads. But if there's anything more serious than that, bring 'em here to the brig."

"I don't know exactly what the procedures are Chief. I mean what if I have to lock someone up?" I said hastily.

"That's taken care of too, see how easy it is?" the Chief smiled. "The Marine Gunny at the brig will take care of all the paperwork; you just drop 'em off and get back out there."

"Aye, aye, Chief!" I said.

"Okay fellas, let's go," I ordered the waiting Shore Patrolmen.

Climbing into the front seat of the van with the driver I wished I was in town having a good time. Instead I was about to face a thousand drunken swabbies and they'd be mighty pissed if I tried to interfere with their fun.

The night was going well, we'd broken up a fight or two, picked up three sailors sitting in the middle of the road drunk and holding up traffic, and chased one guy who was running stark naked down the street. When we grabbed the nude runner, he claimed he was chasing after some local fella who had stolen his wallet while he was with a hooker.

It was after midnight when we got the word that a brawl had broken out at *Yokohama Mama's,* and by the time we got there a couple of dozen sailors were punching, kicking, and wrestling each other. The Mama-San was trying to get her booze bottles out of the way of the melee, and her girls were still trying to get off the stage.

I ran in blowing my whistle with my squad right behind me. What I thought would happen, happened. The first guy I tried to grab swung a haymaker at me; instinctively I ducked, then came up and hit him square in the jaw. The stab of pain ran from my neck clear down to my toes. I staggered back holding my shoulder.

"Jesus Christ!" I yelled, the pain almost unbearable.

"Sorry Boats, I should've nailed that mother for ya," shouted one of the squad, as he jabbed his billyclub hard into the brawler's stomach.

"Clear 'em out!" I ordered, trying to stay on my feet, starting to feel woozy.

The brawling sailors started to hightail it once they saw the billy clubs, armbands, and heard the whistles. It was impossible to hang onto them all; the squad had managed to arrest only about eight or nine.

"Get 'em in the van, we're taking these assholes to the brig," I said, still in pain.

"Hey Boats!" one of the squad hollered from the backstage area. "Y'all gotta take a look at this."

Going backstage, I looked to where he was pointing. I couldn't believe my eyes.

There was Rabbit; he was hiding behind some curtains, his stupid buck-toothed grin trying to mask his embarrassment.

I started to laugh, but as I pulled the curtains aside, my amusement turned to rage. Rabbit had his pants down around his ankles and behind him was a naked little girl.

"You fucking piece of shit Rabbit!" I screamed. "This time I swear I'll do you in." I pulled my pistol out and ran the slider back, at the same moment grabbing Rabbit by the throat.

"Whoa, Boats!" my squad member said as he grabbed my arm.

I could see nothing except that ugly face of Rabbit's, the flashback of the terrified little girl in the Philippines, and now the look of fright on the face of the child behind him.

The Mama-San came out of nowhere yelling in Japanese, grabbed the kid by the arm, and then hauled ass out the back.

"She's just a Jap kid Boats," the squad member said. "It's not like they feel anythin'; they ain't the same as us…are they?"

Ignoring his stupid comments, I pressed the muzzle of the 45 up Rabbit's nose as far as I could, until he started blinking wildly in pain and panic.

"Jake, Jake!" Rabbit whimpered. "Don't do it man, please."

"Don't do it Boats!" added another squad member who'd come backstage.

"I won't kill you," I sneered with hatred, "but this time I'm turning you in."

After we took all the brawlers we'd managed to arrest to the brig, and that included Rabbit, I went to the infirmary and asked for whatever painkillers they could give me. I took twice the dosage and sat in the front seat of the van and tried to rest.

The rest of the night was fairly quiet. I think the farm boys rounded up a few stragglers and returned them to their ships; another fistfight was broken up. I don't remember much; I was doped up with the painkillers. But that was Near Year's Eve. Today it was a new year, it was 1951.

Chapter Ten

I was sitting at my desk a couple of days into the New Year, when I heard the familiar sound of Chief Van de Broeke's voice.

"I need to see you Rickmeyer," he hollered through the door, "come on in here!"

"What's up Chief?" I asked, stepping into his office.

"You did a good job the other night, helped me out no end," he began, "but I need something else from ya." I waited in silence for him to continue, wondering what else he wanted from me. "You hauled in a Petty Officer named Tyler Dicks the other night," the Chief said. "You wanted him charged with raping a child. I want you to withdraw the charges."

"What!" My mouth dropped open; I couldn't believe what I was hearing. "You don't know this creep, Chief. I pulled him off a little girl in the Philippines for the same thing. He got away with it then, but not this time."

"I understand what you're saying," the Chief continued, sounding sympathetic. "But the Navy don't want this to get into the press. No one seen any rape take place, just a naked kid; and incidentally, the kid can't be found now either."

"Chief, this guy's an asshole of the first order," I pleaded. "The Navy would be better off putting his ugly ass in Portsmouth Naval Prison for fifty years."

"I appreciate that Rickmeyer," he said firmly. "But we're returning him to his ship. He'll probably get charged with being drunk and failing to report back aboard on time."

"You're telling me to drop it?" I asked in disbelief.

"You're hearing me right," the Chief said. "Sign this charge withdrawal sheet. It says you're not sure of the exact circumstances upon reflection and are withdrawing the original complaint."

I knew I couldn't do a thing about it; my complaint didn't mean shit if the Navy wanted it dropped. If I demanded the charges stay on the book, I'd only dig a hole for myself I'd have a tough time climbing out of. Holding in my rage, I signed the paper the Chief laid out for me.

"Will that be all Chief?" I said, as sarcastically as I could without provoking Van de Broeke's anger.

"That's all," he said, then added as I went out the door, "If it's any consolation, I ordered *Yokohama Mamma's* placed off limits to all service personnel."

I sat at my desk pissed off for the rest of the day. I thought again about how guys like Bugeye and Billy Smith and thousands just like them hadn't made it, while scum-eating assholes like Rabbit kept slipping out of every fix they ever found themselves in.

The next couple of months passed without incident. My shoulder was as good as new. Van de Broeke was easy to work for, and he lived up to his word and wrote a glowing report and placed it in my records. It was confidential, but Sims had shown it to me before he filed it away.

In April I got the word I was rejoining the *USS Warhol*. I couldn't have been happier; shore duty was for the birds. I went in on my last day to say goodbye to Van de Broeke, Sims, and my other shipmates at the office. It had been where I'd spent every day for the last three months.

"Goodbye Chief," I shook Van de Broeke's hand firmly. "It's been an experience, but I'm a blue water sailor, not used to riding a desk."

"It's been my pleasure Jake, wish I could hang onto ya," the old Chief said sincerely. Then as I walked out the door he added, "And call me Dutch. I'll see ya around Jake."

Sims shook my hand and held the door open for me as I swung my seabag over my shoulder. I took one last look around, and then walked briskly over to the motor pool.

I couldn't find the *Warhol* at first. I found the right berthing pier, but no sign of her. I asked a sailor standing by the gangway of the *USS New Jersey*, moored at the same pier if he knew where my ship was.

"If she's a tin can, she's outboard of us," he bellowed. Tin Can was the nickname given to all destroyers.

"That would be her," I replied. After one long look down the immense length of the battleship, I climbed the gangway, saluted the officer at the head of the gangway, and requested permission to cross over.

The *New Jersey* was huge. I had seen the *Missouri* close-up several times at sea, but now walking across the quarterdeck of one of these Iowa Class battleships was an experience; it was like crossing a football field. I looked down at the *Warhol* tied alongside; she appeared toy-like compared to the mighty battlewagon.

"Permission to come aboard, Sir?" I asked, as I saluted the duty officer smartly.

"Permission granted!" replied Ensign Carter Bilts. "Good to have you back Boats."

I dropped my seabag and took the hand he'd offered me. "It's good to be back, Sir," I replied, returning his grin.

"You know Humpteller," he continued, nodding at the petty officer on watch with him. "He'll help you below and get you squared away."

"Hello Ben," I said. "It's good to see some familiar faces. Shore duty in Japan is not all it's cracked up to be," I laughed as Ben and I headed for the ship's office.

We sailed from Yokosuka in company with the *New Jersey* and two other ships. We were to join up with some cruisers and supply ships off the East Coast of North Korea, and then form Task Force 95. The Task Force would then commence the bombardment of North Korean targets. Shore bombardment had been going on for some time. The *Missouri* had hit communications targets at Chong Jin, which was only thirty-nine miles from the Chinese border, raising fears about a possible war with China itself. Task Force 95 would start shelling around Wonsan, an area I remembered only too well.

The action had not been without casualties on the Navy's part. Shore batteries at Songjin had damaged the *USS Charles S. Perry,* as well as several other ships since bombardment of shore targets had begun in the summer of 1950.

Task Force 95 commenced hitting targets off Wonsan. The *Warhol's* role was to get in close to shore and act as a spotter for the *New Jersey's* 16-inch salvos. After one target had been hit by 16-inch shellfire and the dust cleared enough to see, the Skipper radioed the *New Jersey* when asked for a damage update, that the target had "disappeared completely from the landscape!"

On May 20th the *New Jersey* and the *Warhol* were both hit by shellfire from shore batteries. I don't think the battleship missed a beat, but we had to withdraw out to sea for a damage assessment.

We had suffered three casualties amongst the crew, none of them serious, and apart from some missing and damaged stanchions, scraped paint, a buckled hatch and dented bulkhead, we were in great shape.

We never got back to Wonsan to join the Task Force though. Orders came for the ship to immediately proceed to Formosa. We also heard that General Douglas MacArthur had been relieved as Allied Commander in Korea the month before.

Sailing south to Formosa felt like jumping out of the frying pan into the fire. The tensions with China were mounting and the Communist Chinese were threatening to invade the island of Formosa. General Chiang Kai-Shek and the Nationalist Army had fled to the island after the Communist takeover in 1949, and President Truman had made it clear the US would assist the Nationalists on Formosa at all costs.

What part we were to play in all this wasn't clear, but we figured the Captain would fill us in when the time came. The time came a couple of days later. The Captain spoke to us over the intercom, but it wasn't the news we were expecting.

"Men, this is the Captain," he began. "The *Warhol* has been ordered home!" He waited a few moments for the cheering to die down throughout the ship, then continued. "And as a bonus we've been ordered to take the long way round. We have been cleared for port visits to Singapore, Israel, and then on to England; from there we'll sail across the Atlantic and home."

The messdecks were filled with yells, yips and laughter. It was over for the *Warhol* and her crew. We were going home; at least we'd be out of it for awhile.

The *Warhol* cruised southeast of Formosa, through the Luzon Strait, passing close to Pratas Island, which was held by the Chinese Nationalists. Sailing close to the island was obviously meant to show the US Navy's support for the garrison stationed there.

We then sailed south, down the coast of French Indo-China, where the Frogs were having their own problems desperately trying to hold onto their former colony.

The communist rebels were gaining ground in the northern part of the country, and the US was giving the French billions in aid in an effort to contain Chinese influence throughout the Indo-Chinese peninsular.

Finally Singapore, the island port on the southernmost tip of the Malay Peninsular.

I had made up my mind I was going to see some of the sites in these exotic places, instead of just getting drunk in the first bar I came across outside the dockyard gates. Most of the guys were talking about the beautiful girls of Singapore and how they were going to leave their mark. One young stud claimed he had the perfect line; he told them he lived in Hollywood and his next door neighbor was Lana Turner. The sights, sounds, and smells of the tropics filled my senses, just as they had done years before; I must have been a beachcomber on a south-seas island in a former life.

Singapore was a fascinating place. It reminded me of Shanghai, the Chinese port we had visited on the *Roe* at the end of WWII. The population was a mix of Chinese, Malay, and East Indian. It bustled with commerce; rubber coming by barge down from Malaya; rice, timber, and spices from the Dutch East Indies.

I heard one remarkable story from a raggedy-assed tout who tried to offer me his services as a guide. He told me about the origins of the "Bogie Man", whom all parents threatened their children with whenever they misbehaved.

The story started with the Bogie people of Borneo. They were notorious pirates, and cutthroats to boot, and had long ago established themselves in these seas as seafarers to watch out for. In fact, a street was named after them in Singapore. It's Bogie Street; and like the pirates it was named for, it's full of pickpockets, thieves, and wayward women. It was also notorious for transvestites, if that was your preference.

Another practice that disturbed me was the "Death Houses"on Sago Lane. The Chinese were practical when it came to feeding extra mouths in the household who were too old or infirm to contribute their share. They placed them in these houses of death, and the old folks simply sat there until they died. If they were lucky, they had a few dollars in a bag around their neck. This was to pay for professional mourners at their funerals, their own families being too busy to attend.

We left Singapore much as we had found it, perhaps with a few extra American dollars left behind in the hands of the East Indian moneychangers around Change Alley, or in the bras of the numerous bar girls.

After leaving Singapore, the *Warhol* made her way north through the Malaca Strait. One morning as I was sitting on a hatch cover near the bow of the ship just forward of the 5-inch gun mount, I was looking ahead at the mirror-calm, reflective, turquoise water.

Suddenly a huge, black form leaped out of the sea ahead of the ship, then fell back into the water with an enormous splash. My mouth dropped open.

"What the hell was that?" I said aloud.

It was a full ten minutes before I finally realized I had just seen a giant Manta Ray. It must have been stunning fish on the surface of the water. The Mantas would leap out of the water to stun schools of fish, and then they could eat the stunned meal at their leisure.

Our journey took us around the northern tip of Sumatra, across the Indian Ocean, to sail south of the large island of Ceylon. The whole crew was looking forward to passing through the Suez Canal, and the excitement mounted as we transited the Red Sea.

The Suez was not what I had imagined; you could almost touch the sides at times. It's fairly narrow and there were Arabs riding camels along its banks. At either end of the canal, there were the types of debased, seedy ports that sailors love to go to.

The area was tense with Israeli and Arab unrest, and our visit to the port of Haifa, Israel, was not without its political message. The ships of the United States Navy were not just used to fire guns at enemy positions; they were also used to signal America's policies and intentions abroad.

I was still determined to stay out of the bars and brothels and signed up for the bus tour of Biblical sites. It was a history lesson I enjoyed very much. This land was so old; there had been thousands of years of wars, invasions, famines, turmoil and strife, and all were evident from Bat Gum, just north of Haifa, all the way to Jerusalem.

Ensign Carter Bilts was also on the tour; he must have been a Southern Baptist. His enthusiasm for the history of the country, and the running commentary of Biblical stories he gave at every site, made me realize he was a well-read Biblical scholar. I had scored points with Bilts without any effort on my part, just being along on the same tour.

"Petty Officer Rickmeyer," he smiled, "I'm so glad to see at least some of the crew have Christian values. I'm glad you have the good morals to stay out of the dens of sin one can find all over the Mediterranean."

"Yes Sir," I replied, smiling to myself. If you only knew the half of it, I thought.

After leaving Haifa, we traversed the Mediterranean towards the Gibraltar Straight and on to England, with an added stop on our itinerary at Gibraltar itself. Gibraltar was the point of land jutting out from Spain that had been a British military outpost for centuries.

The *Warhol* entered the ancient port through the North and South Moles, passed the old coaling piers, and tied up at the Royal Navy Docks. My self-control was still strong enough for me to plan to spend my time touring, instead of gallivanting around the hot spots.

Ensign Bilts was once again a hive of knowledge as we rode up the cable car to Signal Hill. Then we visited St. Bernard's Hospital, tramped around the Tower of Homage, and looked through the Governor's Residence with, of course, the opportunity to feed the Gibraltar Apes.

Those damn monkeys shit on my uniform when I tried to hold one up for a photograph.

That was the last tour for me, though. When we reached England I was going to drink a pisspot full of good English beer. Ensign Bilts would be disappointed when I didn't do the tour of the Tower of London with him, but

I needed my ashes overhauled. The *Warhol* cut a fine figure as she sailed through the straight between Morocco on the North African coast and Spain on the mainland of Europe, out into the wide Atlantic.

We arrived in England and tied up at the Royal Navy base in Portsmouth. This was the port so many men and ships had left from and joined the invasion of France on D-Day during World War II.

This time I accepted Ben Humpteller's invitation to hit the pubs. Ben was starting to think I'd been hit in the head as well as the shoulder at Wonsan.

We were on our second pint of beer in the *King's Shilling* when I noticed a well-dressed woman giving me the eye. I'd heard the English women had been easy for Americans in the last war and hoped that was still the case; maybe I'd get lucky.

"Hi," I said, trying to turn on the charm. "Would you care to join us for a drink?"

"I think that might be nice," she replied, smiling pleasantly. "I'm meeting a friend here soon."

"Oh, I guess I'd be interfering," I said, disappointed.

"It's not what you think," she replied quickly. "It's a lady friend, and she would suit your shipmate nicely."

Oh boy! I thought, this is going to be all-goddamn-right.

"My name's Sara," she said, sitting down at our table. "Where do you come from in America?" she asked.

"I'm from Chicago, the name's Ben," Humpteller said, rising slightly up off his chair. "Jake here's from…."

"From Hollywood," I cut Ben off in mid-sentence.

"Oh, how amazing!" Sara said, sounding excited. "Do you know any film stars?"

"I live next door to Lana Turner," I replied quickly, before Ben could get back in the conversation.

"I don't believe it!" Sara laughed. "Is that true, Ben?"

"Yes Ma'am!" Ben replied, catching on fast enough to avoid disaster.

After several more beers with scotches for the ladies, Sara and I left the pub and went back to her place.

It was not long before we'd left our half-finished cups of tea in the living room, stripped each other naked, and were in bed.

After we'd made love, Sara started to ask me all about my life, family, what it was like in America. We lay there in each other's arms talking for hours. Is this what I had been missing all my life? The intimacy of a woman I could hold and love and need? I started to feel myself falling for this delicate English lady. We made love again, and then drifted off to sleep.

The next morning found us laughing over breakfast. "What do you want to do today?" Sara asked, fondling my dick teasingly. "I bet you can't catch me before I get into the bedroom?"

I had her before she'd reached the kitchen door and laid her down right there on the cold linoleum. After all this time without a woman, I was horny enough to go all day and all night. I had a 48-hour pass and did not need to get back aboard the ship until the next day, anytime before five o'clock.

After our frantic lovemaking in the kitchen and a hot bath, Sara talked me into going to the countryside for lunch at a country pub. We took the train towards London, then got off at some little village halfway there. The streets were still all cobblestones, and the houses all looked to be from King Henry the Eighth's time.

"Oh Darling, isn't this wonderful," Sara said, as we walked along a path beside the stream running through the village. "I never knew life could be this good."

"Neither did I," I said, wanting to tell her that I loved her. But I didn't know if Sara would just think I was using another line on her. I wanted this woman more than I'd ever wanted anything in my life.

We found our way to an old mill beside the stream, complete with its own slowly spinning water wheel. The mill had been converted to a cozy little pub, and Sara and I sat with the locals and had shepherd's pie with tomato sauce, all washed down with a pint of ale.

Never had such simple food and company felt so right. I decided I would tell Sara I loved her, maybe tomorrow, before I went back to the ship.

The afternoon drifted into late evening as we caught the train back to Portsmouth. We had been behaving like silly teenagers all day long. We were still laughing and giggling as Sara opened the front door to her flat. "You Yanks," she tried to speak through her laughter. "I've never had so much fun, really."

"Neither have I!" I was also laughing, at what I didn't know or care. I picked Sara up after the door closed behind us and carried her into the bedroom; our passions couldn't be contained any longer.

Afterwards we fell into a sound sleep, waking sometime before dawn. I rolled over and spooned into Sara, her body fit so well with mine, it was almost has if our bodies had been molded as a matched pair. Her well-rounded ass was the perfect shape; her legs long and slender, her breasts fit my hand, with the rosettes pink and inviting my caress, the nipples stiffening under my touch.

Sara was on top and moaned as she pushed herself back onto me. This has to be it; life doesn't get any better.

My mind was racing. I would check with the Captain about what I needed to do about getting married. Ben could be my best man. Could it be arranged in the next couple of days? This is crazy! I drifted off to sleep.

The next thing I remember Sara was shaking me. "It's almost lunch time, get out of bed you lazy bugger," she laughed, pulling the pillow out from under my head.

"Who wants lunch," I yelped, "when I can eat this!"

Sara shrieked as I pulled her back onto the bed. "You bloody naughty boy, we'll never get to the pub for a drink."

It was great every time with Sara; I couldn't get enough of her. I'd made up my mind, I would try and get someone to fill my duty spot tonight and get back ashore to be with her.

The *King's Shilling* was packed when we finally got there. The place was full of Limey sailors and a couple of dozen guys off the *Warhol*; everybody was having a good time. The English love to sing when they're drinking and the walls resounded with *Underneath The Arches, There'll Be Bluebirds Over The White Cliffs Of Dover,* and every other war-time song they could think of.

I hadn't drank more than a pint all afternoon, five o'clock came around all too soon, and I had to get back aboard. I left Sara at the corner and sprinted the last one hundred yards. I stepped onto the quarterdeck breathless, raising the eyebrows of Chief Quartermaster Rowans, who was officer of the deck.

"Welcome aboard Boats," he grunted. "Fifteen minutes late, but given the effort you put in running down the pier, I'll look the other way."

"Thanks Chief," I saluted, as was custom when a chief petty officer was designated Officer-of-the-Deck. I headed for the mess to see whom I could get to take over my duty watch tonight. I had the gangway from eight to twelve midnight.

Wouldn't you know it, everyone who wasn't on duty was ashore or was already filling in for someone else. "Damn it!" I growled, going back to my rack and changing into undress blues. I would need to get some chow, and then straighten up and fly right. I still had my duties to perform.

Several times during the hours before midnight I tried to call Sara from the ship-to-shore phone installed at the gangway; she wasn't home or wasn't answering. When I came off watch at midnight, I thought about going to her flat, but I had the duty again from eight in the morning until noon and I needed some sleep. I would go ashore tomorrow afternoon. I needed to think anyway; this was moving too fast.

I tossed in my rack all night and got up at six in the morning, showered, shaved, and ate breakfast. While I was having a second cup of coffee with Ben, I told him about my plans to marry Sara. He didn't say much, but I got the impression he didn't think it was a good idea.

"We'll be shoving off day after tomorrow. You think you can get something arranged by then?" he asked.

"I'll move heaven and earth if I have to," I replied, as I put my empty mug on the food tray and got up to leave.

The four hours of the morning watch dragged. Just as soon as I was relieved, I changed quickly into my best blues, pinned my ribbons on, slapped on some of Ben's aftershave lotion, squared my hat at a cocky angle and headed for Sara's. I knocked several times before Sara answered, when she came to the door she looked like she was dressing to go out.

"Looks like I got here in time to take you out dancin'," I joked.

"Jake," she said, surprised to find me at the door, "I didn't know we had plans for today."

"I just figured you knew I'd be back as soon as I got liberty again," I said, surprised in my turn by her behavior. "Listen Sara, I thought you knew how I felt. I know it's pretty soon…but…I think I love you!" I struggled to say it, but finally got it out.

"Jake," she said slowly, gathering her thoughts. "I don't know how to say this, but our time together was just that…time together."

"Sara, am I hearing you right?" I began, feeling the shock of her words. "You felt nothing…other than a couple of nights of good screwing?"

"I wouldn't put it as crudely as that Jake," she said. "I never thought you would get so serious. Look, I like you a lot, an awful lot, but that is it Jake."

"I love you Sara." I started to grope for the right words, "Doesn't that count?" I kept pleading, "I want to marry you, take you back to the States with me."

"Whoa, hold on there," Sara's voice was becoming agitated. "Marry? You must be crazy sailor, we only met two days ago."

I just stood there paralyzed, my fists clenching and unclenching.

"Look Jake, be a good lad and hop it," she said, looking past me up the street. "To tell you the truth I'm expecting someone."

I was devastated, heartbroken, and unable to move from the spot where I was standing.

"Sorry love," she said, closing the door.

I turned from the doorway and slowly walked back toward the harbor like a mindless zombie, those half-human creatures from the island of Haiti. Before I realized it I was back on board, the one place in this world I felt safe. Like the talks with my late Grandpa in the past had been a refuge, now the twenty-five hundred tons of gray-painted steel that was the *Warhol* was the one place I could turn to; somewhere I couldn't be hurt.

The next afternoon, after I came off the morning watch, I changed and went ashore. I walked to Sara's flat and just stood across the street, staring at her place, wondering if she was inside. I must have been there for a long time; a light drizzle started to fall and the droplets on my face must have brought me back to my senses.

I wandered back down the road and went into the *King's Shilling*; maybe she would be there, maybe we could forget yesterday and start all over again. I ordered a pint, but the taste was sour in my mouth. I left it half finished and walked out. On the way to the docks, a kid on a bike rode up and asked. "Hey Yank, you got any chewing gum?" I told him to "Fuck off!"

I spent the remainder of our time in Portsmouth lying on my rack. The next morning we sailed; I was relieved and glad to be heading to sea again.

I'd have been better off taking the museum tours with Ensign Bilts. At least I'd have left England with better memories than the bitterness I now felt.

As we sailed out of the medieval harbor of Portsmouth, I reflected on the number of sailing men over the centuries who must have left this port with heavy hearts. Some leaving behind wives and children, some their parents, family, home, hearth. Others like me, after romances that had ripped the guts out of them; Damn! Damn! Damn!

Chapter Eleven

The trip across the North Atlantic was smooth -- at that time of the year storms were few and far less violent than in the winters when gale force winds and high seas could make it a nasty crossing. Our destination was the Naval Air Station at Quonset Point, Rhode Island, where the crew would be relieved and the *Warhol* scheduled for an overhaul, probably down the coast at Norfolk, Virginia.

I hadn't talked too much to anyone, stayed mostly to myself. I had spoken to Ben a few times, but I felt so humiliated. It was hard to get back to that old camaraderie we'd had before.

I'd made a complete ass of myself and that's something I'd have to get over; no one was harder on themselves than I was when I knew I'd fucked up. I swore I'd think twice before letting my emotions be rubbed raw by a one-sided love affair again.

Along with most of the crew I had a four-week leave coming. We had been away eighteen months; men and ship were all in need of a break.

My plans didn't include going back to Oklahoma. The only letter I'd had from my Mom was to say she had finally found the man of her dreams, and he was moving in with her. I guess that's one thing my Mom and me had in common, always falling for the wrong one.

I wanted to get out to Oakland and see Dory and the kids; she had answered the letter I'd written her while I was laid up in Japan. Dory had moved back in with her mom in Oakland, and was having a hard time handling Bug's death. I decided that's where I'd spend my leave.

I traveled by rail as far as Chicago with Ben; that's where he was from. He tried to talk me into staying a few days with him and his family.

"Come on Jake, stay a coupla days," Ben pleaded.

"No thanks Ben," I answered, my mind on getting back out to the West Coast as quickly as possible. "I'll do it next time I'm back this way. Right now I have to get over to Oakland." We parted the best of friends. That's one thing about saying goodbye to a ship or a shipmate; you never knew for sure you wouldn't be back together again sometime.

By the time the train pulled into San Francisco I'd been completely around the world. I'd left Alameda in April 1950, returning to the same spot in September 1951. I'd taken a little more than eighty days to do it, but I had sailed the seven seas.

Walking up the drive of Dory's mom's house was like coming home. The kids had been looking out the window all morning, and when they saw me they burst through the door and sprung on me like monkeys.

Dory had received the wire I'd sent from Chicago giving her the details of my arrival. She hugged and kissed me, and then her mother, Doris, did the same.

"Unca Jake," the kids screamed. "Jake, Jake, Jake!" Dory kept repeating.

"God, you don't know how good it is to see you all," I laughed.

"Come on in Jake," Doris tried to lift up my seabag from where I'd dropped it in the drive. "What the hell to you sailors put in these things?" she puffed, dropping it back down again.

"Leave that Ma," I grinned, "I'll bring it in." This was the family I'd never had of my own. "I'd like to sleep on the couch tonight if you don't mind. I'll get a hotel room somewhere tomorrow."

"Nonsense," scoffed Doris, "we've got the kid's room ready for you. The little-uns can sleep in my room with me."

"That's great Ma." I swung the seabag up with one hand, lifted Dale up in the other arm, and followed Doris and Dory into the house.

I played with the kids most of the afternoon; Roy and Dale were just balls of energy. Roy had those same damn, confounding, unblinking eyes just like his dad; Dale fortunately took after her mother and was the prettiest little thing.

That night after Dory had put the kids to bed, she joined Doris and me in the living room, where I'd stretched out with a cup of Dory's great coffee, laced with whisky.

"I guess you two have some things to talk about," Doris said, wise woman that she was. "I'll get to bed myself, I think."

We talked about my adventures overseas for awhile, then Dory finally got around to asking me what that last night with Bug was like.

"Did he say anything at all?" Dory questioned.

"He just laid there peaceful like, didn't say anything," I answered. "I know he was thinking of you, that's all he ever talked about; you and the kids, you and the kids, he would go on for hours."

"Oh, poor Desmond," Dory sobbed, as she fell into my arms and cried. "I miss him so much Jake."

We stayed like that until she had cried all the tears she was going to cry, then she perked up, wiped her eyes, smiled at me and said, "What about you Jake? I'm sitting here feeling sorry for myself and you were hurt too. How bad was it"

"I'm fine, fine," I sounded like a bird chirping. Dory had caught me off guard with her question. I was still thinking about Bug, what a cruel master war was; this lovely family torn apart and still finding it hard to accept Bug's death. I made up my mind to get across to Alameda in the next couple of days, and see if I could get back in the boat pool there. I felt at home here with Dory and the kids. They needed someone to take care of them for awhile, especially since Dory's father had died the previous year. That hadn't made things any easier.

I wasn't surprised when I found old Chief "Black Bart" Hoffman still running the boats over at the base. I had purposely worn all my ribbons, with the Purple Heart pinned at the top. I was going to plead my case and go all the way to the base commander if necessary. I intended to have my request for a transfer approved.

That didn't prove necessary. One thing about the Navy, knowing a couple of old chiefs was the way to grease the skids. Chief Hoffman was now Senior Chief Hoffman.

"Congratulations on the step up Chief," I smiled, as I was ushered into his office. Senior Chief Hoffman almost jumped across the desk. He put his arm across my shoulder and shook my hand till it nearly fell off.

"I'll be goddamned," he whooped, "I never thought I'd see you again Jake. I heard about you bein' shot up along with Bugeye Millington." He continued solemnly, "I had to go break the news to Dory myself, bein' as how I knew them both."

"Yeah, it must have been rough," I said. "That's why I came across to see ya." I told Hoffman about my existing orders to return to Quonset Point at the end of my leave, and about my hopes of staying in the Bay area to help out Dory and the kids.

"I can use a boatswain's mate for sure here Jake," Hoffman said, after I'd laid out my reasons for wanting to stay for awhile. "Mainly at the small-boat school we got goin'. How'd ya like to teach the boots how to handle a whaleboat without smashing it into the ship's side or scuttlin' it?"

"Can you get me transferred from here, so as I don't have to go all the way back East?" I was excited already; a shore job close to Dory and the kids would be perfect.

"I can and I will," he stated, his face breaking into a wide grin. "This war in Korea may only be the start of it. We need ship's crews who know what they're doin'." Then he added, "That means having people with experience trainin' these pimply-faced goofballs!"

"I can report aboard whenever you want me, Senior Chief."

I had always hated sitting around and after only a week I was ready to get back to doing something.

"Don't be too anxious Jake," he went back around and sat down behind his desk. "I'll need a day to cut the request, then it'll take some time to get it back."

"I'll drop by next week and check with you. I'd like to look over the boat school anyway." Then as an afterthought, "I'll stay on base too, Senior Chief. I think Doris will be glad to get her bedroom back; the kids are getting to be a handful."

"I'll push things as fast as I can Jake," Senior Chief Hoffman said. "Just as soon as the paperwork hits my desk we'll get you back to work."

Things worked out perfectly. My transfer came through and I moved over to Alameda. We were just like a regular family. I worked all week and spent the weekends in Oakland at the house. I helped out with the bills, and the kids were becoming attached to me; I couldn't go anywhere without them.

I did get to take one trip to Hawaii on a troop transport, which was in April 1952. The negotiations between the UN and North Korea were on again, off again all the time. I guess they were planning a buildup just in case they had to launch further amphibious landings to reinforce South Korea.

The transport had loaded troops on board over at the huge embarkation piers near Fort Mason. My job would be to help get the landing craft crews ready for real work in Korea. There hadn't been enough time to train them before they got the word to load and sail.

The plan was we would hold lectures and demonstration lessons on the trip across, then once in Hawaii we'd run one or two live exercises. This would also give the Army a chance to train their troops in beach landing techniques. It worked well in theory, but the reality would prove quite different.

We sailed out of San Francisco Bay, passing by the Faralon Islands. One spot near the islands known as the Potato Patch was notorious for heavy swells. Captains delighted in testing the sea readiness of their vessels at this spot, checking for loose gear and badly lashed down cargo. But I always felt the real reason was to get the greenhorns good and sick, and hopefully help them gain their sea legs. The entire boat crew personnel were spewing their hearts out, along with the battalion of Army dogfaces. This was definitely not the way to start off our training sessions.

Every morning after chow found us in the lower deck cargo holds lecturing at the blackboard; we moved up on deck, near the boats, when the weather warmed up.

We had a fairly well-schooled crew by the time we hit Hawaii; the day of the live exercises, though, was disastrous. Two boat crews never left the side of the ship. They collided with each other and had to be unloaded to assess the damage. One boat reversed into the transport's stern, the force of the impact throwing a crewman to the deck and breaking his arm.

The worst accident, though, was when a boat nearly sank near the beach. The crew had lowered the bow ramp too soon and when the craft broached, a wave swamped the well deck. Soldiers wearing full packs were flushed out into the water like so much flotsam. Most made it back aboard when the wave cleared the well deck, and some got loose of their gear and swam to the beach, but two drowned.

There was a full investigation into the accident. Insufficient training was the verdict, but no one would face court martial. No one person was to blame. These things are unfortunate, but a necessary part of training for war.

The next two exercises went off a lot better, with only a few miner mishaps. The transport tied up in Pearl Harbor after our last live exercise and everyone was set for a well-deserved liberty ashore.

The four petty officers, who had made up the training detail with me, along with the lieutenant in charge of the whole thing, would be flying back to San Francisco as soon as we could hop a military transport aircraft.

They were still fighting in Korea. The North Koreans were attacking every time the peace negotiations broke down, and the US would then try to force them back to the table by resuming air attacks. That August saw the heaviest US air raids yet on Pyongyang.

November 4, 1952, Dwight D. Eisenhower was elected the new President of the United States, and I got my second four-year service stripe; eight years of exemplary service in the United States Navy.

Things dragged on in Korea for another eight months, and then finally the Armistice was signed at Panmunjom on July 27, 1953.

Chapter Twelve

I could have stayed in the San Francisco Bay area for the next ten years; it was a real Navy destination. Alameda had huge carrier piers and a Naval Air Station, Mare Island was growing as a submarine repair facility, Hunter's Point was building, repairing and modifying ships of all types.

I was working at Hunter's Point now, which is on the City side of the Bay. At Hunter's they were working on some designs for larger landing craft and I was in the driver's seat to train in them. At the same time I was taking various advanced classes in seamanship and boat handling. Getting back over to Oakland required hopping a Navy ferry, which wasn't all that convenient at times. I found my visits to Dory and the kids becoming less frequent.

"Hi, Unca Jake!" shouted Dale as I got out of the taxi and walked up the drive. I had an overnight bag and was planning to spend the weekend.

"Hiya Toots!" I swung Dale up on my shoulders and skipped up the front steps.

"Come on in Jake," Doris had the door open before I reached the top step. "We don't get to see near enough of you lately."

"I know Ma," I said lamely, "I'm just too busy with this classroom stuff. If I'm going to make chief one day, I'll need the schooling." Then added, "How's the new job working out for Dory?"

"Oh, Jake," Doris said, perking up, "she's a new woman. It was the best thing she could have done."

"Well things sure will change around here now," I went on, as I wrestled with Dale on the floor. "How's Roy doing in kindergarten?"

"As rambunctious as ever; in another year we'll have Dale in there too, then I might be able to put my feet up." Doris was looking tired. She had given a lot over the last couple of years. Taking care of Dory's frequent bouts of depression, looking after the kids most of the time.

"You deserve a break Ma." I left Dale and got up off the floor and put my arms around Doris, giving her a hug. "Dory doesn't know how lucky she is to have you; you've been the strong one that kept it all together."

"Now, now, you smooth talking sailor," Doris laughed. "If it weren't for you helping us out with the bills, and being…well…just being the man around the house, we never would have made it. I mean that Jake!"

"You know Bug and Dory were my best friends," I said, getting a little teary. "I was just doing whatever I could to help out." Then adding with a laugh, "And of course falling in love with you was the bonus."

"Get out of here you pirate!" she laughed. "The only thing you fell in love with was my cooking; speaking of which I better get supper ready."

"I'll wait with Dale for Roy to get off the bus, then take them for ice cream." I looked at Dale and she shrieked with delight.

"Yaaaaaaa," she whooped.

"Okay, honey!" Doris yelled from the kitchen. "Take your time; just be back by six."

"Hey, Uncle Jake," Roy yelled, as he got off the bus. "How'd you know I was coming home on the bus?"

"He knows you come home on the bus every day, silly," Dale answered for me.

"I asked your Grandma," I said to save Roy the embarrassment of his younger sister's taunt. "Come on, we're going over to Palooka's for ice cream." Dale would have the brains in the family; Roy would just get by on street smarts, kinda like his old man. It was great spending time with the kids again; I had missed that over the last few weeks. Now with Dory working they would need all the attention they could get.

"Hi, we're home," I hollered out to Doris, who was still in the kitchen when we got back to the house. "That smells good, whatever it is," I added.

We were washing up for supper when Dory arrived home. She came in bubbling and full of news about her new job. After we'd eaten and the kids were put to bed, Dory sat down with me in the living room.

"Jake I want to tell you something," Dory began. "I'm not sure if it's wrong or not...I've met a man...he's just so nice Jake. But I can't help feeling I'm being unfaithful to Desmond."

"That's great!" I said, glad Dory had found someone; I knew it would happen sooner or later. I loved Dory only as a friend, yet for a moment I felt a pang of jealousy.

"I'm so glad you think it's all right. I was worried you wouldn't approve," she sighed.

"Of course I think it's all right," I smiled. "The kids will have a full-time dad, and you're still a young and attractive woman Dory. Why wouldn't I think it's okay?"

"He's such a nice guy. I know you'll like him." Then added with apprehension, "I just hope the kids love him like I do."

"They will, and I know Bug wouldn't want you spending the rest of your life alone. He loved you too much for that." Dory started to cry and I held her tightly.

84

"You know how much Desmond meant to me," Dory said between sobs. "It is okay, it is all right, isn't it Jake?"

It was okay. Bug had meant the world to me, but he had been gone for three years and it was time to move on. I wished Dory the best and made the usual joke about dancing at her wedding.

John Cooper, Dory's boyfriend, did turn out to be a great guy. They were married six months after they met and things couldn't have worked out better. The kids adored him, Doris was happy to get her home back, along with some peace and quiet, and I knew I always had a home there whenever I needed one. In turn, I'd always be there for them; they knew that too.

I was still in San Francisco, over at Hunter's Point Naval Shipyard when I got word my Mom had passed away. It was 1955. I'd been in the Navy ten years, had made Boatswain's Mate Second Class, and thought I was bulletproof as far as my career in the Navy was concerned.

I picked up my compassionate leave orders from the Administration Office and grabbed a lift to the downtown train station. I knew the funeral would be over by the time I got there, but it would give me time to think, and I hadn't been back to the old place for a long time. I had only seen my Mom once since I'd left, when I had first gotten back from the Pacific in 1946. I'd spent a week of my leave at home in Hodskins, even then I knew I didn't belong there any more.

My Mom didn't have much to say while I was home, and my old pal Lionel was away working in Oklahoma City. Even when Cecelia Summers made it known that she would be more than happy to entertain me, I didn't feel comfortable; the town had become just a faint memory, no longer part of my life. Now, here I was going back to pay my respects at the grave of the last person that tied me to it.

The train trip had been uneventful, and I arrived in Hodskins feeling dirty and tired; I was walking to the drugstore, intending to use the phone to call my Uncle Joe, when suddenly the screech of tires stopped me in my tracks.

"I'll be goddamned if it ain't the wandering sailor, back from the seven seas," a familiar voice called out. It was Lionel Shanks, ten years older than when I last saw him, but not much changed.

"Lionel, you old son-of-a-bitch!" I cried out with surprise, as Lionel got out of his pickup and threw his arms around me.

"I heard about your Mom. Sorry to hear it; that's why you're back eh?" he said, holding me and patting my back like you would to comfort a child.

"Yeah, did the funeral go okay?" I said, trying to gently release his hold on me.

"It was pretty quiet I heard," he said apologetically. "I didn't go Jake, I felt bad afterwards. I'm sorry man, I shoulda gone."

"Forget it! How have you been?" I said to get us off the subject. "What are you doin' with yourself? You workin' around here? Still livin' at home?" I asked the questions in rapid succession.

"First, you're coming home with me, get you cleaned up, and I guess then you would want to visit the cemetery." Lionel threw my bag in the back of the pickup and continued, "I'm married, got three kids; can't hardly make ends meet, but still manage to keep enough food on the table and a roof over our heads."

We drove out to a small house on the edge of town. As we got out of the pickup, Lionel slapped me on the back and grabbed my bag. We walked up the drive to the front door; when it opened I couldn't believe my eyes! There stood Cecelia Summers with a baby in her arms.

"You remember Jake, honey?" Lionel said to Cecelia.

"Of course I do, how are you Jake? Sorry to hear about your Mom," Cecelia said, pushing another child's head out of the way as it suddenly appeared from behind her skirt. "This is Lucy," she said, holding up the baby, "and this is Beth," pulling out the head from behind her skirt again. "Little Jake, he's named after you, is out playing somewhere."

"Jake can sleep in Little Jake's room for a couple of days till he gets organized," Lionel laughed. "Goddamn it's good to see ya man!"

After I showered and put on some jeans and a shirt Lionel had lent me, I borrowed the truck and went out to the cemetery. I found Mom's grave easy enough, the ground was still freshly dug and the flowers on it were still not completely withered.

It all came rushing back to me in flashbacks: Grandpa's death, my Dad's accident, my Mom's troubles; the night I had to leave the house in a hurry and run off to join the Navy; the long, hot summers with Lionel and Cecelia down by the river. I guess I hadn't cried enough over the years, because now I couldn't stop crying. I knelt by the grave and cried until I didn't have a tear left, all I had were dry sobs.

I finally stood up and walked over to Dad's grave; it was one over from Mom's. I pulled out a couple of weeds, remembering how he used to love hunting grouse in the fall. Then I grinned as I looked over at Grandpa's grave, it was under the only tree in this damn desolate place. I walked over, sat down by the grave and talked to him like I used to. I hadn't done that for a long, long time and it felt good.

"You remember Jake Rickmeyer?" Lionel asked everyone we met in the bar that night. "This sailor is a hero, fought in goddamn Japan, and in goddamn fucking Korea."

We were getting a little drunk and starting to wear out our welcome. I had already broken up two potential fights Lionel had tried to start. "Let's get a bottle and go have a quiet drink somewhere," I finally said, after Lionel had threatened to punch out the biggest guy in the place. That monster was fixing to mop the floor with both of us, and it was definitely time to go.

"I got something in the truck to show ya," Lionel slurred. "Remember your Grandpa's old long-barreled pistol?" He reached under the seat, and handed me the old revolver butt first. "I had it cleaned up for ya, and had the gunsmith check it out. Careful, it's loaded!" he added quickly, as I took the gun and turned it over in my hands.

"I had forgotten all about this," I said, starting to tear up.

"Remember you asked me to get it from the barn the day you left town?" he said as we drove off, swerving and almost sideswiping a mailbox. "I went up there early one morning, checked that the bastard was still asleep, then climbed up in the rafters and there it was, right were you said it would be."

"Damn Lionel! Thanks man, this is great!" I was choking up. "What ever happened to that fucker anyway?"

"He was gone one day about two months after you left, never heard of him again. That's when your Mom moved back into the house," he said. And then added, "Let's go down by the river, drink a little, and get in some target practice."

"Let's go pardner!" I yelled, and gave a rebel whoop that would have awakened the dead.

Bang! Bang! That old pistol almost busted your eardrums when you fired it. I don't think we hit a single bottle Lionel had lined up, and we'd damn near emptied a box of shells. I finally fell back on the cool riverbank and laid the gun on my chest.

"Tell me buddy, how did you and Cecelia ever get hitched?" I laughed. "Been wanting to ask you that ever since I got here."

Lionel lay back and laughed too. "She got knocked up and I thought I'd best marry her. No one else seemed to give a damn," he continued to laugh. "Hell, it may not have been my kid even, but I didn't care, that was Little Jake. Cecelia's idea to name him that, not mine."

"Well, I'm mighty proud," I slurred, my head starting to fuzz over.

The next thing I knew it was morning and flies were crawling over my face. I felt like shit as I turned over to take a look around and saw Lionel. His mouth was open with flies buzzing in and out, he'd thrown up sometime during the night and was laying in his spew. The muck had dried on his face and clothes.

"Goddamn Lionel, wake up!" I said, hardly recognizing my own voice. "We got to get home, Cecelia will kill both of us."

"Fuck off!" Lionel belched, as I tried to get him up. "Shit!" he groaned, as his head started to clear. "What the fuck did we do last night?"

I knew it was time to go. It had been a time to reflect, visit familiar places and see old friends, but already Cecelia was starting to bitch about me getting Lionel into trouble. There was one thing I still had to do, however. The old house and land had been left to me and I needed to take care of some details.

There was still money owing on the mortgage, but I could handle that easily enough. I figured I might as well hang onto it. I'd been to see the lawyer and the bank and gotten all the paper work taken care of. The title and mortgage would be transferred into my name, and I had arranged with the bank an allotment out of my Navy pay. The bank would take care of the details, that way I'd never have to worry if the monthly payments were being paid on time.

"I'll be leaving tomorrow," I told Cecelia when I got back from the bank. "I'll take you and Lionel out to supper tonight. I got somethin' to tell you both."

"You don't need to go so soon Jake. I've been mad at you sure, but stay on a while longer," Cecelia said, surprised now that I was finally going.

When Lionel came home and Cecelia told him, he was upset and pleaded with me to stay longer. "I've never had so much fun since ya left the last time. You know you're like a brother to me; stay just a few more days."

That night at the only restaurant in town worth eating at, I broke the news about what I wanted done with the old house. "It's all arranged. You two can live there as long as you like. I don't want no rent; just pay your bills and keep the place up. The taxes will be taken care of as well, don't worry about a thing."

It had already been a somber evening; now Lionel was teary and Cecelia was balling. She said she didn't mean the nasty things she'd called me that morning, the day Lionel and me came home hung over. The night ended with more tears and statements of undying love.

It was a relief the next afternoon to catch the train out of Lawton. I'd taken Little Jake out to look around the old place that morning; and the look on his face and his laughter as he explored the barn and outbuildings convinced me the choice I'd made was the right one.

I boarded the train and picked a seat near the back of the car, where I thought I wouldn't be disturbed. Sleep was the only thing I had on my mind. There was a newspaper stuffed into the pouch of the seat in front of me. I unfolded it and the headline leaped out: "Edward Morrow Jr., son of the late Senator Edward Morrow, wins seat in State Legislature..." the article went on, "Morrow, a Navy veteran and participant in the invasion of Okinawa..." I laid the paper back down.

I lay back in the seat, and a smile crossed my lips as the train pulled out of Lawton. I was a happy man.

Chapter Thirteen

It was coming up to my twelfth anniversary in the Navy, November 1, 1956. Senior Chief Hoffman was still my mentor and he himself was about to retire in two weeks, after forty years service in the Navy. He had joined back in 1916 at the age of fifteen; he was designated a "Boy" back then, in those days young boys were still being admitted into the Navy. And he'd told me there were kids younger than he was in the service back then.

"Jake, my boy," Hoffman said with pride, "I want the honor of swearing you in when you ship over for another hitch."

"That would be fine with me, Senior Chief. I couldn't think of anyone I'd rather have do the honors."

We had known each other since the days off Okinawa on the *USS Roe*. And although he freely called me Jake, I would never have taken the liberty of addressing him by anything other than his rank, let alone ever calling him "Black Bart".

Now with three service stripes on my arm, a couple of stars on my Good Conduct ribbon, and my Second Class Petty Officer rate, I cut a fine figure of a sailorman.

From being on top of the world to being brought low, this was becoming the story of my life.

A short couple of weeks after Senior Chief Hoffman retired, he died of a heart attack. I was stunned! He had been like a father to me in many ways, and I certainly owed my career in the Navy to him. He was the one responsible for getting the requests filled out, which allowed me to stay in the Navy when I didn't have much to offer.

Senior Chief Hoffman was given a full military funeral at the National Cemetery on the grounds of the Presidio. That old, famous Army Fort, south of the Golden Gate Bridge, was the final resting-place for many well-known military men; the Chief would be in good company there.

Dory and the kids were at the funeral, along with her new husband, John. It was the first time I'd seen them since their wedding. The kids and Dory looked great; they were a happy family again.

"Unca Jake!" the kids whispered to me during the solemn ceremony, "When are you coming over to play with us?"

"Shush!" Dory said quietly. "We'll all go home after this and have dinner together."

John and Dory now lived in their new home in Sausalito. He was a successful accountant with his own growing business. John was friendly to me, yet never seemed totally relaxed.

Maybe he envied me the days when Bug and me were the only things in Dory's life. Dory always talked about Bug when I was around, and that had to wear on a man's nerves after a while.

It was time I went to sea again. I'd been around the Bay area ever since I got back from Korea, at one spot or another. I wanted to make First Class Petty Officer and I'd need to put in some more sea time to qualify.

Of all things to happen, just after I'd put in my request for sea duty, a cruiser arrived at Hunter's Point Navy Yard. The cruiser put in for minor modifications before leaving on a tour of South East Asian ports. The skipper of the cruiser was Captain Sullivan P. Rooks.

Sully was now a full four-striper and was continuing to climb the Naval ladder. This was going to be a pleasure cruise judging by the scuttlebutt. An Admiral would be aboard and the ship was going to make goodwill visits to New Zealand, Australia, India and then sail back, with stops in the Philippines and Pearl Harbor.

The admiral's name was Gridley H. T. Sumpher. Admiral Sumpher had made his name as a member of Admiral Chester Nimitz's staff in World War II. He was coming up for retirement, and this cruise would be a chance for him to visit old military friends in those countries on the stopover list.

Unknown to me, Sully had kept his eye on me over the years and knew I was now at Hunter's Point. Why he was interested in keeping tabs on me, I didn't know. I would have thought he had better things to do. But when I received orders to report aboard the cruiser, I met his personal yeoman who told me the whole story.

"I have a special file on you Rickmeyer," he said, "and that file was passed on to me by the Captain's former yeoman."

"I know the Captain thinks he owes me, but that was years ago. I don't know why he thinks he still has to do me any favors." I liked the fact Sully looked on me as a friend, but it was hard to explain to your low-life swabbie shipmates at times.

"Count yourself lucky," the yeoman continued. "Captain Rooks is the kind of officer who keeps a file on many people, helps him know who's where around the fleet."

"Well, I take it he had my request for sea duty in mind when he got me ordered aboard here in a hurry." I still felt uneasy in some way; I guess it felt like the FBI was tailing you.

"Don't sweat it, this is going to be the cruise from heaven," the yeoman said, as he put a copy of my orders away in the Captain's personal files.

I stowed my gear aboard, checked out my new surroundings, took the pick of the available racks, selected a spacious locker, and then reported to my division chief for duty.

The Chief Boatswain's Mate was a crusty old fart and I took an instant dislike to him.

"Don't think you're going to be treated any different Rickmeyer," he started. "The whole ship knows you and the skipper go way back, but that don't mean nothing to me."

"Aye, Chief," I said, "I'm not expecting any special treatment."

For all the Chief's tough talk, I knew I could jump up on his desk and piss all over him, and he still wouldn't complain.

An enlisted man that had a full captain looking out for him had the run of the ship and everybody knew it.

"Well, I'm glad you feel that way Rickmeyer," he grunted. "I'll not be needing you for anything until we sail. Take the time to look around, get to know the ship."

"Aye, Chief," I said, "I've been mostly on destroyers and amphibious ships, saw lots of cruisers and battleships in Korea; never got to sail on one though."

"Well, now you will," he said, still grouchy. "Carry on Rickmeyer."

I left the Chief's office and started my tour. I always liked to walk the length of a new ship from the pier. It gave you a better idea of her lines, her size, and her power.

The *USS Junction City* was a Boston Class cruiser having the distinction of being one of the first guided missile ships in the Navy; brand new, straight off the slips of the Shipbuilding Corp. in Camden, New Jersey. She was a magnificent 673 feet long, 70 feet wide, 16,700 tons. It would take five or six *Warhols* to make up her tonnage. Four boilers drove four giant screws that powered the *Junction City,* and 1,200 sailors manned her.

The ship's armament was designed to pound a shore or ship target to oblivion. She had six 8-inch guns in two triple turret mounts, another ten 5-inch in five twin turret mounts, and a further twelve 3-inch in twin mounts.

Then there were the missiles, two Terrier surface-to-air launchers were positioned aft, and they could be fired at fast moving incoming missiles or aircraft. I climbed the gangway slowly back to the quarterdeck, smartly saluting the flag billowing from the stern flagstaff.

93

Leaning on the rails to the left of the flagstaff was a Marine Corps Gunnery Sergeant. He seemed to be lost in his thoughts, staring off over the choppy waters of San Francisco Bay.

"Feeling lost Gunny?" I said, as I approached. Marines were stationed on board capital surface ships in the US Navy mainly for ceremonial functions and they provided security for senior and flag rank naval officers.

The Marine looked around at the sound of my voice. "Hi," he said none too friendly, but I was in need of someone to talk to.

I stood alongside him, putting my hands on the top strand of the railing and my right foot on the bottom strand, much as they used to do in a saloon. The stance was Navy style. Why it made you feel "salty" I don't know; but it did! "Been aboard long?" I asked, matter-of-factly. "She looks like a fine ship."

"Been on board since we left Norfolk," he replied, without looking at me. "Hit some nasty weather south of Florida; she came through it okay. I've been on some buckets that would founder in a bathtub."

"I know what you mean Gunny," I laughed. His drawl tagged him as being from the Deep South. "Where you from?" I asked.

"Alabama," he started to warm up, "Sweet little town called Blossomville."

"Sounds like you miss it," I kept looking out across the water.

"Goddamn right!" he continued. "We call it possumville. Just a hoot and a holla from Mobile. How about you?"

"Just a country boy from Oklahoma," I answered. "The Navy has been my home for over twelve years."

"Sounds like me," he held out his hand. "Davis Carlson, good to know ya!"

"Jake Rickmeyer," I shook his hand firmly, and immediately felt the strength of this big man in his grip.

"Attention on deck," the PA crackled, "Captain coming aboard."

The Gunny and I turned and snapped to attention, facing the gangway. We saluted as soon as the Captain's feet hit the quarterdeck.

Captain Sullivan P. Rooks looked much as I had remembered him from that day he visited me on the hospital ship *Repose.* If anything, he looked fitter and more in command of himself and his surroundings.

He returned the salutes from the deck watch, then noticed me standing at the fantail as he gave the ship's topside the once over.

"Jake, good to see you," he said, as he strode over to the stern area. He put out his hand after returning my hurried salute.

94

"Good to see you too, Sir." I shook his hand, feeling uncomfortable with the Marine Gunny standing stiffly at attention beside me. One thing about Sully though, he quickly put people at ease.

"Good day Gunny," he spoke directly to the Marine. "Carlson, isn't it?"

"Yes, Sir," replied the Gunny, obviously taken aback that the Captain already knew who he was

"Don't look surprised," Sully said good-naturedly, "I make a point of knowing who's aboard my ship and when they came aboard. Isn't that right Jake?"

"Yes Sir, it is." I could never figure Sully out exactly. Was he really one of the greatest officers you could have in command? I'd served under a couple, and no one came close to Sully's concern and attention for men under him.

"Good to have you aboard Jake. I've got a special job for you," Sully said. "I'll explain it just as soon as I have time to go over it with you."

With those words, he turned and started to walk off, the Gunny and I saluted again. Our salute was returned by the young lieutenant JG, hurrying to keep up with the fast-moving captain.

"Dang! That's the first time I've had a Navy Captain speak to me personally." Davis Carlson, the Marine from Blossomville, was now under the spell of Sully. "I guess you've served with him before?"

"Never served on the same ship with him, just kept running into him," I grinned. "First time was back in World War II, then again off Korea. Where you been, you never had a Navy Captain speak to you before?" I joked.

"I've been in the Corps ten years, but this is my first sea deployment on anything other than assault ships. I always made it my business to avoid the brass whenever I could." He took out a smoke and offered me one.

"No thanks, Davis," I said, "I don't use 'em."

Two days later I got the word to report to the Captain. The Marine guard outside the Captain's cabin snapped to, and after knocking on the door and announcing my presence stood aside and ushered me through the open door.

"Jake, come in," Sully was seated at his desk behind a stack of files and papers a foot high. Standing to the side of the desk was his yeoman, holding another pile of papers. "Get those typed up ready for my signature Rosewell; that will be all."

"Aye, aye Sir." Rosewell sounded like the kind of efficient clerk someone like Sully would have. I was beginning to realize Sully was someone who didn't tolerate sloppiness of any kind under his command.

"Sit down Jake." He waved to a chair, "We've been around too long to stand on ceremony in private." He continued, barely looking up, "You probably already know we will have an admiral on board with us, for what is essentially a farewell cruise."

"Yes, Sir," I said, feeling uncomfortable sitting in the presence of a senior officer.

"My goal during this cruise will be to make it the most memorable I can for the Admiral. Your job will be to handle the Admiral's Barge," he finally looked up at me. "Jake, I want you to handpick a couple of seamen for your crew. I want the Barge ship-shape, spic-and-span, ready to go the moment the Admiral calls for it. You and your crew will be in full dress uniform whenever the Admiral is using the Barge. I want you clean, trimmed and starched whenever you take the Barge out. The Barge, in other words, will sparkle Jake."

"I understand completely, Sir." I wasn't going to mind this; it could be a smooth tour for me. I loved boats, and now I was going to be responsible for an Admiral's Barge.

"Another thing Jake. Get over to Woolworth's or someplace and buy a hundred or so little American flags. You know, the type kids wave at Fourth of July parades." Sully was serious, "I want you to have them stowed on the Barge and hand them out to all the Admiral's guests whenever they're on the Barge with him. Better draw from stores a couple of extra Stars and Stripes for the stern. I want the flag changed at the first sign of tattering. And make sure you draw several three-star admiral flags too, and fly them whenever he even looks like using the Barge.

"Aye, aye Sir," I answered. I was getting the idea; kiss the Admiral's butt at all times.

"Jake, make the *Junction City* proud," he went on. "You know what I'm expecting from you."

Aye, Sir," I stood up, sensing the meeting was over. "I will give it my full attention Captain."

"I know I can rely on you," he said, businesslike as he pressed the intercom button on his desk. "Rosewell, issue Petty Officer Rickmeyer fifty dollars from the ship's petty cash account. And see that he has authorization to draw what he needs from base stores. He'll need chits for extra flags, etc."

"Aye, Sir," Rosewell's voice answered in a monotone.

"Okay, Jake," Sully said, as he stood up and lent across the desk putting out his hand. "Good to have you aboard with me."

"I'm glad to be aboard Sully," I said, testing the Captain's previous permission to use his first name in private.

He threw his head back and laughed. "That's all Jake, just be ready when you're needed."

The Admiral came aboard with full pomp and ceremony. I'd never seen so much brass in one place. Admiral Gridley H. T. Sumpher was a three-star admiral, fourth generation Navy going all the way back to the Civil War. All hands were assembled on deck in full dress blues. The Marine detachment was lined up, dressed smartly and very impressive with rifles at "Order Arms." The Admiral was piped aboard, and it seemed like half the Navy's captains and admirals were gathered here for the send-off.

I stood ramrod straight, and felt that tingling sense of pride that you feel only on occasions that awaken extreme patriotism.

The *USS Junction City* slipped her lines and moved away from the dock; a tugboat nosed her bow around. The cruiser soon took a bearing and headed out to sea, gliding through the waters of the Bay and passing under the Golden Gate Bridge. The Captain wisely choosing to avoid the Potato Patch, this was going to be a kid-gloves operation all the way.

Chapter Fourteen

The Pacific was as smooth as we could have hoped for; the weather got warmer as we sailed in a southwesterly direction. We stopped briefly at Midway Island for refueling. Nothing had changed there since the island was attacked during World War II. It had been built back up, of course, but it was still an isolated place, not on the "A" list of postings.

At Midway we got the word there had been a last minute addition to our itinerary, Tonga. Tonga was an island still ruled by a king, protected by Britain and part of the British Commonwealth.

This would be my first call to have the Barge ready for the Admiral's use.

By the time we arrived off Tonga, the Barge was polished, fueled, and manned by the tallest, straightest, best looking young seamen I could find. She was all decked out with the American flag flying proudly at the stern, and the Admiral's personal jack at the bow, displaying his three stars.

We took the Admiral ashore first. It was protocol for visiting dignitaries to seek audience with the King at his palace. Then the next day we ferried the King and his court out to the ship for a tour and lunch with the Admiral.

On the return trip at the end of the day, I dutifully gave the King and all his officials a small American flag as they left the Barge; they were delighted! And the Admiral, who had accompanied the King back to shore, beamed his satisfaction.

I didn't get a chance to see much of Tonga. The Barge was in almost constant use, taking members of the Royal family and other Tongan officials to and from the anchored cruiser.

During one lengthy function at the palace, I did get a chance to go see the fruit bat colony just outside of town. The bats had a wingspan of about four feet and were considered sacred by the islanders. The colony, and the spot where Captain James Cook landed hundreds of years ago, were all I got to see.

I checked out the Barge thoroughly after we left Tonga, making sure she was ready to go when we reached our next stop. We'd be arriving in Auckland, New Zealand, in a couple of days.

I got together with Gunny Carlson whenever I could. We got on well together; I think the thing we had in common was our attachment to the service. I had no family, he had twelve brothers and sisters. Strangely, we both felt alone except for our extended military families. "What have you got planned for New Zealand?" I asked him one evening.

"I don't think I'll be doin' too much," he replied. "The plans are for full-dress ceremonies on at least four occasions. One when the US Ambassador pays his respects, another when the top brass of the New Zealand Navy visits the Admiral, then at least two functions ashore with fucking New Zealand politicians."

"I may get a chance to get my ashes hauled," I laughed. "The Chief told me I may be able to stand down the Barge's crew and get in some liberty if the Admiral does all his socializing ashore."

"I wish I could do the same," Davis complained. "These damn shipboard ceremonies are going to drive me nuts."

"If we're tying up dockside and no harbor tours are planned, then I'll be happy to sink a few of those New Zealand beers for you. And they tell me the Kiwi women are ready and willing," I added for good measure.

"You asshole!" Davis moaned, as he playfully punched me in the belly.

New Zealand was as similar to England as you could get; as I wandered the streets of Auckland it reminded me of the time I was in Portsmouth. The people were friendly, and I had no problem meeting a pretty girl and inviting her for a drink.

We were trying to have a quite beer in the lounge, as they called them there, when all hell broke loose. Customers of the pubs in Auckland stand at small, waist-high tables drinking from large bottles. The drinkers were mostly Maori, the native people of this island nation. They were notorious for fighting with each other or, even better, with strangers if they were available -- in this case fifty or so American sailors.

"Fuck you, Yank!" was the first indication trouble was brewing. Bang! Crash! Glass started breaking; chairs and tables were being knocked over.

"Let's get out of here!" my ladyfriend said.

"To a hotel room?" I asked, hopefully.

"Somewhere better," she replied, grabbing her purse, "Much more private."

We hailed a passing cab and she gave the driver directions I hardly understood. We drove for about twenty minutes, during which I had a hard time keeping her from undressing me. We stopped at an apartment building and I paid off the cab.

"Come on love," she was panting, "Hurry up!" We climbed two flights of stairs and tumbled through the door of her apartment laughing hysterically.

She was undressed, and helping me with my clothes before the door had slammed shut. I never quite got my jumper off before she pulled me onto the bed. "Come on, come on," she was speaking in short, sharp breaths.

She spread her legs and raised her knees up, grabbing me by the Johnson and guiding me into her.

"Jesus!" I yelled, as she gave my testicles a squeeze.

"Oh my God! Oh my God!" she kept screaming as I frantically tried to maintain rhythm with her. She groaned with pleasure, and then I finally exploded. I pressed gently against her, completely spent. What a wild ride that had been; never had I been so ready for sex, not even with Sara during those wild times in Portsmouth.

"Oh darling," she whispered, "please make love to me again."

She started to rub her pelvis against me and reached under to guide me into her once more.

This had to be a dream; this wasn't happening to me!

After our second go-round, I was ready for a beer. "Let's go get a beer…oh no! I just realized, I don't even know your name."

"We can't. It's after 6 o'clock and the pubs close at six," she said, walking into the bathroom, "and my name's Mucky."

"Mucky? What kinda name is that?" I said, as I pulled on my pants and straightened myself up.

"It means messy…you know, mucky," she called from the bathroom.

"Well, Mucky," I answered, wondering whether I'd told her my name or not. I must have! "What should we do, go out and eat or something?"

"Let's go get some fish and chips," she giggled, as she bounced out of the bathroom ready to go. "There's a little fish shop on the corner."

An Italian guy was cooking in the shop, and I didn't know the difference between the schnapper and the shark, or chips from chaff.

"Make that three pieces of schnapper and sixpence worth of chips," Mucky said with authority. "The shark is cheaper, but it's bloody bony," she whispered to me.

We ate our fish and chips overlooking Auckland Bay. I couldn't remember when I'd eaten a more tasty meal. The fish and chips came wrapped in newspaper and you had to eat them with your hands. The messy fingers just needed to be licked at the end of the meal, that's all, because they didn't give you any napkins in New Zealand. We were a long way from the dock area of Auckland, and I knew I'd have to be thinking about getting back.

"Mucky," I began, "I have to get back to the ship and see if I'm needed tomorrow. If I'm not, I'd like to see you again."

"Oh, that's wonderful," she said, all excited. "I was hoping you'd say that…and I have a confession to make."

"What's that?" I was expecting her to tell me she was married, or had a kid or something.

"I don't know your name either," she giggled. "Isn't that bloody stupid?"

I laughed to myself all the way back to the docks in the cab. "Christ!" I thought, this world could be crazy sometimes.

After reporting aboard, I headed for a hot shower and some rack time. I hadn't felt this contented for a long, long time.

"What's the shit-eating grin on your face for Jake?" Gunny Carlson said. He was leaving the head with a towel over his shoulder just as I was entering.

"I just jumped the bones of the sweetest little Kiwi girl you could imagine," I continued, still with that shit-eating grin on my face, "and I'm going back for more tomorrow."

"Goddamn you Rickmeyer," Carlson gave my ass a flick with his towel in passing, "I'll even this up yet!"

I wasn't needed the next day, but the Chief kept us standing by until early in the afternoon, then he finally cut us loose.

"Have a good one Boats," my motorman said, as he headed ashore. "If I see you uptown, I'll buy you one."

"Okay," I waved him off; I had no intention of going anywhere except to Mucky's place.

Mucky opened the door before I had a chance to knock. She'd watched the cab pull up and saw me half-run to her building. "Oh Jake," she said, almost in a panic, "I thought you weren't coming. I've been waiting all day."

"I'm sorry, I couldn't get away any sooner," I replied, scooping her up in my arms. I then realized she had been seriously concerned about me. This was something new for me; I was usually the one being left in the dust.

"Never mind," she wiped a tear from her cheek. "It's all right now. I've made us some tea…I mean…what do you call the evening meal?"

"Dinner Mucky, we call it dinner!" I felt like an old married man already, and it was only the second date with Mucky.

We made love after dinner, then cuddled up together talking. Mucky had fallen for me she said, and wanted to come down to the ship to see me off. We were sailing the next day and she wanted to say goodbye.

"I hate good-byes," she said softly, "but I want to see you once more before you go."

"Okay, honey," I said, as I slipped out of bed, "I have to be on board by midnight. If you really want to come down that's great. We shove off at ten in the morning."

"I'll be there," Mucky said, all teary eyed. "Will you be able to come ashore?"

I'll get ashore," I answered. "I'll keep a lookout for you."

The next morning was bright and clear. I had been dressed for departure since 0700 and had been up on deck looking for Mucky.

Finally, there she was! Walking down the wharf, looking up at the huge ship's superstructure, searching the hundreds of faces lining the rails for mine.

I checked with the officer-of-the-deck and got permission to go ashore. I bounced down the gangway and met Mucky has she ran towards me. Throwing our arms around each other, I lifted her off her feet and we kissed; the crowd around us erupted in applause.

"My word, this is just like in the flicks," Mucky said, through her tears. "You will write me Jake? I need you to write me."

"I will," I looked over my shoulder for the signal to get back on the ship. "That address I gave you, your letters will catch up with the ship wherever she is."

It was hard to break away from Mucky's embrace; she was in love with me. I didn't know how I felt, but I did feel something. I kept telling myself to slow down, I was in no hurry to get burned again.

Quite a few hearts had been stolen on this visit; a couple of dozen girls and women were waving frantically as we moved away from the wharf. Mucky looked so small and fragile standing there, the wharf diminished as we pulled away; she seemed to disappear into the crowd as the *Junction City* picked up speed.

"Bye Mucky," I said, whispering her name. Damn! I missed her already.

Sydney, Australia was the next stop on our tour. I had already gotten the word that I'd be needed full time while in port. The ship had been instructed to anchor off the Garden Island Shipyard.

The Admiral was delighted; he thought the ship would look splendid moored out in the harbor for all of Sydney to see.

He was right; Sydney is one of the most picturesque harbors in the world. Dozens of ferries were crossing from one side of the bay to the other; and hundreds of small yachts were sailing all over the vast expanse of blue water.

The plan was to take dignitaries out in the Barge and slowly circle the ship, while the Admiral talked at length about the use of missiles in today's Navy.

The old cronies were mostly retired military types the Admiral had known during his time here in World War II. I don't think they particularly gave a shit one way or the other about missiles. On one trip, though, when we had some young, uniformed officers on board, I noticed they paid close attention to the Admiral's description of the ship's capabilities.

The missile crews were standing by, and when we hove to at a spot where we'd get the best view, the Terrier Missiles were slid out on rails and loaded onto their launchers. This action took place so quickly, it left some spectators gasping, and then the launchers were moved rapidly from side-to-side and up-and-down, leaving all the young Aussie officers impressed.

I dutifully gave out the little flags after each group left. Most of them smiled and politely accepted the gesture of goodwill; others just looked annoyed. At least the Tongans were enthusiastic and they had left the Barge waving the flags above their heads.

At the end of the day we tied the Barge to the small, floating dock moored alongside the ship. I spent some time checking the craft over before satisfying myself that she was ship-shape, and then climbed the ladder to the cruiser's deck.

"Damn Boats! Did you see those old farts today?" the motorman grinned. "I swear one was asleep with his eyes open."

"One more day Mac," I said, as I headed for the crew's quarters, "then we can get some rest."

"I'm pissed Boats," he complained. "This is supposed to be a great liberty port, and we're out with the Admiral all day long, while he goes around farting like a hero."

"Let's get some chow." I ignored his complaint. "We're up at 0530 again tomorrow morning."

That last day we must have done four or five trips, the last two without the Admiral; he had functions to attend to ashore, so the Gunnery Officer conducted the tours.

We hoisted the Barge back on board after the last run, making her ready for the ship's departure the next day.

The word was passed that the itinerary had been changed again. Due to some minor political bickering between India and the US, our visit there had been cancelled, and we were now headed for Subic Bay in the Philippines.

"Damn!" That meant the letter from Mucky I was hoping would be waiting for me in Bombay, would now be playing catch up all over the Pacific. Probably catching up with me weeks after we got back home.

I decided to write a quick note and get it in the last mailbag going ashore; at least she'd know I was still thinking of her.

Chapter Fifteen

My usual period standing at the railing on the quarterdeck was still part of my routine at the end of every day. Now my regular companion was Gunny Carlson. One evening while we enjoyed the warmth of a tropical sunset steaming through the Philippine Sea we swapped yarns, getting to know more about each other, our families and friends back home, our interests, hopes and dreams.

"My brothers and sisters will probably never git more'n a dozen miles from Possumville...in any direction," Davis spoke with a slow drawl that made you want to kick him in the ass and hurry him up sometimes. "Damned if two of my older sisters ain't knocked up already," he continued, drawing deeply on his cigarette.

"What do they think of all these places you get to go to?" I tried to get on the subject of our upcoming visit to Subic Bay.

"They wouldn't know Tonga from Chookamonga," he flicked his butt over the side.

"Maybe we'll get to have that beer together in Angeles City," I said. "Word is the Admiral will be entertained full time by the brass at Subic; should give us some good liberty time without all the bullshit."

"Yeah, our Lieutenant said the Marines stationed at the base would be handling all the ceremonial duties." He perked up, "Good to have some competition for the Admiral's attention, eh?"

"I know what you mean Marine," I replied. "If I have to miss out on the pleasures of a cold San Miguel beer and some fine topless dancing, I'll be a mite upset!"

Subic Bay Naval Base as I remembered it in 1945 was totally changed. The piers were alive with men going about the business of repairing, maintaining, fueling, stocking and just general fussing over ships and craft of all sizes. Two carriers were docked at the base, along with ten or fifteen destroyers. There were tankers and supply ships moored at wharves or anchored out in the Bay.

The huge floating dry-dock that had been captured from the Nazis and towed to the Philippines after World War II, had a submarine docked for repairs. The enormous cavity of the dry-dock looked big enough to handle a battleship, with room to spare. There was a gang on the pier ready to take our lines, and in short order we were secured. The Marine band on the wharf struck up *I'll Be Seeing You In All The Old Familiar Places;* brass was all over the place decked out in dress white uniforms, complete with medals and swords.

I was thankful the Admiral would be attending dinners ashore and giving farewell speeches full-time while we were in Subic. Now maybe Davis and I would get to have a drink or two together. Normally I'd be thinking of that cute little Filipina tail so readily available, but I still had Mucky on my mind.

"Let's go Jake," Davis was already heading below to change into liberty dress.

"Right behind you." I was already untying my neckerchief as I ducked through the hatch. "Let's go downtown!"

Senior NCOs were permitted to go ashore in civilian clothes and both Davis and I put on the fancy shirts we'd bought in Tonga. Mine was as loud as I could find, red and yellow Hibiscus covering the entire front and back of the shirt, Davis had a sunset and palm trees on his.

Angeles City had expanded and rebuilt since the destruction of the war; now it was one dive after another. The place was crawling with servicemen, those in uniform, and those dressed in slacks and shirts; the ones in civilian clothes stuck out as American more than the uniformed guys did.

We let ourselves be ushered into one sin palace by the barker. He was describing the pleasures to be found within to anybody who would listen.

"Come on in, fellas," he yelled at the top of his voice. "What you want? Girls, cold beer, good steak dinner; all inside, your ship she come home sailors."

The inside was dimly lit and we stood for a moment before our eyes adjusted. Several girls grabbed us by the hands and tried to steer us towards a table. We were both savvy enough to know that that was the way to get billed for a dozen drinks in one hellava hurry. The girls would get you seated, sit on your lap and order whiskey. Before you knew what was happening, a tray of drinks had arrived and you'd get stuck with the bill. The whiskey was usually cold tea to add insult to injury.

"No thanks, sweetheart," Davis said, as we freed ourselves from the girls' arms and took a seat at the bar.

"San Miguels, pardner," I said, returning the bartender's nod. I spun around on my chair to take in the floorshow just getting underway.

Two men slid a round wooden platform out onto the dance floor. They then removed the drape that had been covering the girl on the wooden stand, and there was fanfare and a drum roll. The girl was in a spread-eagled position strapped securely to the platform.

"Okay," bellowed the bandleader over the microphone. "This is how the game is played. Anyone wants to volunteer can come up and try to fuck the girl. If you can do it, you'll win the girl for the night and all the beer you can drink!"

The platform's height was a little below waist level and was not as easy as it looked. The trick was you had your hands fastened behind your back, and any pushing against the girl, or the wooden stand, sent the highly polished platform sliding away across the floor, leaving the unfortunate volunteer looking ridiculous with his pants down around his ankles. There was no shortage of volunteers, and several half-drunk sailors tried their luck without success, all to the shouted whoops and laughter of the crowd.

"Jesus," laughed Davis, "I've never seen anythin' like this in all my born days."

"I heard about it." I was laughing too. "Never seen it though!"

I thought I heard a familiar laugh coming from somewhere around the other side of the bar.

"Just a minute," I said to Davis, "I know that laugh." I got up and walked around the partition at the far end. "Fuck!" I halted in my stride, "Rabbit!"

That idiotic, slobbery laugh of his hadn't changed. He was spitting and spluttering all over the table as he yelled encouragement to the guys on the dance floor. He spotted me and yelled out before I had a chance to get back to my seat at the bar.

"Hey Jake, you ol' son-of-a-bitch!" Rabbit shouted, his voice carrying above the din. "Come on over, have a drink."

I stepped over to the table and almost pushed Rabbit's face into the pitcher of beer.

"No thanks, fuckface," I sneered, holding myself in check. A fight here could mean big trouble. The two guys on either side of Rabbit started to get up off their chairs, then I sensed Davis standing beside me. Davis was a half-head taller than me and twice as ugly. The two guys wisely sat their asses back down.

"Okay, Jake," sputtered Rabbit, "suit your fuckin' self."

"One of these days Rabbit," I couldn't resist taunting him. "One of these days you and me are gonna finish this."

Davis and me walked back around the bar and ordered another beer.

"What was that all about?" Davis asked.

"You don't wanna know," I said, sipping my beer. "That prick is the lowest piece of shit I've ever known."

"You usually get on with everybody Jake," Davis said, as he took a swig of his beer.

"Not that dickhead," I erupted in laughter as the play on words suddenly hit me. "That's his fuckin' name...Tyler Dicks...dickhead," The tears were rolling down my face I was laughing so hard.

"I don't get the joke," Davis said, his mind on other things. "I'm gonna make a date with that there little girlie slidin' around the steel bar," he started down the bar to talk to the Mama-san. "You comin'?"

"Nah," I finished my beer, "I think I'll go back on board and write a letter to Mucky."

The visit to the Philippines was soon over and a flood of memories came back to me as we slipped from our pier in Subic. Billy Smith, Bugeye Millington, Ed Morrow, Bully Bulow; the first time we came here, we were all young, happy, wet-behind-the-ears kids. The only face from the old days I'd seen lately was that shitface asshole Rabbit.

A day out of the Philippines I got word to report to the Captain's cabin. The Marine sentry outside the door recognized me and knocked on the cabin door.

"Enter!" a voice replied. Sully was seated at his work desk and looked up as I came in. "Sit down Jake."

I sat down on one of the over-stuffed chairs in the Captain's cabin.

"How are you Jake?" Sully said cheerfully.

"Fine, Sir, " I replied, "and you Sir?"

"I couldn't be better," Sully smiled. "This cruise has gone off like clockwork so far, and I'll thank every man-jack after we disembark the Admiral in San Diego. But I would like to thank you personally for your work on the Admiral's Barge."

"I'm glad everything went off without a hitch, Sir." I was happy to hear that Sully was satisfied. I had a good idea things had gone well. The Admiral had spoken to me on several occasions and he was always friendly, a sure indication of his approval. I'd have been keelhauled if he'd been pissed off in any way.

"The Admiral said he thought the Barge tours in Sydney were the highlight of his trip, and the crew of the Barge were a credit to the Navy." Sully continued, "You've been promoted to Boatswain's Mate First Class, and I've put your name forward for a Navy Achievement Medal."

"I...thank you, Sir," I stuttered, lost for words.

"Jake, I'll tell you something," Sully began, "This tour was more than just babysitting an admiral. It put me in line for promotion to flag rank, possibly within four or five years. I've never forgotten what you did for me, and now it seems you've come through for me again, helping to keep the old boy happy. If things had not gone well, I would have been on the receiving end of the Admiral's notorious temper. Then I would have had COMPAC chewing my ass. I appreciate your help Jake."

"I was happy to serve as helmsman of the Barge, Sir," I replied. "That'll also look good on my records in the future."

"Good," Sully stood up, signaling the meeting was over. "Let's get the formalities over in Pearl, then we can finish with the Admiral in San Diego, and get back to the real business of the Navy."

Aye, aye Sir," I stood at attention for a moment, then turned on my heels and left the cabin.

"Thanks again Jake," Sully called after me as I walked through the door.

"Congratulations sailor," Davis said, after I'd told him about my meeting with Sully. "You'll be thinking of going off to Officers' Training School next," he kidded good-naturedly.

"I may be friends with one of the up-and-comers in the Navy, but I don't really care for officers," I responded to the jib, then added, "I never have."

I picked up some Boatswain's Mate First Class patches at the ship's store, and sewed them on my dress whites before we arrived at Pearl. I knew we'd be getting liberty and I was still enough of a kid to want to show off my promotion.

Pearl Harbor, how I loved the place. If ever I retired from the Navy, this is where I'd want to live. I loved everything about it -- the climate, the mountains looming behind the base, the color of the native Hawaiian dress.

I couldn't make up my mind whether to wear my whites with the new rate, or get myself the loudest shirt I could find in Honolulu and do the bars along Hotel Street.

That dilemma was settled for me, the Admiral wanted his Barge to take him around the harbor for a close up, personal tour of all the old familiar sites one more time. I wore my whites with the new patch and after we got back from that trip and hoisted the Barge, my whites were soiled and sweaty. I showered and changed into my loud Tongan shirt and headed into town with Davis.

Hotel Street was the same as I'd remembered it that night Ed Morrow had tried to make a move on me. I hadn't heard much about him lately, but knew he was still into politics. I still received information from the Oklahoma Republican Party now and again, although I rarely voted.

Davis and I slid onto bar stools in one of the dozens of places that were the favorites for servicemen stationed in Hawaii or passing through.

It was going to be a slow night; both of us had been busy all day and were washed out. As the bartender poured us beers he inquired if we'd like some instant pussy. "How much?" Davis asked.

"Only a dollar," replied the bartender, as he put down the beers in front of us.

"Come on," Davis groaned, "You're kidding?"

"No, I'm not," the bartender was insistent.

"Okay!" we both said, "Here's the dollar."

The bartender picked up the dollar and placed a glass of water on the bar. Then he handed us a package. On the label was written these instructions: "Place contents in water—wait five minutes—be amazed as a hairy pussy appears!" I opened the package, placed the rolled up object in the water; there was hair sticking out of each end. So far, so good, I thought.

We waited five minutes, nothing...five more minutes, still nothing! Just as we were about to give up...the wrapping dissolved and before our eyes...A CAT! It was the hairy shape of a cat with its back arched and its tail in the air.

The bartender threw his head back and laughed. I smiled; Davis finally got the joke and curled over with laughter.

Mid-way between Hawaii and San Diego, the Captain came on the P.A. system and addressed all hands, "I would like to personally thank every member of the ship's crew, both officers and enlisted men, for their contributions to this farewell cruise for Admiral Sumpher." He then went on to talk about the disciplined behavior throughout the voyage, the dedication to duty by the ship's company, and all the other niceties captains thank their crews with.

Two days later the Admiral came on and gave much the same speech. Everybody knew it was mostly bullshit, but lapped it up anyway. One thing to the Admiral's credit, he did stop and talk to a number of the crew, particularly the younger guys during the last days before we reached San Diego. That was the thing men remembered most about good officers, how they talked to you one-on-one; the more senior the officer, the longer you remembered it.

The harbor at San Diego had its share of history; it was dug into the very hills. As you sailed around the north end of Coronado Island on the submarine-pen side of the harbor, you could see huge circular shaped hollows. These were coal storage pits, dating from when the Navy used coal to fuel the boilers in its first steam ships. In those days the pits were much larger; now after years of erosion they had filled in some. I had always enjoyed the history of California, from the early Spanish settlements, to the US participation in the revolt of 1849.

We closed on the piers jutting out in endless rows on the city side of the harbor; a tug came along and took over, nudging us into our berth at Pier 3.

A Navy band struck up *Anchors Aweigh,* and the brass gathered for the ceremonies. The Admiral gave one final speech to the crew from the fantail, a final round of handshaking, then he was piped ashore, with all hands lining the decks in dress uniform. I was always a sucker for ceremony, and I had tears in my eyes as the haunting sound of the Boatswain's Pipe shrilled.

I had one job to complete; that was the release of the Admiral's Barge. The Barge is basically a motorized launch much like a captain's gig or other Naval launch. How it is distinguished is by the colors showing the rank of the admiral and a ton of extra brass and silver fittings. The one we'd used on the trip needed to be offloaded and then replaced with a regular gig for the Captain's use.

It had been made clear to me by that miserable Chief Boatswain's Mate on the *Junction City,* that I could kiss my ass goodbye if there was as much as a scratch on it when it was signed back in at the warehouse; after that he couldn't give a damn.

My heart was in my throat as the dockside crane lifted it from the skids, where we'd lowered it, and onto a waiting truck. I accompanied it to the warehouse, saw it unloaded without incident, and then had the supervising chief sign off on it. At the end of the operation I gave a sigh of relief. Now I had to get back to the ship and get the gig hoisted aboard.

Mucky's second letter caught up with me just before we sailed from San Diego. I had never received the first, so God only knows what had happened to it.

In the letter Mucky spoke of our short time together, and how she was desperately trying to find a way to come to America to be with me. I had written her a long letter from the Philippines and a hurriedly scrawled postcard from Hawaii. I hadn't said too much about the future in my letter because I didn't know where, or when, we'd ever get together again.

"I love you desperately," her letter ended. I could feel her anguish in the neatly written words.

"God Almighty!" I thought, what the hell do I do about this?

I talked to the base chaplain in Dago about the procedures for getting assistance from the Navy. He wasn't much help at all; in fact, he was downright discouraging.

"The Navy can't do anything until after you're married." He spoke in that holier-than-thou tone that aggravated the hell out of me. "I can't see how you can be serious, anyway. How long did you say you were together, two days?" He continued, "Why don't you just put it out of your mind? You'll have forgotten all about it in a month or two."

"With all due respect, Sir," I tried to reason with him, "we're in love and want to get married. The problem is if the Navy doesn't help her get over here, how can we get hitched?"

"The only experience I've had with foreign brides is that they were already married to the servicemen before applying for expatriation to the United States," he said, playing with the pen on his desk.

"Every time the Navy visits ports around the world there is always some young man falling in love," he continued with his lecture. "In time the young man gets over it. How would it be if the Navy spent all its time bringing Chinese, Filipinas, Japanese and every other foreigner here eh? Just because some lonely boy gets a crush on a girl."

"Sir, it's not like that with me," I pleaded. "I know how I feel."

"You think you know how you feel," he spoke to me like you would a child. "Take some time, you'll get over it; then you'll thank me for this chat. You'll see."

I knew I was getting nowhere with him, and in danger of losing my temper. "Yes Sir," I finally said, "I'll take your advice. Thank you for your time, Sir."

"That's what I'm here for, Petty Officer Rickmeyer," he smiled smugly. "If you need to see me again, the door is always open."

I left the chaplain's office feeling depressed and confused. "Maybe he's right," I thought. "Maybe it was just a schoolboy crush."

I was glad to leave San Diego and be at sea again. The *Junction City* was headed for her new assignment. She would pass through the Panama Canal and sail up to Norfolk, Virginia. There the ship would be tied up for four weeks, giving home leave to the crew; then the cruiser would take aboard replacements, stores, carry out any necessary repairs, and then deploy to the Sixth Fleet in the Mediterranean.

Chapter Sixteen

"I've got a job for ya," the Chief said as I reported in to his office.

We'd been in Norfolk a week and things were really quiet with most of the crew ashore.

"There's a delegation of Congressmen from Washington paying a visit to Norfolk." The Chief always looked to me like he had a boil on his ass; he continually twisted his face muscles. "These bigwigs are from some committee responsible for Navy funding, so we need to treat 'em right," he grimaced.

"What do you need from me Chief?" I asked.

"Your specialty," he explained. "You take 'em for a water tour up and down the shipyards using the Captain's gig."

"How many of them are there?" I asked, wondering what I needed to prepare for.

"Only four; the others will be entertained on one of the new aircraft carriers." Sounding like he was happy to palm this off on me, he continued, "You'll be ready at 0900 tomorrow, take the boat around to the inboard ladder. There a Lieutenant Reynolds will be waiting. He'll accompany them and give a running commentary of the work that's going on in the shipyard."

"Do I need to make out an itinerary," I asked, "or will the Lieutenant have everything organized?"

"The Lieutenant will tell you where he wants to go," then added, "just be sure to get over to the Newport News side and give 'em a look at that new amphibious assault ship under construction."

"Aye, Chief," I answered. "Will that be all?"

"That's all Rickmeyer." He looked pissed, but then he always did.

"I'd better get a crew together and check the boat out," I said as I left the office. That grouchy bastard never got it. I loved taking people on boat tours; looking at ships and shipyards, he always thought he was giving me shitty details.

"Hold her steady there!" I ordered the seaman handling the line holding us fast to the ladder. The Lieutenant and the Congressmen were making their way down the ladder to the boat. I saluted smartly as the Lieutenant stepped onto the deck, followed by the first of the Congressmen. As the second man stepped from the ladder, he almost lost his footing. I reached out to steady him.

"Jake!" he exclaimed, "I don't believe it!"

"Ed...Ed Morrow!" I exclaimed in return.

"This is Jake Rickmeyer, everybody," he announced to the rest of the party. "We were on a destroyer together off Okinawa! God! How long ago was that...thirteen, fourteen years?"

"You're looking great Jake," he said, shaking my hand firmly. "The Navy life has been good to you."

"You're looking good, too, Congressman," I replied, not knowing how to address him.

"It's Ed, Jake," he laughed. "We went through too much together to bother with formalities."

"You're right about that," I laughed with him.

"Umm...perhaps we should proceed," Lieutenant Reynolds said, giving me a glare. He was not happy I was taking the attention away from him. "Cast off Petty Officer, and then head upriver towards the submarine pens."

"Aye, aye Sir," I answered crisply. "Cast off for'ard!" I ordered the seaman at the bow.

I backed away from the ladder and swung about in a slow, smooth turn, passing close to the three cruisers moored at the pier.

The tour of the Naval Base and the shipbuilding slips at Newport News took about two hours. I took my lead from Lieutenant Reynolds, trying to anticipate where he wanted to take the Congressmen next. The only suggestion I made was the Chief's about the amphibious assault ship under construction.

The Lieutenant would have poo-pooed it, but the Congressmen thought it would be of interest. I got the impression Lieutenant Reynolds was getting pissed at me, especially since Ed kept asking me the questions Reynolds should have been answering.

"All right, Petty Officer," Reynolds said, at the end the tour, "let's go back to the landing."

"Aye, Sir," I responded immediately, and turned across the river to return to the Norfolk side.

"Jake," Ed came back aft after we'd made fast to the ladder, "I want to get together with you. I'm pressed for time, so dinner tonight would be our only chance. Can you make it?"

"Well..." I stammered, not knowing where he planned to have dinner. "I won't be able to join you at the Officer's Club, if that's what you had in mind."

"No, I know the old bullshit protocol," he laughed. "I was an enlisted man too, remember?"

"Where are you staying?" I asked.

"The Towers Inn," he replied. "Let's say seven-thirty tonight…meet you in the cocktail bar?"

"Okay, fine Ed," I said.

"I'll be looking forward to it," he called over his shoulder as he started up the ladder. "We've got a lot of years to catch up on."

"The boat's released Petty Officer, thank you," growled Reynolds as he followed the last Congressman up the ladder. He gave me a parting look that would have soured milk. He was going to be one of those officers who thought enlisted men should just follow orders and keep their mouths shut otherwise; asshole!

I got the evening off, compliments of Chief "prune-face". He had already gotten the word that the Congressmen were more than happy with the day's tour. That would put a feather in the Chief's cap, too, especially since he was coming up for promotion to Senior Chief.

I caught a cab to the hotel and made my way to the cocktail bar. I'd dressed in the only civilian suit I owned. It was dark gray and I'd bought it for Dory and John's wedding and hadn't worn it since.

I sat at the bar and ordered a drink. It was a little before seven-thirty; I always liked to be early. It was a habit I'd started that first day I signed up in Lawton and the Chief said I'd go far. He'd meant it as a joke, but I'd gotten used to the practice.

The drink just arrived as Ed came in.

"Jake, you don't know how good it is to see you," Ed put his hand on my shoulder and sat down beside me. The gesture didn't make me cringe as I thought it would. That night in Honolulu was a long time ago. We'd both put in a lot of years since then, and there was no need to bring back that episode.

"Tell me all about yourself," Ed said, smiling. "You're still in the Navy, so what about it?"

I talked for a while, filling Ed in on my failed marriage to Barbara-Jean, the Korean action where Bug had been killed, my wound, the time spent in Japan, and then we went in to dinner.

"I'm going to have the lobster Jake," he looked up from the menu. "Have whatever you want, it's on me," he added with a grin, "at least the American taxpayer, anyway."

"The sirloin steak, medium rare," I told the server waiting by the table to take our order.

"The lobster for me," Ed ordered, "and a bottle of Mollet, thank you."

"Oh, I have to tell you this." I suddenly remembered that Ed had known Rabbit too. "You remember that asshole we used to call Rabbit?"

"Of course...Rabbit," Ed reflected. "Yeah, he joined up with us in Lawton."

"Well, I bumped into his sorry ass in Japan." I was really enjoying reminiscing.

"What was he doing there?" Ed asked. "Is he still in the Navy?"

"He is, and he was up to the same old tricks with little girls," I continued. "And then, believe it or not, I ran into him again in the Philippines a couple of months ago!" I told him about the scene in the bar.

Ed was laughing, "I can't believe this," he was wiping the tears from his eyes with his napkin. "Remember you and that Rabbit in Yuma, when we were on the way to boot camp?"

We were starting to draw attention from the other diners with our laughter.

"What about you Ed?" I asked through a mouthful of steak. "You going to run for President?"

"I don't think so," he said as he sipped his wine, "not yet anyway." With a smile he continued, "I plan to run for the US Senate when the seat is up for election two years from now. After that, it will be trying to get on the right committees in Washington."

"Well, that's out of my league." I was finishing the last of my steak. "Politics is something that has never interested me."

"It's something that doesn't interest most people," he was sucking the meat out of the lobster's claw. "That's why power-hungry assholes like me keep getting elected."

We both laughed; I almost choked on the last mouthful of mashed potatoes.

It had been a great evening. I hated to have it end and it was obvious Ed felt the same.

"Jake," he shook my hand for the tenth time as I got in the cab, "if there's anything I can ever do for you, don't hesitate to get in touch with me; I mean that!"

"Thanks Ed." I hated to end the evening. "I'll always remember that."

As the cab drove off, I looked out the rear window. Ed was still standing at the curb holding his arm up in farewell.

"I wished we had more time to spend together old buddy," I said to myself. "Maybe next time."

I was just finishing my letter to Mucky when I heard the P.A. announce that the Captain was coming aboard. Sully had been away for the last week working at the Pentagon.

The brass in the Pentagon were always drawing up war plans. The big fear was the Russians were going to start something. The *Junction City's* deployment to the Mediterranean would be right on the front lines of the cold war.

Leaving Norfolk wouldn't be the worst thing for me, apart from the dinner with Ed; I hadn't exactly enjoyed my stay here. Mucky was on my mind all the time. Was the chaplain right? Should I just move on?

It did seem like the distance between us was just too vast. Her last correspondence had been full of plans for us to marry and set up a home someplace. "I'll wait for you forever, darling. You don't know how much I love you," she had ended her last letter.

Chapter Seventeen

The Mediterranean in 1958 was a sort after deployment for Navy ships. Port visits every couple of weeks to Greece, Italy, Spain, Turkey. The trouble was keeping enough dough in your pockets. The dollars went a long way in those places, but there were a lot of places to go.

Davis and I had drank more unpronounceable drinks, in more unpronounceable bars and restaurants, than you could shake a stick at. It looked like being a dream cruise until one day we were placed on high alert. A coup had taken place in Iraq and the ship was dispatched to standby off the coast of Lebanon.

The Middle East had been unstable ever since World War II, and now the President of Lebanon was asking Uncle Sam for help to keep his fragile government intact. President Camille Chamoun had asked the US Government to send American troops to his country. The Sixth Fleet had at least a battalion of Marines from the 2nd Marine Division stationed on ships throughout the Mediterranean. Several Beach Landing Teams (BLTs) had been mustered under Brigadier General Sidney S. Wade and deployed to help maintain order and to send the message that the United States was prepared to defend the pro-western government of Chamoun.

The situation that first week looked like it could erupt at any time, and the *Junction City,* as well as other ships, was ordered to evacuate civilians from Beirut. At first we were taking off only US Citizens; then other governments started asking for the Navy's help.

The evacuation was orderly, with families being loaded aboard landing craft from amphibious ships off the coast, then moved onto ships that had room for them.

Our ship's role in the evacuation had been to intimidate any potential rebel groups from taking action against the evacuees. We remained close enough in to shore to make clear the power of the cruiser's armaments.

There were Muslims, Christians, and other groups all looking for a power grab. Beirut was a dangerous place, and thank God the Marines had landed and taken control.

"Now hear this…Boat parties close up," a voice summoned over the P.A. That meant me. I still had control of the deck boats and I hurried to my station.

"Boats, get a motor cutter over the side," said the XO, arriving with the Chief Boatswain. "Take one crewmen and two armed Marines for cover. We need to get a boat to the beach south of the City. There are some Italians isolated there, and they can't make their way to the evacuation location."

"Aye, aye Sir," I replied. "Unlash and swing her out!" I ordered the boat crew. The Marine lieutenant arrived with a squad, armed and with full battle packs.

"Lieutenant, pick two men to go ashore with the boat, they'll provide cover if that becomes necessary," the XO ordered.

"Aye, Sir," the Lieutenant replied. "Gunny, you and Shaw go in, check your weapons, make sure you have enough ammo."

The boat was lowered and I got everyone aboard. As soon as we were ready to shove off, the XO yelled down, "Keep your walkie-talkie handy. I'll relay any instructions; just head to the northern end of the beach, and report back when you see them."

"Aye, aye!" I yelled back as we shoved off and headed north up the shoreline.

Davis yelled back at me, "What the fuck are these wops doing running around on the beach anyway?"

"How the fuck do I know?" I hollered back.

"There they are Boats!" the young seaman at the bow shouted, "looks like two guys and a woman."

"I see 'em!" I replied, picking up the walkie-talkie to call the ship, "Boat party to mother."

"Mother here, go ahead boat party," came the crackled reply over the radio.

"Have civilians in sight," I spoke into the mouth piece, "three people, repeat three."

"Roger boat party," the voice on the radio replied. "Proceed with extreme caution. We have report of a possible sniper."

"Roger that!" I hooked the radio back on my belt and called out to Davis. "Gunny, there's a sniper somewhere on the beach, heads up!"

Davis waved an acknowledgment and pointed towards shore as he spoke to the other Marine, who promptly raised his rifle and held it to his shoulder.

I gunned the boat towards shore then slowed. As soon as the bow hit the beach the crewman jumped over and held her steady.

Bang! Ping! A bullet ricocheted off the gunwale. Davis and the other Marine jumped over and ran a short way up the beach, and then they dived in the sand, bringing their rifles to a ready position.

"Get aboard!" I yelled at the Italians, who were standing there with panic on their faces.

Bang! Another shot from the wall overlooking the beach; the woman screamed and slumped to the ground. Davis and Shaw started to return fire in the general direction of the wall. The two Italian men picked the woman up and lifted her into the boat, at the same time the crewman started to push the boat off.

"Davis!" I shouted as loud as I could, "Let's go!" I was starting to slowly reverse off the beach. Davis and Shaw ran back in a zigzag pattern and waded out to the cutter, which was now broadside on to the beach.

Bang! Another round fired by the sniper.

"Shit!" Shaw yelled and clutched his arm. I grabbed him with one hand, holding the tiller with the other, while Davis got him under his backside and threw him bodily into the boat.

Davis then turned and fired a full magazine at the unseen gunman, then swung himself up, diving headfirst into the cutter. I was already gunning the motor and starting to put as much distance between the beach and the boat as I could.

"How is she?" I called out to the Italian nearest me.

"She is bleeding, but all right, I think," he replied, while trying to tie his shirt around her chest.

Davis had cut open Shaw's sleeve, and was applying a first aid bandage; they both looked okay.

That evening, standing by the quarterdeck railing in my usual spot with Davis, I asked him what he was thinking.

"Wondering about that woman, about Shaw, glad they're both okay; thinking how I would have handled being hit myself," he said, almost in a whisper.

"Funny, isn't it," I said, looking at him fumbling with his cigarette pack. "It's all over in a second and you never have a chance to think; you just react. It's later on when your hands start to shake."

"I know it!" he smiled, "Big tough Gunny and I can't even get a cigarette out of the pack!"

I didn't offer to get one out for him; I just let him work through it himself.

The sunsets in the Mediterranean could be as beautiful as those found anywhere in the world, and I never tired of enjoying them.

The next day Gunny Carlson, Seaman Boeser and myself were ordered to report to the Captain's cabin. It was for that "well done" speech I figured.

Captain Sully Rooks was in a good mood, it seemed he was touched with "fairy dust". The *USS Junction City's* daring rescue off the beach in Beirut had made headlines in the International Press.

More important for Sully was the fact that ComSixthFlt, the Joint Chiefs of Staff, and the Secretary of the Navy would be reading about it. The other ships had evacuated hundreds of men, women and children. We'd only picked up three, yet that is what's meant by "fairy dust". To read the headlines, the *Junction City* was the only ship off the beach.

"Gunnery Sergeant Carlson, Petty Officer Rickmeyer, Seaman Boeser," Sully began, "for your efforts in the rescue of civilians from a hostile environment ,the Navy commends you," he continued. "Corporal Shaw, who is doing well in sickbay, will be recommended for a Bronze Star for his selfless efforts to complete the mission while under hostile fire. I have recommended the rest of the rescue party for Navy Commendations."

It was now being called a mission. What had been the pick-up of three civilians who shouldn't have been where they were in the first place had now turned into a mission, all because the press had picked up the story.

"We're headed for Naples to return our civilian guests to Italy." Sully was still standing in front of us, "And we'll be able to get hospital care for the young lady. I would like to thank you three dedicated men personally, and can assure you the Navy also thanks you. And I'm quite sure the good people you saved thank you."

"I would also like to say well done," added the XO, who was part of the group in the cabin.

I looked at the Chief, who was also there. If he was smiling, I couldn't tell. Only a slight curl of his left lip gave any indication of a change in his facial expression.

We left the cabin ramrod straight after shaking hands with the Captain and XO. I noticed the Chief do a double take when Sully called me Jake as we shook hands. If that lip curl was a smile, it was now gone.

"Wow Boats!" exclaimed Boeser, "A Navy Commendation! Wow, wait till I write my folks."

"How about you Davis?" I kidded. "Feel any different now that you're a hero?"

"Nah, feel like I got it under false pretenses," Davis drawled. "I was firing blindly at the top of the fucking wall, never even seen the fucker. A Bronze Star for Shaw sounds a little over-done."

"You'll learn to take the fluff and praise the system," I said, feeling cynical about the whole thing myself. "Play along...to get along."

"Will you be needing me before the evening watch Boats?" Boeser asked. "I'd kinda like to get that letter written to my folks and mail it when we hit Naples."

"You're relieved for the rest of the day Boeser," I smiled. "Take your time, write down the details before you forget."

I was happy for the kid, and happy for Davis and Shaw. I don't know why I was feeling so down about myself. Once again I'd be getting medals pinned on me, once again my records would bloom with praises of outstanding performances. After fourteen years maybe I'd had enough, maybe I wouldn't ship over next time.

The mountainous landscape of Italy came slowly into view as the cruiser's slim bow cut through the opaque waters of the Tyrrhenian Sea. Naples…La Bella Napoli…it was straight out of the storybooks.

As we entered the Bay of Naples we could see medieval castles, buildings built high up on the sides of hills. We'd just sailed past the fabled Isle of Capri, and now dead ahead was Mount Vesuvius the famous volcano.

Two lengthy breakwaters with equally lengthy names sheltered the Navy facilities in Naples. They were called Diga Porania Emmanuele and Molo San Vincenzo.

Before we'd tied up, the press bulbs were popping all along the pier. The Italian Press was there in force, and the Navy had Photographer's Mates running up and down trying to get pictures of the ship as she docked.

The fun began as the Paparazzi went wild when the Italian men ran down the gangplank into the waiting arms of their families. Then the insanity kicked up a notch as the wounded Italian woman was taken off on a stretcher. The Navy photographers got into the fray as Corporal Shaw was helped ashore to a waiting ambulance. I stood at the railing and took it all in.

"Wanna hit some wop hot spots tonight?" Davis lent over the railing beside me.

"Why not," I replied, "some Italian food and a little wine to celebrate our heroes welcome. Why not?"

"With all these Catholic mothers around here, probably no chance of getting into their daughters' pants," Davis winked.

"Let's forget the dames for once," I said seriously. "Let's go see some of the historical sites."

"You like history, I'll tell ya a little Marine Corps history," Davis began. "Did you know the Marines have been fighting in the Mediterranean for a coon's age?"

"Something about the shores of Tripoli?" I said. I knew how the Marine Corps Hymn went.

"In 1805 a Marine Lieutenant named O'Bannon raised the flag over Derna, in Tripoli, after defeating the ragheads there," he said matter-of-factly, "and the Marines have been keepin' an eye on things ever since."

"Well, we got time to get dressed and go take a look at Pompeii," I offered. "That'll give us a history lesson before we tackle the spaghetti and vino."

"I'm game," Davis slapped me on the back. "Let's go!"

Pompeii had been a place I'd always wanted to visit. I remembered the history teacher telling us all about it in junior high, about how Mount Vesuvius had erupted in 79 AD, completely burying the city of Pompeii and covering its inhabitants with ash.

The cab ride to the ancient city had taken longer than we'd thought; the volcano had looked so close from the harbor. Our driver was jabbering in a mixture of lousy English and Italian, all the while trying to maneuver his beat up old Fiat through the bicycle traffic.

"How mucho?" I tried to pay in dollars.

"Fiva dollar," he answered. "It'sa longa way froma the boat, no?"

"Bullshit!" chimed in Davis "Take two you lousy dago!"

"Fungu bastardo!" the cabby raised his arm and slapped the elbow with his other hand.

"Same to you, ya asshole!" Davis yelled back, flipping the bird to the driver.

The ruins were preserved better than I had imagined. Some houses were intact, and some even had paint still on the walls. But the most profound objects were the bodies, or what remained of them.

"These are fake," Davis said with a smirk. "Looks like cement to me."

Davis' drawl made the word cement sound like see-ment.

"They're not fake," I tried to explain. "It's how the ash replaced the actual cavities left by the bodies, and then it set like cement." I was having a hard time convincing him.

"I'm about ready for a drink," he sighed. "I've seen enough of this bullshit!"

It was clear Davis would not replace Ensign Carter Bilts as a sightseeing buddy. The Ensign and I had a lot in common as far as a love of history was concerned.

I hadn't seen nearly enough, but it was no use trying to hold Davis' attention any longer. We caught the same cab back into town, the cabby and Davis glaring at each other the whole way.

Some of the greatest little restaurants in the world can be found around Naples, most run by ordinary families. The constant yelling from the kitchens, the sound of pots banging on stoves…and the mouth-watering smells!

"This goddamn wop food is great, isn't it Jake?" Davis was digging into his second bowl of pasta, and washing it down with rich red Chianti.

"Yeah Davis," I said. "It doesn't get any better than this."

It had been a great day and we headed back to the ship after a night of eating, drinking, and lousy attempts to sing love songs to the local girls as they walked past our table at the restaurant.

The next morning I checked with the ship's mail office for any letters from Mucky. I hadn't received any for a while and was starting to sense a change in the tone of her letters. There was a letter! I took it and hurried back to my rack and lay down; the corner where I slept afforded me what little privacy that you could find on a ship.

It started off with the usual small talk but the ending was missing her usual statements of undying love. I guess the distance and the time we'd now been apart was taking its toll. Better to let it go, I thought. I'd sent a hurriedly written postcard the day before; I didn't think I'd write to her again.

Chapter Eighteen

The *Junction City* showed the flag up and down the Mediterranean for the next couple of months. We'd seen Athens and Istanbul, visiting both ports to show no US favoritism between the two countries. Greece and Turkey had been squaring off over real and imagined grievances.

Malta was also a popular port for visits and we tied up there after about two weeks at sea. I'd pulled gangway duty, so would not be getting ashore this visit.

I sensed trouble when Davis had gone ashore with a couple of Marine friends. He looked pissed when he'd left the ship that evening, and only mumbled a reply when I'd spoken to him.

It was just before midnight when the British Military Police (Red Caps) brought Davis back to the ship in handcuffs. The Red Caps didn't bring him up the gangway, figuring their jurisdiction ended on the pier. They stood there waiting for us to take over. The Officer-of-the-Deck was livid.

"Boats!" he turned to me, "Summon the deck watch and get that man aboard!"

"Aye, aye Sir." My heart sank. This would mean big trouble for Davis. I spoke over the P.A. system, "Duty deck watch to the gangway...on the double!" I added, seeing the dark look on the duty officer's face.

They arrived within two minutes and hurried down the gangway and relieved the Red Caps of their prisoner.

"Take the Gunny to the brig," the young officer ordered the petty officer in charge of the deck crew, "and post a guard. The master-at-arms will take care of the charge formalities tomorrow."

Turning back to me, he said sharply, "Go down and get the facts of the offense from the MP's and extend the US Navy's apologies and thanks for bringing the offender back to the ship." He was an up-and-comer and didn't care for trouble on his duty watch.

"Aye, Sir," I threw him a quick salute and hurried down the gangway.

My report to the Officer-of-the-Deck, a copy of which would go to the master-at-arms, was that a fight had broken out between some Marines and British sailors; the Limeys were off a Royal Navy submarine. The military police had settled the argument, restored the peace, and dismissed the participants. Then Gunnery Sergeant Carlson had become agitated and head-butted a Red Cap corporal.

With the military policeman's nose broken and bleeding profusely, it was impossible to dismiss the incident. They had no alternative than to arrest Gunnery Sergeant Carlson.

The Red Cap detail had been apologetic and said they realized we'd been at sea and that men needed to let off steam. But regrettably, the assault on the corporal could not be ignored.

"Damn right it couldn't be ignored!" the Officer-of-the-Deck repeated, his face red. "Enter in the log that Gunnery Sergeant Carlson is being charged with assault on a Military Policeman, disorderly conduct, and being out of uniform. He'll be held in the brig pending Captain's Mast."

"Aye, Sir." I made the entry, logged the time and initialed it. It looked like Davis was going to get the book thrown at him. The out-of-uniform charge was because he'd been brought back without his cap. I'm sure the young officer would think up a couple of other charges before morning.

After I was relieved, I went below to the brig to get Davis' side of the story. Davis was looking pretty sorry for himself. He was disheveled from the pushing and shoving he'd received getting handcuffed and brought back to the ship by the Red Caps, who hadn't been gentle. I suspected he had struggled all the way; a few bruises and scratches were evident on his face and hands.

"What the fuck did you do?" I asked. "You have been charged with assault, and you're headed for Captain's Mast; the master-at-arms is certain to recommend a court martial."

"Those fuckin' Limey fags!" he was still fuming. "Those fuckers tried to make a move on a couple of Marines, and then those fuckin' Limey Red Caps just laughed it off!"

"Why'd you head-butt the military policeman?" I asked, still not believing how this thing had gotten so far out of hand.

"He told me to go back to the hills, hillbilly, and fuck your sister!" Davis put his head in his hands. "I'm fucked now, I'll do time in Norfolk and get a dishonorable discharge."

"Maybe not," I tried to cheer him up. "The Captain may go easy on you."

"And what?" he looked up. "Bust me back to private? I might as well get thrown out."

Davis dropped his head again. I knew the Corps meant everything to him; he was like me…a lifer!

"Captain's Mast won't be till we sail day after tomorrow," I spoke softly, feeling sorry for him. "They'll hold you in here until then. Can I get you anything?"

"Nah, what's done is done," he mumbled into his hands. Looking up at me, he added, "Thanks anyway Jake."

I waited in the companionway near Sully's cabin in the hopes of catching him on his way down from the bridge. This was the first chance I'd had following our departure from Malta.

"Jake!" he said, as he came down the ladder. "You look like the world just landed on your shoulders."

"It has in a way, Sir," I replied. "Could I see you privately Captain?"

"Of course, Jake," he nodded to the sentry as the young Marine opened the cabin door for him. "Come on in."

"Sir..." I began, trying to sound as serious as I could. "It's about Gunny Carlson."

"Oh yes." He looked up after throwing his cap on the desk and sitting down. "Not what I wanted to see from the Gunny; he had what it took to be a good NCO I thought."

"Captain, you once said if I needed anything to ask..." I hated being in this position, but I kept going. "Can you reduce the charges and let Gunny Carlson off with a verbal warning only?"

Sully sat there staring at me for a full minute.

"Jake, you're asking me to look the other way on a serious breach of discipline here." He was not happy with my request.

Another minute of silence followed. I was starting to have second thoughts about coming to Sully.

"I'll review the case," he said deliberately. "If I can find a way to let it slide, I will."

"Thank you, Sir," I let out the breath I had been holding.

"That will be all Jake," his words dismissing me. Then added as I turned to leave, "Don't do this to me again Jake."

"Aye, Sir." I left with a bad taste in my mouth; it had been a lose-lose situation for me. I hated putting Sully on the spot to ask for favors. On the other hand, I couldn't let Davis go down the tubes.

I said nothing to Davis or anyone else. I just hoped this would work out.

An hour after Captain's Mast, two days out of Malta, I was sitting in the mess having a coffee, trying to study the Navy's handbook on regulations. I was hoping to make Chief when we got back from this deployment.

"Jake, you ain't gonna believe this!" Davis sat on the bench beside me. "The Captain tore me a new asshole...lectured me about disgracing the good name of the United States Marine Corps...how we're all ambassadors while in foreign countries...and how, as an NCO I should be setting an example...on and on. Then he dismisses me with only a verbal reprimand and the loss of a month's pay!"

"That's great Davis," I heaved a sigh of relief.

"Man, I thought my ass was in a sling for sure." He had a grin from ear to ear, "I'm feeling so lucky, I may try to find me a poker game somewhere."

"I'd count my lucky stars and stay out of trouble for a while if I were you." I couldn't help smiling at the change in Davis, especially after seeing him that night in the brig.

The ship took part in exercises in the Adriatic Sea with naval units from the North Atlantic Treaty Organization (NATO), just to tick off the commies in Yugoslavia, I think. We transited between Albania and the heel of Italy into the Ionian Sea, then after further exercises with the Limey and Italian Navies in the waters around Sicily, we turned our bow west and headed through the Straits of Gibraltar out into the Atlantic.

It had been a long deployment, extended twice because of the unrest in the region, and our involvement with the Marine landings and evacuation of civilians from Lebanon.

Chapter Nineteen

Crossing the Atlantic in late 1959 we hit one nasty weather front after another; these were not ideal cruising conditions. We'd rigged the foul-weather safety lines along the topside open deck area anywhere personnel had to carry out necessary activities. It was wise to remain below; the high seas would occasionally send waves crashing over the ship that could sweep a man overboard in an instant.

It was fascinating, almost mesmerizing, to be up near the ship's bridge and watch the bow dip and rise, sending huge sprays of water up over the superstructure.

"Boats, better keep any activities on the deck to those absolutely necessary," the officer on watch warned me. "We don't want to lose a man over the side."

"I've secured the deck crews, Sir," I replied to his unnecessary order; I'd been on the deck of a ship in storms before. "I'll rig a lifeline on myself and check the safety lines one more time, Sir."

"Good!" he said, cautioning me. "Make sure you have a man watch you until you've cleared the deck, then have him pass the word back to me."

"Aye, Sir!" I replied.

"Watch me all the way aft. You'll be able to see me enter the aft section hatchway from here," I ordered a seaman just inside the signal bridge entrance.

"Gotcha Boats!" he said, helping me get into the foul-weather gear and rig the lifeline I'd need for safety outside on the open deck.

As I left the signal bridge between bow dips I was almost blown away, the winds were so strong. I attached my lifeline to the rigged safety ropes before I started my way back aft.

Just as I reached the aft section hatchway, a large swell lifted the stern of the ship almost clear of the water, at the same time turning her broadside to the storm. I lost my hold on the rope, and as the next wave hit I was lifted up and left hanging over the ship's side, secured only by my lifeline, as the wave swept on over me. The ship dipped low in the water and I was totally submerged for probably three or four seconds; to me it seemed like eternity.

When I was lifted clear of the water as the ship rolled, I sucked in the biggest breath I'd ever taken; I knew I'd be submerged again on the next roll. There was no way I could get myself back onto the deck. It took all my strength just to hold the lifeline securely around me. I must have been dunked twice more, and as I cleared the water each time, I exhaled and inhaled the deepest breath I could. Finally, I felt myself being pulled up and hands hauling me over the railing.

I was thrown heavily through the hatch and a couple of bodies tumbled in after me.

"Jesus Christ!" one of my rescuers exclaimed fastening the hatch dogs. "You just lost one of your nine lives there sailor!"

I was unable to speak for a few minutes, just looked at my rescuers nodding my head up and down.

"Get him down to sickbay," an officer suddenly appeared. "Good job men, get yourselves dried off and take a hot shower." Looking down at me he added, "I thought you were a goner Boats!"

The bunk in sickbay was warm and dry. It had taken me a full hour to warm up enough to stop shivering. The pharmacist's mate had piled a half dozen blankets on me. "Any more," he'd said, "and you'll suffocate under the weight!"

"Holy shit!" I heard the familiar voice of Davis. "What the fuck were ya trying to prove being out on deck like that?"

"Checking lines that maybe didn't need checking," my teeth started chattering again.

"Well, I'm glad your sorry ass didn't get flushed away," he said with a seriousness I'd seldom heard from him before.

"Okay Gunny," the pharmacist's mate said, "that's all the time you get…he'll be released tomorrow morning. You can catch up then."

"See you tomorrow," Davis said, giving my shoulder a squeeze.

I winced! It was the shoulder I'd been wounded in; the cold water had started it aching.

My next visitor was Sully. I was glad he'd stopped by; we hadn't spoken since I'd asked him for the favor concerning Davis.

"Seems I'm always visiting you in hospital beds," he began, looking down at me with concern. "That old hag of a sea harpy is always trying to claim us, eh Jake?"

"For the last time I hope, Sully," I said. "Maybe it's time to get a shore job."

"I'll make sure of that," he replied. "I'll be handing over command of the *Junction City* when we tie up in Norfolk. If I don't have time to get back to you, it's been a pleasure to have had you under my command Jake."

"And it's been an honor to have served under you, Sir," I answered truthfully. Sully had been a good captain. He'd commanded the *USS Junction City* by the book, but had been fair and shown real concern for the men serving under him.

"If I don't see you personally before I leave," he took my hand from under the blanket, "good luck, and I look forward to our next meeting."

"So do I, Sir," the warmth of his hand cheered me. As he turned to leave I found myself whispering those words again, "And good luck to you too Sully."

Norfolk was crowded with the welcoming committee, a Navy band, the wives of the married guys, the little kids waving flags, some dressed up like tiny, miniature sailors.

"I just got the word, I'll be transferring to Camp Pendleton in California after I complete my home leave," Davis said, taking his usual spot beside me after we'd secured. "Any word on where you're goin'?"

"Not yet," I said, not taking my eyes off the sailors and their wives as they hugged and kissed. Thoughts of Mucky suddenly came back to me, that time when we'd been on the pier in each other's arms.

"I think I'll take whatever leave I've got, maybe take a trip out west," I replied, still deep in my thoughts about Mucky.

"To visit the family of your dead friend?" he asked.

"Yeah, they're the only family I've got," I said with a touch of melancholy. "I've got to deliver all these cheap nick-knacks I've been collecting for the past couple of years."

"Let's get ashore for a coupla beers," Davis sighed. "I've got to shove off first thing in the morning."

Another goodbye! The Navy was the longest running soap opera in the world. It was an unending procession of friendships, bonds, and partings.

Three days after we'd arrived back in Norfolk, Captain Sullivan P. Rooks had completed the handover procedures with the new skipper. Only thing left was the formal deck ceremony and the piping over the ship's side for the departing captain.

All hands were assembled in full dress blues, and the ceremony went off with all the pomp that the Navy has had for the last one hundred and eighty years.

Damn, I loved it! The color, the tradition, the attention to form and detail; plus it gave me an excuse to wear all my ribbons, now making up an impressive four rows across my chest.

I was sorry to see Sully leave, but he had his career path all mapped out for him, had ever since I'd first met him. He was marked for the top.

I started to wonder when I'd finally get off this bucket. I was ready for some home leave. A week later that question was answered. The *Junction City* was going up on the slips for hull maintenance.

Chief "prune face" called me in and handed me my new orders. "You'll take a month's leave, then report on board the Naval Amphibious Base at Little Creek, Virginia."

"Thanks Chief," my head was spinning. "Little Creek eh?"

"You'll be instructing probably." He closed a folder and pushed it to the side, "Should be a good billet for you. Most of the instructors there already have chief's rank."

"The landing craft Chief," I was already thinking ahead. "They have some on the drawing boards that will be fun to drive. That's always been my ambition, to captain my own boat, one that's big enough to shove all the others out of the way, maybe an LCT."

"Well, you've done all right," he looked at me with that curled lower lip. "How old are you now…thirty-two?"

"Yeah, Chief," I said. I wouldn't be thirty-two until next October. I always had to remember I'd lied about my age when I first enlisted. That thirty-second birthday would also mark sixteen years service for me. Man, the time had gone by so fast.

"You've got a damn impressive record Rickmeyer," the Chief's voice brought me back. "I'd say you could go a long way in this man's Navy."

"Never have been over-ambitious though, Chief." This was the longest conversation I'd ever had with "prune face". "I just love the boats!"

"Okay, Rickmeyer," he ended our conversation. "You're relieved effective midnight tomorrow night; good luck to ya."

I shook the Chief's outstretched hand and left his office with a spring in my step.

I called the Naval Air Station and inquired about getting on any transport planes that were headed for the West Coast. The Navy and Marine Corps had aircraft flying back and forth continuously, and if there was room servicemen on leave could hitch a ride.

I managed to get room on an old Navy DC-9 that had been flying since World War II. The plane was carrying containers of ship blueprints and other files out to Alameda in California. The destination was perfect for me; the long, uncomfortable ride wasn't.

I'd spent years at sea and hardly ever felt squeamish. Now like a dryland-greenhorn I was about to throw up. The first time the plane hit turbulence I was heaving. The crew had given me a bag of sandwiches and I'd half eaten one when I felt my breakfast coming back up; the only container handy was the sandwich bag, which I violently spewed into.

I started to feel better, and famished. Unfortunately, the sandwiches were now covered in puck. I laid my head back and went to sleep.

The navigator came back and woke me up; he said we were fifteen minutes out of Alameda.

He twitched his nose, "Don't tell me you threw up Boats?"

"Sorry," I said, feeling embarrassed and humiliated.

"Don't forget to take that smelly bag with you when you get off," he ordered, holding his nose with two fingers as he went back to the cockpit, just to rub it in a little more.

Alameda looked the same as I caught a cab down to the ferry docks. I'd catch the ferry over to Fisherman's Wharf, then grab the regular one to Sausalito. I took another cab when I got to Sausalito and arrived at Dory's house ten minutes later. It was late afternoon and the kids were home from school already. Dale ran out and put her arms around me; she was ten now and cute as a bear's ear. Dory held back until I'd finished hugging Dale, then she threw her arms around me and almost squeezed the breath out of me.

"It's so good to see you Jake," she said, with tears in her eyes. "You were a little slack with your letter writing."

"I know," I laughed. "Forgive me?"

"You know I will," she smiled, wiping her tears.

"Where's Roy?" I asked, looking around. "He's not home?"

"He's home," chirped Dale, "he's just too shy to come out and meet you."

Dale was still the confident one I could see. "Well, let's go in and find him; I got some things for you guys."

"Come out scaredy cat," Dale taunted Roy, who had crawled behind the sofa to hide from me.

I figured the best thing to do was let him come to me in his own time. "How about a coffee for this traveler?" I asked Dory, hoping she would take the hint and offer me something to eat too. I was hungry and as dry as a popcorn fart.

"Why don't I make us a real drink," she offered.

"That's even better," I replied, as I dug through my bag for some of the gifts. "Here honey, a late Christmas gift." I handed a little Filipana doll to

Dale; I'd picked it up in the Philippines on my last visit and had been hauling it around ever since. I dug out a curved knife with a carved ivory handle that I'd bought in Turkey for Roy.

"Mom, Mom!" Dale went running out, "Look what Uncle Jake gave me. She's got clothes and an umbrella and everything!"

I noticed a face peering out from around the sofa; I turned back to digging in the bag, and pretended I hadn't seen it. A moment later I felt a touch on my arm.

"Hi Uncle Jake!" Roy said shyly. He was now eleven and still had that innocent, wide-eyed look of Bug's. He was going to be tall, though, and goddamned skinny.

The three weeks with Dory and the family were some of the best I'd had in a long time. Dory and John had made a good life for themselves and the kids. I couldn't have been happier for them.

The time to leave came around way too fast. The kids had bonded with me again and wouldn't leave me alone for a second. I didn't mind at all, and wondered what I would have been like as a father. What if Barb hadn't lost our baby that time, what if we'd stayed together; too many ifs!

"Come on guys, let's go over to Fisherman's Wharf!" I announced the morning before I was due to leave. It was a Sunday and my last chance to spend the day with the kids. "We'll have shrimp and sourdough bread at the Grotto, then go take a look at that Ripley's Believe It Or Not museum.

"Yaaaa!" Dale squealed, "I want to see the baby with two heads in the glass jar."

God, it was going to be hard to leave. I hadn't had too much time to spend alone with Dory, but she seemed content with her life. We did get a chance to go over to Oakland and spend the day with Doris a couple of times. Doris was now showing her age. She seemed lonely; once you lose your partner and the kids move out, it gets tough.

Dory drove me down to the ferry in Sausalito the morning of my departure. I was glad the kids weren't there. It had been hard enough saying goodbye to them when they caught the school bus.

"I hope you enjoyed being here as much as we enjoyed having you," Dory had started to cry.

"You know how much I have," I started to get teary. The deckhand started pulling in the plank on the ferry as I hurriedly kissed Dory goodbye and jumped on.

"I'll write more, I promise," I called out, "and I'll send the kids postcards more often."

"Bye Jake!" Dory called, blowing me kisses, "God bless!"

"Bye!" I yelled over the ferry's rumble. She probably couldn't hear me as we backed out into the Bay.

I had allowed myself a couple of days to get to Virginia in case there were no immediate flights I could get myself on. This time I was lucky; there was a plane heading back that afternoon. This one was rigged for passengers and made for a more comfortable trip. The only problem was the guy sitting next to me.

He was a Master Sergeant from Graves Registration, and for the next six hours I had to listen to how they'd advanced the techniques for identifying bodies, even checking back over ones that previously had been impossible to identify. The Graves Registration Division was responsible for gathering, identifying, transporting and interring men killed on the battlefield; military accidents as well. In fact, anywhere there was death you'd find them.

"Teeth!" he went on, "take teeth. They can survive when the rest of the body has been almost totally destroyed by fire."

He droned on and on, his voice penetrated now and again as I half-dosed.

"And bodies that have been laying out in the open for weeks...especially in the tropics. Now that is when you really..."

Chapter Twenty

Little Creek, Virginia was the largest amphibious base in the world. It had been nothing but swampland when the Navy took it over during World War II and developed it to train the tens of thousands of troops needed to invade Europe.

The beaches on the base were ideal for all types of landing craft; large Landing Ships Tank (LST) came right onto the beach and offloaded their cargoes of trucks, tanks, jeeps and every other piece of conceivable equipment needed on a battlefield. It was amazing what those things carried in their tank decks and topside. Wherever they could fit something in, that something was fitted in there.

The base also had every other class of landing craft, from the small ones I was familiar with, to the newer, larger Landing Craft Mechanized (LCM); they had both the LCM-6 and the LCM-8 here.

The LCM-6 was the smaller, carrying only about 80 troops with a top speed of 9 knots; the LCM-8 was faster and could carry 200 troops. Plus, they were constructed of welded steel, a lot different than the plywood-hulled craft we had used in Korea.

I was going to like it here. I had been given comfortable quarters, sharing a room with one other petty officer by the name of Ernie Nuefeld. From what Ernie had told me about himself, he had been around boats as long as I had.

"You know they're building new amphibious landing ships. You won't need to hoist boats over the side like in the old days," Ernie was telling me one evening after chow. "The ship will pump water into compartments in the stern, lowering it below sea level, and simply flood the well deck. The stern doors will open and the landing craft will just float out, already loaded up and raring to go!"

"Yeah, I already seen them," I answered. "They'll carry those big, new Landing Craft Utility (LCU) aboard."

Shop talk among boatswain's mates, it could go on like that for hours.

One Saturday, after I'd been on base long enough to find my way around, I decided to go into town. I don't know why, I wasn't in the mood.

I went to a Bunny's restaurant, ate a mushroom burger and fries, lingering over a couple of cups of coffee. I sat there at the counter watching the team of short-order cooks. It was a busy time, and there were four cooks working on the grille. They all had their jobs, and never said more than a couple of words to each other, yet they worked like a well-drilled rifle squad. This one was flipping the eggs, that one was doing the hashbrowns, another the burgers, the fourth the toast and buns. Yet, together they were turning out dozens of completed meals every couple of minutes.

That's what I called teamwork; never once did those bastards fuck up!

I decided to wander down the street and try out a bar I'd passed earlier. It was almost empty, just a lone black sailor sitting at the end of the bar, and two loudmouthed rednecks playing dice for drinks with the bartender.

I glanced at the black sailor, checking out his rate by habit. He wore the patch for a Petty Officer Third Class Boatswain's Mate, my kinda guy, I thought.

I sat down, ordered bourbon and 7-Up, strolled over to the jukebox, and selected *Blue Monday* and *I'm Walking to New Orleans* from the limited selection. I loved Fats Domino. I sat back down on my stool and sipped my drink. With nothing better to do, I started reading the labels of the bottles stacked on shelves behind the bar, just another lonely Saturday night.

No sooner had Fats started singing "...Blue Monday....how I hate blue Monday....got to work like a slave all day...." when one of the rednecks made a crack about nigger music. I looked out of the corner of my eye towards the colored sailor. He seemed to be ignoring them, although I knew he must have heard the remark.

The two rednecks got louder and louder with their wisecracks and racially charged insults; meanwhile, Fats kept pounded out his rhythms, filling the room with his unique style of rock and roll.

When the second Fats record ended, I walked back over and put another dime in the slot, and selected the same two songs. What was I trying to do, deliberately bait these assholes?

"What the hell do ya think ya doin'?" one of them said to me. "We have to listen to that goddamned nigger music all night?"

"Turn that shit hollerin' and squawking off!" the other chimed in, then moving closer to me said, "Hey buddy, y'all like that nigger bullshit?"

"Maybe that's his date down the end of the bar," the other one laughed. "Y'all know how these Navy guys are."

The one closest to me started laughing at his friend's joke, revealing his lack of a front tooth. The problem was they had bumped into me on the wrong day.

I carefully calculated the distance between them, then grabbed the closest guy behind the neck and slammed his face into the edge of the bar. With the same motion I covered the three paces to the other one and caught him with a right jab, just as he was starting to get off the stool. He staggered, but came back at me swinging. I took a glancing blow on the chin as I threw my head back to avoid the punch. I straightened back up and swung, hitting him square on the nose with all my strength.

Both men were now sitting on the floor with stunned looks on their faces. The one I'd slammed into the bar had blood streaming from a gash over his eye. I threw a dollar on the bar to pay for my drink, and walked out to the fading sounds of Fats Domino "…but I've got to get my rest…cause Monday is near…"

"Hey, wait up!" a voice called from behind me.

I stopped and turned; it was the black sailor from the bar.

"Damn that was fun to watch." He held out his hand, "My name's Charlie Sparks."

"Jake Rickmeyer," I replied, taking his outstretched hand. "I guess I came into town looking for that!"

"I know what you mean," he laughed. "I was feeling that way myself."

"Why didn't you bang their heads together before I did?" I asked.

He looked at me with a quizzical expression. "I guess you're not from around here. This is the South and a poor black sailor-boy would be in the hoosecow if I even looked sideways at those white crackers!"We started walking together and he continued, "Not good for my service record to have the Shore Patrol come get me from a jail cell; know what I mean?"

"I hear ya," I was warming to his easy-going manner. "You over at Little Creek?"

"Yeah, taking Boat Handling and Control classes," he replied.

"I'll probably be doing some work with ya." I grinned, "I'm an instructor at Little Creek."

We went into the next bar two blocks down the street. It was still early, and it sounded like a good idea to get shitfaced and trade a few sea-stories.

Charlie Sparks told me all about his life; he was a talker once he got going. He was from Richmond, Virginia, the youngest of twelve kids. He'd got into some trouble and the family's long-time pastor had managed to get the charges dropped on condition he went into the military.

That was five years ago he told me. Now he liked the Navy so much he'd signed on for another hitch.

Charlie talked about what was happening in the South with the Civil Rights movement, the struggles taking place in Alabama and Mississippi. The whole night was an education for me. This was 1960 and things were different in this part of the country once you got away from the base. I had no idea this shit was going on; I'd spent too much of my life worrying about boats.

Little Creek was easy duty. The instructors answered to a Lieutenant Commander through a Master Chief. Both the CO of the school and the Master Chief were at the end of their careers, so had no bones to pick with anyone.

We had a well-thought-out curriculum for classroom work, followed by practical time out driving the landing craft. I managed to find my niche doing the practical instruction, leaving the boring classroom lectures to a couple of the older chiefs.

I did receive a couple of letters from Dory, and managed finally to get one short reply off to her, but I had sent the kids postcards whenever I could. The first eighteen months at Little Creek passed without losing any men or damaging any landing craft, at least none that couldn't be repaired.

I'd kept in close touch with Charlie Sparks, and had gone up to his home in Richmond one time to spend a weekend, and then again to spend Christmas with his family.

Charlie's family was the happiest, rowdiest, largest group of people I'd ever met. They made me feel right at home, and I even became attracted to one of Charlie's sisters. She was the opposite to Charlie and the rest of the family. They were all big, but Suzie-girl was as petite and pretty as they came.

We went to a movie or two, but the glares and remarks that were directed our way hurt too much, we decided to just stay friends and never let our emotions get involved.

I would be thirty-four this coming birthday and didn't think this would ever work out for either of us. Suzie-girl understood only too well, and Charlie admitted he was about to ask me to end it. He was thankful there was no harm done and we could still all be friends.

Chapter Twenty-One

Orders came through in June 1962 for me to report aboard an LST. I had been hoping to remain at Little Creek for a while longer. I hadn't made a lot of close friendships, but I liked my job and the people I worked with.

My new billet was aboard one of the new DeSoto/Suffolk Class Landing Ships Tank, the *USS Carson County LST-1165*. Only nine of these ships had been built in the late fifties, they were basically the same design of ship that had been so essential to the landing of equipment in World War II and Korea. They were a little bigger, that's all.

The *USS Carson County* had been handed over to the Navy from the builders and commissioned in September 1958.

A new class of LST was already being added to the Navy's roster, and they were making ships like the *Carson County* obsolete before they'd been on the books long enough for the paint to dry. The new LST was the bigger, faster Newport Class.

Despite her outdated design, she was still a thing of beauty to me -- 455 feet long, with space for 650 Marines and all their equipment, plus living space for the 14 officers and 160 enlisted men making up her ship's company.

I joined the LST as acting-chief and would be responsible for the deck and the two LCVP boats she carried.

The ship was assigned to pick up a battalion of Marines at Radio Island, near Morehead City, North Carolina. This was the embarkation/ disembarkation point for Marine Corps units stationed at Camp Lejeune, North Carolina.

We were to transport the Marines to the Caribbean for exercises; the islands of the Caribbean had many excellent areas that were ideal for beach assaults. The bonus was there were also great liberty ports at the conclusion of the war games -- San Juan, Puerto Rico, Jamaica, Bahamas, and the Dominican Republic. I'd never been down there, so I was looking forward to it.

The embarkation of the Marines was routine and we shoved off from Radio Island in the late afternoon. That night I was restless and couldn't sleep. It was sometime during the mid-watch, about 0200, when I finally got up and went on deck.

I stopped by the galley and poured myself a cup of "Joe"; the strong, black, shipboard coffee reminded me of that old chief in Lawton that morning I'd enlisted. Navy coffee was something you had to acquire a taste for. It was welcome on a cold night though, I can guarantee you that.

Phosphorus streaks lit up the *Carson County's* wake as I stood by the stern rail, taking gulps of hot coffee and staring out into the churning water.

"Evening Boats!" a voice said, the young sailor on duty as the After Lookout was in the shadow of the stern anchor winch.

"Yeah, good evening," I replied to his greeting.

"You can see the lights all along the shore," he commented. "Can't be far out from the coast eh?"

"Nah, they stay fairly close in." I took another gulp of coffee, glad of his company, "You know the German submarines in World War II saw the same thing. That's how they would line up the ships; silhouette them between the sub and the bright lights along the coast."

"No kidding?" he said. "I'll be goddamned! Is that right?"

He was glad of the company too and we chewed the fat for about thirty minutes. I started to feel sleepy finally; bidding him good night I headed below to my rack.

October 18, 1962, I awoke to the buzz of scuttlebutt. The word was the Soviets had been installing missiles on Cuba and were aiming them at the United States. I got dressed and reported to my division officer's cabin.

"Scuttlebutt's right Boats," he said, busy ticking off a checklist. "The ship has been ordered to join the *USS Independence* and her attack group off the Florida coast."

"Are we on high alert?" I asked.

"Not quite yet, the ship has been ordered to maintain a high state of readiness." He was young and excitable, "We could go to General Quarters at any moment."

"Jesus Christ!" I thought aloud, "We're talking nuclear missiles here."

I called the deck watch together and told them what I knew, which wasn't much.

"What happens when we join up with the aircraft carrier?" asked a seaman apprentice.

"I don't know," I told him, "but things will change from one minute to the next if this turns serious."

"Does this mean we won't be doing the exercises?" asked another dickhead.

"Yes, Garcia," I said sarcastically, "it means there will be no-fucking-Marine-fucking-exercises!"

Things began to change rapidly just as I'd predicted. The *USS Enterprise* had left Norfolk with destroyers and cruisers as escorts, under the command of Admiral Robert Dennison. The group we were part of would join them and make up Task Force 135. The word we were getting was that President Kennedy had ordered a quarantine of Cuba, and was forbidding any Russian merchant ships from crossing the quarantine line. There were to be no more deliveries of anything to Cuban ports. Task Force 135 would position itself between Cuba and Florida and launch aircraft for cover if an invasion of Cuba became necessary.

The Task Force had only just formed up when the *Carson County* was ordered to break away from the group and proceed at top speed to Guantanamo Bay on the south east coast of Cuba.

The United States Navy had maintained a base at Guantanamo since 1903, following agreements with the Cubans after the Spanish American War of 1898. The Marines we were carrying on board would now be used to reinforce Guantanamo's defenses.

The *Carson County* arrived at "Gitmo", as the base was affectionately called, on October 22nd. Marines from the First and Second Divisions had already been arriving by air from the States. Our battalion would join them beefing up the perimeter.

From what was to be a two-week exercise in the Caribbean, and then back to their warm beds in Camp Lejeune, had now turned into the possibility of war with Russia. The young leathernecks were holding the line at Guantanamo, soaking wet from the heavy rains and wondering whether they would be the first casualties of World War III.

The LST's work had only just begun. The need now was to get the more than 2,000 dependents and civilian contractors safely off the base. Four other ships were already loading civilians, as many as they could carry. The *USS Duxbury Bay*, *USS Hyades*, *USNS Upshur*, and the sister ship of the *Carson County*, the *USS DeSoto County*.

Together they had lifted almost all of the dependent families, and were starting to shove off from the piers that had such names as Wharf Bravo and Southwest Pier Lima.

The *Carson County* picked up the last 118 dependents, which included two pregnant women, and three dozen children.

That was the day President Kennedy made his radio and television address to the Nation. All of the ship's speakers were tuned to the radio broadcast and we listened in silence to the news that the Soviets, under Nikita Khrushchev, were refusing to dismantle the missiles, as Kennedy had demanded.

I didn't know too much about nuclear warheads, but I was in the Pacific when they dropped the bombs on Hiroshima and Nagasaki and knew from those reports it would be all over if the US and the Soviets started lobbing missiles on each other.

I felt sorry for the wives and children of the servicemen left behind to defend Guantanamo; they were leaving, not knowing if they would ever see their husbands or fathers again.

The *Carson County* sailed out through the entrance to Guantanamo Bay, the women and children lining the rails waving. Then as soon as we'd made open water, we headed southeast, almost to Haiti, then north, and finally northwest through the Straits of Florida between Cuba and the Bahamas. The ship hugged the coast as soon as we reached the landmass of Florida and from there we sailed north, destination Little Creek.

A week later, on October 29th, it was announced over the intercom that the crisis was over. The Soviets had agreed to dismantle and remove all the missiles they had on Cuba. President Kennedy and Nikita Khrushchev had pulled the world back from the brink of nuclear war.

The *Carson County* still had her assignment to complete, and we had several more days sailing to Virginia.

Going from the Caribbean to the mid-Atlantic in October meant the weather was getting cold and most of the evacuees were short of warm clothing. They had been ordered to pack only one suitcase of essentials and then get on the buses taking them to the wharf area.

We did what we could, issuing whatever clothing we had in store; as well many of the crew gave what they had in the way of jackets and sweaters.

It was comical seeing ten-year-olds running around in large-size pea coats. It reminded me of those scenes of children playing dress-up.

One of the pregnant passengers started going into labor late one night, and our ship was without medical personnel. *Carson County's* pharmacist's mates had been left behind on Guantanamo. They would be needed there if the base came under attack and it became difficult to get further personnel into the base once hostilities started.

"Wake up Boats!" one of the duty watch whispered, shaking me.

"What the hell's up?" I was instantly awake, having spent years being woken at all hours.

"There's a problem with one of the women!" he said, backing away from the bunk as I jumped up.

"What are you telling me for?" I asked, confused. "Notify the Officer-of-the-Watch."

"I did," he continued. "He told me to call you. You're in charge of the deck and the civilians fall under that."

"Jesus," I mumbled, as I pulled on my clothes, "what's wrong with her?"

"I think she's having a baby!" he said, slightly embarrassed.

"What!" I exclaimed. "What the fuck do I know about having a baby?"

The area where we'd quartered the pregnant women was small and cramped. Several other ladies had things under control when I got down there. They knew what they were doing, but I thought maybe we could get her to sickbay in time, and make things more comfortable for everyone.

"Go get a stretcher and bring it down here," I ordered the young sailor who had woken me up. Then turning to the older of the women who were helping, "I think we need to get her into sickbay; we have a table in there and medical bandages and shi…" I stopped myself in time.

"Good idea," she said, very calm and businesslike. "My name's Sheila, and this little mother-to-be is Caroline."

"Jake!" I introduced myself. Then talking to the young woman, "Okay, Caroline," I said gently, "we'll get you comfortable and everything will be just fine."

As soon as the young sailor got back, I helped him lift Caroline onto the stretcher and we carried her to sickbay. Luckily it was on the same level and we didn't have to go up any ladders.

Once we got Caroline off the stretcher and onto the table, Sheila and one of the other ladies took over.

"Jake, we'll need blankets and towels, and something soft to wrap the baby in," Sheila took control.

"Okay, they have most everything in these cupboards." I started to rummage through the storage spaces and drawers, mumbling to myself.

"What's going on?" the Captain said, sticking his head in through the hatch.

"Nothing we can't handle," Sheila shot back. "Jake, Mrs. Randolph and I have things under control, thank you very much!"

"Is there anything I can do?" the Captain asked, over the clanking of the basins I was frantically throwing about.

"Yes!" Sheila ordered. "Get out of here and give us some room!"

"Umm," the Captain mumbled, a little taken aback by someone telling him what to do on his own ship.

"Very well," he said gruffly. "Keep me informed Petty Officer Rickmeyer."

"Aye, Sir," I yelped, jamming my hand in the drawer as I pulled out towels.

It was all over in twenty minutes. Caroline had her baby without complications and without any further interruptions from the Captain. It was a boy, and she said she'd call him Carson, after the ship.

Congratulations were expressed all-round, Sheila thanked me for all my help, Caroline thanked me with a kiss on the cheek, and the Captain shook my hand as if I were the father.

"Good work Rickmeyer!" he said, shaking my hand till it nearly fell off.

"I really didn't do anything, Sir," I said humbly. "The ladies did all the work; they deserve the thanks."

"I like that Rickmeyer," the Captain smiled. "Give all the credit to someone else, very commendable; yes, very commendable indeed."

The seas had been calm the entire trip back to Little Creek, thank goodness. It could have been very uncomfortable for the evacuees, in cramped quarters, with children needing constant attention, not to mention our youngest crew member, Carson!

We pulled into the Little Creek Naval Base on December 7th, and all our charges were disembarked into the waiting arms of relatives. There was some fanfare and press coverage, as the dependents evacuated from Guantanamo were considered casualties of war.

After the hype and tensions of the Cuban Crisis, everyone was relieved that it was over. The dependents from "Gitmo" were being treated like heroes.

Once free of the civilians, all hands on the *Carson County* then turned to; we had to load stores, refuel, and get back to Guantanamo. The Marines we had left there would be re-embarked and brought back to Camp Lejeune..

In the last couple of weeks we had seen a mass mobilization of US Forces; damn near World War III, frantic evacuation of US Citizens and dependents, and the birth of a healthy baby boy named after a proud ship.

Chapter Twenty-Two

After returning our Marine battalion to Radio Island, North Carolina, we sailed up to Norfolk and tied up in time for Christmas.

Charlie Sparks had invited me up to Richmond, and I had accepted the invitation without hesitation. Apart from the way his family always made me feel at home, it was his Mom's cooking and the fun of spending time with Suzie-girl.

It was damn cold this December and the train trip from Norfolk to Richmond was miserable. I grabbed a cab from the Richmond station, and got to Charlie's place in time for their Christmas prayer service before dinner.

I ate too much and drank too much, and couldn't remember Charlie taking me home to his cousin's apartment. That's where I always stayed when I visited. Charlie's house was already crowded from deck-to-overhead with visiting siblings and their own families.

The next morning I felt like shit, my breath smelt like a gorilla's armpit, and I had a blinding headache. I was still in bed when Suzie-girl and Charlie came by to pick me up.

"Don't you remember last night?" Suzie-girl said. "We all agreed we'd go listen to Dr. Martin Luther King Jr. speak at the rally downtown."

"Shit!" I groaned, "I don't remember anything about last night."

"Well, get up sleepyhead," she pulled the blankets off me. "You, too, Robert; you agreed to go too!" she yelled at her cousin.

Robert, Charlie's cousin, was in no better shape than I was. We both got out of bed reluctantly, and staggered towards the bathroom, colliding as we both tried to get through the doorway at the same time.

"I'll get the coffee on!" Charlie volunteered. "You two look like you could use some."

"And I'll go get something to eat from the corner store," Suzie-girl called, going out the front door. "Y'all be ready when I get back."

It was damp and chilly at the downtown rally where Dr. Martin Luther King Jr. was speaking. There were thousands of black people there, and a few white like me. Some of them only curious, others had some conviction for what was happening in the Civil Rights movement.

I really didn't know a lot about it, other than what I'd heard at the Sparks' home. Charlie and Suzie-girl were the most vocal. I did know that things were changing. Coming from Oklahoma I hadn't had too much exposure to Black America. In my early service years there was segregation, but it had never really registered with me.

Then President Truman ended segregation in the Armed Forces. Everybody seemed to get on well enough, at least in the commands I served in, although I can't say I'd made many Black friends aboard ship.

Now, here I was learning about the injustices and discrimination that Blacks were still suffering from, a century after their freedom from slavery.

The convincing manner in which Dr. King Jr. spoke had the crowd shouting and cheering, including me. The rally ended with pledges of solidarity and a commitment to meeting the movement's goals.

"It's so funny!" Suzie-girl exclaimed. "Here we are in Richmond, the old Confederate Capitol, and this is going to be the first place to start making changes!"

She was fired up all right, but that's what made her fun to be with. I was just glad my old buddy, Gunnery Sergeant Davis Carlson, wasn't with us. He'd been named for Confederate President Jefferson Davis.

My short couple of days with the Sparks family was over and it was time to start back to Norfolk. I always left with a warm feeling, having been treated so nicely, and somehow just a little changed in my views on the world. I had Suzie-girl to thank for that, she was persuasive all right; I had the feeling as I caught the train that she was becoming heavily involved with the movement.

Charlie, who still had his Navy career to think about and had just made Petty Officer Second, needed to keep his nose clean if he wanted to advance any further.

The thoughts on Charlie's promotion brought me back to my own Navy career. I was a selectee for Chief Petty Officer and had completed most of the tests and examinations required.

I needed to make arrangements when I got back aboard ship to take the one on leadership, tradition and professionalism; that one would be my last.

I'd read the "Bluejacket's Manual" cover to cover a half dozen times over the years, I was considered well qualified on all types of small craft, my "Charge Book" had years of activities logged, and I was qualified as far as sea time and length of service. With my combat experience in two wars, plus the commendations and evaluations I'd gotten over the years, it was a sure thing.

152

Like everyone else though, I had to appear before the Selection Board. They would review my life in the Navy; look at test scores, records, qualifications, superior officers' evaluations, and comments as to my qualities of leadership and dedication.

If the Selection Board recommended me for advancement to Chief, then the announcement and ceremony would take place in September; meantime, I had to get that last written test completed.

The Officer-of-the-Deck wished me well as I left the ship heading over to the Education Division's classrooms. I had been up since before dawn, reviewing the sections I'd been studying for months.

I had a lot of deck smarts and confidence, and had been shot at in action, but sitting there waiting for the test papers to be laid in front of me left me in a cold sweat. My mind sometimes went blank, and the questions I fouled up on, I remembered the answers to the moment I left the room.

The young officer looked like he was fresh out of college. I would only be thirty-five this year, but I felt old. There were several others there to take the same test; I didn't recognize any of them thank goodness. I was not in the mood for renewing old acquaintances at this time.

"Okay men," the young officer began, "You know the rules, but I'll give them to you once more."

I stared straight ahead, feeling my palms starting to get sweaty.

"You'll each get the test and a pencil; do not turn the test over..." he continued, droning on in a monotone.

"Come on...come on!" I was thinking, getting more nervous by the minute.

"...When I tell you to, turn over the test. Upon completion, hand the test back to me and quietly leave the room..." he kept droning.

"Do these assholes think we're schoolgirls," I thought, getting more nervous.

"...Once you've left the room you will not be allowed to return..." he kept it up.

"Oh, for Christ's sake!" I said to myself, wiping my hands on my pant legs for the fifth time.

"...Good luck!" he finally concluded.

"Thank God!" I gave a sigh of relief. My back was ramrod straight, and I was as tense as I'd ever been in my life.

The test turned out to be a breeze; I'd almost worried myself to the point of blowing it. Of course, after the fact you always second-guess every question, but I felt confident I'd done well as I handed in the completed papers.

I didn't feel like going immediately back aboard ship, and no one would miss me until late afternoon, so I hitched a ride on a workboat going over to the Newport News side of the river. On the slips was one of the new Amphibious Transport Docks (LPD) and I wanted a look at her.

The new ships were large, with a combination of functions; they had a flight deck for helicopter operations, and a well deck for landing craft. They would be able to carry Landing Craft Utility (LCU) or the LCMs I'd been instructing on at Little Creek. The LPDs would also carry the experimental Landing Craft Air Cushion (LCAC), now being tried out off Atlantic beaches.

Nine hundred fully equipped Marines, as well as six transport helicopters (CH-46 or CH-53), would be carried on board to give them mobility.

Still under construction, I couldn't go aboard, but I was able to get a real good look at her from a distance. The crew, I learned from looking at the specifications, would include 30 officers, 20 chief petty officers and around 350 enlisted men.

Helicopters were becoming a more important part of Marine amphibious assaults, but I knew boats would always be part of the Navy/Marine team. A boatswain's mate just had to keep up with advances in new technology. I was wondering about these new air cushion craft, maybe I'd get to take a crack at them.

Feeling relaxed now, after the morning's test ordeal, I had one last look at the LPD's stern gates. They were lowered, revealing the vast, empty cavern of a well deck.

The workboat was making her return run to the Norfolk side, so I jumped aboard. The helmsman was talkative; he told me these new ships would be joining the fleet within eighteen months. He'd also seen them testing the air-cushioned craft up the river, and claimed they were the coming thing.

I was back aboard the *Carson County* by chow time, and heard there'd been a phone call for me from Charlie.

I called Charlie back as soon as I'd eaten and gotten squared away. He said he'd received orders to join a destroyer about to deploy to the Seventh Fleet. He'd be heading for San Diego in a couple of days.

"I'd hoped y'all could get up before I leave," Charlie said. "The movement's got another big rally downtown planned."

"Yeah, I hate to miss that," I lied. I was beginning to realize these Civil Rights demonstrations were getting out of hand. I'd heard there had been trouble on buses and in restaurants all over the South.

"I'm sure Suzie-girl will be in the thick of it!" I said. "How about you? Happy to get a destroyer headed for the Pacific?"

"Yeah, I guess so," Charlie said, with hesitation. "Sure hate to miss all the fun, though."

"Well, you need to get back to doing what a boatswain's mate is supposed to be doing," I lectured good-naturedly, happy that Charlie was getting away. I had a feeling in my bones that these Civil Rights protests were not going to ease up until something big had happened.

"Okay, I got to go," I said. "You take it easy and say hi to everybody up there in Richmond."

"You betcha Jake," Charlie laughed. "I'll see y'all when we catch up with each other."

"Okay, buddy," I responded. "Take care of yourself!

Through the course of the next six months we spent our time embarking and disembarking Marines from Radio Island, sailing to the Caribbean for drills and exercises. Each time the ship would sail close enough to Cuba to count the coconuts on the trees, but not close enough to cause an incident. It was just Uncle Sam showing the commies he was still King of the Caribbean.

I wondered what old Columbus would have thought in 1504 when he discovered Cuba; that the paradise he'd found would four centuries later be the focus of so much world attention, perhaps the flash point that could have launched the world into a war; a war that would have destroyed us all.

The Caribbean was ideal in many ways. Its weather, apart from occasional hurricanes, was balmy all year-round; some islands were mountainous with lush green vegetation; others just a few feet above sea level, created from the remains of ancient coral reefs.

Not much is known about the original inhabitants. Apparently there was a tribe of Indians called the Caribs, from which the Caribbean takes its name, but by the time Columbus' gold hunting crews, land hungry settlers, and other riff-raff had finished with them, the tribe was extinct. Now nobody even knows, or cares, about those long-gone people who had called these islands home for a thousand years.

After the last trip to the Caribbean, we had gone into dry-dock for routine maintenance. There one morning my past and future crossed over like flotsam caught in a crosscurrent. I had picked up my mail from the base post office, and the first letter I opened was from the Selection Board. I had been successful and was to advance to Chief Petty Officer.

After I'd taken a deep breath in relief, I glanced down the other names on the list.

"No!" I shouted out loud. On the second page under the Ds, the name came off the page and hit me in the face like a ton of bricks... Dicks, Tyler J. advanced to Chief Gunner's Mate (E-7) from Gunner's Mate PO1 (E-6).

"Tyler Dicks!" I almost spat, "Fucking Rabbit, how in the hell did he ever make it?"

I was still fuming when I opened the second letter. It was from Lionel and Cecelia in Hodskins. They were wondering if I had any objections to them building an addition onto the old house.

The kids were getting big and they needed more room. Lionel also said he was doing all right now and working most of the time. They mentioned the kids were doing great; they'd had two more since I last saw them.

"Damn Lionel!" I thought. "Why do some people never seem to get a break!" I imagined the addition would probably be one room, with most of the work being done by Lionel himself.

I was happy to see that Little Jake was now working as an electrician's helper, and was planning on taking the electrical certification exams.

I folded the two letters and put them back in their envelopes as I walked slowly back to the *Carson County*.

I hadn't thought about the old place for years; there was not a snowball's chance in hell that I would ever go back there to live. I had about 8,000 dollars in the bank, and my needs were few. Shit! Why don't I just sign over the place to them? They've taken care of things for almost ten years, why not? I climbed back aboard, got my important addresses and other notes from my locker, and went ashore to the little office we were using on the dockside.

I answered Lionel and Cecelia's letter and told them I was notifying the lawyer in Hodskins, and planning to sign over the property deeds to them. Next I wrote a letter to the bank manager, where the deeds were still held in the vault, and advised him of my plans. The mortgage had been paid off years ago, but the bank had kept the final mortgage papers and deed in safekeeping for me.

I told them of my intentions, and for them to draw up whatever papers were necessary and send them to me for my signature. That done, I walked back to the post office and mailed the two letters; with a sense of well-being I went back aboard.

The final bit of the flotsam in the cross current came when I was notified I was being transferred to the Recruit Training Center (RTC) in Great Lakes, Illinois.

What a day! First the good news about the promotion, then the upset about Rabbit making it on the same promotion's list, then the great feeling I had after making the decision to give the old place to Lionel and Cecelia; now the unexpected and unwelcome news of the transfer.

"Any chance of getting out of this?" I asked the XO, when he'd stopped to ask about the condition of the anchor chain I was working on. I'd had the chain run out and had gone over every link, checking for corrosion or damage of any kind.

"You're now a chief petty officer," he told me, looking at the chain. "They need men with experience and maturity to show these young recruits what the Navy's all about."

"Can't they get them from somewhere else?" I continued pleading my case, "I'm a blue water sailor. What am I going to do wiping the asses of a bunch of Boots?"

"I'm sorry Chief, I know the Captain would rather have you stay on the *Carson County*," he said, looking me straight in the eye, "but we didn't make the decision in this case." Then pointing his clipboard at the line of chain he asked, "Now what's your report on the anchor chain going to look like?"

I looked smart in my new chief's uniform as I stood on the station platform, my four bullion service stripes sewn on the lower left sleeve, the bullion Chief Boatswain's Mate patch on the upper arm, my chest full of colorful ribbons. The brimmed cap still felt awkward and uncomfortable; I'd worn the "Dixie cup" white hat for so long.

The train leaving for Chicago was on time and I'd accepted the fact that I was going to be a Boot-Pusher.

Everyone claims they remember where they were, when they heard the news that JFK had been shot; in my case it was etched in my memory for all time. I'd heard some people in the seat near me talking about the shooting. Becoming concerned, I asked the conductor. He gave me what information he had from radio reports, and by the time we had reached New York the papers were already announcing: **"President Kennedy Assassinated in Dallas!"**

After reading the sketchy details of the assassination in Dallas, I turned to the second page and saw pictures of a Civil Rights demonstration in Richmond. It had gotten out of hand and the rally had turned into a riot. There in the picture, struggling with police as they dragged her to a waiting paddy wagon, was Suzie-girl! That petite, little lady had a look of pure hatred on her face as the two beefy policemen hauled her off in handcuffs.

I was sickened by the fact that Suzie-girl was headed for jail. At the same time I was glad Charlie had been deployed. He would certainly have been there in the thick of it. An arrest for civil disturbance in that situation would probably have resulted in his discharge from the Navy.

I felt Charlie had too much going for him as a Boatswain's Mate, and hoped he'd stay out of all the racial conflicts taking place right then, even though I thought I understood his passion for Civil Rights.

Chapter Twenty-Three

Traveling to the new posting at Great Lakes couldn't have been more depressing. What was I going to do marching a bunch of recruits around? How the fuck could the Navy do this to me!

Chicago's train station was as cold and miserable as I felt. I threw my bags down on the platform and looked around at the milling crowds. Where were all these people going? Where were they all coming from?

The P.A system announced that a Chief Petty Officer Rickmeyer had a party waiting at the main lobby information booth. That would be my pickup.

I followed the signs through to the main lobby and spotted the lanky sailor standing there. He was eyeing all the tail as it paraded past.

He damn near shit his pants when I tapped him on the shoulder from behind. Turning, he saw all that bullion on my uniform and almost snapped to attention and saluted, catching himself just in time.

"G…Good afternoon Chief," his words scratchy in his dry throat. "Let me take those bags for you."

"Sure," I replied, letting him do his job.

"We've got an hour's drive ahead of us," he said, hoisting my bags. "Pretty scenery, though, once we get out of the city."

"How'd you get stuck with this driver job?" I asked, trying to make conversation.

"I'm waiting for a billet at the new electronics school in San Diego," he said. "I was division leader and finished my boot training two months ago. I got hung up waiting for my evaluation to get to the right office. They're trying to get people who are good at math assigned to the school."

"Electronics school," I nodded. "Yeah, everything's going electronic. Gunnery, missiles, navigation, old sailors like me are only good for boot-pushing I guess."

What the fuck was wrong with me? I had never felt this sorry for myself in my whole life. I had to get out of this shitty detail of recruit school boot-pusher. My mind was spinning, trying to make out a mental list of who owed me a favor.

The Recruit Training Center at Great Lakes, Illinois, is a collection of parade grounds, barracks rooms, classrooms, medical facilities and administration buildings. There are fourteen barracks buildings, each housing twelve divisions, with each division having about eighty-eight recruits.

159

Mathematics was never my strong point, but that's over fourteen thousand snot-nosed, home-sick, hormone-raging dickheads! Christ!

Before I started pushing my first division though, I had to complete an intense eight-week course myself. Once the course was completed, I would get to wear a red rope around my left shoulder, which distinguished me as a Recruit Division Commander.

The training course for me was the longest eight-weeks I'd ever spent. Christmas and New Year's came and went with the customary turkey dinner and a bunch of old farts swapping sea stories in the Chief's mess hall.

The only thing I was looking forward to was the three weeks leave at the end of it; then I'd have to report back on board to start work with my first division of recruits.

I had already decided I was going out to Frisco and visit Dory. The kids had sent me Christmas cards, but they'd just made me feel lonelier.

I couldn't have picked a worse time to travel. February in Chicago was brutal; the wind howling in off the Great Lakes felt like it was coming directly from the North Pole. When I got to San Francisco it was even chillier. I had flown commercial with TWA. It was a lot faster then getting around by train or bus, and I hadn't felt like waiting around for a spare seat on a military aircraft.

Dory and Dale were at the airport to meet me, and for the first time in months I started to feel like life wasn't too bad after all.

"Uncle Jake," squealed Dale, as she gave me a big hug.

I returned her hug; almost cracking her bones I was so happy to see them. She had shot up and now stood a half-head taller then Dory.

"I keep forgetting you're fourteen now," I said, amazed at the changes taking place in this little girl. "I keep seeing a little ball of energy chasing me around on the living-room floor."

"Wait till you see Roy!" smiled Dory, throwing her arms around me and giving me a kiss on the cheek.

"This is just great!" I almost cried. "You guys don't know how good it is to see ya."

"John's making dinner for us," Dory laughed. "He's been taking culinary courses and can't wait to show his skills off." Then added, as we got in the car, "Oh, there'll be another guest tonight, someone you knew a long time ago."

"God! Now I've got to spend the rest of the afternoon wondering who it is," I said good-naturedly. "You never change do you Dory?"

The drive from the airport to the car-ferry and across the Bay to Sausalito brought memories flooding back to me. They came faster then I could assemble them in any order, not the least was the image of Bug, laughing as he drove those boats all over the base. I always thought of him whenever I spent time with Dory. I never brought Bug up with her any more. I knew she was happy with John; she could keep Bug's memory alive in her own way.

"If you hadn't joined the Navy…" Dale's voice brought me back from my own thoughts.

"…You might have been in there," she continued, pointing over at Alcatraz Island.

"Oh, Dale," Dory scolded.

"I just finished reading all about a big escape attempt in 1946…seven convicts held hostages for three days…and two of the convicts were from Oklahoma…that's where you're from aren't you Uncle Jake? Their names were Clarence Carnes and Sam Shockley…did you know them? Clarence Carnes was from McAlester, Oklahoma…is that near where you lived?"

"That's right honey, I guess that's where I would have been headed if I hadn't joined up," I said, putting my arm around Dale's shoulder and giving her a squeeze. She had been talking a mile a minute all the way across. It was good to be back!

John and Roy were waiting for us on the front porch. John took my hand and shook it firmly, while Roy just stood there looking at the ground and shuffling his feet. He was almost as tall as I was, but still as skinny as a split-rail fence.

"I'd best get back in the kitchen," John grinned. "I've got prime-rib for tonight, with a horseradish sauce that I developed myself." Slapping me on the back he added, "Good to see you Jake."

"I'll go fix us a drink," Dory called after him. "Dale, will you see if the room is made up for Jake okay?"

"Sure Mom," Dale went skipping into the house.

"Well, how are you?" I said to Roy, who was still standing on the porch looking at the ground.

"I'm, I'm…fine…Uncle Jake." Roy eventually got it out, "How have you been?" he said, finally looking up at me.

"Oh, you know Roy," I tried to sound salty, "the Navy always has a surprise or two up its sleeve."

"I was hoping to ask you about the Navy," Roy said, hesitantly. "I think I want to join up."

"Wow!" I replied with surprise, "You still got to finish high school, but you could do worse I guess."

"That's what I've been thinking," he said, picking up my bags and going inside the house.

I came out of the bathroom after washing up, looking forward to that drink Dory had waiting.

There was still one more surprise in a day full of surprises; sitting on the sofa in the living room was Barbara-Jean.

"Jake," she smiled broadly, "you haven't changed a bit."

"B..b..b..arb!" I felt like a stupid kid stumbling over my tongue. "How have you been?"

"Good Jake, good," she nodded.

I sat down in the chair opposite and looked at her; she did look good. Her hair was pulled straight back in a tight bun, and she was wearing very little makeup.

"Glad to see you two have already met," Dory said, as she bounced into the room with the drinks. "The chef told me we only have time for one before dinner is served."

We all laughed; it was just like old times.

John's prime-rib was delicious. I didn't think his horseradish sauce was all that great, but I praised the meal to the high heavens anyway. It was good to watch his face light up when I rubbed my stomach, and complained I'd eaten enough to sink a battleship.

Barb hadn't said much during the meal, but she laughed at all my stories and seemed really relaxed. That had surprised me. She seemed so mature and in control of herself; what a difference from the last time I saw her fifteen years ago.

"Why don't you two sit in the living room and have another drink," Dory offered. "John and I will do the dishes and Dale and Roy have their homework to get done."

"Arrr Mom," they both complained, but got up dutifully and went to their rooms.

When we were alone, I asked Barb what she'd been doing all these years. It was as if she had been waiting for me to ask her that question all evening. It came like a flood in a non-stop monotone, all about her failed relationships, the problems with the booze and the drugs, the failed attempts at rehabilitation. And finally about her success, she'd been straight for the last six years.

162

"I really feel good about myself now Jake," she concluded, wringing her hands together and looking at me for a reaction.

"Sounds like you had it rough." I didn't know the right thing to say. "You do look pretty tonight," I added, trying to sound upbeat.

"Thanks Jake," she smiled, looking a little uncomfortable, "I was hoping you'd say that."

John and Dory joined us for another round of drinks, and then Barb said she'd better be getting home. She had a job as a bank teller over in Oakland and needed to get her beauty rest, she had joked.

I walked Barb to her car, feeling like she wanted me to put my arms around her, but something held me back. I had the urge to pull her to me and kiss her passionately, but the memories from the past still haunted me. We said goodnight shaking hands, both of us feeling awkward.

I watched her drive away; wondering what demons still tormented her. I hoped she'd found peace, I felt no malice towards her. That time had long passed. The times when I'd cursed the day I'd ever met her were over!

Barb and I went out to dinner one night and to a movie on another occasion, both times with Dory and John as company. It was funny how we just seemed to all get along.

I was starting to look at her in a way I wasn't sure about. I did know she was capable of stirring those hot desires in me still, now even more so.

I wasn't sure of my feelings; I thought we'd better stand back from it for a while, give both of us a chance to think. I couldn't stand the thought of her relapsing into those manic depressive bouts from the past. I didn't think I could handle that.

"You know, Barb asked me about you every time I'd bump into her," Dory said one night after we'd come home from a show. "Every time I got a letter from you, I'd telephone and give her all the details."

"Why didn't you tell me you'd been in touch with her all these years?" I asked, rolling my drink around in my hands.

"She was out of touch during the worst of her times," Dory continued. "I went to see her once in the rehab center, it was awful Jake. And, of course I knew about the marriage with that jerk, and all the other affairs."

"Do you think she's over all this mess?" I asked. The question had been on my mind all night.

"Jake, you know I can't answer that," Dory said kindly. "I only know she has been sober and clean for almost seven years. And I know she's never stopped loving you Jake."

With the emotional confusion of the last couple of weeks still bothering me, I wasn't in the mood to discuss Barb and me any more that night. In an effort to change the subject, I brought up Roy's idea about joining the Navy.

"I think it might be good for him," John said, the first time in fifteen minutes he'd had a chance to get into the conversation.

"Well, I don't," Dory snapped back. "I don't want him hurt. You've heard about this trouble in Southeast Asia?"

"President Johnson is not going to get involved beyond supporting the Government down there," John replied.

"Jake, you must know what's going on?" Dory turned to me.

"All I know is that the US has been sending advisers," I said, trying to calm what looked like a heated discussion they'd had before.

"Well, I heard some of those advisers had been killed." Dory was getting upset, "And I just heard they were sending more ships down there."

"It doesn't mean anything," John said. "President Johnson isn't stupid enough to get us into some silly war. Where the hell is this place anyway?"

"Vietnam!" Dory said. "I looked it up. They've been fighting each other for years, now some group wants to overthrow the Government."

"I remember sailing down the coast of Vietnam coming back from Korea," I interjected, trying to stop a potential flare up between John and Dory. "The locals were fighting the French at that time; then after they got the French out they split the country in two."

"And now there's a group called the Viet Cong trying to overthrow the Government President Johnson is supporting," Dory was still upset. "We have no business there; let them fight it out amongst themselves."

"Look Dory," I said, moving closer to her and placing my arm around her shoulder, "Roy is only fifteen. He has three more years before he's eligible for the draft."

"That's right honey," John added, realizing Dory was not going to calm down. "Hell, in three years that storm-in-a-teacup will be all over!"

"Right!" I said, "Then Roy can join the Navy before the Army can draft him. He'll probably spend a couple of years sailing around the Mediterranean chasing pretty girls and getting a suntan."

"If he does go in," Dory laid her head on my shoulder, "promise me Jake, you won't let anything happen to him!"

I looked at John, then down at Dory, who was starting to sob quietly. "I promise to do whatever I can," I said, knowing if Roy joined he would go wherever they sent him.

"I couldn't live if anything happened to him," she sobbed. "I couldn't take what happened to Desmond all over again."

164

That was the first time I'd heard her talk about Bug in front of John in a long time. Roy's talk of joining the Navy must be bringing back all those half-forgotten memories.

I didn't know much about this Vietnamese buildup, but I didn't think Dory would have much to worry about. Better for Roy to join the service of his choice, than to get drafted into the Army and sent God knows where.

My visit was over, time again to say goodbye to Dory and family. The kids were doing well in school, John's accounting business was prosperous, even old Doris was still hanging in there; she'd now outlived one husband and one live-in boyfriend.

Dory stopped by the bank in Oakland, picked up Barb, and then the three of us had lunch together. This was our last chance before Dory drove me to the airport.

I couldn't get over the change in Barb, she seemed so bright; the stirring in my loins when she hugged me goodbye made me feel uncomfortable, yet excited at the same time.

The flight back to Chicago was uneventful, the weather had improved over the last couple of weeks, and I relaxed reading the newspaper. I noticed the news item on the Tribune's second page as I skimmed through the stories, "Two aircraft carriers sent to patrol the coast off Vietnam…"

Chapter Twenty-Four

The barracks at the Recruit Training Center were all named after ships; the *USS* this and *USS* that; all designed to give Boots the feeling they were already part of a ship's company. My first division of trainees was housed in *USS Carr*; and I would be working the division with two other chiefs. The first couple of days were hell! Some of these kids didn't know their left from their right, as the old Army drill instructors used to say.

After a few weeks, though, I started to warm to some of them, picking out the ones with potential and the ones who would be working in the trash compactor room for the rest of their Navy careers.

The recruits in the division started to come to me for all kinds of advice. It was part of the Recruit Division Commander's job to help develop these raw shitfaces into well-disciplined, mentally and physically fit young men, with the basic training needed to become useful sailors and join the fleet.

I laughed myself sick when three of them came to me the night before they were to get out on their first liberty.

"Chief Rickmeyer," one of them said, "what do you think about us getting tattoos?"

"Why would you want to get tattooed?" I asked, building up to the punchline.

"Because most of the guys are getting them," chirped up the short one.

"Well, I think it's a great idea," I smiled. Then added with a growl, "Get a tattoo of a football on your asses…then when you get back, I'll kick it all over the parade ground!"

They just stood with their mouths open.

"Now get the fuck outta here!" I ordered.

As soon as they'd gotten out of the office, falling all over themselves, and the door closed, I curled over laughing. Damn! I had wanted to do that so bad, ever since I heard a chief use the same line on another bunch of shitfaces.

My attitude toward my assignment at the Training Center hadn't changed, but I did feel proud when the basic training had been completed for my first group of recruits.

The division was ready for the Pass-In-Review parade and the graduation ceremonies. It was almost as if they were all my own kids, and they had worked their tails off to make me proud of them.

From the home-sick young men that had stood, shaking in their steel-studded boots that first day, until this last day; when they stood, a well-disciplined group of tall, straight, smartly uniformed sailors, with a look that made me feel confident I'd done a good job. They all looked impressive as they marched past in review.

I also had concerns for them. On August 4th North Vietnamese gunboats had attacked the *USS Maddox* in the Gulf of Tonkin. President Johnson had then ordered retaliatory strikes against North Vietnam, where men and planes had been lost in action.

Three days later, Congress passed the Gulf of Tonkin Resolution, giving President Johnson the authority for the build-up of US Forces in the area.

My next division of recruits was no more capable than the last group during their first few weeks, the same assortment as before; tall, short, thin, muscular, blond, dark, black and white. I felt the same frustration and a feeling of being trapped on this land-locked "Ship", with its endless musters, sick calls, mindless repetition of drills and lectures.

The word was passed to me early one afternoon to report to the CO. I quickly ran a mental checklist of what I may have done to piss the Old Man off, but could think of nothing.

My first division of Boots had graduated third overall out of the divisions completing boot camp that summer. I was more curious than apprehensive when I reported to his office.

"Chief Boatswain's Mate Rickmeyer!" the yeoman announced, as he knocked and opened the CO's door.

"Chief," Captain Bannack looked up, "Come in."

"Good afternoon, Sir," I said, snapping to attention.

"At ease Chief," the Captain smiled. "Looks like we'll be losing you. Orders just came in reassigning you to Camp Pendleton, California."

"Effective when, Captain?" I could hardly control my excitement. "I've just started a new division of trainees, Sir."

"As soon as you can hand over to your relief," Captain Bannack said. "I don't like to lose good Division Commanders, and you looked like you were going to do a lot for these young recruits."

"I'm glad I could set an example for them, Sir," I said, wanting to get the best evaluation from the Old Man I could before I left, but not pushing it too far in case he tried to get my orders changed.

"You advanced from a Seaman Recruit with a grade of E-1," he began, "to a Chief Petty Officer with the grade of E-7. Your record is impeccable, and the scuttlebutt is the young recruits look at you as someone who came into the Navy through the hawsepipe. You know what a compliment that is for a career sailor?"

"I do, Sir," I raised my eyebrows in surprise. That was something you didn't hear very often any more. It meant you'd been in the Navy for a long time and were as salty as a sailor could get. "That is a compliment, Sir."

"You've done a fine job Chief," he said, looking me straight in the eye. "I also know you weren't exactly happy here."

"Well…" I said, trying to be honest with him, "I have always felt my job was at sea, Sir."

"You're going to get more sea time than you can handle Chief," the Old Man said with a twinkle in his eye. "You're going to join an instruction group in beach assault for the Marines at Camp Pendleton. The Marines are gearing are up for Vietnam. You may be sent over."

"On the boats is where I belong Captain," I said, wanting this over with.

"That will be all then Chief," he said, shaking my hand, "Good Luck!"

I snapped to attention and turned to leave, then stopped as Captain Bannack added, "Be careful what you wish for…you just might get it!"

I couldn't have been happier. At chow that evening I didn't know whether some of the other instructors were envious or whether they were feeling sorry for me; either way I got stared at all during the meal.

The US was getting more and more involved in Vietnam. Every day you heard stories of attacks by Viet Cong guerrillas. The constant skirmishes were making news and being written about in every newspaper.

Camp Pendleton eh? I wondered if Davis Carlson was still there. Maybe I'd get a chance to spend more time with Barb; San Francisco was not too far from Pendleton. I couldn't sleep that night, anxious to get these last few days over with and be on my way.

Chicago never looked so good as when I said goodbye to it. The summer with its humidity was just as miserable as the cold winter winds.

I could smell the Pacific 20,000 feet up, as the Navy transport began its approach, descending to the air station on Coronado. I'd be stationed there for a while at the Naval Amphibious School; specifically, the Landing Craft Control School.

The plan was to get a team together and spend time at Pendleton, using the beaches off the base to give us lots of area to play war games.

My excitement at getting my feet wet again was complete when Charlie Sparks, now wearing a Petty Officer First rate, met me at the terminal.

"Welcome to Coronado!" Charlie grinned, taking my hand in both of his and shaking it for a full minute. "Damn it's good to see you!"

"Jesus Sparks!" I laughed, grabbing Charlie by the shoulders, "What the hell are you doing here?"

"I'm on the same detail," he laughed. "I'll be driving the LCM-6's along with you."

"Let me report in and get squared away," I whooped, "then we'll get caught up over a drink."

"I'm ready for that!" Charlie laughed, hoisting my bags, "Let me help you with your gear."

Chapter Twenty-Five

The beach landing assault team we put together consisted of three LCM-6s and three LCM-8's. The LCM-6s were 56 feet long and could handle 68,000 lbs. of cargo or 80 troops. The LCM-8 was about 20 feet longer, faster, and could carry an M60 tank or 200 troops.

With the big LCM-8 being about 3 knots faster than the LCM-6, it required a well-rehearsed and disciplined effort to get the team working together.

Each boat had a four-man crew, with a Boatswain's Mate First in charge, a Motorman PO and a fireman, as well as a seaman to handle the lines and fenders.

Next up the chain were three chiefs, of which I was one. We had charge of two boats apiece. We, in turn, answered to a lieutenant who was the group's commander. It was a well-chosen team; even the seamen and firemen had several years sea time and knew their jobs.

The group spent several weeks at the Landing Craft School in Coronado before we left on our first trip up to the boat basin at Pendleton. I was anxious to check whether Davis was anywhere around, or whether anyone knew where he was. Gunnery Sergeants in the Marine Corps were easy to track down.

The landing craft were very sea-worthy, the trip up the coast was smooth, and we made excellent time. Our CO, Lieutenant Ortega, was a young, ambitious officer who knew his stuff. Everybody had the kind of respect for him that made for good enlisted-officer relations.

Lieutenant Ortega, in turn, showed respect for everyone under his command, listening to suggestions for any improvements in the operation from even the lowliest swabbie in the group.

After securing the boats in the basin at Pendleton and getting the crews squared away in their billets, I strolled over to the NCO's canteen. I ordered a beer and asked the couple of sergeants sitting around a table if any of them knew Gunny Carlson.

"Yeah, I know that son-of-a-bitch," one of them said. "He's due back from a fleet deployment in February."

"That's great," I said, "we served together in the Mediterranean. I'm looking forward to hitching up with him again."

I took my beer over to an empty table and started to thumb through a copy of the Navy News. Funny how the older you got, the faster you turned to the obituaries. I wasn't that old, but sometimes it felt like I'd been in the Navy fifty years, instead of the twenty I'd have the next anniversary.

Two names I recognized, both brought back a mixed bag of memories. Captain Abe Poser retired, my skipper from the *USS Roe*, passed away quietly at his home in Florida.

And another name I could never forget, Chief Master-at-Arms "Dutch" Van der Broeke retired; the obituary stated he'd died from a self-inflicted gunshot wound at his home in Baltimore, Maryland.

No other details were given and it left me wondering what men like Van de Broeke and old "Black Bart" Hoffman must feel when they are retired out. The Navy was the only thing they knew, and when it was time to go, they went kicking and screaming.

Many finished up drinking themselves to death, or doing what "Dutch" Van de Broeke had done. Veteran Administration hospitals around the country were another dumping ground. God! I hoped I didn't finish up like that when my time came.

I had used some of my spare time in Great Lakes to qualify for my expert rifle and pistol qualifications. The old flat-sided M1911A1 was my favorite handgun. The M1911 had been the standard sidearm of the military since the troubles in the Philippines in the early 1900's. It was modified slightly in the 1920's and designated the M1911A1.

The story on its acceptance by the military was that the Army needed something that could stop a charging Moro fanatic dead in his tracks. The Moro tribesmen would get hopped up on drugs and charge the American soldiers in their trenches.

There were countless stories of Moros being shot a half dozen times, and yet they would still keep on coming, swinging their murderous machetes. The damage they did in the closely-packed trenches was horrendous.

The 45-caliber slugs that the M1911 fired were not only heavy enough to stop the charging target, they actually knocked the man back on his ass.

All branches of the military during World War I, World War II, and Korea had used the M1911 and the M1911A1; the hard-hitting sidearm was still in service going into Vietnam.

Beach assaults usually began from ships offshore, with Marines going over the side and climbing down nets into the waiting boats below. Now things were changing; with the new Amphibious Assault Ships men and equipment were being pre-loaded, the landing craft then floated from the well deck through the lowered stern gates. This was safer, quicker, and much more efficient.

The weather off the California coast was beginning to get unpleasant by October. The Navy and Marines, however, had to be ready to go in all conditions. So you just grinned and bore it, and made sure there was lots of hot "Joe" on hand.

We must have picked up and dropped off thousands of Marines without serious mishap during our daily exercises. Things couldn't have gone better.

Of course, with the real thing there was always the element of confusion that appeared when the stress of noise, raw nerves, and fear affected men.

Barb was coming down to San Clemente to attend a seminar the bank was conducting. San Clemente was just outside the north gate of Camp Pendleton, so we'd arranged to have dinner together. Fate stepped in and the weekend she'd be in San Clemente was the week after my twentieth anniversary in the Navy; another reason to celebrate.

I met Barb in the lobby of the hotel and we went arm-in-arm into the dining room. She'd already arranged with the Maitre 'D' a nice table by the window.

"I remember when we all went out together on your fourth anniversary," Barb laughed. "Remember, you couldn't wait for me sew on your first service stripe?"

"Yeah, I do remember," I smiled, thinking back. "I had also just made Boatswain's Mate Third."

"And I had to sew that stupid patch on too," she was enjoying this as much as I was.

"Life was pretty good then." I kept thinking about the details of that night. "Damn! Dory and Bug used to be fun to go out with!"

I was just about to order a bottle of wine when I remembered Barb's drinking problem. She saw my hesitation as the wine waiter stood by to take my order.

"Go ahead," she said touching my hand, "I won't have any, but you go ahead and celebrate."

"Okay, just a half-bottle." I ordered the wine, and then sat back taking in the beauty that Barb seemed to project.

"I see you wasted no time getting your fifth service stripe sewn on," she said, noticing the five stripes on my uniform.

"I guess it's still the little boy in me," I replied. "Just want to show off and be the center of attention."

We both laughed and ordered the fillet mignons for dinner.

After coffee sitting in the hotel lounge, we reminisced on times past; somehow we both knew that the moment for a decision had come. It would be now or never if we wanted to renew our relationship.

I just couldn't make the first move. Barb sensed the lack of confidence in me and reached across for my hand.

"I want you to come up for a while," she said throatily.

"Okay," I managed to say through my suddenly dry throat.

Being in each other's arms felt so right, we lay together for a long time just feeling the touch of our skins.

Then as we kissed and caressed each other it became urgent. We couldn't wait any longer. Barb rolled over and sat atop me and we moved in frantic, breathless motions, grinding and moaning. It was as if we'd spent the last years of our lives yearning for the chance to do this one more time. My face twisted in passion as I reached my climax, Barb had already called out my name several times, lost in her own ecstasy.

We lay together till almost dawn, talking quietly. I was still not sure about all this, I'd confessed. Barb said she understood and there was no point in rushing into anything. "Let's just play it by ear," she had said.

I left the hotel feeling like I was walking on air. The night doorman gave me a knowing wink as he hailed me a cab. I felt a sudden flash of anger at his smart-ass gesture and almost cold-cocked him then and there.

"Ahhh, what the hell!" I thought. "I won't let anything ruin this day!"

Christmas rolled around again and I'd made arrangements to go visit Dory. Now, of course, Barb was also in my plans. I would be able to spend time with her, though neither of us thought it a good idea for me to stay at her place yet; better to have a long, old-fashioned courtship.

I'd talked Charlie Sparks into going up with me, and Barb had arranged for one of her friends from work to date Charlie. That way we could all go out together and he wouldn't feel in the way.

With Vietnam starting to heat up, there was a non-stop procession of military aircraft flying up and down the coast. Charlie and I had no trouble getting from Camp Pendleton to Alameda. We had scored a couple of seats on a big Marine cargo plane.

"There's no doubt we'll be heading down to 'Nam soon enough," Charlie said over the noise of the engines.

"Fucking guerillas just attacked some air base called Bien Hoa," I said. "Several Americans killed and a bunch of aircraft blown up."

"You don't think we're training all these Marines for nothing do you?" Charlie continued. "I'm telling you this is going to get messy."

San Francisco was all lit up for the Christmas season. We hadn't bothered Dory about picking us up; Charlie and I just took a cab to Barb's place in Oakland. From there we planned to drive with her over to Sausalito.

"Hi'ya sailors!" Barb said, with mock sauciness as she opened the door, "Come on in boys."

"Barb," I began, after I'd given her a hurried hug, "This is my friend Charlie Sparks."

"Pleased to meet you, Charlie," Barb took Charlie's hand and led him into the living room, "And this is my friend Akima."

Akima was a stunning young black woman. I could already feel the vibrations from across the room as Charlie's mouth dropped open.

"How do you do?" Akima said, holding out her hand delicately.

"Fine...and you?" Charlie was captivated. That big lug had met his match this time.

"Let's get organized and drive over to Dory's," Barb said cheerfully. "John has been working on this Christmas Eve dinner for three days."

We arrived at Dory's with a full load of gifts and goodies. Roy and Dale were more excited about the arrival of their Uncle Jake, and his giant black friend, than they were with the Christmas activity of opening presents.

Dory and John were as pleasant as always, and we all enjoyed a Christmas dinner that would have made the gods of Mount Olympus envious.

"What's the latest on the Navy?" I asked Roy, pushing the empty plate away after my second serving of dessert.

"I still want to go in Uncle Jake," he replied, still fascinated with Charlie sitting at the end of the table.

Charlie filled out his uniform nicely. He was wide-shouldered, big chested, and had several rows of ribbons. Petty Officer Sparks looked so damn good he should have been on recruiting posters.

"I can't talk him out of it," Dory started clearing off the table.

"He's still two years away from his eighteenth birthday," John said, offering Charlie another helping of his special ice-cream dessert.

"No thank you John," Charlie said. "I like to burst here!"

"The meal was wonderful," said Akima, getting up to help Dory clear away.

"Oh, you go and sit down in the living room," said Dory, strutting around like a mother hen. "The kids and I can take care of this."

"Yes," added John, getting up, "I'll put on some coffee."

John was beaming with pride at the compliments he'd received from everybody about the meal; even Roy had commented on the dinner. Dale was always the little lady and kissed John on the cheek, telling him it was the best Christmas Eve dinner she'd ever had.

"When do you have to go?" Dory called from the kitchen.

"We just got three days," I replied, "then Charlie and I have to hightail it back!"

"Oh, that's a shame," she answered over the sound of running water.

"Sorry I didn't tell you how short our visit was going to be," I said, turning back to Barb.

"That's the Navy for you," Barb said. "Never get mixed up with a sailor." She looked toward Akima and they both started to laugh.

During the flight back down to Pendleton, Charlie hardly said a word.

"Anything wrong?" I inquired, knowing damn well that he was smitten with Akima.

"I'll tell you Jake," he said dreamily, "that girl is going to be my wife! My wild-woman chasing days are over buddy!"

"I didn't think she was much," I joked. "Thought she was a little on the butt-ugly side."

"You goddamn motherfucker!" he grabbed me playfully and yanked my hat off my head.

Chapter Twenty-Six

That year saw the continued buildup of forces in Vietnam. The first two months found us training for battalion-size beach assaults.

In February, Davis got back from his sea deployment; he'd been on board a carrier. When he got the word I was at Pendleton, he'd left a message for me to join him at the NCO's canteen.

I couldn't believe how fit he looked, just as tough and mean as ever, though.

"Goddamn it's good to see ya!" he drawled. "Damn Navy just about convinced me to join the Air Force this last trip."

"Bad ship or bad weather?" I grinned, holding him by the shoulders, and then I shook his hand till my fingers went numb. He was still the strongest guy I'd ever met, and when he shook your hand you knew it had been shook.

"Son-of-a-bitching skipper had a full kit inspection every week," Davis complained.

"I'll get you a beer," I offered, getting up. "What the hell have you been up to since…when was it…five or six years ago?"

"I married me a little filly down in Alabama," his voiced carried clear across to the bar. "That lasted all of ten months; after that I swore off women…until I got amongst that Aussie poontang on a trip to Sydney."

"You got down to Sydney again?" I said, returning with the beers.

"Yeah," he took a swallow that emptied half the bottle. "That was a dream cruise compared to this last shit trip."

Just then Charlie Sparks came in. He saw me and came over to the table.

"Hi Jake…can I buy y'all gentlemen a beer?" he asked, glancing at Davis.

"Sure," I said, getting up off my chair. "Davis, this is Charlie Sparks, a friend of mine; Charlie, this is Gunny Carlson, we sailed together a few years back."

"Gunny," Charlie held out his hand.

I sensed the change in Davis immediately, so did Charlie. Davis took Charlie's outstretched hand, but he hardly held it for two seconds, and there was none of the power that Davis possessed in the shake.

"Yeah you too," Davis mumbled. "Look Jake, I got to get squared away, I'm on the boats tomorrow morning at cock's crow."

I was embarrassed for Charlie; it was obvious Davis didn't want to have a drink with him.

"Yeah, sure Davis," I said, "I'll catch up with you."

Davis finished his beer and walked right past Charlie as if he didn't exist.

"I'll get that beer," Charlie said, with a hurt look on his face.

"Jake!" Davis slapped me on the back as I was supervising the securing of the landing craft about a week later, "I haven't had a chance to jaw with ya. How about a beer or two tonight?"

"Sounds fine," I said, still unable to make up my mind on how to judge Davis' behavior.

"That's if you haven't got plans to meet your nigger friend," he added sarcastically.

"Now wait a minute Davis," I flushed. "Charlie Sparks is one hell of a guy!"

"Just another nigger to me," he sneered, "and a squid to boot!"

"You know Davis," I was really pissed now, "I don't think I want that beer after all."

"Suit yourself," he turned and walked away, hoisting his backpack and rifle onto his shoulder.

The television had been repeating all day the coverage of the Civil Rights march that'd turned into a riot in Selma, Alabama. The images of the sheriff turning fire hoses on the marchers and letting dogs loose was not going down well with colored Marines and sailors at Pendleton.

The attempt to march across the bridge on March 7th had turned into a disaster. Martin Luther King and thousands of supporters had tried to cross the bridge in Selma against the orders of local authorities. The sheriff and local police had broken up the march with over-aggressive use of force.

I was having a beer with Charlie and watching the TV news when Davis and two other Marines came in.

I felt the tension in Charlie as Davis headed for our table. Charlie set himself in his chair and I noticed his fist ball up.

"I see you porch monkeys are doing your best to fuck with my State," Davis said to Charlie.

"You motherfucking racist asshole!" Charlie replied, starting to rise.

"I'm from Alabama," Davis' face was set, "and my advice to your Martin-fuckin'-Luther-fuckin'-King is to leave us alone; get the fuck back up to Washington!"

"Now hold on you two!" I yelled, getting between them.

"My sister is marching with King down in Selma," Charlie was up out of his chair, "If you motherfuckin' redneck crackers hurt her I'll…"

"You'll do what?" Davis' face was now twisted with hatred, "You fucking porch monkeys need to keep your place!"

I saw the blow coming but couldn't get out of the way, taking the full force of Charlie's balled fist to the side of my head. My legs buckled and I hit the floor, my head ringing.

"Jesus Jake!" Charlie was trying to pick me up. "I'm sorry man!"

My head cleared in time to see Davis walk away with a disgusted look on his face. At least I'd prevented a fight that would have meant charges brought against both of them, and probably got several others involved as well.

Friendship has its price, I thought. My head felt like a hundred jackhammers were at work inside.

By April of that year, troop strength in Vietnam had grown to 60,000 men. The Marines we had been training with were all slated to leave soon, first to Okinawa and then in-country to bases in Vietnam; to places with names nobody could even pronounce.

I hadn't seen Davis since that night in the canteen, but wanted to square things with him if I could. I didn't want the bad feelings between us to be taken to war. You never knew whether you'd get back in one piece or not.

I never got to see Davis before his unit was shipped out. I felt troubled. Although I never agreed with the kind of racism that Davis displayed, he was still someone I had been good friends with. Thinking back to when we served together on the *USS Junction City*, with the good times on liberty in all those European ports, and the hairy times like off the beach in Lebanon.

It didn't set well with me, I never wanted conflict with friends, and maybe that's a weakness in me. I'd rather walk away leaving problems unresolved sometimes, than stay and work them out, avoiding the unpleasantness.

Maybe it had been my fault that Barb and me had failed in our marriage. Maybe it was my fault I never understood my Mom's problems… maybe…maybe.

I didn't have long to dwell on it. I received orders to pack my bags and fly to Pearl Harbor; both Charlie and I were going to join the same ship. The *USS Pocatello* was a brand new Austin Class Amphibious Transport Dock (LPD) and we were both excited about the transfer.

Charlie was scrambling to get up to Oakland and see Akima before he left, and he wanted me to go with him. We'd been given three days leave, but I told him I couldn't make it.

I knew Barb would be unhappy with my orders and I also knew Dory would be frantic. She was terrified that Roy or I would be sent to Vietnam. I didn't want to say goodbye under these circumstances. All I knew for certain was it was another example of me taking the easy way out.

When I called Barb to break the news to her, I made the excuse that I had some urgent personal things to take care of before I left. That wasn't a complete lie; I needed to sit down and make out my will.

Things had changed for me, and now I thought I'd leave everything to Barb. Maybe it was guilt on my part, or maybe I just thought it was about time she got a break; either way I didn't want to see her before I left.

Barb and I had been writing on a regular basis, and I hoped that would continue while I was deployed to Vietnam. I looked forward to her letters, which always had lots of news and were written with endless humor.

Charlie only just made it back before we boarded the charted TWA airliner to Hawaii. On the flight to Pearl he told me that he and Akima had decided to get married.

"I want you to be my Best Man," he said, all serious. "We didn't have time to do it in Oakland, so she's coming to Honolulu and we'll get hitched before we sail."

I knew we'd be at least two or three weeks in Hawaii before our deployment, so that would give them more than enough time.

"Will you?" his words brought me back.

"Of course I will Charlie!" I responded. "I'd be proud to stand up for you."

"And Barb is Akima's maid-of-honor, so y'all can get together one more time too," he added.

"You know we're gonna be busy those last couple of weeks," I told him. "You better make sure your arrangements coincide with the Navy's."

"Jesus!" I thought. I hadn't even thought about Barb since I called her two nights ago, she'd be coming over to Hawaii too.

"We're just planning on them coming in late on a Friday night, we'd get married on Saturday." Charlie continued telling me his plans, bouncing around in his seat like a kid. "Then they'll have to fly back Sunday. They can't get any time off work and they got to be back Monday."

"They have Chaplain services at Pearl," I said, trying to get him slowed down. "Have you thought about being married on base?"

"I hadn't, but I guess that'd work," he answered, his head in the clouds.

I could see Charlie hadn't thought much about any formalities. I guess that was one more thing I'd have to take care of when we got to Pearl.

The flight across seemed short with Charlie bending my ear non-stop. We were down on the ground before I knew it. A bus took us to the harbor and the *Pocatello*.

As we approached by bus driving down the pier, seeing the ship for the first time gave me a feeling of pride. She was enormous, having the capabilities of being a troop transport, attack cargo ship and helicopter carrier all rolled up in one.

She could carry 900 battle-ready Marines, as well as 2,500 tons of heavy equipment. On her flight deck she had helicopters ready for vertical deployment of Marine assault teams, and in her well deck she housed four LCMs for water-borne operations.

Her stern gate weighed 7 tons, and it lowered to reveal a well deck 392 feet long and 44 feet wide. The difference between the earlier stern lowering Landing Ship Dock (LSD) and the newer Amphibious Transport Dock (LPD) was the LPD's ability to carry helicopters on a flight deck built over the mammoth, floodable well.

The lowering of the stern section of the ship was made possible by pumping 2.3 million gallons of water into her ballast tanks.

The *USS Pocatello* had been handed over to the Navy and commissioned only two months earlier. Since then the ship had been rapidly completing sea trials before she joined elements of the Seventh Fleet off the coast of Vietnam.

In fact, that's one of the things still left to complete, the final testing of equipment and signing off to the civilian contractors, some of whom were still on board.

That afternoon after I'd reported aboard and stowed my gear, I walked the length of the ship along the dock.

My routine hadn't changed from the first ship I'd served on. I'd always liked the look of a new ship from the outside. I liked to look at the shape and lines, the bow straight on and her height from the ground up.

I had the feeling this was going to be a good billet for me. Meantime, I had to get my duty assignments, find out where things were on the ship, who the senior officers were, and try and get a weekend organized when Charlie and Akima could get married.

Time would soon run out and we would be sailing off into the sunset.

Chapter Twenty-Seven

"Chief Rickmeyer," Commander O'Reilly, the executive officer, began, "We have a visitor coming aboard, Rear Admiral Sullivan P. Rooks. The Admiral will be joining us for a three-day shakedown cruise before we sign off on the ship."

"Admiral Rooks, Sir?" I asked, not surprised.

"Yes, lower half," the XO replied.

Sully had gotten his first star, Rear Admiral lower half; now he warranted his own flag.

"The Captain wants an arrival ceremony, Side Boys and a Boatswain to pipe the side," he explained. "Can you organize that? I hate to drop it on you at short notice, but you are the in-port duty chief."

"I can organize it," I said. "When is he coming aboard, Sir?"

"Tomorrow morning at 0900. I want the forenoon watch without a hair out of place." The XO continued to give me my instructions, "All on-duty personnel will be required to "man the rails" at 0845."

"I should mention Commander," I was warming to the whole idea of the ritual, "I have known Admiral Rooks for many years."

"That's wonderful Chief," the Executive Officer grinned. "I'll inform the Captain. He'll be relieved to know we have someone on board who knows the Admiral. The Skipper's just a little apprehensive about having a Rear Admiral looking over his shoulder when he's trying to get a new ship in shape."

"I'd like to pipe the Admiral aboard myself, Sir," I volunteered. This was a chance to do something I'd never done before. I'd been a Side Boy a few times, but never had a chance to use my skills on the Boatswain's Pipe.

"Excellent Chief," the XO was beaming. "You'll have the authority to get what ever you need, just tell me what you want."

"I'll get the guidebook out and start organizing the detail immediately, Sir," I said.

"Good," he nodded. "Make sure everything is as it should be. My office is open to you at any time, anything you need Chief, anything at all. The Captain wants to start off on the right foot with this visit."

"It will be done right Commander," I assured him. "My first job will be to round up the white lanyard and silver pipe."

"Very well Rickmeyer," the XO was smiling with relief now, "Carry on!"

The whole ceremony of piping aboard high-ranking officers was as old as the Navy itself. Two rows of sailors would line the gangway, these were the Side Boys. Originally they were there to hoist the ropes raising the visiting high-ranking officer's boat. Nowadays they lined up and held the salute while the Boatswain blew the arrival signal on his pipe. The Boatswain wore a white lanyard around his neck, attached to it was the pipe. All personnel would be required to stand to and line the rails. It was very impressive if done right, and this was going to be done right!

I had made arrangements with the Pearl Harbor Chaplain's office to perform the marriage ceremony for Charlie and Akima. The Chaplain wasn't too happy. He wanted to discuss things with the couple before performing any marriage.

But the Vietnam conflict had changed things; a lot of servicemen were getting married before going overseas.

That was a mistake as far as I was concerned. Why get married? You may never get back!

I guess some people thought it would bring them luck, maybe they thought it would hold their love until they got back. In my experience that was another myth. I could count in the thousands the sailors who had been cheated on by their wives while they were away.

I guess the number of sailors who also cheated on their wives, in every bar and brothel from Tokyo to Tangiers evened up the score; either way it was still a bad idea as far as I was concerned.

"Charlie!" I called out to him as I saw him walking past the boat supply locker, "You need to be at the Chaplain's office tomorrow at ten."

"Shit Jake," he complained, "Why the hell can't they just do the job? Why fuck around with all this bullshit?"

"Don't complain," I said. "He's doing you a big favor; normal procedure is for both you and Akima to attend these sessions. He's been fair in understanding that Akima is in California and can't get over until the wedding day."

"Fuck it man!" he groaned, swinging his head from side to side. "You got no idea of all the crap that preacher fills my head with."

"Just be off the ship before 0800 in the morning," I laughed. "After 0800 the gangway will be closed for all except essential arrival and departures."

"Yeah, I know," he looked at me and smiled, his white, even teeth a walking advertisement for Colgate. "Good luck with the big show."

"Thanks," I said, "I'm looking forward to the Admiral's arrival a lot more than your disorganized wedding I can tell you!"

184

The morning cleared about 0630. I thought the rain we'd had all night was going to screw up the ceremony we'd worked so hard to get ready.

I'd been up most of the night practicing my pipe signals down in the well deck. In that space, which was the equivalent of two basketball courts, the pipe's shrill notes sounded like the charge of the light brigade.

Several times during the evening watch, and at the start of the mid-watch, the roving patrols checked in to see what all the noise was about. "Fuck off!" I yelled at them.

I grabbed an hour or two in the rack after my practice, then I was up again checking and re-checking all the details, just to make damn sure we had it right.

I couldn't check the Side Boys and the Forenoon Watch until they reported for duty. But I would be checking them over carefully. They'd better be ship-shape, spic-and-span and dressed in Class A whites.

I had personally selected the Side Boys, making sure they were all as close to the same height as possible.

A hurried breakfast gave me heartburn; after that I paced the quarterdeck waiting for time to tick off second by second.

0900 came soon enough. The Captain, XO and Officer-of-the-Deck were all waiting impatiently for the Admiral's arrival. The Side Boys were lined up, I was at the head of the gangway, and the railings were lined with hundreds of swabbies in starched whites.

I was trying to keep my mouth from drying out so I didn't fuck up when it came time to blow the pipe.

The fleet of black cars pulled up and the P.A. speakers called the men lining the rails to attention.

Admiral Rooks stepped out of his car when the driver opened the door with a flourish and threw a smart salute.

The other cars emptied with an assortment of staff officers and three civilians...

Was that Ed? I caught a glimpse of a familiar figure. Keep your mind on the ceremony goddamn it! I thought, as I raised the pipe to my lips.

Sully walked slowly up the gangway followed by his aide-de-camp, when he reached the head of the gangway I snapped to and blew the signal on my Boatswain's pipe. Sully stood at attention as the Side Boys all saluted in one single, tight, synchronized action.

I noticed a slight flicker of recognition cross his face as he caught sight of me, but he never wavered in his rigid conformity to the occasion.

The last shrill notes of the pipe faded across the quarterdeck and the Side Boys held their salute. Sully stood stock still for a long moment, and then he returned the salute with as much precision as I'd ever seen one returned. Then as he stepped onto the deck, the ship's bell rang, announcing his "arrival".

The Captain and other officers stepped forward to salute and shake the Admiral's hand, and then lead the party forward to the wardroom.

The civilians in the party did include Ed Morrow, though why he was here I didn't know. Maybe he was on another Navy inspection tour from Washington.

He made a motion to step forward and say something to me, but when he saw the tight lines on my face he realized that would have broken protocol, so he hurried forward to rejoin the others heading through the hatchway.

The arrival had gone off without a hitch. I dismissed the Side Boys and the rest of the ceremonial detail. The ship's company was ordered to stand down and they went back about their own business.

"Very well done Chief," the Officer-of-the-Deck said, "Pass the word to the Side Boys. They were a credit to the ship."

"Thank you, Sir." I didn't realize how tense I'd been until I felt one leg almost give way.

"Captain Sarnoff will no doubt thank you personally when he gets time," he continued, "after we finish the tests and get the Admiral back ashore. Until then, everybody will have to be on their toes."

"Aye, aye Sir," I saluted, turned-about sharply and went below. I needed to take a piss in the worst possible way!

I kept my Class A's on. We were shoving off at 1400 and I would have to stand with my division on the flight deck as we departed Pearl.

Just before I went topside, there was a knock on the bulkhead of the tiny office that the boat division used. "Excuse me Chief," a young black sailor said, standing in the hatchway, white hat in hand.

"Yeah, what's up?" I answered, waving him in.

"I'm Seaman Apprentice Washington, Chief," he said nervously, twisting his hat around in his hands.

"Oh," I looked on the boat crew roster, "Yeah, you're assigned to this boat section."

"I don't know whether you remember me Chief," he went on, "but I was in your boot division at Great Lakes."

186

"I'll be damned!" I said, my memory starting to put the face with my time at the Recruit Training Center. "You'll be pleased to know you're one of the only divisions I ever got through boot camp; I had just one solitary division."

"Well, I'm sure glad to be working for you Chief," he said, starting to relax. "My last boss was about as much fun as a case of colon cancer!"

I almost knocked over my coffee I began to laugh so hard.

"Where the hell was this?" I asked, in between laughing and trying to catch my breath. "Where'd you go after Great Lakes?"

"To the boat control school in San Diego," he said, with a smile that would disarm even the toughest old salt. "I was transferred to the *Pocatello* when she stopped at Coronado for refueling." He continued slowly, "The school was okay, but then I spent time in the barracks waiting for my sea billet."

He was about eighteen or nineteen, but looked twelve. He was small, probably rejected by the Marines, that's why the Navy got him. He had a face that had never seen a razor and wouldn't see one for several years to come.

"Who was running the transient work detail?" I asked.

"A Chief that would have given ice-cream a headache!" he grinned, glad that I was enjoying the tale, "Name was Chief Dicks!"

"Fucking Rabbit!" I exclaimed, almost knocking my coffee over again.

"What's up Chief?" the kid stepped back.

"Nothing," I said, recovering myself, "I've come across him before that's all."

I didn't want to start bad-mouthing Rabbit in front of this kid. Chief petty officers crapping on each other was not good for discipline in the lower ranks.

"I'll put you on Petty Officer Sparks' boat," I said, making a note on the list in front of me. I liked this kid and I knew Charlie would be fair to him.

"Let's get topside, we'll be shoving off in fifteen minutes." I grabbed my hat and started out the door.

"Did you see Charlie Sparks get back?" I asked the petty officer standing by a locker as we walked down the companionway.

"Yeah Chief," he said, hurrying aft, "he's been back for a while."

The *Pocatello* slid from her berth and was turned in a graceful arc by the assisting tugs. Pearl Harbor never lost its attraction for me, although I'd been in and out of here for twenty years.

As soon as we'd cleared the mouth of the harbor and stood down, I hurried below to change into other clothes. We'd have a lot of work to do over the next couple of days.

"Charlie," I grabbed him as we passed in the space leading to the berthing deck, "I need to see you in the office as soon as you get changed."

"Okay Jake," he was smiling. The meeting with the Chaplain must have gone all right.

"Get the other boat drivers there too, will you?" I asked him.

"Already on it!" he replied, he was undoing his black neckerchief as he hurried away.

Charlie was a damn good man; he worked hard and knew what needed to be done before you asked him to do it.

"Tomorrow starts the speed tests for the main power plant," I began my get-acquainted talk with the boat crews. "They should be done by early afternoon, and then they want tests of the ballast tanks' flooding and draining capabilities. Each time they lower the stern gates we'll take the opportunity to run out the boats."

"With a load?" asked one team member.

"We'll go empty. All we're trying to do is see how well the boats behave. My understanding is they haven't had their keels wet yet," I replied to the question, speaking in the tone of authority I'd learned at Great Lakes.

I knew these guys knew what to do, but I was not about to leave my ass exposed and hanging out in the wind.

"There will be no fuckin' "gundecking" on reports!" I said, raising my voice a notch. "If the rudders are sticky, write it down. If the engines are overheating, write it down. If the boat feels heavy in the water, write it fuckin' down."

"What about the firemen and seamen assignments, have you made them out yet Chief?" Petty Officer Allbright asked.

"Yeah," I answered, passing out copies of the crew roster. "Remember, some of these kids are still wet behind the ears, so you'll be training them the way you want, turning them into reliable hands; that's part of your job too."

"What time are we mustering?" a petty officer motorman asked.

"0630," I said. "I know it's early, but we have an admiral aboard and some mucky-ducks from DC. I'm sure the Captain will have a long memory for any department that fucks up and makes him, or the ship, look bad."

There was some shuffling of chairs; otherwise the room was quiet.

"That's all, see you in the morning," I said, over the suddenly noisy boat teams.

"How'd the meeting go?" I asked Charlie at evening chow. It was the first time we'd had a chance to talk since the night before.

"All right, my man!" Charlie grinned, his white teeth sparkling. "I think we can pull this off right."

"We get in on Thursday, then leave again the following Tuesday," I said. "Did you contact the girls and check if they're all set for next weekend?"

"That I did Jake baby!" Charlie was behaving as if he'd pulled off a coup.

I suspect the Chaplain and his wife had taken care of most of the details, including reminding him about the phone call. Charlie had been too strung out to remember it on his own.

A new breed of Navy Chaplains was now in the fleet, with more concern for men's personal needs, rather than the Navy's needs. The old fire and destruction they used to preach to you, trying to keep you from making mistakes that your folks would complain to the Navy about.

Much had changed. I remembered how I'd pleaded for help when I'd asked the chaplain about getting Mucky over from New Zealand. He didn't lift a finger.

Just as well though, I'd moved on in my life and now Barb was increasingly on my mind.

"Excuse me Chief," a member of the duty watch taped me on the shoulder, "the Admiral would like you to report to his sea cabin."

"What the fuck have you done now Jake?" Charlie rolled his eyes in mock concern.

"Not a thing," I said, pushing my food tray away, "just my old buddy wanting to chew the fat."

"When you come into the Navy through the hawsepipe you know every motherfucker!" laughed the sailor who'd brought me the message. "Anyway, the word is to report when ready."

"Aye, thanks," I said to the messenger, appreciating Sully getting the word passed to me quietly. The ship would be abuzz with stories about the Boatswain and the Admiral soon enough, without summoning me to his cabin over the ship's P.A. system.

I spruced myself up a bit, and then went forward into "Officer's Country"; the sea cabin Sully had been given was roomy and well furnished. The *Pocatello* had the amenities and communications equipment necessary to make her a Primary Control Ship if required.

The Marine guard knocked and announced my arrival.

"Enter!" Sully's voice boomed from within.

The Marine held the door open for me and quietly closed it after I'd entered the room.

"Jake, so good to see you again," Sully was sitting in a large, padded chair opposite Ed Morrow. He rose and shook my hand as I smiled and nodded first to him, and then to Ed.

"Good to see you too, Admiral," I replied, "and congratulations on your first star," referring to the flag with its solitary star hanging from the stand behind his desk.

"Hi Jake," Ed got up from his chair to shake my hand.

"I couldn't believe it when I saw you coming aboard this morning Congressman," I said, still surprised to see Ed.

"It's now Senator Morrow," Ed laughed. "And my duties as the chairman of the subcommittee on defense keep bringing me back to my old friends in the Navy."

"Sit down Jake," Sully pointed to an oversized chair beside him. "It's hard to believe you two pulled me out of the water all those years ago!" Sully was looking at Ed for a reaction.

Ed laughed and grinned at me, "Maybe we should have left you to the sharks. You were just another dumb "Airedale" who couldn't find his way back to his carrier."

Sully laughed at the joke; my reaction was to grin to cover the fact that I didn't find it very funny.

"Right now the Navy would like to be throwing me to the sharks!" Ed emphasized, looking at Sully.

"What Ed is talking about Jake, is the fact that we need a supplemental spending bill for extraordinary funds," Sully explained, "to cover the shortfalls we're experiencing with this Vietnam business."

"And I have to go back to Washington and try to explain the Navy's needs to the Senate Appropriations Committee," Ed was warming to the discussion.

"And I have to satisfy my boss that we're doing everything possible to get you on our side," Sully answered.

The boss he was referring to was the Commander-in-Chief-Pacific (CINCPAC). I was in the middle of a discussion that was going way over my head. I'd feel more comfortable just making my manners, and then getting back down below where I belonged.

"The Senate Budget Committee sets the funding limits for the fiscal year," Ed was starting to sound like he was making a political speech. "The twenty-eight members of the Appropriations Committee have to match their expenditures to the limits set by law!"

"And the Secretary of the Navy, through CINCPAC and others, have to impress on you that defense needs extra funds to compensate for these high priority shortfalls!"

"Sorry Jake," Ed looked over at me. "I can see we're talking shop, when we should be catching up with you. How have you been?"

"Fine, fine Ed," I said. "I don't mind, it's good to get to see how government works."

"I must tell you how much pride I felt coming aboard this morning Jake." Sully had lowered his voice, "I know you love the old Navy traditions as much as I do, and just for your information, that was the first time I've experienced an arrival ceremony as an Admiral."

"I'm glad the ship made you feel welcome, Sir," I replied. "The Navy's moving so fast nowadays, it's good to put on a full-dress shebang now and again."

"I'm sorry I can't offer you anything more than coffee," Sully said, as the Filipino steward came in, placing a tray with a silver coffeepot and fine porcelain cups on the table, "But you both know the regulations about liquor on a US warship."

"I think I may have to decline Admiral." I took the opportunity the break in the conversation gave me, "I have to get all my ducks in a row for tomorrow morning."

"I understand completely Jake." Sully stood up and offered me his hand. "I wish some of our ship commanders had the same dedication to duty."

"Thank you Sully," I took his hand. "I do appreciate you taking the time to say hello; I know you're very busy."

"My pleasure," Sully smiled. "I only wish we had more time, our meetings are always much too brief."

"And I add my thoughts to that," Ed said, putting his hand on my shoulder. "We must have dinner together again. Unfortunately, not on this trip; I'll be flying back to Washington just as soon as we return to Pearl."

"And I may not get to do any more personal visits either Jake," Sully said apologetically, "but we'll meet again before long."

"I know we will Admiral," I said, momentarily standing to attention as protocol demanded. I turned and headed for the door; the Filipino steward was there before me and opened it.

"Thank you," I said to the steward, and his face burst into a wide smile.

"Bye Jake," Ed said, as I left. He was looking tired and worried.

"Bye Ed, good to see you again," I replied. "Goodnight Admiral," I added.

I went out on deck to clear my head, and to go over my impressions of the meeting with Ed and Sully. It was obvious they were both under pressure. The higher up the ladder you went, the greater the responsibilities; some people thrived on it, others caved in.

I wished at that moment that I smoked. The night was so pleasant and I could still smell the sweet tropical scents of Hawaii on the night breeze. Wouldn't it feel good to light up, stick my foot on the rail and take a deep drag on a cigarette? Maybe not. If I started smoking, I'd just finish up coughing and wheezing like the other dickheads I saw walking around.

A sailor with a coffin nail sticking out of his mouth was one of my pet complaints; a glass of good, ice cold beer, now that was different!

The day started off badly, with delays during the speed trials. Then when we finally did get up to flank speed for the test, a vibration developed in one of the shafts.

The boat teams had been in the well deck most of the morning and were starting to get crabby. The ballast tests finally did get done, and we got to do our boat sorties. They went off like clockwork; the drivers put the craft through their paces as if they were competing at the Indy 500.

They'd completed the boat runs successfully, but things didn't go so smoothly as they returned to the ship. Charlie brought his boat in too fast.

"Fenders!" Charlie shouted at Seaman Otis Washington, the young sailor I'd assigned to Charlie's LCM.

Otis couldn't get the fenders over the side fast enough, and the minor collision scrapped about six feet of paint off the starboard side of the boat.

"Jesus H. Christ!" screamed Charlie, "Don't you know to get those fenders ready?"

"I'm sorry Boats," Otis replied, looking like he was about to cry.

"Sorry?" Charlie said, still in a rage. "Sorry doesn't cut it! Look at this motherfuckin' boat!"

I felt Charlie had come in a tad fast and it wasn't all Otis' fault, but I couldn't intervene. Charlie was responsible for the craft and the crew aboard it.

"Make this motherfucker fast, goddamn it!" Charlie was still tearing into poor Otis, "Secure the boat, and then you better check with the paint locker. I want that scrape painted over before I take her out again."

"Aye, aye Boats!" Otis responded to Charlie's orders. He jumped up on the walkway and started sorting the hoisting cables.

"A mothfuckin' admiral on board," Charlie was still on fire, "and you want me to take this boat out looking like she's been tore up by some dumb, motherfuckin' deckape?"

I felt Charlie was becoming a little more agitated than the accident warranted. I put it down to nervousness over his upcoming marriage next Saturday.

After our boat tests that day, the team spent the remainder of th checking hoisting equipment, pumps, damage control, fire hoses ɛ boat gear; everything that operated, moved, or took up space in the v was checked, rechecked and a written report turned in.

I'd only seen Sully once during the three days and that was from a distance. He and his entourage walked across the flight deck looking over the helicopters. When we finally made Pearl, all the ship's company from the Captain on down to the fireman apprentices, were ready for a break.

The ship hadn't been tied up at the pier for more than twenty minutes before Sully, Ed, and the rest of the Admiral's staff and other officials had disembarked.

There was no talk of a sendoff for the Admiral; pressure was on to get back to the meetings with CINCPAC.

"Charlie," I called, after the ship had secured and I saw him in the after companionway, "when do you have to see the Chaplain again?"

"Tomorrow Jake," he yelled back, "and he wants you there this time too."

"What time?" I asked.

"Sometime in the forenoon watch," he answered. "I'll call to confirm the time."

I knew I'd better get all the reports and other paperwork done before I started thinking about the wedding. The Command Master Chief and our Division Lieutenant were both sticklers for detail. I wouldn't be able to use Charlie's wedding as an excuse not to have everything completed and turned in on schedule.

Charlie and me sat twiddling our thumbs in the Chaplain's office that Friday morning. I planned to take Charlie for a bachelor's night out that evening, nothing big, just a few beers at some of the joints on Hotel Street. The place hadn't changed much over the years, and a group of the guys from the boat teams would meet us at Harbor Lights to celebrate.

Akima and Barb would be arriving at around eleven that night and I'd booked a room for them at the Waikiki Hilton. Akima didn't want to see Charlie before the wedding because she was superstitious, so the first we'd see of them would be Saturday at 1430, when the marriage would be solemnized at the Base Chapel.

We got through the meeting, as boring as it was, with the Chaplain. And that night the bachelors' party went off without anyone being arrested by the Shore Patrol, although young Otis Washington did throw up on the table at one point in the evening's festivities and spent the rest of the night sitting quietly; his face pale enough to pass for a white man.

"Do you, Charles Sparks, take this..." the Chaplain's words were only dimly registering. I was looking at Barb. She was radiant, and I had never seen her looking more beautiful.

I found myself thinking about what we'd do that night, after Charlie and Akima had gone to their honeymoon suite.

"And do you, Akima Lucilla Brown, take this man..." I was only half-listening to the words. We'd only have the one night together; the girls had to catch an early afternoon flight back to the mainland on Sunday.

"I now pronounce you Man and Wife!" The ceremony was over, time to come back to reality and stop fantasizing about Barb.

"Congratulations Charlie," I shook his hand. "May I kiss the bride?"

"You sure can," Charlie responded, pumping my hand until it hurt.

I gave Akima a light peck; I didn't want Charlie getting jealous on his wedding day; that man could do you damage just looking at you.

Barb kissed Charlie, and then put her arms around Akima giving her a hug.

"Well, I guess the next stop is the photographs!" I had arranged for one of the ship's photographers to take a few wedding day memories, then we headed for the Chinese restaurant for the reception.

I had invited the boat crews and their dates; I just hoped everyone would behave. Getting a bunch of swabbies together and giving them free beer and wine was a recipe for disaster.

China Gate was one of the more popular restaurants in Honolulu. It catered to a wide range of customers, from local Chinese to visiting movie stars. And, of course, their relationship with the Navy went all the way back to when the US Fleet used Hawaii as a coaling station for their battlewagons.

Several of the crew were there waiting when we arrived. Petty Officers Abalite and Harkwood had two of the worst looking hookers I'd ever seen hanging on their arms. Then Seamen "Smitty" Smith, Billy Rogers and Otis Washington arrived shortly after we'd taken our seats at the table.

They were all decked out in Class A's and had their hats squared. The three of them stood at attention, and "Smitty" read from a poem they must have been working on all night. They'd never make poets, but Akima and Charlie appreciated their effort.

"That was so cute!" Barb said, as she lent forward and gave me a kiss. "Wait till later baby!" she whispered in my ear, darting her tongue quickly in and out. The courses kept coming; pork dishes, chicken dishes, noodles, rice, seafood dishes, all washed down with Chinese green tea and good old

Primo Beer. Johnny Chan, the grandson of the original owner, fussed over Akima and Charlie and kept pouring champagne into their glasses.

It was quite an evening, with everybody managing to behave himself or herself somewhat. Harkwood's hooker date started criticizing him when he didn't hold her chair out as she got up to go to the bathroom.

"If you were a fucking gentleman..." she slurred her words, "You'd pull the fucking chair out for a lady..."

The time had come to end the evening's festivities. Charlie and Akima looked like they were ready to head out, and the rest of the gang were starting to feel the effects of the evening's drinking.

Harkwood had told the hooker to pull her own chair out, to which she had replied, "Go fuck yourself!"

Now "Smitty" and Otis were starting to weep on my shoulder, telling me I was the greatest Chief Boatswain's Mate they'd ever served under. Barb quietly hugged them, patting them on the backs like children.

"God!" I thought, "I hope these kids don't get hurt over there."

"Oh, shit!" it suddenly hit me. I hadn't booked a room for Akima and Charlie to spend their wedding night.

"We'll just have to let them use the room Akima and I had at the Hilton," Barb said. "We can get something else."

Finally the Bridal Couple left the restaurant amidst a wild medley of whoops and slaps on the back.

The boys took off for Hotel Street for some more carousing, while Barb and I settled the bill and used Johnny Chan's telephone to try and get a hotel room somewhere.

"It was a great day," Barb said, as we strolled along Waikiki Beach.

"I know," I replied dreamily. We hadn't been able to get any accommodation, so we'd have to spend the night on the beach.

"This is so romantic Jake." Barb looked up at me, "If we find a secluded spot somewhere..."

"I've got my eye peeled for one," I laughed.

It was about two in the morning when we found a spot between two catamarans on the beach. We lay down and began to embrace passionately with an urgency that had been building since our last time together. There was haste in our lovemaking, not much else, but we both needed it.

"Where do you see us going Jake?" Barb asked, her face pressed against my chest.

"I wish I had the answer darlin'," I replied truthfully. "I want to say let's try it again, but I'm scared."

"Don't be scared honey," she said, lifting her head. "I want you to be sure, and I'll wait until you feel you are."

She rolled onto me, gently kissing my eyelids, then she moved down to my nose, then my lips. We started to make love again, this time gently, lovingly.

"Oh, Jake sweetheart," Barb said throatily, "I'll wait for you to be sure!"

I awoke to a dog's wet nose on my face.

"Quick Barb!" I said. "I can see the dog's owners running up the beach, get your clothes on!"

"Oh, shit," Barb laughed, as she struggled into her underwear. "I'll never forget this night!"

Barb and I made our way back to the Hilton and ordered breakfast in the outdoor cafe. Several stares were directed our way. It was obvious we'd spent the night on the beach. After a reasonable time, given the circumstances of Barb needing to shower and change, we went to Charlie and Akima's room and knocked.

To our surprise Akima and Charlie were up, dressed, and had just finished a nice room-service brunch.

"Sorry to disturb you," Barb apologized, "but I need a shower and some fresh clothes. Then we'd better be thinking about getting to the airport."

"Is it time already?" Akima said, looking dreamily into Charlie's eyes across the breakfast table.

"It will be by the time I get my face on!" Barb replied, on her way to the bathroom.

"I can't thank you enough Jake," Charlie said, after we'd seen the girls off at the airport. "It was one fine day in my life, I can tell you."

"I was glad to do it," I said, "and it gave me a chance to get together with Barb again too, don't forget that."

"I don't know man," he added. "Being married makes a man think differently."

"Save the philosophizing for later," I said, turning him towards the airport exit. "We've got to check up on the boys, see if they got back all right last night." Then added, "We shove off on Tuesday; we need to get squared away."

The June morning we left Pearl Harbor for deployment to Vietnam was a turning point for me. I had been thinking about Barb, and had decided to ask her to marry me when we got back. I could probably get a good shore posting, maybe in the San Francisco Bay area. That way Barb could keep her job, and we'd be close to Dory, John and the kids. Maybe Akima and Charlie would stay in the Bay area too.

Chapter Twenty-Eight

The coastline of Vietnam looked mountainous and green, with the tropical heat haze distorting its features. It was the wet season and had been raining on and off all day. Someone had told me that the haze you always saw on hot days was not pollution, but oil molecules rising into the air from the vegetation, and when the sun shone through these molecules it created the haze effect.

Cam Ranh was our port of entry to Vietnam, and I was amazed at the activities that could be seen as we sailed around the point, and moved farther into the bay.

The Seabees had built a major port here, with warehouses, piers, sheds, and a large anchorage; heavy-duty dock cranes could be seen unloading cargo from ships, and a fleet of forklifts swarmed around the wharves.

The military had planned to make this the main port for re-supply and entry of new personnel into South Vietnam. Cam Ranh was north of Saigon and to the south of Da Nang, where we would be headed next.

I kept hearing about the beach at Vung Tau, where a lot of guys were spending R&R. It had miles of unspoiled white beach, with the whole South China Sea to swim in.

At first we thought we might get some time off on arrival. Now we'd heard things were heating up at the Marine bases south of Da Nang, and we'd be moving troops and supplies north almost immediately.

After transferring some personnel off the ship and taking on others, refueling, and loading extra fuel and ammunition for the choppers, we sailed north.

While still at sea, the *Pocatello* joined other ships heading for the Marine base at Chu Lai, where reinforcements were landed on August 14th. The Second Battalion, Fourth Marines (2/4), and Third Battalion, Third Marines (3/3) were needed to beef up the existing forces at the base.

Increased Vietcong activity had been observed in the area, then on August 15th a Vietcong deserter had given up information about a major offensive planned against the base at Chu Lai. The Marine base was relatively isolated, and the Vietcong must have been planning a quick, decisive victory.

Rather than wait for something to happen, the commanding general at Chu Lai, General Lewis W. Walt of the Marine Corps, planned a preemptive strike against the Vietcong forces digging in to the south of the base. On August 17th when an attack on Chu Lai became imminent, he put operation Starlite into effect.

The Operation began the morning of August 17th with patrols scouting the area where three landing zones had already been selected, 12 miles to the southeast of the base and about a mile inland.

The beach selected for the sea-borne assault was a mile-wide sandy stretch, north of the Song Tra Bong River mouth.

The Marine 3/3 Battalion was embarked in the afternoon to ships offshore. The flotilla then moved slowly south overnight, arriving off the assault beach at 0500 the next morning. H-Hour, the time when the beach assault would begin, was set for 0630.

The Marines would be landed onto the beach by landing craft, and helicopters would carry other units to the three landing zones inland.

Offshore the *USS Cabildo LSD-16*, acting as Primary Control Ship, would direct the assault. Other ships, including the cruiser *USS Galveston CLG-3*, would provide fire support with her impressive array of big guns. A reserve battalion of Marines would be held aboard ships in case further forces were needed after the initial landings.

At 0615 all hell broke loose, as naval gunfire and artillery from Chu Lai opened up on the area inland from the beach. Marine and Navy fighter jets flew in and added to the bedlam. The sudden, loud, overwhelming attack was frightening. I stood there on the deck in the early morning hour awestruck. I could only imagine what it must be like to be a Vietcong guerrilla in the bush, and been awakened by this show of impressive firepower.

The shelling eased off and the assault began at 0630 with the Marine 3/3 Battalion heading for the beach. The assault troops aboard the *Pocatello* were being held in reserve. We stood ready to launch reinforcements at a moment's notice.

Reports of retreat from all along the Vietcong positions started to filter in and the Navy was asked to cut off any fleeing VC using sampans to escape.

"Chief," the Lieutenant ordered, "Take an LCM with a squad of Marines into the river estuary and sink anything that even looks like it's carrying VC!"

"Aye, aye Sir!" I was glad to be doing something at last. "Charlie, stand by to take out your boat!"

A young Marine second lieutenant came trotting along the catwalk with a ten-man squad; they were all loaded down with heavy weapons.

"I'm Lieutenant McBride," he said, in an even tone not displaying any nervousness or excitement.

"Get your men on the boat," I said, slapping him on the backpack.

"Load up!" the young officer shouted to his men. "Take the Boatswain's direction on positioning yourselves!"

Everything was happening at once. The Marines were clamoring aboard, Charlie was shouting instructions to his crew, and I was giving a thumbs-up signal to the boat commander standing by the stern gate.

"Cast off!" Charlie shouted to Otis, who was handling the bowlines. The motorman was standing by and the Marine squad was crouching down in the well. The craft sailed out through the lowered stern gate and into the bright sunshine. We immediately headed for the river estuary, giving a wide berth to the ships that were still providing fire support for the Marines on shore.

I took the 45-cal. pistol from my shoulder holster. I'd started wearing a shoulder holster ever since we'd arrived at Cam Ranh. I released the ammo clip, checked that it was full, slammed it back into the grip and pulled the slider back, loading a bullet into the breach. A chopper pilot had told me how the shoulder holster was less cumbersome in tight spots, better than the standard hip holster.

The river we were heading for was the Song Tra Bong, just one of the dozens of rivers of Vietnam. The rivers had been dumping silt into their estuaries for centuries. This ensured that the estuary and bay bottoms were mostly sand, good for flat-bottomed boats because you didn't have to worry about hitting anything that could damage the keel.

I was taking in everything as we plowed through the water, trying to anticipate what we could expect if we encountered any sampans.

Charlie had been acting strangely ever since we'd arrived in Vietnam. He'd been moody and seemed pre-occupied. I'd left him alone and he seemed to prefer it that way.

Now I noticed as we headed closer to the shore he was wide-eyed and mumbling to himself. "Shit!" I thought, "Don't tell me Charlie is going squirrelly on me!"

"Look!" a Marine standing in the bow shouted, pointing to a spot on the beach. "Two of the fuckers! You see 'em, Sir?"

"Yeah, I see them!" the Lieutenant shouted back. "Mayberry, get your B.A.R on the lip of the ramp!"

"Aye Sir!" the Marine with the large caliber B.A.R replied, as he set the barrel of the heavy weapon on the ramp top.

"Bang, bang, bang…" the B.A.R. bounced as it sent a dozen rounds towards the two fleeing figures. It was as if we were watching an event from far away, in slow motion. The two running Vietcong were flung over on their backs, the black-glad figures falling long after we'd heard the loud report of the rifle.

"Outstanding!" the young lieutenant yelled, "Good job Mayberry!"

The sergeant standing beside the B.A.R. rifleman slapped him on the back, turned and yelled back, "Lock and load! Keep your eyes peeled; they could be anywhere!"

I kept glancing back at Charlie. I felt an uneasiness in my gut that couldn't be explained.

The mouth of the river we sailed up emptied into a large, horseshoe-shaped bay called Vung Dung Quat, the land curled around to the east ending in a long, narrow spit of land. There were numerous fishing hamlets as we moved cautiously up the river. Most seemed to be devoid of any life; maybe the people had taken cover once they'd heard the shelling start.

At a point some one hundred yards upriver, out from underneath some overhanging trees, a sampan suddenly appeared traveling slowly.

"Charlie!" I yelled, "Get to him, cut him off, swing wide to port!"

"I can't go any faster!" Charlie shouted back.

"Bullshit!" I yelled over the noise of the engines, "Open 'er up!"

Charlie was holding back. We'd have to move faster to cut the fleeing sampan off before he got too far upriver.

"Man the sides and prepare to open fire on my command!" Lieutenant McBride ordered. He was getting his men into position along the starboard side of the boat. "Cooper, get your M-60 loaded and take out the wheelhouse when we get within range!"

I was becoming excited with the drama, and knew we'd now get to them before the fleeing Vietcong could round the sandbar; that's what they were trying to get around to reach the middle of the river.

"Otis!" I yelled, "Get your fuckin' ass back here and keep your head down!"

"Shit Chief!" Otis yelled back. He was scrambling aft, crouching low, "We ain't gonna ram 'em are we?"

"No!" I grabbed him by the arm and sat him down hard behind me. "Stay down, let the Marines do their job."

Charlie had swung too far to port and now had to make a wide turn to intercept the sampan, but the Vietcong had lost their one chance to escape.

202

"Cooper! Take out the wheelhouse!" McBride ordered the Marine with the M-60.

"Thump…click…thump…click…" the M-60 made a hollow thumping sound as the Marine fired it, launching the grenade. He reloaded and fired again. Before the first one had hit, two more grenades were in the air.

They were direct hits and the wheelhouse exploded in a thousand slivers of wood and glass.

"Open fire!" the order was screamed over the grenade explosions.

The ten Marines opened up with everything they had; it was pure, adrenaline-rush overkill.

The sampan and its occupants literally disintegrated in a hail of large and small caliber bullets.

"Whooee…!" the Marines were yelling as they poured it on. I couldn't help feeling the rush myself; the action affected everyone on the boat.

"I can't believe it!" Otis said, lifting his head up and looking over the side of the LCM. "They killed 'em all! Motherfucker!"

"Cease Fire!" McBride ordered.

"Check! Check! Check!" the Sergeant repeated the Lieutenant's command.

The water was littered with bits of boat, clothing, and mangled bodies; whiffs of smoke were rising from some of the larger pieces.

There was no doubt this was one VC sampan that wasn't going anywhere.

"How many you count?" the Sergeant said to McBride.

"I'll go with an even dozen Sergeant. That'll look good on the body count report," McBride answered. "Outstanding Marines!" he added, as his squad reloaded and checked their weapons.

We could still hear the ongoing battle to our north, rapid small arms fire, with occasional loud booms from incoming close fire support. The artillery at Chu Lai and the offshore ships were still selecting targets.

"Turn her around Charlie," I ordered. "We're far enough upriver to get caught with our pants down if we're not careful. Let's get out!"

Charlie didn't need any urging. He had the boat turned around and this time I didn't need to tell him to pour it on.

By the next day the Vietcong were in full retreat, with only isolated firefights with small groups of enemy guerrillas. The fighting continued for another seven days, but the major actions of the first day had routed the Vietcong, giving the Americans their first victory in a face-to-face confrontation with a large body of enemy troops. The Marines had lost 45 men killed in action and over a hundred wounded.

Close air support, artillery and naval bombardment had played a major role in the coordinated fighting. The Navy had done her part, with almost two thousand rounds fired from offshore. The various units had sunk a total of seven sampans, and fleeing Vietcong troops had been pinned down along the beach and held there until ground forces took care of them.

General Walt commented on the fact that air support had been invaluable. In some cases it had been called in to within 200 feet of American forces that were under heavy attack at the time. The Battle of Chu Lai was over, and we'd all had our first trial by fire in Vietnam.

The *Pocatello* sailed north to Da Nang to disembark our remaining Marine forces. I was still worried about Charlie and decided to talk through whatever problem he had that was bothering him. I'd arranged to meet him in the well deck by the boat hoists. It would be quiet there and we could talk privately.

"Hi Charlie!" I greeted Charlie as he walked up. "You know your behavior has been concerning me, don't ya?"

"I got to get outta here man!" Charlie was rubbing his arms as if he was chilled. "I got a bad feeling and all I want to do is get back to Akima."

"You should have thought of that before you got married," I replied, a little pissed. "If you keep your head up your ass like you did the other day, you'll get someone killed."

"My hitch is up in December," Charlie said, "and I ain't shipping over!"

"Think about that Charlie," his words caught me by surprise. I'd thought Charlie was in for life. "You'll make Chief next year, especially with combat service on your sheet."

"I don't give a fuck about making Chief." Charlie had made up his mind. "Akima's uncle lives in Memphis and he can get me a good job on a tugboat."

"Why don't you think about it?" I tried to reason with him.

"Nothing to think about Jake. I'm not shipping over and that's that!"

"Okay Charlie," I gave up. "How's Akima?"

"She's as upset as I am Jake," he looked directly at me. "You've got to understand, we just want to live a normal life. This fucking mess down here is nothing but shit. Man, you seen those crazy Marines up the river the other day, they were nuts!"

"Maybe you're right," I was troubled by the way I'd felt that day myself. The fascination with watching men being killed; from where within us do these demons come?

"I know you wanted John Wayne out there with you Jake," he said emotionally, "but I realized all I want is to get back to Akima, have a coupla kids and come home to a nice, quite family meal every night."

"I understand Charlie," I said. "Just try and not do anything stupid until your hitch is up."

"I won't," Charlie replied. "And thanks for letting me get this off my chest."

I shook his hand, adding, "Go get some chow; you've got the evening watch tonight."

"I'm glad we talked buddy, I've been worried about how you'd take it. I mean, me wanting out," he crushed my hand in his big mitt. Turning, he added, "By the way, Suzie-girl said to say hi. She's a teacher now, all married up and living in Richmond."

Suzie-girl. I started to think back to the years of good times with Charlie and his family back in Richmond, how they'd made me feel so welcome and at home. Charlie needs that family life. The Navy is for loners like me.

I hoped Charlie would stay healthy and get back to Akima in one piece. Maybe take that job in Memphis, tugboat eh? That sounded like just the ticket for a Boatswain's Mate retiring from the Navy.

Chapter Twenty-Nine

For the next four months the *Pocatello,* and other ships with amphibious capabilities, moved men and material up and down the coast. The ship's boats and helicopters were constantly on the move, like worker bees buzzing around a hive.

The area around Chu Lai still had Vietcong sympathizers in many of the villages and hamlets. Some villages were hotbeds for recruitment and also a refuge for small groups of VC.

The *Pocatello's* LCMs were called upon to assist and check for sampan activity in all the nearby rivers on a regular basis. One day we were ordered to check out the Song Ben Van River to the north of Chu Lai.

"We know that the supplies are coming down river by sampans, and then making their way to the Vietcong groups scattered throughout the area to the East of us," the Marine Major was briefing the team in the operations room. "If we can disrupt this supply line, even for short periods of time, it will give us a better chance to flush some of these VC out. We'll force them to make more frequent visits to the villages to get food," he explained, pointing to various spots on the maps he had displayed on the wall behind him.

"What is the operating procedure for stopping and searching sampans?" a Marine lieutenant asked. It was McBride from the action up river last August, the time we'd destroyed the sampan.

"Have them heave to," the Major said. "Then board and search. If they are carrying any contraband, arrest the occupants and sink the sampan."

"What if the sampan doesn't stop, or shows hostility towards us?" another Marine officer asked.

"Then stand off and open fire," the Major said. "Be sure they are avoiding or ignoring you before you open fire. Of course, if you see any guns on deck or they fire on you first, that's self-explanatory!"

"Any other questions?" the Major asked after a long pause. He was anxious to end the briefing and get on with the mission.

There was some shuffling of chairs and clearing of throats.

"Okay!" he concluded. "We shove off in forty-five minutes; the boat assignments with their squads are marked on the board. We'll pre-load in the LCMs and launch three hundred yards off shore…Good luck!"

The boats were all idling with lines singled up waiting for the Marines to board. I hadn't seen Charlie since the briefing, but the motorman on his boat had checked things out. Young Otis and the fireman were standing by at their stations.

"Chief Rickmeyer," the Boat Commander called me over, "Petty Officer Sparks has reported to sickbay complaining of abdominal pains. They're keeping him in for observation; they're worried about appendicitis."

"Jesus, Lieutenant!" I said, "We're shoving off in ten minutes!"

"Is another boat driver available at short notice?" he asked, looking at his watch.

"Not one that was at the briefing," I replied. "I'll take her out myself. I know the boat and I know how these Marines like to operate."

"Damn!" he looked at me with concern on his face. "I need you here to coordinate boat traffic, but we don't have time to fool with this."

Just then the signal sounded for the Marines to board the LCMs.

"You're right Chief," the Boat Commander said, hitting the railing hard with the palm of his hand. "You take her out!"

I jumped on the afterdeck of the craft, entered the box-like wheelhouse and quickly looked over the control panel; everything was good to go. Otis gave me a thumbs up from the bow, the motorman glanced up, a look of surprise crossing his face when he saw me, then everyone went about the business of launching.

The Boat Commander signaled for the LCMs to go and we moved out in our well-rehearsed, orderly manner.

The brightness of the tropical morning momentarily blinded us as we cleared the stern gate of the ship. God! It felt good to be at the controls of your own boat, breathing the fresh salt air, feeling the vibrations of two 600 horsepower diesel engines under your feet.

The LCM-6 was ideal for poking around these rivers. It had a shallow draft, only 4 feet, and they could cruise for 130 miles at 9 knots without refueling. I'd set course for the shoreline when Otis came aft to speak to me.

"Glad to see you at the controls Chief, but where's Petty Officer Sparks?" he asked, with his usual wide innocent grin.

"Sick," I answered him, my eyes still fixed on the distant river mouth.

"Can't say I'm sorry Chief," Otis continued. "He's been hell to work for lately."

"What do you mean?" I asked, knowing how Charlie had been irritable for months. I knew the junior members of his crew must have been feeling it.

"Everything I do," Otis complained. "Lines ain't coiled right, well-deck ain't washed down good enough. I thought he would start complainin' 'bout the way I wiped my ass next!"

I laughed. Otis could make a great day even greater. "Sparks is not shipping over, so you'll be getting a new boat driver in another couple of weeks," I told him.

"No foolin'?" Otis smiled broadly, "I don't have anything personal against the brother, it's just he's so goddamn cranky!"

"Meantime, go on back to the bow and watch for any movements along the shoreline," I nodded towards the river.

"Say Chief," Otis shouted back as he went forward, "you know what a West Virginian's idea of fore-play is?" He yelled loud enough for the motorman to hear because Petty Officer Bates was from Clarksburg, West Virginia.

"No!" I shouted back the expected reply.

"Shut up Bitch! And get in the truck!" Otis delivered the punchline to the loud laughter of the Marines.

"I'll kick your ass, asshole!" yelled Bates good-naturedly. He liked Otis as much as I did.

I slowed as we entered the river, staying in the middle as much as possible. Shallow sandbars sometimes forced me to get right in close to the banks, but I'd get back out as soon as I could. We cruised for about twenty minutes until we reached the junction of several tributaries flowing into the river.

The two other LCMs each took streams to left and right, while we stayed with the main river. It was starting to get spooky as we went farther north, the banks at times were overhung with forestation and the river had multiple bends and twists.

"What do you think Lieutenant?" I called down to McBride who was commanding our squad of Marines.

"Looks too quiet," McBride said, as he climbed out of the well deck and stood by the wheelhouse. "Listen for any loud monkey cries. I learned they were a sure sign that something was going on."

It was another fifteen minutes before we saw anything, monkeys or no monkeys. A sampan was floating alongside the eastern bank, not doing anything, just sitting there as if it was abandoned.

I slowed and moved farther over towards the opposite bank.

"I don't see anything Chief," McBride called up. "Better take us over, though; we're going to have to check it out."

"Aye, aye Lieutenant," I slowly crept towards the sampan, keeping my hand on the throttle ready to gun the motor if I had to.

"Get ready on the sides," McBride had started to whisper. "Hold your fire until I give the order."

It was the last thing he said. Suddenly shots rang out from the underbrush! McBride was flung back with blood gushing from a throat wound; the Sergeant grabbed him and desperately tried to stop the flow with his bare hands. The other Marines opened up on the unseen snipers in the brush; the mission had turned to chaos in a split second.

I jammed the boat in reverse and started to back off; the craft seemed to take forever to respond.

"Get us the fuck out!" the Sergeant shouted, looking up from the bleeding officer.

A second Marine was hit and fell back into the well deck, then another slumped forward near the bow, losing his helmet and rifle over the side.

I was turning the boat into midstream and starting to crank the throttle wide open. It was all happening at once. Otis jumped up onto the bow ramp, grabbed the Marine dangling over the side, and attempted to pull him back inside. As Otis was pulling the wounded man in, he was flung back suddenly, his head jerking violently.

I had to concentrate on getting the boat out of there, but my face was already contorting with disbelief as the image of Otis being hit affected my focus.

"Bang…ping…" bullets continued to hit the boat as I gunned the LCM downstream. "Shit!" I yelled, as the bullets hit the wheelhouse.

I felt the burning in my arm; a slug had ricocheted off the steel bulkhead and hit me. The pain was hardly noticeable; my heart was pounding like crazy, but I felt the wetness of blood running down to my elbow.

I ran the LCM at full power, getting everything I could out of the engines all the way back to the river junction where we'd split from the other two LCMs. Swerving wide to dodge a sandbar I headed straight on and out to sea.

The radioman had already called in our condition to the ship and medical help would be standing by as soon as we made the *Pocatello*. It was only a short two hours since we'd left that morning, feeling bright and cheerful. Now we were back with dead and wounded men on board, including Otis, the youngest and brightest of our crew.

Lieutenant McBride was going to make it. He had lost a lot of blood, but they had stabilized him. There was no shortage of volunteers of his blood type for all the transfusions needed.

It was decided not to airlift him by helicopter. He was resting and we were on our way to Da Nang. The other wounded Marine had a shattered shoulder, but was not critical. The young Marine who Otis had tried to pull back into the boat was dead; the one other fatality was Otis.

He had been shot neatly through the forehead, as was the dead Marine. This ambush was not a bunch of gooks recruited from the rice paddies. They were well-trained snipers and they knew how to shoot and when to shoot.

My arm had been stitched up; the bullet had torn a wide, deep gash just below the shoulder. Other than the stitches I needed, I was okay.

"A Purple Heart for you Chief," the corpsman bandaging my arm said, not meaning any harm.

"Fuck you!" I erupted. "I get a Purple Heart for a scratch and Otis gets a Purple Heart and he's over there in a body bag! Fuck you!"

"I'm sorry Chief," the corpsman jumped back. "I didn't mean anything."

"I know," I calmed down. "Sorry, I need to get some rest."

"You best stay overnight here," the doctor said, coming over when he'd heard my outburst.

"I'll be all right, Sir," I said softly; "I need to get some fresh air."

"Make sure you come back if you have any further bleeding or any sudden pain," the doctor ordered.

"Yes, Sir," I slipped down from the table where the corpsman had been treating me. "I apologize for my outburst," I said, putting my hand on the young corpsman's shoulder.

"That's okay Chief," he replied, looking at me with sympathy. "I know how you must feel."

Charlie had looked for me in the Chief's mess and had been told I was on the flight deck. I had gone up there to get some air and try to get emotionally squared away. My hands trembled whenever I thought about the morning's events.

"How you doing Jake?" Charlie said, as he joined me on the flight deck.

"Okay I guess," I replied, not looking at him.

"I know what you're thinking; that I was faking it this morning!" he said. "I know it looks like I chickened out of the mission, but that's not true!"

"I believe you Charlie." I looked at him, "You didn't know we'd get bushwhacked." I was shocked by Charlie's appearance. He looked drawn and haggard; his eyes had lost their sparkle and they looked lifeless.

"If I could bring Otis back I would," he rambled on. "You know I would Jake!"

"You had nothing to do with it!" I replied, trying to bring him some solace. "The boat would have been ambushed and Otis killed whether you or I was driving today."

"I can't get it off my mind," Charlie's head was hanging on his chest. "I know you put Otis with me because you wanted me to take care of him. At first I thought you were sticking him on my crew because he was black. Then I figured, nah…not Jake, he's trying to watch out for this kid."

I turned Charlie around, held him by the shoulders and looked him straight in the eye. "If you don't let this go, you'll be no use to Akima, yourself, or that life you've got planned. Let it go!"

"I'll try Jake," he was sobbing quietly, "I'll try man!"

The wounded were taken off to a waiting ambulance as soon as we docked in Da Nang. The bodies of Otis and the Marine were carried down in body bags to another waiting van. They were headed to the morgue for preparation before being returned to the States.

"Damn it Chief," "Smitty" Smith said, tears rolling down his cheeks, "Why'd it have to happen to Otis?"

We were all standing by the railing watching the vehicles leave, Abalite, Harkwood, "Smitty", Billy Rogers, Bates and me. Charlie was standing alone farther down the deck.

"It ain't who you are in this war," Bates said philosophically. "That old "Grim Reaper" ain't particular."

Bates spoke with the soft drawl of the West Virginian; it only reminded me of the joke Otis had told that morning, just before the attack. Otis had imitated that accent of Bates' perfectly.

Chapter Thirty

Christmas 1965 was spent on the *Pocatello,* heading for Subic Bay in the Philippines through choppy, nasty seas. With nearly six months on station, the ship needed a mini-overhaul.

The *Pocatello* was not being rotated back to the States, only given a reprieve for a month in Subic. She was then going back on station off Vietnam.

Charlie was technically a civilian two days before we reached the Philippines, and he would be mustered out at the base and flown home. I hadn't talked to him much, but we'd all tried to enjoy Christmas dinner together.

It was hardly ideal, the plates were sliding all over the place, trays had been dropped on the deck where sailors had slipped over; the turkey was cold, and the coffee was so hot it couldn't be held to your lips. I couldn't even take my customary evening air on the fantail. The sea was so bad spray continually soaked the open decks.

The activity in Subic Bay had picked up considerably since Vietnam started to escalate. Carriers and their escorts arrived and left on a regular timetable. Supply ships were keeping warehouses stocked with everything from fuel oil to suntan oil.

I had been given the use of a jeep while in port under the guise of needing to check warehouses for spare parts. Things could be stocked anywhere on the huge base and it was impossible to get around otherwise.

My arm had been bothering me. It was itchy and needed constant scratching, so when Charlie had to go to the base hospital for his service separation medical, I decided to drive him over and get my arm looked at.

"You'll be home before you know it," I grinned at Charlie as we zipped into the parking lot at the hospital.

"Anything you want me to take back?" he replied. "I'll be in Oakland for a couple of weeks until Akima gets organized, and then we'll leave for Memphis."

"I just got a letter from Barb. Maybe I'll have a reply for you to take back," I said, as we walked through the front doors. Charlie was looking better. He had lost a lot of weight, but now he seemed to be getting back to his old self.

While Charlie was going through the slow process of examinations, tests and paperwork, I went across to the X-ray department.

"I'm Chief Petty Officer Rickmeyer," I told the technician. "You had word from the *Pocatello* to take a look at my arm."

"Yes Chief," the technician said, picking up a file. "Follow me and we'll get you done."

The X-rays showed a small piece of metal still in my arm, perhaps a piece of the slug or a sliver from the steel bulkhead. It could have been stuck to the ricocheting bullet and implanted in the wound.

A doctor came in while I was still putting my shirt back on, and announced he'd dig it out the next morning.

"Then we'll have you back good as new Chief!" he said smugly.

I hated Navy doctors; funny thing was they were the only doctors that'd ever treated me!

Charlie and I went out one evening and had a few beers. He was anxious to be on his way and I felt the experience of the last couple of months had changed both of us. So much so that I thought we needed time to find out where our friendship stood right now.

I had unlimited use of my jeep, so I drove Charlie all the way out to Clark Air Force Base. He was leaving on a big C-130 back to the States.

"Goodbye Jake," he said, swallowing the lump in his throat. "I think you should start thinking about coming with me to Memphis."

"I might do that buddy," I said, with the same lump in my own throat. "Meantime take care of yourself!"

The flight was called and he hurried across the tarmac to the waiting plane. He looked back and waved from the top of the stairs, then disappeared through the aircraft's hatch.

I laid on my bunk after I'd returned from seeing Charlie off, and re-read the letter from Barb. She wanted to know whether I'd thought any more about our talk in Hawaii. She mentioned how excited Akima was that Charlie was coming home and their planned move to Memphis. The usual stuff, her job was doing fine, she'd had another raise, how Oakland was becoming a black community, how radical black groups were making the news headlines all the time. It was ten pages long and I could see Barb sitting at the kitchen table, in her neat little apartment, as she sat there and wrote it.

I'd also had one from Dory. It had caught up with me and was waiting when I returned to the ship. I opened it, and looked forward to reading some more news from home.

The sad news was that poor old Doris had passed away. She had died peacefully in her sleep, Dory had written, and they'd given her a quiet funeral. The good news was that John and the kids were doing great. Dale was almost sixteen and had been on her first date; Roy had turned seventeen and was still determined to join the Navy after his next birthday. I let the letter drop on my chest as I drifted off to sleep.

During one of my frequent jeep trips around the base, and to other military facilities in Manila, I decided to try and put a trace on Gunnery Sergeant Davis Carlson.

I dropped into the personnel section of the Marine Corps offices one day and went looking for the nearest Master Sergeant; I knew how to find things out in a hurry. He was a crusty old bastard, just as I'd expected, but if you wanted to find out anything they were the best source.

"Good morning Master Sergeant," I said, trying to sound pleasant. "I was wondering if you could do me a favor?"

"Mornin' Chief," he replied, giving me the once over. "What kinda favor?" His voice sounded like his throat was lined with sandpaper.

"I'm trying to locate an old friend of mine," I said; "Name of Davis Carlson, Gunnery Sergeant Davis Carlson."

"You know I can't give out that kind of information," the old jarhead croaked, "unless you have official business and have authorization."

"Nothing official Sarge," I tried to be honest and sound casual. "The Gunny is an old friend of mine and I know he was heading to 'Nam. Just thought I might catch up with him when we get back over there."

"Mmm…" The old Sergeant looked me over from head to toe. Old Marine hands were pretty friendly to Navy chiefs; the lower ranks were looked upon as inferior and naval officers were considered lower than squid shit.

"Give me his name and rank," he sat back in his chair. "I'll be able to tell you whether he's in-country or not. Give me an hour or so."

"Thanks Sarge!" I stuck out my hand. "I appreciate it."

He rose and shook my offered hand, nodding his head. I guess I'd met with his approval.

I had a long drive back to Subic, so I thought I'd just kill the hour the Sergeant had asked for by looking at some of the historical sites of Manila.

The city was old, it had modern trappings, but buildings dating back to colonial days were still plentiful. There were some beautiful old Catholic cathedrals dating from Spanish times, as well as the original fort built by the Spaniards at the mouth of the river. I easily filled the hour and then some;

touching the ancient walls of the fort and sensing strange feelings, perhaps the ghosts from centuries past.

Walking back to where I'd parked the jeep, I came across some squatters living in cardboard shelters along the edge of the bay.

I stopped and returned the greetings they had offered so politely. We chatted for a while and then they invited me to share their meal with them.

I was humbled. Here were people who wore clothes that were ripped and torn, lived in cardboard-walled shanties, and they were offering to share what little food they had with me.

"No thank you, I've already eaten," I replied politely. I knew this was a display of good manners in their culture. I was tempted to offer them money, but realized that would have been insulting under the circumstances. They were poor, but still proud; I left them with their dignity.

I returned to the Marine Corps office and went over to the Master Sergeant's desk. He looked up at me and reached for a slip of paper.

"This is all I can do for you," he rasped. "Gunny Carlson is in-country, got there months ago. He's with the Third Marine Division. I don't know what company or even battalion, you can follow that up if you get to Da Nang." He handed me a piece of paper, "Here's the name of a staff sergeant in personnel there. Tell him I sent ya!"

"Thanks for all your help Sarge." I took the paper and tipped my hat with my finger. That was as close to a salute as one enlisted man could give to another.

"You're welcome Chief!" He didn't change his expression, but his voice sounded a little less gruff.

When I got back on board I found the replacements for our boat teams had arrived. There was a Petty Officer named Spence to take over Charlie's boat, and another fresh-faced seaman apprentice to fill Otis' billet. "Ringo" Bertram was his name, Billy Rogers told me, because he looked like a member of some Limey rock group called the Beatles.

I got them squared away and sent their orders through to the Boat Commander's office.

They had arrived aboard just in time. We were scheduled to leave at 0630 the next morning on our way back to Cam Ranh.

Chapter Thirty-One

Vietnam, 'Nam, in-country, by any name it was the same fucked up place.

I had seen the huge numbers of ships, planes, and men at the end of World War II; the mobilization of forces during the Korean War. Now Vietnam was keeping every factory in America busy making something to send over here.

Ships were unloading hundreds of helicopters, armored personnel carriers, tanks, trucks, artillery, crates, sacks, cartons, and men.

In May 1966, North Vietnamese troops crossed the Demilitarized Zone (DMZ) and clashed with Marines of the Third Division near Dong Ha. Once again, the Marines were victorious with the help of air power and the guns of US ships offshore. The Marines finally drove the North Vietnamese back across the DMZ, but only after three weeks of heavy fighting.

Davis Carlson would be somewhere amongst that; I had to find out where he was. We were heading north to what was called I Corps. Most of the Marine forces were based in this area; it was closest to the DMZ.

At Da Nang, I found the staff sergeant in personnel the old jarhead in Manila had told me to look up. The staff sergeant told me the unit Gunny Carlson was with was still in foxholes up at Dong Ha.

"You're welcome to go up and look for him there," he joked.

"I'll check with you again," I said, disgusted with this fruitless chase. There were over 300,000 troops in-country, and another fifty or sixty thousand sailors off-shore I thought. What the fuck was I thinking!

The *Pocatello* became part of the Combined Action Program (CAP). Squads of four or five Marines, plus Navy Corpsmen, began spending time in villages from Chu Lai north to the DMZ.

The boat team's job was to take these squads up the rivers where their assigned villages were, or close enough to where they could walk to them from the river drop off. Or, where the villages were too far inland from the waterways, they went in and out by choppers

The expression, "all alone in Indian country," was first used on these CAP forays.

"The plan is to move with two boats up the Song Tam Ky River. You'll be running parallel with the coast, so it'll be a cakewalk," the Marine Captain coordinating the CAP in this area announced. "We don't expect any trouble; most of the villages the squads are going into have been friendly for some time. You may pass through some spots where small groups of VC are operating, so the word is, watch your asses," he concluded.

This guy thought of himself as someone who was making a difference in this war, and they were the dangerous kind; all Gung Ho, at least with other men's lives.

I was to command the two-boat flotilla, while the individual squads had their own orders. Our job was to drop them off as close to their assignments as possible, then return to the ship.

I knew this area well and had been up the Song Ben Van River before; the Song Tam Ky flowed into the Ben Van. Any of these rivers and estuaries had a hundred ambush sites, and the VC had become expert at picking their spots. They got their intelligence from fishermen, who knew as much about our movements as we did ourselves most of the time.

We had loaded extra water and food rations in case the teams got marooned in bad weather, and we were unable to get back in and get them out on schedule.

The little flotilla entered the Song Ben Van River system and chugged north, veering to the east at the junction of the Song Tam Ky.

The lead boat dropped off its first team, then with waves and thumbs up we continued on north up the river.

I was in the rear boat because I liked to keep everything in front of me, and it also meant I didn't have to constantly look behind me for the other boat. I'd learned that trick on previous forays. It would also give me a better vantage point to direct a rapid withdrawal if we ran into trouble.

Wild hooting suddenly erupted from a heavily overhung bend up ahead, the noise interrupting the quiet sounds of the river.

"Jesus!" I exclaimed, "Monkeys!"

I grabbed the walkie-talkie hanging from my belt. "Harkwood!" I ordered, "Come about! Come about, right now!" Harkwood looked over his shoulder at me for a split second, and then swung the wheel hard to starboard. The LCM slowly turned and started heading back.

"Spence!" I ordered the driver of the boat I was on, "Follow him out!"

"What's up Chief?" Spence yelled, throttling back to start the turn.

The Marine squad was looking at me as if I'd gone crazy. Just then the first mortar was fired.

"Woomp...woomp," the Vietcong started opening up with their mortars the moment they realized we were turning back.

Harkwood gunned his boat as soon as he heard the noise; he was pushing past our boat as the first explosions threw water and spray thirty feet into the air off his stern.

The Marines on board opened fire in the direction of the gunfire and mortar pops coming from a tangled mess of trees.

Spence was turning quickly and Harkwood's boat was well away. One mortar round landed just off our port quarter, and we felt the concussion through the metal sides of the LCM.

"Fuck!" I realized the trap had been sprung, and heard gunfire from farther downstream, from the spot where we'd dropped off the first squad.

"Harkwood!" I called over the walkie-talkie, "Keep going. Take up a position at the junction and cover us as we clear this fuckin' river!"

"Got it!" came back Harkwood.

"Corporal, get your guys on the sides. We're going to pick up the first squad!" I yelled.

"Aye, aye Chief!" the Marine Corporal responded, sliding back the bolt on his M-16 rifle. "Get ready to pour it on if we have to cover our guys!" he ordered the other Marines lining the sides.

The sounds of battle grew louder as we reached the spot where we'd dropped off the CAP team. I ordered Spence to run the boat up on the bank and lower the ramp two-thirds.

The first indication we had that the team was still close by was when two of them came out of the brush, one carrying the other.

The Marines jumped off the ramp and made a perimeter defense around the bow. The Corporal helped the two returning men back aboard.

"Where're the others?" I grabbed one by the arm.

"They're fighting their way back, fifty or so yards behind us," he gasped. He lay down on the deck exhausted. He'd carried the seriously wounded Marine on his shoulders all the way out.

I had my pistol out and was waving it around like a Wild West gunslinger. I told the boat crew to back out and haul ass, just as soon as we had everyone accounted for.

Two more Marines broke from the brush, one dragging a wounded leg. The injured Marine limped aboard and yelled back at the Corporal crouched by the ramp, "They got Jeff and the corpsman pinned down!"

The Corporal on the shore looked unsure of himself. He looked at me hoping for guidance.

"Give me two men and a rifle. I'll go back in for them!" I took charge. "You hold a defensive position here and cover the boat; without it none of us are gettin' out!"

"Spence," I yelled back as I started into the brush, "Don't wait forever; get out if they fire on you."

"Aye Chief!" his voice boomed out in reply.

Everything became suddenly quiet as we penetrated into the bush and got to where the team had been ambushed. We saw the two men hungered down at the base of an old mangrove tree; they looked back in our direction when one of the Marines with me whistled.

The VC knew we were mounting a rescue and were holding their fire, waiting until we came out into the open. They knew we'd break cover to reach the trapped men.

"Jesus," I whispered to the closest Marine to me, "We've got to cause some kind of diversion."

"I'll get around to the flank and throw a couple of grenades behind them," he suggested. "You'll have to make a run for it. I suggest Tony stay here and support you with covering fire when you bring them out!"

"Good idea. You hear that Tony?" I whispered over to the other Marine.

"Yeah," Tony whispered back. He was licking his lips with the tension and kissed the crucifix hanging around his neck.

"Okay," I continued to keep my voice low. "When I hear you toss the grenades, I'll get in and get them out. You can fire off a couple of rounds Tony, but make sure they're well over our heads."

Tony nodded, and snuggled his M-16 tightly into his shoulder.

"Okay!" I spat. "Let's do it!"

I crept forward as far as I could without breaking cover and waited. I could hear Tony breathing heavily behind me.

The other Marine was somewhere to my left. I heard him grunt as he threw the grenade; seconds later came the explosion. I raised myself up into a crouching position and ran forward.

Firing broke out to my left and then came another explosion. I reached the two men at the base of the tree. The corpsman was all bloody and he was holding a dressing down on the chest of the other man. I wasn't sure whether the corpsman had been hit, or it was the wounded Marine's blood.

"Can you move?" I asked the corpsman.

"Yeah," he replied. "But we're gonna have to carry this guy out!"

"Then let's go!" I yelled. "They can't hold 'em off forever!"

Tony had started to fire steadily over our heads and I heard another grenade boom. We picked up the Marine and half dragged, half carried him back towards Tony. From out of nowhere a figure suddenly appeared and stood in front of me staring. His rifle was pointing at me, but he looked to be in shock. I saw blood coming from his ear and realized the grenades had concussed him.

Holding the wounded Marine with one hand, I lifted my rifle up and fired point blank from the hip; the black-glad figure flew backwards like a rag doll.

Tony was suddenly beside us and we were all running back towards the river. As we broke the brush and reached the ramp, the grenade-throwing Marine burst out off to our right. Helping hands threw us bodily on board, and the LCM's engines roared as Spence backed her off.

"Let's go! Let's go!" the Corporal was yelling, as the Marines lining the defensive perimeter fired a burst into the undergrowth and clamored aboard.

"Give me the walkie-talkie," I said breathlessly to Ringo, who'd been standing by the ramp ready to shove off.

"Harkwood, are you there!" my throat was bone-dry.

"Go ahead Chief, I copy," Harkwood's voice came back.

"We're headin' your way...look for us to break south," my orders were broken as I fought for breath. "Follow us out...have you contacted...contacted the ship, over?"

"I have," replied Harkwood, "Birds are on their way. They have the position of your last contact with the VC."

As we broke out of the Song Tam Ky, the distinctive sound of Huey helicopters could be heard. Then we saw them clattering overhead, following the path of the river, so low we could make out the faces of the gunners sitting in the doorways.

That night I searched in the troop accommodations for the Marine who had thrown the grenades to cover me that day. I found him in the middle of a bunch of jarheads, recounting the day's events blow by blow.

The wounded had been airlifted from the *Pocatello* to a hospital ship off Chu Lai within minutes of us getting back, and I'd been busy writing out reports since then.

"Hi Chief," he grinned, as he saw me come in.

"Hi," I replied, "I realized I never even got your name today."

"It's Goldwin, Chief," he said, self-consciously, "PFC Barry Goldwin."

"Good to know ya, and thanks," I said, holding out my hand.

"You're welcome Chief," he replied to the hoorahs of the other young Marines.

While the *Pocatello* was still in the area of Chu Lai, I decided to pay a visit to that hospital ship and see how the wounded men were doing after the ambush. The Boat Commander gave me the okay to use a boat under the pretext of doing a run to check engines.

As we approached the white-hulled ship with the big red crosses on the sides, I noticed her hull number. It was AH-16. I'll be damned, I thought, it's the *USS Repose*!

Funny how my life seemed to go around in circles. Here was the *Repose*. I'd seen her at Ulithi during World War II, then I'd been treated on board her off Korea; now here she was in Chu Lai bringing succor to other young men, in another wasteful war.

Chapter Thirty-Two

After the ambush in the Song Tam Ky, the *Pocatello* settled down making runs from Cam Ranh up to Da Nang and back.

Transferring supplies and replacements for the Marine units now suffering increased casualties every day. In fact the Army, Air Force, and every other branch of the military were taking increased losses.

The week following the attack the Executive Officer, Lieutenant Commander O'Reilly, called me in and announced I had been recommended for a Silver Star. It was for my actions that day on the river.

Apart from the recommendation for me, awards were going to some of the others involved, including a Bronze Star for the Navy corpsman, and Purple Hearts to the wounded. I couldn't help thinking about Bugeye whenever talk of medals came up, and now the face of Otis, with his wide mischievous grin joined the procession.

During one stop in Da Nang we picked up a company of Marines just in from Dong Ha. I asked if anyone knew Gunny Carlson and where his whereabouts might be.

"That son-of-a-bitch!" a black sergeant growled. "I know him, spent a month with him at Dong Ha. He's just a mean, ugly, nigger-baitin' bastard!"

"That sounds like Carlson," I held back a smile. "You know where he is?"

"Yeah," he replied, "Company B. They just got moved down to Chu Lai. What ya want with that cracker anyhow?"

"Just had a message for him," I lied, not wanting to admit that Gunny Carlson was a friend of mine. Not to this Black Marine anyway. I could tell he had a hard-on for Davis and I didn't want his anger re-focused in my direction.

"Chu Lai eh?" I shrugged my shoulders and walked off. Damn! I thought, I was just in fuckin' Chu Lai!

It was nearing the end of the year and the *USS Pocatello* was overdue for rotation back to the US. We had just picked up a battalion of Marines and were transporting them to Okinawa.

We'd take a couple of days to restock, fuel, and transfer some of our personnel. After that the ship would set a course for the good old USA.

"XO wants to see you Chief," the messenger caught up with me relaxing with a coffee.

"Where, in his cabin?" I asked.

"That's right Chief," he replied, hurrying off to take care of other errands.

I finished my coffee, rinsed the mug and placed it back in the rack, grabbed my hat, and headed for "Officer Country".

"Come in," the XO ordered after I knocked. "Good to see you Chief, sit down," he added after I'd snapped-to in front of his desk.

"The Captain will be formally presenting you with your Silver Star when we get to Okinawa," he began. "Captain Sarnoff will read out the citation on the flight deck with all hands present."

"Thank you, Sir." I wasn't expecting this.

"You should be very proud Jake," he continued. "The Navy is proud of you."

"I don't know what to say, Sir." I was moved. "I am proud of this decoration."

"And so you should be," O'Reilly went on. "Chief, the good news is you're scheduled to be rotated home. You've done all that was expected of you, and no one deserves to go home more than you do."

Oh, oh! I thought, I'm being buttered up for something. I hadn't spent over twenty years in the service without knowing a snow job when it came along.

"There's a new force being implemented," he started to cut to the chase, "It's called the Mobile Riverine Force and will involve elements of the Navy working with the Army. The main area of activity will be in the south, around the Mekong Delta in IV Corps."

"The Navy and the Army, Sir?"

"The Marines are massed in I Corps to the north, and that's where they'll stay concentrated. IV Corps, that's the Army's preserve, but they need help in the waterways of the Mekong Delta. It's impossible to move Army units around there without water craft of some kind. There are hundreds of canals, swamps and bogs."

"What would I be doing Commander?" I asked, wondering what the Army would need with me.

"Small boats of all types Jake!" Commander O'Reilly began. "Your specialty LCMs, they'll convert them for all kinds of tasks. You'll be teaching the teams boat handling and river tactics. You're starting to gain a reputation, and the Army thinks they can use the knowledge you've gained in the rivers up north."

"I had planned on getting married, Sir." I wanted to get home, yet the thought of this new river force excited me.

"You won't be alone Chief," he kept up the sales pitch. "It's a large undertaking; there will be lots of people involved. And there's a promotion to Senior Chief Petty Officer in it for you."

"When do you need my decision, Sir?" I asked, already knowing what my answer would be.

"Right away," he gave me the standard Navy reply. "If you volunteer for another tour, you'll be flown to the US from Okinawa, have Christmas at home, enjoy three-weeks of leave, then they'll fly you right back to Saigon."

"With twenty-two years in and retirement on my mind," I was thinking out loud, "That Senior Chief's rank will just about set me up for life."

"Then if that's a yes, congratulations Senior Chief," the Commander was on his feet. "The Navy needs more like you Jake. You're a credit to your country."

"Thank you, Sir," I shook his offered hand.

I'd done it now, might as well enjoy the perks. Christmas with Barb and Dory's family would be nice; Barb would probably skin me alive. I'd said in my last letter that I'd try and get a posting to the Bay area or retire out.

Okinawa was nothing like I remembered it. When we'd escorted the invasion forces back in World War II, it was nothing but blackened landscape, noise, confusion, smells, and the horrors of the Kamikazes.

It now looked like any other beautiful tropical island as we sailed past Kudaka Island and into Nakagusuku Bay.

We had approached the island from the south, through the Philippine Sea, staying well to the east of Taiwan. China was hostile towards the Taiwanese again and making noises demanding one China. They wanted Taiwan returned to the mainland, bringing it under the umbrella of the communists.

The decoration ceremony was scheduled for the next day, and I'd heard the boat crews were planning a surprise celebration afterwards.

It would be good to relax with the men I'd lived with, fought with, cried and laughed with over the last year and a half.

The *USS Pocatello* had been a good billet; I'd remember her for a long time.

The flight deck was lined with sailors in dress blues. The Captain and XO were bedazzled with medals and ribbons, and I was standing ramrod straight in my best uniform, already with the Senior Chief Boatswain's Mate patch festooning my left arm. I was never one to delay in getting my rank and insignias updated.

Captain Sarnoff had never had much to do with me; I suspected it was because of my friendship with Admiral Rooks. He probably thought I was reporting back everything that happened on the ship to the Admiral.

Now here on the open deck, for the entire world to see, I had more medals on my chest than he had, which pissed him off even more.

The Captain read out the citation, giving the details of the action and my part in it. Captain Sarnoff then walked forward to me, pinning the medal on my chest and shook my hand; he then stepped back saluting smartly.

The ceremony was over, and I have to admit I enjoyed the spotlight. Any Navy official occasion was an emotional event for me. I had a hard time not tearing up; a moist eye is acceptable, sobbing uncontrollably is not.

Petty Officer Harkwood called on me in the chief's mess after I'd put my medals away in their boxes. He asked me ashore for a beer, thinking I hadn't heard about the get-together. I played along acting the dumb ass.

He'd arranged a taxi to take us into the city for the evening, so I just sat back and enjoyed the ride.

Lying back, with my head on the headrest, I daydreamed with a jumbled mixture of thoughts taking me back to that day on the *Roe*. The day the gun mount was blown away, then Billy Smith came into my thoughts, then Bug appeared with him, laughing his usual infectious laugh, his bulging eyes popping out. I wished they were here now, heading ashore for a beer with me.

Harkwood had the taxi stop outside a restaurant in Naha as if it was just one he'd picked out on the spur of the moment. The street was full of restaurants.

We went in, sat at the bar and ordered a drink. Suddenly a loud chorus from behind a bamboo divider split the silence.

"Surprise!" the whole crowd were there, Harkwood, Bates, Abalite, Spence, Billy Rogers, "Smitty", "Ringo", Lieutenant Birkdale the boat commander, and his assistant Chief Wieners.

They slapped me on the back and made the customary jokes, wished me well in my new billet in the Riverine Force. Then after a couple of drinks Lieutenant Birkdale and his assistant shoved off, leaving us to do some serious drinking.

"Ringo" finally got drunk enough and stood up to do a Beatles' impression.

He spoke in a phony British accent for the introduction, then "Smitty" and Billy Rogers stood up beside him, and they started playing imaginary guitars while "Ringo" slapped the back of a chair for the drum beat. *"Oh…I get by with a little help from my friends…mmm…gonna try with a little help from my friends…"*

It was late and "Ringo" was slumped in his chair passed out; Harkwood and Abalite were arguing about baseball, neither one making any sense. Spence had his arm around "Smitty" and was advising him on the best way to pass his exam for Petty Officer Third Class; he wasn't making a lick of sense either. And Billy Rogers was his usual melancholy self, telling me in slurring, tearful words how I was the best Chief Boatswain he'd ever worked for, how I was an American hero, on and on. The restaurant owner politely asked us to leave for the fifth or sixth time, so we lifted "Ringo" up, left a generous tip, and took a couple of taxis back to the ship.

The next morning with an aching head, I borrowed a jeep and driver, and went to Camp Lester Navel Hospital for a quick once over before I headed back to San Francisco.

I must have drank ten cups of coffee that morning trying to clear my head. The problem was trying to stop peeing once the cup was full, rather than the usual struggle to start the flow. Damn! The cup overflowed and I frantically tried to redirect the stream into the bowl, at the same time trying to prevent the cup from spilling, all this with shaking hands as a result of my hangover.

Once the medical people had finished with me, I managed to get a phone call in to Barb in Oakland before I left the hospital.

"Hi, where are you?" Barb said excitedly. "Are you here already?"

"No, I'm in Okinawa," I replied. "Good news is I'm flying out of here tomorrow. I'll call you from Alameda when I get in."

"Oh Jake," she sounded so happy. "How are you?…I mean…is everything okay?…what's wrong with the ship?"

"Nothing's wrong," her questions were coming a mile a minute. "I've just been promoted, and part of the deal is getting home for Christmas!"

"I can't wait sweetie," she was on a roll. "I'll call Dory and tell her you're coming…I'll have to get my hair done tomorrow…I'll…"

"Whoa, slow down," I laughed. "I can't talk any longer now, but I'll be there late tomorrow night your time."

"Okay darlin'," she squealed, "I'll wait up for your call…bye now…take care!"

"Bye Barb," I said. I stood for a moment looking at the phone receiver as if Barb had been inside, the guys behind me waiting their turn on the phone started to get impatient; I hung up and left the hospital.

The lumbering transport rolled down the runway at Kadena Air Force Base and lifted into the cloudless, bright blue sky over Okinawa.

It had been a morning of shaking hands, best wishes for Christmas, and promising to look each other up back in the States, the usual ritual of sailors saying goodbye to a shipmate. I was happy to be leaving the ship on her homeward deployment; the guys had completed their tour in-country and deserved to go home. They'd be posted, after some generous home leave, to other ships and bases.

Probably transfers to the Sixth Fleet for the junior hands, maybe to training posts ashore for the senior guys. Their knowledge of handling boats in tight situations in environments like the rivers of Vietnam was invaluable.

Too bad all the guys weren't getting to go home. A lot of kids were dying out there, and it was starting to become confusing as to why they were.

The lights of San Francisco looked like a fantasy world after the dark countryside of Vietnam. The buildings were all lit up with Christmas decorations. It looked spectacular as we made a wide circle over the city, slowly losing altitude on our flight path into Alameda.

Chapter Thirty-Three

I headed for the nearest phone as soon as I got inside the terminal. The trip back had been quiet; the other passengers had been mostly Air Force guys coming home. I'd slept most of the way, never realizing just how tired I was after Vietnam, or how good it felt to be heading home to Barb.

I had to wait in line; there were four guys ahead of me for the booths. My turn came and I had to ask the guy behind me for a dime. I didn't have any American change in my pockets. I'd have to get my head out of my ass; I was only thinking about one thing.

"Hello Barb...yeah I'm here," I told her. "Yeah...a good trip back...everything okee-dokee!"

"I'll be there to pick you up in fifteen minutes," Barb was bubbling. "Where will you be?"

"I'll wait outside the main gate," I said. "That way you won't have to screw around trying to get on base."

"Okay, I'm on my way!" she hung up.

It was a chilly night around the Bay and I hadn't thought to have a heavy coat handy to put on. I was dancing up and down to keep warm; that wind just whipped off the water and went right through to the bone. After all that time in the tropics it was even worse. The guard at the gate noticed my distress; he also saw my ribbons, including the two Purple Hearts.

"Hey Senior Chief!" he called out, "Come on in, we've got a heater goin' in here." I trotted over, my head pulled down into my crunched up shoulders, my hands jammed into my pants' pockets.

"Just get back?" he asked.

"Yeah, came in on an Air Force flight," I replied. The shack was warm and cozy.

"I'm shipping out in two weeks," he continued. "What's it like over there?"

"Bad if you're a grunt and in the bush. What ship you billeted to?" I asked.

"The *USS Hancock*, she's on her way to relieve the carrier on Dixie Station," he said with an air of pride.

Dixie Station was where the carrier next in rotation waited for the relief carrier coming from the States; when relieved, that carrier then moved north to what was called Yankee Station. It was closer to North Vietnam.

The carrier relieved from Yankee Station then rotated back to the States. The operation meant at least two carriers were always available, with two more at sea in transit one way or the other; a tremendous display of seaborne air power.

"You'll be okay," I said. "The carriers operate far enough out there's no threat from shore, and they're too big for attacks from North Vietnamese gunboats. Six months over there letting the jet-jockeys do their stuff and you'll be home again telling war stories."

"I'm looking forward to it," he was only half-convincing. "They say if we make a liberty port like Sydney or Manila, the girls go crazy for American sailors!"

"That's what I hear," I grinned. "But watch out for the Dragon's Tail!"

"What the hell is that?" his eyes widened.

"The worse dose of clap you can imagine," I lied. "They say you can never get rid of it!"

"No kidding?" the kid was hooked.

"Yeah, I knew a couple of Marines got it!" I was having fun with this greenhorn. "They shipped them back in straight-jackets. They was itchin' so bad, it drove them insane!"

"Jesus Christ!" he exclaimed.

Just then Barb drove up. "There's my ride," I told him, "thanks for the hospitality."

"You're welcome Senior Chief," he said, still petrified at the thought of catching the Dragon's Tail.

Barb jumped out of the car and ran towards me, leaping into my arms almost knocking me over. "Oh, Jake, Jake!" she repeated between kisses. "Let's go home and get out of the cold."

"Good idea!" I was shivering uncontrollably.

Barb's apartment was still as neat and tidy as I'd remembered it. I noticed a gift-wrapped box on the living room table as I dropped my heavy bag on the floor.

"That's your Christmas present, don't open it until tomorrow night!" she said, hanging her coat up in the closet.

"I've got something for you too," I smiled. "It's only small, I didn't have a lot of room in my bag."

"Never mind, we'll do some last minute shopping tomorrow." She put her arms around me and led me to the bedroom.

It had been a long time and our passions were running high. We rolled over and over on each other, almost falling off the bed. Barb pushed herself down on me and frantically kissed and thrust her tongue deep inside my mouth. I wanted to get my complete body inside her, wanting to become one with her, unable to get close enough. I felt her softness, her heat, her wetness, her breath, and her life.

"Wake up sleepy head!" Barb touched my ear with her lips. "We've got a lot to do today."

I rolled over and stretched. It felt good to be snuggled up under the warm blankets. "Last night was really something eh?" I said, still pleasantly tired from the night's lovemaking.

"Never mind that," she laughed. "I've already got pancakes on the griddle, so get up!" she said, hitting me over the head with a pillow.

I pulled on a pair of skivvies and walked into the kitchen yawning.

The smells from the breakfast cooking made my stomach start to growl. It was only then I remembered I hadn't eaten since the meal on the plane, and that was 24 hours ago.

Barb and I spent the day shopping for things to take over to Dory's later that night. Christmas Eve at Dory's was becoming a tradition and I was looking forward to seeing her and the kids again.

I hadn't written much to any of them during my time away and was now feeling a little guilty. Dory would want to know all about it and I wasn't yet ready to talk.

We hadn't stopped for lunch, so by the time we got to Dory's the smells of John's cooking were intoxicating. We smelled them as we stood on the front steps waiting impatiently for someone to answer the doorbell.

"Come in, come in," Dory said, her face beaming as she took the bundles and boxes from us at the door.

"Jake, how are you?" John called from the kitchen. "Merry Christmas!"

"Merry Christmas to you too!" I yelled back. Dory placed the presents and foodstuffs we'd brought on the hall table and threw her arms around me.

"Jake, you're looking well," Dory said, planting a sloppy kiss on my cheek. "Come in you two!" she said, hugging Barb and taking her coat.

"Hi Uncle Jake!" Roy appeared, he was over six feet tall and filled out. He'd grown into a man since the last time I saw him.

"Well, I'll be doggoned!" I exclaimed, looking him up and down. "I guess you won't be wanting to crawl around the living room floor playing with cars with me any more." Roy looked embarrassed and glanced down at the floor. I went over and hugged him anyway, "Where's your sister?"

"She'll be along any minute; she's bringing her boyfriend over," Roy said, looking disgusted with the thought of his sister dating.

"I keep telling her not to get serious," Dory added, as she took my hand and led me into the living room. "You know kids nowadays!"

"Jake!" John came out of the kitchen and shook my hand. "I can't leave my sauce, this is my latest creation."

"Barb, honey, how are you?" he added, kissing Barb on the cheek keeping his spoon out of the way of the embrace.

"Oh, for God's sake John, get back in the kitchen!" Dory fussed, placing a drink in my hand.

"Uncle Jake," Roy said, sitting down beside me. "I don't know whether Mom told you, but I've been accepted into the Navy. I'll be leaving for boot camp in six weeks, day after my birthday."

"I gave up trying to talk him out of it," Dory threw up her arms dramatizing her words. "I've got one leaving for the Navy and another wanting to play house at seventeen."

"Well it's probably the right thing to do," I tried to sound positive. "No one wants to wait for the draft. I was talking to a young sailor last night at the base gate; he was about to join an aircraft carrier. Now that's the way to spend this war, hot meals, warm bed, good liberty calls."

"Let's not get Mom started," Roy pleaded.

Just then the front door opened and in came Dale. She was quite the young lady and pretty as a picture. I gave the young boyfriend a critical once over.

Dale was like a daughter to me and I didn't care much for his appearance. He looked sloppy with hair sticking up all over the place; now this guy should go into the Army, they'd straighten him out real quick.

"How's my favorite Uncle?" Dale leaned down and kissed me on the cheek. "This is Willy," she said, introducing her friend, "and Willy, this is my famous Uncle Jake!"

"Dinner is served!" John came out of the kitchen, bowed and made the announcement.

The dinner was excellent as always and I made sure John knew how much I'd enjoyed it. After dinner we all went into the living room for coffee and drinks.

Dale excused herself. She said they'd planned on taking in a movie and Dory seemed okay with that. Funny how whatever Dale did was fine with Dory, but poor Roy couldn't even wipe his nose without her complaining.

"Have you heard about this Black Panther group?" John asked, filling my cup with his special blend, home-ground coffee.

"No, can't say I have," I responded.

"It's a group of black thugs," Dory chimed in.

"They started in Oakland," Barb joined in the conversation. "Last year two Blacks, Huey P. Newton and Bobby Seale started it off. They said Blacks should have their rights no matter what it took to get them, including violence against the "White Man's System" if it came to that!"

"Yeah, they are pretty radical," John added.

"I haven't heard of them," I said, realizing how little I knew of what was going on in the States these days. I remembered how I was surprised when I learnt about the Civil Rights movement in Richmond after I got to know Charlie and Suzie-girl. Now Black groups were talking about violent uprisings in the streets.

The evening ended with hugs, kisses and wishes for a great holiday season. I had brought back little knick-knacks from around Asia for everybody. These included a Kris, which is an Indonesian ceremonial knife, for Roy's collection; colorful silk sarongs for Dory, Dale, and Barb; John got a set of Japanese chef's knives from Okinawa.

The box I'd noticed on the table when I'd first arrived at Barb's contained a cashmere sweater that I'd immediately put on. Dory and John gave me the customary bottle of Johnny Walker scotch whisky.

The next week passed with days spent lounging around the apartment.

I went with Dory one day and visited Doris' grave and took some flowers. Doris had been nice to me, especially in the early days of my traumatic marriage to Barb. I had been saddened when Dory had written me about her death.

The second week went by with Barb and I spending a couple of days at a little motel up the coast. We walked on the beach daily talking about everyday things, and then the conversation finally came around to where I was to be stationed next.

"I know you don't want to hear this Barb," I began, "but I'm going back to Vietnam for another tour."

"What?" Barb stopped in her tracks. "Jake, you said you…"

"I know I said I'd try and get a shore posting," I cut her off. "But this is an important job, something that needs doing."

"Oh no, Jake!" Barb cried, tears filling her eyes. "I had thought this would be it."

"It's a new task force being formed," I tried to explain. "It'll be small craft working the rivers all over the Mekong Delta."

"How many times are you going to risk your life? And for what?" Barb looked away. "Let's go back to Oakland, I'm not enjoying this any more."

It was quiet around the apartment after that; neither of us had much to say. We both came to realize there were only a few days left of my leave, and things started to warm up between us.

"I know you think I'm unreasonable Jake, but I want some kind of normalcy in our lives," she said. We were dressing to go over to Dory's.

"I hear what you're saying, honey," I said, trying to get her to see it my way. "Twelve, eighteen months; I'll be back with almost twenty-five years in, maybe that offer of Charlie's would work then."

Akima had written Barb about the success they were enjoying. Charlie had spent three months as a deckhand on the tugs, then passed his certification exam and was now the skipper of his own tugboat. Akima had mentioned there would be opportunities for me there, too, and Charlie wanted me to come down.

"I'll write and tell Akima to pass on your thoughts to Charlie," Barb said sharply. "Meantime, let's enjoy tonight with Dory and John. You leave day after tomorrow."

The dinner was prime rib, something John did to perfection. After the meal we were drinking John's home-ground coffee and sipping on French cognac. John's culinary pursuits now included everything French. He talked about how the greatest chefs in the world were French, even the one at the White House.

"Anyway, Jake, you may be better off down there," John changed the subject, "the way things are going here. Malcolm X was assassinated two years ago and we're still having trouble with the Black Muslims, and now the Black Panthers here in California."

"How can you say Jake would be better off?" Dory asked, coming in from the kitchen. "There's a war on down there. How do you think it makes Barb feel?"

"All I meant was we'll probably have a war in the streets here soon," John backpedaled. "A war in the streets of America; a racial war!"

"That will happen only if people keep listening to that kind of radical race talk," Barb joined in. "This war in Vietnam is dividing the country. People have different ideas about it, and it's time the government started to listen to the people."

I started to feel left out; what was happening here was not the country I remembered growing up in.

Spending all that time away made you lose touch, and even when I came home I was insulated by the military's umbrella. As much as I hated to think about it, I was looking forward to getting back down to 'Nam.

234

"Jake," Dory began, "if Roy does get down there, will you look out for him?"

"I'll do what I can Dory," I tried to sound convincing. "Let's just see where he gets billeted. He may finish up painting buoys in the Caribbean or someplace."

The evening ended on a happy note, Dale came home and entertained us with the retelling of the movie she'd just seen. Barb and I left with sex on our minds; somehow we both sensed the need we both were feeling.

"Oh darlin'," Barb whispered, as we lay locked together. Our lovemaking had been gentle, without the usual desperate need to satisfy each other. "Will you propose to me...please!"

"I can't honey," I replied, my voice low and raspy. "Not until I come back. I've seen too many guys get married just before they leave. It's bad luck."

"You think so?" she burbled in my ear.

"Something like that," I rolled over on my back and began to lift Barb's hips rhythmically up and down.

San Francisco International Airport was hectic. It was a main hub for incoming commercial flights across the Pacific, plus now there were numerous military charter flights using the airport.

Barb and I had gotten there well before departure time, and now we sat quietly not saying much. Her head was snuggled into my shoulder.

Barb wept softly when my flight was called, her head buried in my chest.

"Jake," she looked up at me, "Promise me you'll be extra careful. I can't imagine life without you. I couldn't bare to lose you."

"I'll be okay sweetie," I said, trying to reassure her. "I've been around a long time. I know where all the light switches are in this man's Navy."

"Time to get on board," the stewardess touched my arm.

"Goodbye honey," I kissed Barb and hugged her tightly.

"Goodbye Jake," Barb sobbed, as I gently pushed her from me and started down the ramp.

The Boeing 707 bounced around as we climbed above the cloud cover over San Francisco Bay. There was a storm coming down from Canada and it was already dumping snow on Seattle and Portland. Our flight was headed directly for Saigon, with one refueling stop on Guam. The rough ride would last for some time the pilot had warned us; lunch would be served just as soon as we'd left the weather behind and were well on our way.

Chapter Thirty-Four

Task Force 117, Mobile Riverine Force (MRF) had been formed as a self-contained amphibious assault group. It would be fully supported with its own repair, supply, and command ships, the only difference would be it would match up the Navy with the Army, instead of the traditional combination of the Navy and Marine Corps.

Combined Army and Navy operations were nothing new; they had worked well in previous wars when the Army needed to be transported across vast oceans. Combined operations had been successful in the Normandy invasion on D-Day as well as in the retaking of the Philippines. Both undertakings involved close cooperation between the services.

My Army "opposite" met me in Saigon when I landed, and after the usual processing, took me to a bar in the nightclub section of town.

He was Master Sergeant Bubba Slats, United States Army. Bubba was from Brooklyn, and he looked and sounded like he'd been a hit man for the mob in civilian life. It turned out he'd been in the Army since he flunked out of his final year in high school.

Bubba also had an "opposite"; he was Master Sergeant Nguyen Tran Vin, Army of the Republic of South Vietnam. He looked the opposite in every way to Bubba. Master Sergeant Nguyen was slight and studious looking, even effeminate I thought. They both sat down at the bar and ordered the coldest beers in the house; it was obvious they were regulars here.

I'd been around bars frequented by military personnel all my life, and one thing you learned quickly was how to brush off the flurry of hookers and bargirls that greeted every new customer, avoiding the scam of loading up your bar bill with iced tea charged as imported whisky.

Nobody bothered the two sergeants, though. They were served promptly with a bow from the bartender, and several other Vietnamese characters at a corner table nodded a greeting at them. Never once did any of the dozens of girls even give us more than a momentary glance. It seemed strange to me, but I thought no more about it. I'd just arrived in-country and life in Saigon was probably a lot different than other places I'd been to.

"I figured you'd want to get your gear stowed, and your sea legs before we started to really show you around," Bubba laughed, his deep smoker's rasp carrying all over the bar.

"Thanks, I appreciate you taking the time for a cold beer," I lifted my bottle in salute.

"Tran's idea," Bubba said, swallowing half his bottle. "We've arranged a chopper to fly us down to Vung Tau."

"I thought it would be better to show you we are just regular guys," Tran said, in impeccable English. "Bubba and I have been working together for the last six months."

"Yeah," chimed in Bubba, "Tran and me know how to get things done, right Tran?" Bubba had turned towards Tran, who nodded his agreement.

"We better be going," Tran said, standing up from his stool. "We'll need the daylight to show you what the Rung Sat Special Zone looks like."

"I'm ready," I said, finishing my beer. I'd already made up my mind about this pair and knew I wasn't going to like them; there was just something not right.

The heliport where our ride was waiting was crowded with choppers of all types, most belonging to the Army of the Republic of South Vietnam (ARVN). Security didn't look too tight to me, but then I was used to working with the Marine Corps. They did everything by the book.

With the amount of bomb terrorizing that had been going on in Saigon, I expected things to be tighter than a gnat's ass.

We climbed aboard, Bubba put on a set of headphones and signaled me to do the same, and as soon as we were strapped into our seats the pilot started up the rotors.

"Can you hear me all right Rickmeyer?" Bubba asked, through his headset.

After a slight volume adjustment, I replied that everything was ten-four.

"Okay, Sir," Bubba spoke to the pilot. "Take us over Cat Lai, then down the Long Tan Channel into Vung Tau. You can fly as low as you think is safe."

"Roger Sarge, we'll stay nice and low," the pilot answered in that calm monotone that pilots always have. "We'll stay around eight-hundred feet. I may have to maneuver sharply if we take fire, so keep fastened in your seats gentlemen!"

The chopper lifted off straight up about a hundred feet, and then banked sharply left and clattered off towards the southeast.

"Look down there," Bubba said, pointing to a complex not far from the city. "That's Cat Lai, that's where most of the ammunition coming in by ship is off-loaded. The ships are too large to get any farther upriver, so they discharge their ammo onto barges; then it's moved to the ammo dumps at Long Binh or up to the storage bunkers at Bien Hoa."

As the helicopter flew farther down the river and canal systems, I began to realize how much of a nightmare this could be for the Army.

We followed the Long Tan Channel into the Rung Sat and it was obvious a modern army, no matter how well equipment, could never mount a massive offensive in there. Vietcong guerrillas could use the muddy, swampy maze for launching raids against installations, then pull back to the Rung Sat with safety, no pursuit could follow them in there.

The chopper left behind the mango swamps and channels and flew over a wide expanse of blue water, tainted brown here and there with the silt washing downriver.

Vung Tau appeared below us. It was a town built around brush-covered hills, the concrete piers on the bay had ships moored alongside, and there were dozens of other ships anchored out.

"There, you see that?" Bubba pointed out an LST docked at the pier. "That's the *USS Whitefield County*. She's one of the MRF's ships. We also have the *USS Askari*; she's another converted LST we use for a repair ship."

I looked down on the ships and other craft anchored, docked or moving in and out. It was a new experience for me. I was used to seeing ships at sea level; from up here it gave you a completely different perspective on everything.

"Where will I be billeted?" I asked Bubba.

"On a barrack ship," he replied. "Self-Propelled Barracks Ships like the *USS Benewah*; they have everything you need on them. Accommodation is air-conditioned, good food, medical and dental care. They house several hundred men with all the amenities."

The miniature world below grew larger as we lost altitude and hovered above the landing platform on the deck of an LST.

The helicopter dropped gently to the platform, and reality returned as I felt the familiar comfort of a steel deck beneath my feet.

The floating barrack ship was adequate; I had a small cabin to myself and shared an office with Bubba and Tran.

The morning after I got on board, the man who would be my boss called me in for our initial meeting. He was Commander Eric Bolton, a midwesterner I thought, who sounded and looked fairly straight.

"Sit down Senior Chief," Commander Bolton said. He seemed friendly enough. "You'll be working with Master Sergeants Nguyen and Slats. The three of you will be primarily responsible for procuring. By that I mean anything and everything we need that we don't already have, or can get from our own military sources, local suppliers in other words."

"Commander," I was surprised by his description of the job I'd be doing. "I was told I'd be needed on the boats, instructing and helping get crews up to speed on boat handling and tactics."

"That may have been so Senior Chief," his tone changed, "but now you're here, and I need your knowledge of boats in the procurement section. This task force will have a number of river assault squadrons; they'll be using converted LCM-6s mostly. You know, these are the most suitable for river transportation. We've found out though they are too vulnerable in their standard configurations."

"What do you mean, Sir?" I asked.

"They are too open," he replied. "Even with their steel construction they can still be damaged by small arms fire from the river banks. We've come up with a number of different versions. All will be covered with extra steel plating to some degree and, of course, they'll be heavily armed. Some we want to cover completely, like miniature versions of Civil War monitors; they'll be used for close in fire support."

"What about the crews, Sir?" I still persisted. I didn't want to be stuck in some procurement job. That wasn't what I came down here for. "Are they ready to navigate these rivers? It looked pretty messy in there from what I saw from the air."

"Don't worry about the crews Rickmeyer," the Commander said, getting on edge. "You start working with Slats and Nguyen as of five minutes ago." He calmed down and added, "Master Sergeant Slats is one of those unique individuals who can find things no one else can, and Nguyen's family is well-connected in the government here. He also knows his way around the Saigon business community."

"Who will I be reporting to, Sir?" I asked, not liking the setup at all.

"Master Sergeant Slats will report to me and receive his orders directly," he leaned back in his chair. "You'll take your lead from him. There will be no need for you and I to see much of each other."

"Will that be all, Sir?" I asked.

"Yes, carry on," he said, making no move to reach out his hand. He just tapped the pencil he was holding on his front teeth.

I stood up, came to attention briefly, and then left his office suppressing the anger I was feeling at his rudeness.

For the first few weeks I might as well have been goofing off in the bars of Vung Tau. Finally one day Bubba and Tran invited me to go to Saigon with them. "We need to arrange for the purchase of some steel platting that the Navy doesn't have on hand, you know what we need to cover those pilot houses on the LCMs Jake."

"Just need your expertise on boat dimensions really," Tran added.

That slope-headed bastard was starting to give me the creeps, both he and Bubba. What was all this bullshit about me knowing the dimensions?

The three of us were leaving by helicopter that afternoon; it would at least give me a break from sitting around the office. All I did all day was answer requests for this fuckin' thing, or that fuckin' thing, or where could I get my hands on those fuckin' things!

The Rung Sat looked as forbidding to me this trip as it did on the first day as we flew up the channel heading for Saigon. I thought I would try to get out on a mission with one of the River Assault Squadrons; I needed to get close to the action down there.

The reports I'd heard from sailors coming and going on the barrack ship was that they were having successes and losses, the usual mixture of ups and downs for a new operation. Fighting the Vietcong in the waterways was like trying to sweep up sand in the desert; as fast as you swept it up, it blew back in again.

The chopper hit the tarmac in Saigon and the humidity hit us. At around a thousand feet the air had been cool, now your clothes just clung to you with perspiration. There was a car and driver waiting, not military, but a nice late model air-conditioned sedan. I guess dealing with local merchants had its perks.

"I think we'll let Tran do the talking Jake," Bubba said, as he squeezed his bulk into the back seat. "Let's you and me go get us a beer."

"I thought you wanted me to give you the dimensions for an LCM-6 pilothouse?" I asked, feeling uneasy.

"Yeah, we do," Bubba answered, "let Tran set it up first."

Tran meantime had spoken rapidly to the driver in Vietnamese and the next minute we were dodging our way through the streets of Saigon. Bicycles, motorbikes, cars honking horns, people hawking everything from cigarettes to sex shows, kids trying to steal the watch right off your wrist.

The car pulled up outside a flashy hotel. "This is the Hotel Caravelle Jake," Bubba informed me, "This is where all the foreign correspondents like to hang out. It has the coldest beer in Saigon too."

I got out of the car when the doorman opened the rear door for me. Bubba made no attempt to follow, but leaned over and said something to Tran that I couldn't hear.

"Tran will be back and join us in about an hour," Bubba said, when he finally got out of the car. "Let's get in out of this fucking heat!"

The Hotel Caravelle still looked like it must have done in French Colonial times, spacious, cool and elegant. The bar was crowded with people, most of them speaking English with a variety of accents. One tall guy with an Australian accent grabbed Bubba and dragged him into the space he'd just made for him at the bar.

"Bubba!" he said, slapping Bubba on the back. "How are ya mate?"

"I'm good Bluey," Bubba replied, obviously enjoying the recognition.

"I'm Bluey Warrington," the Aussie introduced himself to me. "I'm with the bloody Sydney Daily, bloody rag of a paper but beggars can't be choosers!"

"Jake…Jake Rickmeyer," I answered.

"Jake's just joined us," Bubba piped up. "He's been in-country before, up around Da Nang. He's a decorated war hero."

"Is that right mate?" Bluey grinned. "Better have a beer on me then cobber." I wasn't too happy with Bubba's swapping war stories on my account; still the beer was cold, it was damn cold!

The afternoon was gone before Tran finally showed up. Bubba had switched to whisky an hour ago, and he and Bluey were well on their way to becoming legless. It was obvious Tran was not happy with Bubba's condition and he looked pissed!

"We can't settle the purchase today Bubba," Tran said, trying to get the big man's attention. "We'll meet again in the morning. It is too late to fly back now. I'll inform the CO and tell the pilot to stand down."

"Hey, that's great Tran," Bubba grabbed the little Vietnamese around the shoulders. "Where're you putting us up?"

"Here is probably the best," Tran replied, turning to the Vietnamese behind the bar and speaking to him rapidly. Tran's orders seemed to carry weight because the bartender disappeared in a hurry towards the lobby.

"Tran has connections everywhere," Bubba said, turning his attention back to Bluey and me. "Hey! What do ya think Jake ol' buddy, ready for a real night on the town?"

"We'll have to stay the night Jake," Tran looked at me, happy at least to see I wasn't in the same condition as Bubba. "The houseboy will be along shortly with your room key. Anything you need he will obtain for you. I have to go back out on business; I'll see you in the morning," turning with a last disgusted look at Bubba he stormed out of the hotel.

What the hell was going on here? This didn't make a lot of sense to me; two guys going and coming as they pleased, staying in hotels in Saigon whenever they felt like it, a helicopter at their disposal. And what the hell was a man of Tran's obvious connections and education doing as a master sergeant in the army?

It all suddenly became clear in my mind, the Black Market! These fuckers must be in it up to their necks and I'm caught in the fucking middle!

But what did they want from me? Were they showing me the good life here in Saigon before asking me into the ring? Five will get you twenty I thought, they'd send a girl to my room tonight, the ol' honey trap never failed.

"Come on over Ding!" Bluey was now as loud as Bubba. He waved over a heavyset guy dressed in slacks and sport shirt. "Ding, this is Jake, and of course you already know Bubba?" he added, spilling his drink all over the floor.

"Oh shit, you fucker!" Bubba jumped out of the way of the splashing drink. Then laughing he ordered another round, including a beer for Ding.

"So Jake," Ding said, sitting down beside me. He was sober and didn't look the type to be amused by the antics of our two drunken friends. "How long you been in-country?"

"This is my second go-round, and I can't say I'm enjoying it!" I answered, deciding to unload my troubles on this guy. "That your real name, Ding?"

He laughed and said, "No, that's just the name I go by; my name's Carlo Campssini." His eyes, although warm and friendly, seemed to penetrate right through me.

"What's the problem, not enough action for you?" he continued. "Maybe procuring doesn't have the opportunities you'd expected?"

"Depends what you mean by opportunities," I answered. "I wanted to be involved in the boat interdiction patrols in the Rung Sat; instead, I'm sitting at a desk with my finger up my ass!"

"Well, I can tell you, there are a lot of guys who'd switch places with you in a heartbeat," he said, ordering another round. Bubba and Bluey had moved farther down the bar and were all over some French female news correspondent. "Sitting here drinking beer, probably going to have a nice big dinner, hotel suite, things must be really good," he continued.

"What is it exactly that you do, Ding?" I felt he was probing. "Are you military?"

"Let's just say I work for the government and leave it at that," he said, smiling. He looked around to check where Bubba was. "Jake, let me ask you something, have you been on any buying trips with Bubba and Tran?"

I didn't like where this conversation was going but felt compelled to open up. "No, they keep me answering the phones back at base. This is the first time I've been out since I got here, and then it turns out they didn't need me; just bullshit and a waste of my fuckin' time!"

"Look Jake, I know about you, at least what's in your records," he said, leaning closer. "Everyone is checked out before coming into these procurement positions."

"What's so special about this job?" I asked, uneasy that this guy knew more about me than I knew about him.

"I'll take a chance on you Jake," he looked deadly serious. "Only because I think you're the all-American boy and may inadvertently do something to fuck up my job here."

"What are you talking about for Christ's sake?" I said, moving my head back from Ding's.

Ding glanced again at Bubba, "I don't want to go into it here. Meet me outside in fifteen minutes; say you're going out for some fresh air."

"Okay," I said, my mouth dry. "Fifteen minutes, where outside?"

"Just turn right when you leave the entrance and walk along the sidewalk," Ding said. Then he got up, went over and put his arms around Bubba and Bluey's shoulders, said something they all laughed at, and then walked out.

I waited fifteen minutes and then told Bubba I was going out for some fresh air.

"Okay ol' buddy, don't get lost now!" Bubba hooted. Bluey was incoherent by this time and Bubba was slobbering all over the rather plain-looking, almost ugly French woman.

The evening air was heavy and for a second I had to take extra deep breaths to get enough oxygen. I looked around, then started walking as Ding had instructed. After I'd walked fifty yards or so, and waved off a half dozen taxis honking their horns at me, Ding suddenly came out of nowhere and was beside me.

"What's this all about?" I was getting nervous and didn't even know why I'd come outside. Maybe curiosity had got the better of me.

"I don't want you getting mixed up in this, Jake," he began. "You've been around, you know about people in positions where large amounts of money can be made at the military's expense. The Black Market here in Vietnam involves American personnel, as well as ARVN and Vietnamese government officials."

"Why are you telling me all this?" I asked. "I might be in on it!"

"You're not," he laughed, "otherwise I wouldn't be talking to you. What I'm afraid of, though, is that you'll see what's going on and start trying to bring it to someone's attention. That could be bad. You see, we're closing the net on these guys and to put it plainly, we don't want some Boy Scout like you fucking it up!"

I didn't know what to say. Was I happy that Ding thought I was a straight-up guy and had taken me into his confidence, or pissed he thought I was such a wimp I'd never have the guts to be in on something like this!

"So…" I asked, "what am I supposed to do here?"

"Nothing," he answered, occasionally glancing back over his shoulder. "They'll wait another month or so before they try to bring you in. This trip was just to let you know what it's like having the booze and the women. They don't take too many chances, so just carry on as if you know nothing. Trust me Jake, I've got enough to hang them, but there are a couple of worms still in the can. I can't tell you any more than I have."

"That's more than I want to know," I said, starting to look over my shoulder as well now. "I'm just a sailor, I don't even want to be here in this Saigon shithole, I'd just as soon get my ass back to the regular fleet."

"Just don't look under any rocks, or more important, don't be perceived as looking under any rocks," Ding said. "Of course this talk of ours never took place."

"Who exactly do you work for, military intelligence? Oh no, not the CIA!" I exclaimed, and it suddenly hit me Ding was a spook.

"Jake," Ding said, stopping and turning me towards him. "Don't ever ask me again what I do. It's always sensitive and always highly classified. We'll see each other from time to time. Let's just be friends, okay?"

"Fine by me," I shrugged my shoulders. "Just carry on as if nothing's happened, I think I can do that!"

"Good," he smiled again, "I've got to get going. Goodnight Senior Chief Rickmeyer."

I nodded my head and shook his hand.

Walking back to the hotel my mind was racing with all this cloak and dagger bullshit. Whoa boy! I finally decided, just forget everything like Ding asked you to do.

I felt a little cocky about being right when I'd come to the conclusion that Tran and Bubba were dirty, without Ding having to tell me.

The bar at the Caravelle was even noisier when I returned. I had made up my mind to have a nightcap with Bubba, and then maybe get something to eat.

"Hey Jake," Bubba shouted loud enough for the whole bar to hear. "Come over buddy and talk some fuckin' parley voo!" he laughed, as he spat bits of shrimp cocktail all over the poor French woman.

What a pig I thought, I'll be glad to see him doing twenty years in Leavenworth prison. Bluey had disappeared and I decided to eat something at the bar, have a drink or two, then call it a night.

"Here's your key," Bubba said, handing me a room key. "The houseboy brought 'em while you were gone," he slobbered. "Where the fuck were you anyway?"

"Just needed some fresh air; I was feeling those drinks," I lied. "What are you eatin'?" I said to change the subject.

"Shrimp cocktail, and this little cocktail is Marieeeee," he held the e sound. I felt sorry for the woman; up close she was just plain butt ugly!

I ate a steak at the bar, putting up with Bubba's constant interruptions and then headed for my room, having had all I could take for one night.

Just as I'd figured and Ding had reaffirmed when he spoke to me, there was a knock on the door five minutes after I got in.

"You like nice lady?" a high-pitched voice asked.

"Go away! I shouted.

The phone woke me the next morning. It was my wake-up call the front desk politely informed me, I hadn't made any request but I figured someone else must have organized it. As soon as I had showered and used the razor and toothbrush that had been provided by the hotel, I went down to find the dining room.

"Good morning Jake." Tran was there already, looking neat and refreshed. "Did you have a good night?"

"I did, yeah thanks," I answered. "That omelet looks good."

"It is delicious, I'll order one for you." He waved the waiter over, "Coffee?"

"Yes, that I need," I said, trying to size Tran up. I now knew for certain that he and Bubba were working shady deals and God only knew who else might be involved with them. My omelet had just arrived and I was digging in when Bubba appeared. He was hung over and looked like he'd slept in his clothes. My opinion of him as a pig was reinforced looking at him this morning. I could tell Tran felt the same way; he wasn't happy at all. When Bubba arrived at our table, Tran really dressed him down.

"We had lots of work to do today, but it's obvious you are in no shape to do business," Tran said stiffly. "I cancelled our meeting and ordered a helicopter to get us back to Vung Tau."

"Fuck you Tran!" Bubba grumbled, sitting down and calling rudely for coffee.

"I'll meet you in the car. We have twenty minutes to make the heliport." Tran left the remainder of his breakfast and stormed out.

It was great watching the behavior of these two, now that I didn't have to figure out what made them tick any more. Why would Tran get mixed up with someone like Bubba? The obvious answer was Bubba was a greedy corrupt pig, I guess. I could see Tran had nothing but contempt for him, only tolerating him because that was the cost of doing business with the United States Army.

Nothing was said as we made our way back to the chopper field. We lifted off; swooping over the buildings at the edge of the city limits and then on back to the LST moored at Vung Tau.

I decided to do as little as possible in the office, spending a lot of time on deck talking to guys about the action up the rivers. The Brown Water Navy, as it was now called, was like an army of ants running everywhere, doing their business, and then zipping back to the nest at night.

The converted LSTs had large booms stretched out from their sides; these booms had boats of all shapes and sizes secured to them. The boat crews were fed, showered, re-supplied and then off they went back up the rivers on the next mission. I liked to hitch rides on the picket boats that patrolled the harbor around Vung Tau. The crews were a great bunch of guys, and they enjoyed chewing the fat with an old salt like me. They even let me take the controls for some slick maneuvers at times.

I'd had a couple of letters from Barb waiting when I came in one afternoon off one of these runs. I took the mail and lay down in my cabin to catch up on the news.

Barb said she missed me and told me what she was going to do to me when I got back. Dale had broken up with her boyfriend and would be going to college in the fall. Roy had gone off to Boot Camp and would be getting his first ship soon. He was planning on being a seaman, just like his dad.

I put the letter down and let myself drift back to San Francisco. It was a chilly evening and me, Barb, Dory and John were sitting around sipping whisky sours.

"Bang…bang…bang!" Barb was banging her head on the table. Wait, no! I came out of my stupor; it was someone knocking on my door.

"What is it?" I called.

"Commander wants to see you Senior Chief!" I recognized the voice of the Commander's yeomen.

"Okay, I'll be right up!" I replied. I was expecting this sooner or later. I'd made up my mind to be as useless as I could because one, it would keep me out of the net closing in on Bubba and Tran; and two, maybe get me transferred out of here.

Over the last six weeks I'd spent as little time as possible with either of them. Bubba had complained at first over my lack of enthusiasm, and then they must have decided if I was that lazy on the job, then they'd be better off without me.

"Enter!" Commander Bolton ordered, as I knocked on his office door.

I entered and stood for a full minute before he stopped reading the papers on his desk and looked up at me. The bastard aggravated me no end, but I bit my tongue. He was still a senior officer and my boss.

"I'll be up front with you Rickmeyer," he said, starting my dress-down. "Your efforts since arriving here have been less than desirable. In short, you're useless to me!" I was expecting this, I was glad my sloppiness had made that much of an impression on him.

"I'm sorry I haven't been of service, Sir," I answered, about to give him a lame excuse for my behavior.

"I don't need assholes around here not giving me one hundred percent," he cut me off. "I'm trying to give you the benefit of the doubt Rickmeyer; your records are exemplary. Maybe procuring is just not your cup of tea, is that it?"

"With all due respect, Sir," I said, my jaw set. "I made that clear when I first reported aboard. If I can get on the boats..."

He cut me off again. "You're not going on the boats Rickmeyer, is that clear?"

"Yes, Sir!" I answered, my fists balling at my sides.

"You're here and you'll do your job," he said with determination. "I want you in that office, working your butt off to purchase the materials this outfit needs to win this war! Is that perfectly clear?" he said with finality.

"Perfectly clear, Sir!" I replied.

"Carry on Rickmeyer," he went back to his paperwork. "And one more thing, no more joyrides on those harbor picket boats!" he added without looking up.

"Aye, aye Commander!" I left with a taste in my mouth that needed to be spat out.

I noticed a change over the next few weeks. I was at the office each day, doing just enough to avoid court martial, but I hadn't seen Tran for days and

Bubba seemed to be depressed. He came in each day acting like a bear, shouting and yelling at the junior yeomen and procurement clerks.

Around eleven-thirty one morning, just before we broke for chow, two burly military policemen marched into the office. They stood Bubba up and handcuffed him, then spread-eagled him across his desk and patted him down. The MPs then half dragged, half-pulled Bubba out through the door and headed topside.

I followed to watch the fun. Here was that big, loud-mouthed pig suddenly deflated. His appearance had changed from Bubba the Bull, to a whimpering, slouching, broken man.

He'd been in the Army long enough to know what Leavenworth had in store for him. Murderers and rapists were treated better than black marketeers in military prisons; they were like a thief on the messdeck, everybody hated them.

I exited the hatch in time to see Bubba break free from the MP holding him; the other policeman had just climbed into the waiting launch below.

Bubba ran towards the stern, and in one motion, stepped up on a bollard and dived headfirst over the railing. It happened so fast no one even moved until he'd gone over.

I ran to the railing with the MP and searched down in the water for any sign of him. Someone was shouting at the launch alongside to cast off, and they were yelling back, not understanding what was happening. It was no good searching anyway. The tide was going out and Bubba's body, if they found it, would be miles away in an hour or two.

"Fuck!" was all the MP standing beside me said.

Around the deck area where Bubba had gone over that morning, and below in his cabin, a small army of military policemen and intelligence types were at work. They were taking statements and collecting all of Bubba's papers, files, correspondence, and all of his personal effects.

I jumped as a hand squeezed my shoulder, "Hi Jake," Ding said.

"Don't creep up on people like that Ding!" I complained. "Or is that the way you always greet people?"

"No, my friend," Ding laughed. "Take a walk along the deck with me, will you Jake." The activity at the stern was still in full swing, so Ding and I walked forward towards the bow.

"It's all over for Bubba," I said. "What did you do with Tran?"

"He slipped away, I'm sorry to say," Ding sounded disappointed. "That's the way it is sometimes. Tran has connections, he must have been tipped off and left his buddy Bubba to take the fall."

"What about the other "worms" as you called them?" I asked.

"We got some," he said, shrugging his shoulders. "Trying to get Vietnamese Government officials with their hands in the till is like trying to catch a falling knife; you have to be very, very careful."

"What's up for you now?" I asked.

"I'll be moving up north. There's always something for me to do," Ding stopped, looking over the bow into the water. "Jake, I may be looking you up in the future. I know about your experiences in the rivers south of the DMZ and may need your help from time to time."

"Doing what?" I looked down at the water, both of us within our thoughts.

"Remember, I told you Jake," he said, turning towards me, "never ask me what the mission is!"

After the hullabaloo over Bubba's suicide, things settled back down to their normal chaotic pace. It was June 1st and I'd just opened a letter from Dory dated May 15th, not bad for delivery time.

She was a little shook up. Roy had been assigned to the *USS Forrestal CVA-59* and she was worried about him. The *Forrestal* was heading for Vietnam and due to leave Norfolk, Virginia on June 6, 1967. The *Forrestal* was a super carrier. There would be no place safer for Roy to be than on this floating behemoth, I thought.

That is what I told her in my reply to her letter and added that, although this would be the first combat mission for the giant carrier, it would be manned with experienced officers, and the crew would be confident well trained and disciplined sailors. So Roy was on his first ship. I'd keep tabs on the *Forrestal*'s whereabouts; maybe I could find an excuse to visit her.

"Commander wants you Jake," one of the office clerks told me as I returned from mailing the letter to Dory.

What now, I thought; this son-of-a-bitch is a pain in the ass!

"Rickmeyer," Commander Bolton said, as I reported to his office. "I want so badly to ship your sorry ass back to the States, but it seems you have the connections in high places."

"I beg your pardon, Sir?" I said puzzled.

"When I received a transfer order for you to report aboard an Amphibious Assault Ship, I tried to have it rescinded," he said with a scowl on his face. "I then got word back that Admiral Rooks, who is in command of the amphibious group, had made out the order personally. So, Senior Chief, you're back where you wanted to be. But I can tell you, my evaluation of you will be as negative as I can make it!"

"I'm sorry it didn't work out here, Sir." I was laughing on the inside and had a hard time keeping the smile off my face.

"I'm glad to see the last of you Rickmeyer," Bolton continued. "Pack your gear and be ready to report for transport to Da Nang tomorrow morning at 0700. That is all, now get out of my sight!"

I went back to my cabin and started packing my bags. Damn! Commander Bolton and I never did hit it off. He was one of the few people I'd met in my life that I couldn't get along with.

The evaluation that he'd write on me and that would accompany me to my next ship would be bad, I knew, but I wasn't worried. My records had enough positive evaluations in there. This one negative could be explained away as a personality clash between an officer and a senior NCO.

It was a crystal clear morning as I boarded the launch that would ferry me to shore. I was to be flown out of Vung Tau on a transport heading north to Da Nang. There I'd pick up my orders and proceed to join up with Admiral Sully Rooks' group. I wondered how he was doing. The last time I'd seen him in Hawaii seemed like a lifetime ago.

Chapter Thirty-Five

Da Nang by June of 1967 had grown into a huge facility -- it had a deep-water port allowing huge ships to transship men and equipment; it had runways, field hospitals, and large areas for troop housing. The security was tight, with the constant fear of VC sappers getting inside the perimeters and planting bombs. It also had the largest air-conditioned space in the world, the morgue.

I'd be over-nighting here in a transit hutch, and I'd arranged to make a phone call to Barb. The lineups for these calls were long, but senior NCOs could book approximate times.

While I was waiting, I decided to try and track down Davis Carlson once again.

"Good afternoon Sergeant," I greeted the Marine in the personnel office. He was not the Marine I'd been dealing with on my past visits and figured I'd have problems. I threw the names of his predecessor and my contact in Manila around, and after looking me over went into the files and started shuffling through folders.

"You've missed him again it looks like," the Sergeant said, flipping through some forms. "I see here, it says there was a message left for you by the last clerk."

"What does it say?" I asked, hopeful I'd catch up with Davis this time.

"Keep your shirt on!" the Sergeant said, juggling the heavy stack of papers. "Here it is!" he added, removing the note and sticking it between his teeth. He put the rest of the files back in the cabinet and handed me the slip, now indented with teeth marks.

The message was scrawled in almost illegible longhand. "Gunny Carlson heading back to States."…I couldn't read the next sentence… "Return Da Nang after home leave and"…I could hardly make out the last sentence…"be back when reassigned and new outfit equipped and running."

"This is great!" I said, looking up from the note. "There's no fuckin' date!"

"You wanted help, ya got it!" the Marine said. "I think you're damn lucky to get that!"

"Okay, you're right." I didn't want to piss off the only source I had. "Thanks!" I added.

"You're welcome!" he said, with a toothy insincere grin.

"Hello Barb…yeah it's me!" I finally got my call through after waiting an extra forty-five minutes. "It's what, early in the morning there?" Barb sounded like she was a million miles away.

"I'm sorry," I apologized for waking her up, "No, everything is fine…I'm joining a new ship…I say…I'm joining a new ship!"

Barb sounded half asleep.

"How are you?" I asked, "How's Dory and family?" Barb then told me about Roy. "Yeah I know…yeah, the *Forrestal* is due on station here sometime next month," I replied to her news.

"He'll be okay…tell Dory not to worry…I miss you too baby!" I replied to Barb's words of affection.

"I can't answer that; there're a bunch of nosey guys listening!" Barb had started to tell me that she was feeling horny.

"Oh, I do baby!" I moaned into the phone. "I've got to go, I love you honey…yeah, bye," I hung up the phone with reluctance. Damn it hurt to hear her voice knowing she was so far away, in another world; the real world.

That night at chow I just picked at my food. I was deep in my own thoughts, thinking about Barb, my failure to contribute to the Brown Water Navy's operations in the south; they were turning into a first class outfit. Some of the greatest people you'd ever meet were involved; it was just my luck I had to get lumbered with Commander Eric Bolton.

"I hear you're heading out to the "Oak" tomorrow?" a voice brought me back. I looked up from my uneaten dinner to see a Chief Petty Officer dressed in khakis.

"Yeah, sit down," I said, gesturing towards a chair. "You being transferred out to her too?"

"Rejoining her," he said, sitting down with his plate of chops and mashed potatoes. "I left her in Sasebo, Japan when she docked there. I had to have a nasty root canal done and they kept me a couple of days in case of complications."

"That sounds pleasant," I said, noticing his right jaw was swollen. "What's she like?"

"A good ship!" he started forking mashed potatoes into his mouth. "She was just commissioned last year. I've been aboard about two months, that was until Sasebo. By the time they'd done the root canal and kept me in hospital a couple of days, she'd sailed."

"I was on the *Pocatello*, she was the same class of ship as the *Oak Island*," I said. The amphibious ship I was joining was the USS Oak Island or as the Chief had affectionately called her, the "Oak".

"I'm Tom Schumacher," he said, wiping his hand on his pant leg before holding it out.

"Jake Rickmeyer," I took his offered hand, he had a firm grip. That was one thing that hadn't changed for me as an Oklahoman; a man can always be judged by the firmness of his handshake.

"Well Jake," he began, "I'm gonna be happy to get back aboard. The chow on the *"Oak"* is first class, not like this crap!" I laughed; Tom was going to be a good shipmate and I was looking forward to reporting aboard.

The large, lumbering Marine helicopter had picked us up at Da Nang, along with a couple of Marine officers and a ton of mailbags. I knew how anxious men were to receive letters from home, so this would be a welcome flight to the guys on board ship.

We flew out over the heavy ship traffic in and out of the harbor, traveling some thirty miles I judged by the air time.

The *USS Oak Island* appeared outside the port window I was sitting at; she looked ship-shape and smart as a tack. The helicopter circled wide, almost making a full circuit of the ship before touching down gently on her flight deck.

The view I had of the *Oak Island* from the helicopter would have to satisfy my habit of walking the pier to look over a new ship. I was starting to get used to flying at low altitudes in helicopters. It could be fun, if you weren't being shot at.

The rotor blades were still turning slowly as we exited by the rear ramp; with heads down we quickly walked over to the hatch and reported to the office for processing.

Tom Schumacher was a Chief Radioman and would be sharing a double cabin with me; I couldn't have been happier. After the formalities of reporting in, a seaman striker took our bags and led us to the Chief's mess.

It was catch up as fast as I could, my duties included being on the roster for Chief-of-the-Watch, Damage Control Leader, as well being slated for instructional duties I hadn't been briefed on yet.

The *"Oak"* was the flagship of an Amphibious Force that would be carrying out assaults with the Marine units in the group. We'd be active where and when needed anywhere in I Corps. The Force consisted of another LHA similar to the *Oak Island*, as well as a supply vessel and four destroyers.

Sully Rooks was aboard, but as yet I hadn't seen him. He was in overall command of this amphibious group and I'd noticed his personal flag now had a second star. Sully had made Rear Admiral Upper Half.

The first week passed before I got the word to report to Sully. I'd been wondering why he'd gotten me transferred if he wasn't even going to say hello. I reported to Sully's cabin and had to get used to Marine sentries once again. On small ships it wasn't necessary, but on capital ships with Marine detachments, captains and especially admirals had guards posted outside their cabins. The Marine corporal knocked and announced my presence.

"Send him in!" Sully's voice hadn't changed; it still carried unquestioning authority with a deep, rich timbre.

"Jake, how are you?" Sully came around the desk to greet me.

"I'm fine, Sir," I replied. "It's good to be serving with you again Admiral."

"And I'm glad to have you with me again," he said. "How have things been since the *Junction City*?"

"A lot of water crossed, Sir," I replied, happy to see Sully looking so well. He seemed more distinguished every time I saw him. Sully seemed to grow larger the more responsibility the Navy heaped on him. I remember picking him as someone who would be an admiral one day, now I was aiming higher, maybe the Joint Chiefs of Staff.

"This is my first command of an amphibious task force Jake," Sully said. "And my first command responsibility in a combat zone. I don't need to tell you how important this is to me. I want this group to be the pride of the Seventh Fleet."

"I understand completely, Admiral, and I hope I can contribute in some way," I responded with enthusiasm. Sully could get you all fired up and Gung Ho.

"You can contribute Jake," Sully said. "I read the reports on the river actions you were involved in with the *Pocatello*; and now your experience in the Rung Sat with the Brown Water Navy. There's no one more qualified to shape my boat crews into efficient first rate units than you."

"I didn't exactly do a lot in the Rung Sat, Sir," I said, trying to get that episode behind me.

"Nevertheless," Sully was on a roll, "I have known you for nearly twenty-five years and you are a credit to your rate of Boatswain's Mate!"

"I appreciate your confidence in me Admiral," I replied, feeling again that I would follow Sully into hell if he led the charge.

"Jake, your responsibilities will be to work with Lieutenant Williams," Sully began in a sober tone. "He's my training officer, and together you'll develop a training program with drill schedules that will turn good crews into great crews. I want an efficiency report on CINCPAC's desk that will make him sit up and take notice!"

If I were a Marine I would have shouted, Hoorah! Sully had the ability to get the best out of men and I was no exception. I knew I'd give it one hundred and ten percent.

"On a personal note," Sully said, changing the subject. "I saw Ed Morrow in Washington recently."

"How is the Senator?" I asked. I hadn't thought much about Ed lately, although I knew he was still very much involved in politics.

"He is a member of the Senate Select Committee on Intelligence; they oversee the CIA amongst other things. The "Company", as the CIA like to call themselves, is more involved over here than I'd like."

"I know," I said, "I met one in Saigon."

"Oh!" Sully perked up. "How did that come about?"

"I was with a procurement outfit that was dirty," I began. "This guy was involved in breaking it up."

"I just hope they don't get any more involved out here than they already are," Sully said, turning serious. "Trouble is, everything they do is classified and we can't control them. Goddamn spooks!"

The phone rang and Sully excused himself while he answered it.

"Admiral Rooks here!" Sully paused, then looked at me. "Just a moment." I knew it was time to go.

"Jake will you excuse me," Sully said, holding his hand over the mouthpiece. "I really have to take this call. I'm sorry we couldn't jaw some more, but we will have more time for that later."

"Of course Admiral," I stood up quickly. "It's good to be back with you again, Sir."

"Thanks Jake," Sully nodded, "I'll get back with you as your training program progresses."

With those words I left his cabin, letting him get on with the running of a very impressive fighting force of ships and men.

Lieutenant Williams was young, bright, and eager to make an impression on me. I figured he'd graduated from college with some kind of Education Degree and should have been home teaching high school kids. He was good at the paperwork, however, and he busied himself writing procedure guides, setting objectives and devising a system of tests we could run the crews through. The kind of paperwork superior officers liked to get across their desks, the very thing I was not good at.

But I knew small craft capabilities and had a knack for getting guys to work well under me. Together we'd get the job done.

The two LHAs each had several boat crews assigned; these crews manned the craft, and they also performed normal deck duties on the ships when not operating the LCMs. We also had reserve crews and general well deck personnel. The men assigned to the well deck were responsible for handling, maintaining, and the overall readiness of the craft. Lieutenant Williams scheduled classes to provide maximum training and drills, with minimum disruption to the regular day-to-day operations of the ships.

Chief Schumacher was an asset to have as a friend; he read everything that came in through the communications room. I'd asked him to keep an eye on the *Forrestal*'s progress as she made her way out.

The traffic reports on all ships in CINCPAC's area were updated constantly; what ships were coming in, what ships going out, what ships were on station, and what ships were passing from Second or Third Fleet responsibility to Seventh Fleet.

The *Forrestal* arrived on Yankee Station July 25th and started immediate combat operations. Her firepower, by way of her fighter aircraft complement, was the equivalent of a World War II battle fleet.

The super carrier was awesome as a fighting unit and her silhouette with the setting tropical sun behind her, was to me, as majestic as any oil painting in the Smithsonian Institute.

July 29th dawned like so many others in this part of the world. The seas were calm, the sky clear, and the air free of the humidity that would envelope us later in the day.

I had been up on deck early, enjoying watching the ships slice through the soft colors of the water precisely on station with the flagship. The second LHA on our starboard quarter, the supply vessel well to our stern, and the destroyers ahead and on our flanks, sitting low in the water like the sleek Man-O-Wars they were.

Later on in the morning as I was lecturing a class, calls of "Emergency crews close up!" blared over the P.A speakers. The calls were preceded by the words "This is no drill!" I immediately dismissed the class and hurried to my Damage Control station, when I reached the station I was told to go back and report to the Boat Commander in the well deck.

"What's up?" I yelled, arriving back at the well deck puffing from my run up and back from the Damage Control station.

"The *Forrestal*'s on fire!" the Boat Commander yelled back. "We're changing course to intercept and assist!"

258

I felt the ship change course at the same time he gave me the news. The *Oak* was slow to answer the helm but you sensed the wheel was hard over.

"What the fuck happened?" I asked, not believing it could be that serious.

"A rocket fired off accidentally from one of the planes sitting on the deck about to be launched," the officer answered. "That's all I know at the moment. Meantime Jake, get everything that will float ready. They'll tell us what's needed when we get close enough to help."

We were an hour away from the carrier and as we got closer more and more reports were coming in.

The initial fire had caused a chain reaction of explosions from other aircraft parked nearby on the deck; the entire aft end of the flight deck was now a blazing inferno. The fires had further been fed by aviation gasoline from tanks fueling other aircraft.

It was the worst possible scenario for a carrier, its flight deck jammed with loaded and fueled fighters ready for a sortie, and fire breaking out on the crowded flight deck.

"Jake," the Boat Commander yelled, hanging the phone receiver back on the bulkhead, "we're launching four LCMs. I want you to take control and coordinate their movements around the carrier. The primary objective will be to pick up men in the water. Watch your movements around any other ships coming in to assist fighting the fires."

"Aye, aye Sir," I acknowledged. "Stand by to cast off!" I yelled at the crews in the boats. They'd been ready and standing by for the past thirty minutes.

"Jake!" the Boat Commander added, "take aboard live men first and get them back here, or any other ship close enough that can provide medical attention. There'll be a lot of burn victims, so warn your crews it won't be pretty."

"Aye, Sir," I replied, jumping aboard the second boat pulling out. I immediately checked radio communications with the other craft as soon as we'd cleared the stern gate and moved off.

"Fuck!" I yelled aloud, hoping Roy was not one of the casualties we'd be pulling out of the water. "Please God!" I spoke the words quietly, "Please let Roy be okay!"

The *Forrestal* had turned into the wind, trying to prevent the flames from moving farther forward on the deck. Smoke and flames were trailing the huge ship as a good headwind blew across her deck.

Our walkie-talkies were capable of communicating with the *Forrestal* and any other ships involved in the rescue. We also had one channel exclusively for communicating within our small flotilla of LCMs.

I assigned one seaman striker to keep a radio on the *Forrestal*'s emergency channel and ordered the other boats to remain on our exclusive channel only. The last thing I wanted was an over-excited boat crew losing contact because they'd forgotten to change channels.

The water was full of debris as we approached following in the carrier's wake. At first we couldn't identify anything; then as we got closer we realized just how many men were in the water. Small boats and destroyers from the carrier's own battle group had been picking up survivors from the get-go. The first reports of men overboard had brought rescue ships hurrying in to help.

Many men had literally been blown over the side by the force of the explosions, and then as the fire grew intense many more had jumped over to escape the flames, unable to stand the heat from the growing inferno.

The first group of men we pulled from the sea was hideously burned. I had ordered the ramp lowered and we began to pull the survivors from the water and give them what first aid we could. Each boat had corpsmen aboard and these medics would administer whatever medical attention was available. That's all we could do for them until we got the injured back to the *Oak*. On board the *Oak* and other large ships, Navy surgeons in fully-equipped sickbays would treat them.

"Keep your focus on the radio!" I yelled at the seaman who was my contact with other emergency units. "That's the only fuckin' job you have!"

"Yyyyes Sir!" the young sailor stuttered. He had grown pale and looked on the verge of passing out; the first two men we pulled on board had their skin hanging off in sheets.

"Jesus Christ!" shouted the corpsman. "Lift them in gently, try not to pull them by the arms!"

It was a nightmare for the men on the boats. Most had never seen seriously injured men before. Now they had to touch bodies that were literally cooked in some cases, with limbs turned into fused stumps.

Others looked untouched, but were in a semi-conscious state concussed by the explosions.

Still others managed to swim over and climb aboard unaided, with only minor injuries or simply suffering from exhaustion from their time in the water.

"Bring your boat alongside," I ordered boat number-two over the radio.

"Dave, take these casualties back to the *Oak*," I ordered the helmsman on the boat I was on. "Unload them and get back as quick as you can!"

"Got it Jake!" he replied.

"Come with me!" I ordered the young seaman with the radio, and together we stepped on to the other boat as it slid alongside.

The rest of the day was spent pulling men from the water, rotating back to the *Oak* to drop off injured sailors, re-fuel when necessary, pick up more medical field dressings, and grab what ever other supplies we needed and return in a hurry.

Taking the radioman along with me I kept jumping from one boat to another, staying on the scene as each boat left on their round-trips back to the *Oak*.

All the boat crews and corpsmen were near exhaustion but they kept working. Everybody knew the *Forrestal* was still fighting for her life. The efforts on the part of the carrier's crew would go on for most of the night.

Ships had been arriving all day to assist. The aircraft carrier *USS Oriskany* was standing off nearby to give support throughout the emergency.

When the frantic efforts to save the injured men in the water were complete, the small boats then had to turn their attention to the search for, and recover of, bodies of dead sailors.

I felt the anguish as I looked on each face as bodies were brought aboard, hoping that Roy's would not be among them. They were young; some looked like they should still be in high school. Many looked peaceful, making you ask yourself the question, "How could this young, healthy kid die?"

"What?" the corpsman asked.

"Nothing," I realized I'd asked the question out loud. "Nothing!" I repeated.

It was twelve hours before the fire on the *Forrestal* was finally contained. The mighty carrier was blackened and scared and began limping her way towards Subic Bay Naval Base in the Philippines.

The carrier would undergo clean-up and temporary patch-up there, and then go home to Norfolk for more lengthy repairs; it would be months before she'd be ready for sea duty again.

It was late and every man aboard the rescuing LCMs was totally beat. Some of the men were asleep on their feet as the last boat came home to the *Oak*. It was carrying the last two bodies we'd picked up. I had looked at their faces under the bright lights searching for Roy and I wished I hadn't. They were both horribly mutilated with parts of their bodies missing.

The *Oak Island* immediately sailed back towards Da Nang, airlifting the serious burn cases by big Marine Sea Knight helicopters to the hospital ships in the area. The walking wounded and uninjured personnel would be offloaded in Da Nang. From there they'd be flown to the Philippines to rejoin the *Forrestal*, or receive treatment and be re-assigned to other billets.

"Keep checking every casualty list you can for me Tom," I kept asking Tom Schumacher.

"I've looked over every list of the known dead, missing-presumed-dead, serious and light injuries a dozen times," Tom said, getting irritated with me. "No Roy Rogers Millington, or Roy Rogers Bakstrom is anywhere on any list."

I'd asked Tom to look up Roy under Bug's surname of Millington, and then realized he may go by John's family name, which was Bakstrom.

"Well keep checking the updated lists will you?" I asked, continuing to pester him. I knew Tom had better things to do than monitor every casualty list communicated to CINCPAC, but I had to be sure about Roy.

The initial report to the Navy Department of the tragedy on the *Forrestal* listed the cause of the accident to the accidental firing of a Zuni rocket from an F-4 Phantom jet. The jet had been parked ready to sortie on the flight deck. The fired rocket flew across the deck and hit the fuel tank of a parked A-4D Skyhawk aircraft nearby, spilling flaming JP-5 fuel from the 400 gallon belly tank on the aircraft.

The spreading flames then caused explosions on other nearby aircraft adding to the inferno. The fire was so hot it burned through the steel flight deck spreading the conflagration below. Berthing quarters directly below became death traps for the off-duty men sleeping there.

The fires were battled for 12 hours before final containment. The casualty list included 134 dead, large numbers injured, and dozens of aircraft destroyed or damaged.

I wondered how Barb and Dory would be taking the news; the reports of the fire would have hit the newspapers back home. The Navy would do their best to keep wild speculations to a minimum, but the Stateside press was becoming anti-war and an accident of this magnitude would be publicized to the hilt.

I needed to get ashore in Da Nang and call Barb as soon as we'd offloaded the remaining injured personnel still on board.

"Attention all hands," the P.A speakers crackled, "This is the Captain speaking. Admiral Rooks has asked me to pass on a Job-Well-Done to all hands for their efforts in assisting the *Forrestal* in her emergency. Many men owe their lives to the quick and levelheaded response of the rescue parties."

There were nods of acknowledgment from the listeners.

"One of the finest traditions of the Navy is to help fellow seafarers in times of peril on the high seas," the Captain continued. "That tradition was evident in our ship company's efforts, working as a team to bring succor and relief to many sailors who may have otherwise perished. I would also like to add my well done to that of the Admiral's. Goodnight and God Bless."

I asked Tom once more to check the casualty lists. It looked reasonably certain Roy was okay.

I wasn't going to take any more chances and would ask Sully to intervene and help get Roy transferred Stateside. I couldn't have faced Dory if Roy had been hurt on the *Forrestal*.

"Come!" Sully's voice commanded, when the Marine sentry announced my presence. I had asked through channels for a meeting and had been granted one immediately.

"I'm glad you could see me Admiral," I stood at attention before the massive desk.

"Not at all Jake," Sully replied. "I don't get to see you often enough. At ease Jake, take a seat."

"Admiral," I began, feeling awkward. "I have a favor to ask and I know it could be seen as seeking favoritism, but I need to ask it."

"If I can help Jake," he said, leaning forward, "Is it problems at home, something on the ship?"

"No, it's a personal request regarding a young enlisted man, Sir." I didn't know how to phrase it. I didn't want to make it look like Roy was getting a free ride home. "A son of an old friend of mine is on the *Forrestal*; as far as I can determine he's all right. But I promised his mother I'd take care of him and feel I can't fulfill that promise."

"Who was his father?" Sully asked. "Knowing you he must have been in the Navy."

"He was, Sir. He was killed in Korea on a behind-the-lines beach operation." I felt a lump in my throat as the memories of that night came back. "It was the kid's dream to follow his father into the service, but I don't think he's really cut out for it."

"Is he in for a four-year hitch?" Sully asked. "If so, I don't like to cut deals for early-outs, particularly with this Vietnam business on."

"Nor would I expect it, Sir," I could see Sully tense. "All I ask is that he finish out his time in some Stateside posting. I wouldn't ask this for me. It's just that his father died in the service and I thought maybe this kid needed a break."

"I've always told you to come to me for anything Jake," Sully said relaxing. "Yet the only times you have come, it's been to ask for help for others. A lot of people would have taken advantage of our friendship."

"That's not what our friendship's about Sully," I said, feeling emotional.

"And that's what I've always admired about you Jake," Sully sounded a little emotional himself, "Your strong sense of decency and loyalty!"

"Well, I'm proud to be your friend Admiral." I couldn't think of anything else to say.

"Men like you and me," Sully said, sounding nostalgic, "the Navy has been our lives; it's where we belong. Our commitment to duty and service to our country seems what we were born for..." he seemed to drift off for a moment, then he came back. "I'll send a back-channel memo to BUPERS (Bureau of Personnel), requesting them to assign the young man to the James River Reserve Fleet in Virginia."

"Thank you Sully," I said, breathing a sigh of relief. "That will make his mother very happy and it will be a big relief to me."

"Give my yeoman his name and rank," Sully said, pressing a button on his desk. "I'll tell him what it's all about and this only goes for one hitch. If he ships-over for another four years, he's on his own," Sully laughed. "Roswell, please come to the office," Sully spoke into the intercom.

"Is that Yeoman Roswell from the *Junction City*, Sir?" I asked, remembering Rosy well. I had talked to him several times when he was a yeoman to a much younger Captain Rooks.

"One and the same," Sully said. "He has been with me through thick and thin!"

"I'll get the information to him Admiral," I said, standing up. "I've taken up too much of the Admiral's time. Thank you again, Sir."

"Glad I could help Jake," Sully smiled his winning smile. "And good work with the boat crews by the way."

"Thank you, Sir," I said, leaving as Rosy came in. Both of us raised our eyebrows in recognition but said nothing. I'd jaw with him later when I gave him Roy's information.

The first chance I got in Da Nang I booked a call through to Barb. While I was waiting I thumbed through a magazine. When my turn came I was excited, anticipating hearing Barb's voice again.

"Hello Barb?" I could hardly hear her. "Please speak up...that's better...how are you?"

"I'm fine…glad everything's okay there," I replied to her question. It was great to hear her sleepy voice; I must have awakened her again. "Did you hear about the *Forrestal*? Is Dory upset? Has the Navy given her any information?" I was asking a string of questions.

Barb replied she didn't know much.

"Listen, as far as I can tell he's all right," I told her. "I've had a reliable guy checking the casualty lists. No, nothing more to add than what the Navy's told her."

Barb continued to ask what else I'd found out.

"What I have done is get Sully Rooks to get Roy a safe billet Stateside for the remainder of his hitch. Whatever you tell Dory, don't tell her that…I don't want Roy to find out!"

Barb said she understood.

"That's right…what about you, everything else okay?" I was hurrying knowing my allotted time was up already.

"I love you too…more than you'll ever know!" I said, hating to hang up.

"Okay, come on will ya!" a guy in line behind hollered.

I hung up and headed back to the *Oak*. I was happy to have spent that little time on the phone with Barb and also relieved Roy would be safe and sound in Virginia, just as soon as the *Forrestal* reached Norfolk.

I didn't care that he would be spending the next three years checking out anchor chains, mooring lines, greasing shafts and pumping out bilges. He'd be dirty and bored, but he'd be safe!

Chapter Thirty-Six

The big Marine CH-46 Sea Knight helicopters ferried Marine assault teams from the ship to locations inland up and down the coast. They tried to catch VC units out in the open and bring them to battle, but the wily VC were rarely where they were last reported to be.

The Marine teams did have some successes, and the command's body count was being compared favorably with other top units in-country. These raids were kept up for the next five months, then the *Oak* received orders to sail north deeper into the waters of the Tonkin Gulf.

The Boat Commander called me in one morning and told me a special operations mission was being prepared. No one had any further details until the special unit arrived aboard; meantime, I was to keep quiet about it.

Finally, after three days of driving myself crazy wondering what was up, a chopper from one of the big carriers farther south landed on our flight deck. Ten military types loaded down with all sorts of equipment disembarked from the helo, including one that I recognized.

"Hello Ding," I said, walking to the hatchway where they were standing sorting their gear.

"Shit!" Ding said, looking surprised. He reached out and took my outstretched hand, "How are you Jake?"

"Fine!" I wasn't going to ask him what this was all about; I remembered his warnings to me in the past.

"Good," Ding said, hoisting a heavy bag onto his shoulder and starting through the hatchway. "We'll be seeing each other real soon Jake."

I didn't have long to wait to have my questions answered. The Boat Commander and I were ordered to the pilot's ready room, which also served as a handy conference space. Present were Sully, the Captain and XO, the Marine Colonel, Ding and one of the guys who'd arrived with him. Then there were the Boat Commander and myself.

"Gentlemen!" Ding began, "What I'm going to lay out for you is classified and not to leave this room."

No one seemed surprised; everyone knew it must be a Black Ops for the CIA. Sully and the Captain would certainly have had some inkling. I remembered Sully's comments about the "Company" having too much freedom in what they were doing over here.

"We need to make an asset extraction from the other side of the DMZ," Ding began. "The asset is a North Vietnamese Colonel. His name is Dinh Bok Bao and the extraction will include his immediate family. He is defecting and we have reason to believe he can give us vital information on the North's long range tactical plans."

"What is our role in this?" Captain Lewis asked.

"Transportation and support basically," Ding said, unrolling a map on the wall behind him. "We'll need to get up river in one of your LCMs as quietly as we can, drop our operational team off. The boat will hole up and wait for us to get back." Ding was running a pointer up the thin black-inked line of a river, "The LHA will cruise offshore at a safe distance and come in and pick us up when we call. Otherwise we'll take care of everything."

"What about discovery?" the Marine Colonel asked. "Will you need helicopter-borne Marines to help get you out?"

"Colonel, in this business you either succeed or you don't get out," Ding said, dead serious. "We'll be going to a pre-arranged extraction point from the landing craft drop off. If we're discovered, or Dinh Bok Bao gets cold feet, we'll be too far in to get out if they're waiting for us."

"I'll need to have some idea of the time element," Sully joined in, his eyes scrutinizing Ding.

"Of course, Admiral," Ding replied. "Launch the LCM as close to shore as practical after dark, our team in the LCM will go upriver to the disembarkation point here." Ding pointed to a speck on the map, "We should be there well before dawn. The boat will find cover and remain secured through the day." Ding turned back to look at us, "We will be back just after dark the following night. If we're not back in enough time for the LCM to get back down the river and rendezvous with the LHA before dawn, then they'll have orders to shove off without us."

"What crew requirements will you need for the LCM?" the Captain asked.

"I want Senior Chief Rickmeyer to run the boat. That's why I asked him here for the briefing." Ding continued, "He has experience in these rivers and knows what to expect if conditions get tight. What he needs to complete the crew, I leave up to him."

All eyes in the room turned towards me, I felt like I was standing in the middle of Times Square naked. "I'd...I'd like to take at least five men," I answered quickly. "They'll all need to be proficient in firearms."

"Arrange whatever you need with the Boat Commander," Captain Lewis said, turning his attention off me and onto the Boat Commander. "Lieutenant, I'll want you to keep me informed whatever you decide."

"Aye, Sir!" the Lieutenant replied, caught off guard.

"If there are no more questions gentlemen, I'll need to talk privately with the Admiral," Ding concluded, looking slowly around the room, locking onto each person's eyes for a brief moment. "We'll be ready for a green light tomorrow night. If it's a go, 2030 hours would be ideal for the launch."

"Well, I guess that's all gentlemen," Captain Lewis said, standing up. "Let me know how the boat preparation progresses Lieutenant."

He nodded towards Sully and headed out the door with the rest of us following in his footsteps. I don't think Captain Lewis was too happy with the way he'd been practically ignored in all this. It seemed Ding had the power, acting for a greater authority in Washington; the rest of us, including the Captain, just had to go along.

"Bullet-head!" I took the mechanic's arm, "I'm heading upriver on a special mission. I want you with me as motor-mac; pick the best fireman you can think of to assist you."

Bullet-head Malone was one of those individuals who looked like he was made up of spare parts. He was big, awkward, his arms were too long and he had a head that was long and narrow; not top to bottom, but front to back. When you looked at him in profile his head resembled a 38-caliber bullet.

"What's up Senior Chief?" Bullet-head asked, wiping his oily hands on the greasy cloth he always had sticking out of his back pocket.

"Can't give you any details yet," I told him, looking over the boat he was working on. "We'll take boat-2. I want you to drop everything and check that boat's engines out thoroughly. Make up a list of spares you might need in any emergency, load a good set of tools aboard, organize two 45-gallon drums of extra fuel and get them stowed. I want everything ready by noon tomorrow!"

"Where're we goin'?" Bullet-head said, looking puzzled by the string of orders I'd just given him.

"It's classified!" I advised him. "I know the scuttlebutt will start soon enough, just you keep your mouth shut, okay?"

"You got it!" he said, packing up the job he was working on.

"How's it going Jake?" the Boat Commander asked, "I'll need to take a progress report to the Captain."

It was late evening, and I'd gotten most of what I wanted organized already. "I have selected the boat; we'll use boat-2. I have a mechanic and fireman picked; we'll take extra fuel in drums and enough C-rations and water for four days. I've selected Petty Officers Randolph and Williams, and a seaman apprentice named Ocha. He's got rifle and pistol expert qualifications." I ran the list off for him.

"Sounds like you've got everything under control," the Boat Commander said, sounding pleased. He'd look good when he reported all this to the Captain; meantime he was happy to let me get on with it.

"Anything I can do?" he asked.

"Yes," I said, handing him a list. "I need your authorization to draw pistols, M-16s, a grenade launcher and plenty of ammo."

"Jesus Christ Senior Chief!" his eyes widened as he looked down the list. "You sure you're going to need all this stuff?"

"We've got to sit in the weeds for almost twenty-four hours. I don't want some wandering North Vietnamese patrol stumbling on us and all we're holding in our hands is our dicks!"

"I take your point!" the Boat Commander said, signing the list and handed it back to me.

Chapter Thirty-Seven

The LCM slid quietly from the lowered stern of the *Oak*. The night was moonless, ideal for a secret operation but dangerous for driving a small boat up a narrow river.

"Jake," Ding said, holding a map lit by the small pencil flashlight he was holding cupped in his hand. "The mouth should be free of sandbars as I pointed out on the ariel reconnaissance photos I showed you this afternoon."

I was keeping one eye on the bow and one eye on Ding's map. The large, blacked-out hulk of the *Oak* faded into the darkness behind us.

"Those photos were a week old. Sandbars can appear and disappear overnight," I said, turning the helm slowly to cut a wide arc towards the river mouth. "Best thing to do Ding is watch for ripples on the surface; they'll be easy to spot with the tide going out."

"Okay Jake," Ding switched his light off and folded the small map. "I'll get my guys ready. I estimate it will be about three hours before we reach the drop-off point. It's black-out and no noise from here on in!"

"Will you send Petty Officer Randolph and Bullet-head back? I need to talk to them," I said in a low voice. "I'll need to get them up-to-speed with what we're doing."

"Roger that," Ding slipped down into the well deck.

Randolph and Bullet-head climbed up onto the after deck and stood by the wheelhouse.

"Okay," I spoke in a whisper, "I can tell you now we're going up river to extract some North Vietnamese Army officer and his family. We'll be about three or four hours getting to the drop point. There we'll unload the commando types and wait until the next night for them to come back out. We then pick up the whole kit-and-caboodle and get back out to the ship."

"Shit," Bullet-head said, "I'm glad I checked the mufflers on this baby. The way you're talking in whispers is scaring the shit out of me!"

"We are also north of the 17th parallel, which means we're in North Vietnam!" I hated to hit them with this now, but I couldn't say anything before. "Bullet-head, you and your helper stand by those engines at all times; be ready to do whatever you have to do if we have problems. Randolph, I want you and the other two deck hands to watch the sides and the bow. Anything, and I mean anything, you see out of the ordinary, give me one long whistle, okay?"

"Got it Jake!" Bullet-head nodded.

"I'll tell the others," Randolph said.

"And everyone check and strap on your sidearm, and check and load your M-16 and have it near you at all times." I ordered them. "And pass the word, there is no talking, smoking, or lights of any kind. If you have to communicate, do it in whispers."

Both men nodded in the affirmative and went back to their posts.

The boat made its way from the wide river mouth into the narrow, meandering bend before I saw ripples off to the side. I slowed and swung farther to port, trying to judge the depth of the channel I'd chosen by pure "gut". My instinct was right and we had no trouble making the bend.

It was quiet so far; the banks looked deserted as we passed several small fishing hamlets. Bullet-head's mufflers were keeping the boat's engine noise to a minimum, and any fishermen still awake would figure us for a motorized fishing boat making our way back upriver.

"Jake," Ding whispered as he came back to the wheelhouse. "Look for an old, ruined temple on your right; we should reach it after the next wide bend."

"Pass that on to Randolph," I whispered back, his face was so close to mine I could feel his breath on my cheek. "Tell him to whistle when he spots it."

Ding tapped my shoulder and went back forward. I saw the bend coming up and slowed; Randolph gave a long, low whistle as we came out of the turn on the other side. The pagoda loomed out of the darkness like a spirit from some ancient civilization. The ghostly appearance of it only made me feel even more a stranger in this foreign land.

Ding was at my side again and pointing to an overgrown stone pier; it must have been the old landing for the temple.

"Don't tie up, just go alongside and drop us off. Remember Jake, tomorrow night if we're not back on the pier by midnight, shove off! Synchronize watches...I've got 0010...now!"

My watch was the same exactly. "Okay Ding, Good Luck!"

He gave me thumbs up and went back to his men. They were standing up and throwing their backpacks on and picking up their array of weaponry.

I guided the boat alongside the landing. Ocha and Williams jumped off and held the boat steady while Ding and his team disembarked, quietly disappearing into the Temple. I backed the boat out and looked for the spot I'd noticed with long, leafy trees hanging over into the water.

I slid the boat under the branches and stopped; Randolph, Williams and Ocha got lines secured to limbs protruding from the banks. I looked in all directions and satisfied myself that we were safe, and then I shut down the engines.

I gathered everyone together in the well. "I'll take the stern and I want Williams to take the bow. We'll keep watch until 0300, then wake up Randolph and Ocha. They'll watch until 0600, then they'll wake Bullet-head and Eddy," I whispered the orders. "We'll keep those three-hour watches all through the day. If you're not on watch, try and rest, save your energy. As soon as it's light enough to see, we'll try and pull some more brush around us. Any questions?...Okay, get some sleep!"

The day was long, hot, and the humidity kept us continually drinking water. I was tempted to slip over the side for a swim but remembered about the liver flukes; they were parasites that got into your body and made a mess of your liver. The evening brought some relief and we all gave a silent pray of thanks when the sun finally set. But then the mosquitoes came out.

"What a fucking, God-forsaken place this is...why the fuck are we fighting over this shithole for anyway?" complained Williams as he slapped his neck.

"Keep your fucking voice down!" ordered Randolph.

"And don't slap any more mosquitoes," I added. "That sound can carry a long way; just squash them with your fingers."

Everybody tried to stay rested, but we were starting to feel the tension mount. We'd have to start the engines soon, and if there were any North Vietnamese around we'd have a fight on our hands. I didn't know how many runs I'd make to the pier and back looking for Ding. I figured I'd start the engines at 2255 hours, then make our first run at 2300. If they weren't there, we'd back off and go in again at 2330. Finally a last run at 2400, then if no one was there, my orders were to leave.

It was 2255 by my watch and time to start the engines. I waved to Bullet-head to stand by and pressed the starter with my heart in my mouth. It purred into life, the relief I felt almost made my knees buckle.

"Okay," I whispered to Randolph who was standing beside me. "Pass the word for everyone to stay sharp, release all the lines except one. We'll slip out at 2300 hours for our first look over at the Temple."

I backed out slowly and started over, bumping softly against the stone pier on our first run. Williams and Ocha jumped off and held the boat fast. We waited ten minutes and no sign from the Temple ruins. I whistled for Williams and Ocha to jump back aboard and I backed off, crossing the river and slowly crept back under our canopy of tree branches.

The nerves of the guys must have been at breaking point, I knew mine were. It was time to make another run over to the stone wharf. Once again, we slipped the line from the branch and glided over to the Temple.

Another five minutes and no sign, I'd almost decided to back off and wait once more. Then there it was; the signal -- two quick blinks from Ding's tiny flashlight. I returned their signal with one long blink from the miniature flashlight Ding had given me.

Three dark figures appeared and took up defensive positions on the pier, followed by three more from the shadows herding five others, three were small, obviously children. The crew helped the group aboard, then three more figures left the safety of the Temple carrying a fourth.

This last group jumped aboard followed by the three who'd stood guard, and I immediately whistled Williams and Ocha to get back in.

I backed off slowly, made a tight turn and headed down river, controlling the terrible urge to open up the engines and head out at top speed.

"Ding said to offer you his thanks," one of Ding's men had come back to speak to me. "He'd come back himself, but he broke his ankle," the man laughed quietly. "Stupid bastard tripped on a mangrove root, the only casualty of the mission," he said, continuing to grin as he patted me on the back.

The trip down river was anti-climatic. It was after midnight and neither man nor beast was stirring along the banks. Ding's radioman had sent off the pre-arranged radio signal to the *Oak*, and there she was right on schedule as we cleared the river mouth and headed into the open sea.

As soon as we'd secured inside the well deck, Ding and his team quickly left with their assets in tow. The XO and Boat Commander were there to greet us and looked pissed when Ding's group just brushed past them.

The mission was a success, however, and all would share in the glory. The XO and the Lieutenant turned their attention to us with handshakes and lots of "Good job...well done!"

After the officers had left, heading as quickly as they could to report to Captain Lewis I figured, I thanked each crew member myself with a long, firm handshake.

Bullet-head blinked his eyelashes, and in a bad imitation of Mae West said, "I'd go upriver with you anytime, Jake honey!"

The rest of the guys burst out laughing, as much in relief after the tensions of the mission, as at Bullet-head's comedic performance.

I sure as hell was relieved, and only one casualty as the man said, and that was only a lousy broken ankle.

We'd been up a North Vietnamese river, snatched an army colonel right from under their noses, and were now off free and clear.

The next morning two large helicopters touched down on the flight deck and Ding and his team climbed aboard, along with their North Vietnamese Colonel and his family. Ding had his leg in a cast and was helped on by two of his beefy teammates.

He saw me watching from the hatchway and nodded a goodbye. No words were necessary, and I could see the gratitude in his eyes.

Chapter Thirty-Eight

Cam Ranh was as festive as they could make it that Christmas and New Year of 67/68.

The *Oak* had tied up after coming south from her last deployment and the crew got their feet on dry land for some well deserved R&R, if eating hot dogs in an open-sided tin shed, and drinking low percentage beer on the beach can be called R&R.

Sully had left the ship for some high-powered meetings at headquarters in Saigon, so the ship would be here at least until his return.

My thoughts drifted once again to that old partner-in-crime of mine, Gunnery Sergeant Davis Carlson.

"Tom," I asked Chief Schumacher, "is there some way you can find out the location of an old Marine buddy of mine?"

"I suppose I could make an inquiry, say it's unofficial, make it plain language," he said, lighting the pipe he had constantly in his mouth. "That way no one should get their noses out of joint."

"I've been checking every time we make Da Nang, and either miss him coming, or miss him going!" I explained.

"You have a name in personnel there in Da Nang?" Tom asked.

"Yeah," I answered, happy that I didn't have to keep going back and wearing out my welcome at the office. I got the feeling last time the sergeant thought of me as another annoying squid.

"Drop the name and anything else off to me this afternoon and I'll send off a brief inquiry," Tom said, drawing deeply on his pipe.

"Thanks Tom, I really appreciate this!" I said. Maybe, just maybe, I might get to have a New Year's beer with Davis. We had a lot of catching up to do.

The lineups for holiday season phone calls home were a mile long. I considered myself lucky to get through to Barb mid-way between the Christmas chaos and New Year's bedlam.

"When was I coming home?" she'd asked the inevitable question.

I'd answered that I'd probably be rotated out in February, or come home with the *Oak Island*. The *Oak* should get us into San Francisco at the end of March or early April.

One bit of good news she had was that Roy had arrived back at Norfolk in September, and after home leave had been sent to James River in Virginia. "Dory," Barb said, "was doing cartwheels, she was so happy!"

"Hey Jake," Tom said, catching up with me in the mess. "I got the whereabouts of your Gunny, he's at some Godforsaken place called Khe Sanh!"

A fresh battalion of Marines had come aboard, and with Sully's return we were headed back up the coast. Things started to pop in the next couple of weeks; we got the word that Khe Sanh was under heavy rocket and artillery attack.

Our first orders were to transfer the Marine battalion we had aboard back to Da Nang for reinforcing Khe Sanh. Then within a week the US Embassy in Saigon and bases and installations all over Vietnam were under Vietcong and North Vietnamese attack. It was the Vietnamese New Year; the Vietnamese called it Tet!

The confusion and changes in priorities as the Tet offensive unfolded had our orders changed once again; we joined back up with our Task Force and were now headed north to help reinforce the city of Hue. The Marines there were under heavy attack and it looked like they may have to pull back. Either way, we could reinforce the city or help in any needed evacuation.

Tet, as far as the Task Force was concerned, was like a dog chasing its tail. No sooner had we gotten into a position to help at Hue, when the Marines started to inflict heavy losses on the VC and were pushing them out of the city and our help may no longer be needed.

For awhile it was being considered that we launch a water-borne assault up the Perfume River, then the ships were ordered once again back to Da Nang. The Marines aboard would be disembarked there to help out at Khe Sanh.

All across Vietnam the Tet offensive by North Vietnamese and Vietcong units had been a failure, and American forces had held their positions and inflicted thousands of casualties on the enemy. Proving that American firepower would prevail any time the enemy came out in the open to fight pitched battles. The attacks on Khe Sanh were continuing and it was now being called the Siege of Khe Sanh, as the base became isolated and cut off.

There were still minor skirmishes taking place in I Corps, and mopping up operations were taking place in other areas. Things were almost over as the *Oak* tied up in Da Nang to disembark the battalion of Marines.

"Jake," Tom looked like he'd seen a ghost. "When I contacted Da Nang for you that time, I included a request to flag Gunny Carlson's name, and asked them to contact me if there was any change in his status."

"So, he's what, heading to Hue now that we've just come from there?" I asked, trying not to believe what I read on Tom's face.

"No!" Tom said, looking away, "He's been killed at Khe Sanh, KIA two days ago. I'm sorry Jake."

The news hit me like a sledgehammer! I felt my body go numb and realized the blood must have completely drained from my face.

"Jake…Jesus Jake!" Tom said, grabbing me and pushing me down onto a chair. "You okay?"

"I'll be okay! I have to get some fresh air and let this sink in," I said, composing myself and tightening my jaw.

"Maybe you ought to sit a while," Tom was holding my arm.

"I'll go topside," I said, getting out of the chair. "I think I need some privacy."

The waters of Da Nang provided that perfect tropical backdrop I'd experienced so many times from the deck of a ship; a gentle breeze brushed my face as I looked out to sea, the scene renewing my spirit.

I remembered the time in Naples, when Gunny Carlson and me got drunk on good Italian wine, and were doing our best to serenade the senoritas from the balcony of the restaurant, the time he got in trouble in Malta and I'd asked Sully to cut him some slack. The time we had been shot at on the beach in Lebanon; the time he'd stood by my side in Manila when Rabbit's pals had tried to intimidate me. So many images of Gunny Carlson, he was a big, tough, son-of-a-bitch, mean and nasty, but a good friend.

Another life wasted in this long, useless, fucking war!

The Tet offensive kept us on station longer than scheduled. But then at last we were ordered to unload what trucks, APCs, extra ammunition, anything else we had on board.

We were heading home, with one stop in Hawaii then on to San Francisco.

Two days out of Pearl I got word to report to Sully's cabin. He looked tired, and I realized just how much this tour had taken out of all of us.

"Sit down Jake, coffee?" Sully said, coming from behind his desk and sitting across from me. The comfortable leather chairs he had in his cabin were a treat to sink into. "Pedro, bring coffee for two, thanks," he called to his Filipino steward in the pantry.

"What can I do for you Jake, as far as a posting?" Sully asked, sighing as he sat down. "No one deserves a rest more than you do, two tours in Vietnam, with hardly a break in between."

"I was just doing what every one else was doing," I said, taking the coffee from the tray Pedro offered me.

"Thanks Pedro, good to see you!" I said, nodding a greeting to Sully's long time steward.

Pedro beamed; he had always liked me. I guess I was one of the few people who took the time to even notice him. He was devoted to Sully and should have been retired by now; but he'd probably serve the Admiral until they rolled him up in a canvas shroud.

"You most welcome Boats," Pedro replied smiling. He had always called me by the traditional nickname for a Boatswain.

"I won't need you anymore tonight Pedro, thank you," Sully took his coffee from the tray.

"You can have your pick of postings Jake," Sully began as Pedro placed the coffee service on the table and quietly left. "God knows I owe you for the job you've done with the boat crews, not to mention that special ops for the "Company". Our part in that did not go unnoticed in Washington, by the way."

"I'm glad everyone got back out okay," I said. "As far as the posting, I'd like something in the San Francisco Bay area, if that's possible."

"You've got it," Sully said, looking pleased that he could do something for me. "You've already spent a couple of stints there over the years haven't you?" he asked.

"Yes, Sir," I answered. "When I got back in 1946 and then again in the fifties; the boat pool at Alameda, instructional work at Hunter's Point, here and there."

"This is good coffee," Sully seemed less tired and more relaxed. "Maybe it's just getting away from Vietnam, the pressures of high command take their toll in combat situations."

"It is good coffee," I added my compliments to his. This was the first time Sully had ever opened up to me about his personal feelings. I guess even Sully needed to let his guard down with an old friend once in a while.

"Ever thought about retirement Jake?" he asked.

"I have, Sir," I replied. We'd been sitting for several minutes, not talking, just sipping our coffee. "Probably put my thirty years in, Admiral. I'd have to do something after that, though. I've seen too many lifers go on the booze or get depressed once they left the Navy."

"I know exactly what you mean," Sully said, going quiet again for a moment. "When you finish your home leave Jake, report to the Alameda personnel administration office. I'll get Rosy to memo BUPERS to set something up," he added, sipping quietly on his coffee.

"Thank you, Admiral," I said, finishing mine and returning the cup to the tray.

"I'll be leaving the Task Force at Pearl. Debriefing with CINCPAC will take about a week, and then I'll be going directly on to Washington. So, I guess its goodbye again Jake," Sully said.

"It's been a pleasure to serve with you once more Admiral," I said, taking Sully's outstretched hand as he stood balancing the coffee cup in his left hand.

"It's been an honor to have had you under my command Senior Chief," Sully said, sounding sincere. "Goodbye Jake, and good luck!" he added as he put his arm around my shoulder and walked me to the door.

"Goodbye Sully!" I replied, leaving with tears welling up in my eyes. Why was I such a fuckin' sentimental bastard!

Tom Schumacher, Bullet-head Malone, Bobby Randolph and I went ashore together in Hawaii and enjoyed the long-established traditions of visiting Hotel Street.

The street was full of young GIs heading for Vietnam, or coming back from there. I noticed guys who'd been over tended to either sit by themselves quietly, or overdid the loudmouth routine; there was no in between. Either way, I knew they'd all been changed by their experiences over there, especially the ones who had spent a lot of time in the bush.

We had all gone ashore in civvies and the usual competition for the loudest, most colorful Hawaiian shirt was evident. Some of us looked like neon signs, but military was still written all over us.

"What you gonna to do now that your hitch is up Bobby," Tom asked Randolph.

"He's goin' fuckin' fishin'!" Bullet-head chimed in.

"It's true, my brother's got a fishing boat working out of the Bay," Bobby said. "I promised him I'd help when I got out."

"Well, I'm lookin' forward to some good Chesapeake Bay crabs. I'll be crackin' shells for the month I'm home, I can tell ya!" Bullet-head said. He was from Baltimore, Maryland and the only thing he ever thought about was food; that was when he wasn't up to his elbows in an oily engine.

"What about you Jake?" Randolph's question brought me out of my half-trance.

"Oh…yeah…well, I'll be transferring to a shore job at Alameda," I said, catching up with the conversation. "I'm in for thirty, so I've got a couple more years yet."

"Yeah, just like ol' fuckin' Schumacher here," Bullet-head said, slapping Tom on the back. Tom almost swallowed his pipe Bullet-head hit him so hard.

"Well I might surprise you one of these days," Tom said. "I can leave this outfit any time, no regrets!"

"Yeah, sure!" Bullet-head laughed. "You and Jake came into the Navy through the hawespipe, and you'll never give it up!"

I didn't really feel like tying one on and went back to the ship after a few drinks.

Bullet-head and Tom were raring to go, they had the whole night planned, including visiting a certain address Bullet-head knew about. I think Bobby had decided to stay with them to keep them out of trouble; he seemed to be pacing his drinks.

I wanted to get back and write a letter to Charlie and tell him I was getting back to Oakland, then wanted to get it posted before we left Pearl the next day.

The Task Force made good time to San Francisco and we arrived to fanfare and cheering families crowding the piers. The big LHA hardly bumped the fenders as she came alongside and berthed opposite the carrier *USS Coral Sea*; the other ships mooring at spaces along the jutting piers as they arrived one after the other.

It took me a while before I could pick out Barb in the crowd. Then I saw Dory and Dale jumping up and down and waving kerchiefs. It looked like they had all made it down to meet the *Oak*, and then I saw John at the back waving his arms like semaphore.

It was good to be home. Now the question from Barb I'd have to face, I knew she would insist this time, when would we get married?

Chapter Thirty-Nine

"Wake up sleepy head!" Barb yelled, shaking me roughly.

"Eh…what time is it?" I groaned, having a hard time opening my eyes; it felt like they wanted to remain clamped shut.

"Noon!" Barb kissed me on the cheek. "You've been conked out for about fourteen hours."

I remembered getting home from the restaurant where we'd all had dinner, and then John, Dory and Dale dropping us off at Barb's apartment around nine.

"I vaguely remember climbing into bed…" I croaked. "After that what did we do?"

"Nothing," Barb pouted. "By the time I'd undressed and made myself pretty you were already sound asleep."

"God, I must have been saving that night's sleep up for a long time," I said, sitting up and shaking my head hoping to clear the cobwebs away. "What have you got planned for today?"

"Breakfast," Barb said, heading for the kitchen. "I've got it started, ham and eggs with Texas toast."

"Great!" I whooped, stumbling from the bed and heading for the bathroom; I suddenly needed to take a leak.

"It was sure nice of everyone to meet me yesterday," I said through mouthfuls of scrambled eggs. "It really felt good to have someone waiting for me."

"We thought it would be appreciated," Barb began. "You know there are a lot of people protesting the war here now. Some returning servicemen are even being spat on by protesters"

"What!" I exclaimed, my mouth full of jellied toast. "That's bullshit! What's the matter with these people?"

"Reality Jake," Barb sighed, standing up and taking her dishes to the sink. "I've got to ask upfront Jake, where are you going next?"

"Good news!" I said, knowing how worried she was. "Sully Rooks is setting something up for me in Alameda, so I'll be working a nine-to-five and get to come home every night like a regular working stiff."

"Oh Jake," Barb started to cry as she came over and put her arms around my neck. "You don't know how happy that makes me."

"Come on, honey," I said, knowing how much this meant to her, "everything's gonna be fine!"

"Jake, I've been worried sick every day you've been gone," Barb sobbed. "So much in the papers about casualties, and photos of flag-draped coffins coming home week in and week out."

Barb started to sob uncontrollably, and for whatever reason I started to cry too. We held each other and cried until we were all cried out and were just holding each other tightly, rocking back and forth.

"Let's get dressed and go for a walk," Barb said, finally breaking my hold on her. "I want to show you the new park they're just now fixing up."

"I need a good, long, hot shower first," I stretched. "Care to scrub my back?"

The first couple of weeks home were taken up with visits to Dory and John, ferrying back and forth to San Francisco and Sausalito; shopping, movies, eating shrimp and sourdough bread at Fishermen's Wharf. One day Barb and I went over to the National Cemetery at the Presidio, taking flowers to place on old Senior Chief Hoffman's grave.

Dale was just finishing her sophomore year at Berkeley and was full of radical ideas. Every time she was home when Barb and I visited, she would attempt to convince me how wrong the establishment was and how things needed to change.

Dory would get pissed and storm off to the kitchen, John would try to argue her down; I preferred to just kept my mouth shut. Dale was young, idealistic, I knew she'd grow out of it. Just so long as she didn't start getting in too deep with some of those long-hairs over at Berkeley.

I dropped in to the Administration Office on Alameda a couple of days before my leave was up and I was due to report in. I was anxious to see what they had me down for.

"Senior Chief Rickmeyer," the yeoman called my name. I'd been sitting along the wall waiting for them to dig out my orders. The office was a hive of activity, typewriters clicking, telephones ringing, doors banging and a general atmosphere of hurry up and wait.

The Navy was good at looking busy, but underneath there was a current of FUBAR (fucked-up-beyond-repair).

"All your records have caught up with you, everything's in order," the yeoman said, flipping through the bulky file. "You're to report to Commander Bilts day after tomorrow 0700; the Commander runs the boat pool."

"Bilts?" I repeated, knowing the name. "That's fine, I know where the pool is, thank you."

"Anything else you need to know Senior Chief?" he asked, anxious to be helpful, eyeing the four rows of ribbons on my chest.

"No, just needed to know everything was in order," I replied, starting to leave. "You know how things can get fucked up?" I added for the benefit of the grouchy-looking Chief Yeoman sitting behind a desk piled high with papers. He had a superior look on his craggy puss I didn't care for.

The young yeoman said nothing, just looked around nervously.

The Chief looked at me over the glasses perched on the top of his nose. I thought he would say something, but to my surprise he just gave his head a slight jerk in my direction, as if to say, "Fucking deck-apes, couldn't find their ass with both fucking hands!"

I was on my way to the boat pool when it suddenly hit me! "Bilts! Of course, Ensign Bilts from the *USS Warhol*!" I said, slapping my head.

Ensign Bilts was now Commander Bilts, and he was to be my new boss. I suddenly remembered what a nice guy he was and the many sightseeing trips we'd taken together. It would be good to chew the fat with him, find out what he had been doing the last sixteen odd years.

The yeoman ushered me into the Commander's office after I'd presented my orders at his desk. "The Commander's been expecting you Senior Chief, please go on in."

I knocked once on the frame of the open door and stood at attention.

"Come in, come in Senior Chief!" he said, looking up from his desk. "I knew it was you as soon as I saw your name on the orders a couple of weeks ago." The Commander came around his desk with a huge grin on his face, "How have you been?"

"Fine, Sir," I said, shaking his hand. "It's good to see you looking so well."

"Well, I would argue with that," he laughed. "Sit down John."

"Thank you, Sir," I replied wincing, "but I prefer to be called Jake. I haven't heard John since I was a boy, Sir."

"Jake it is then," he smiled. "What have you been doing since the days on the *Warhol*?"

"Oh, probably about the same as any other sailor," I replied. Then I began to tell him briefly about the various ships I'd been on, about my last Vietnam tour.

"I never stayed in the regular Navy. I got out in 1955 but stayed in the inactive reserves. Of course when Vietnam got really started I was activated in 1965. I'll be in until this is over," he said, still grinning.

285

"I think a few of us will be in until this is over," I added. Wondering if it would ever be over.

"Excuse me, Sir," the yeoman said, popping his head in the door. "I've been holding your calls, but the base CO is on the line."

"Okay!" Bilts said, "I'll take it."

"I'll let you get on with your work Commander, where do you want me?" I said, getting up.

"Just take a couple of days to get familiar with things Jake. See me next Monday morning, okay?" he said, lifting the phone from its cradle and putting it to his ear.

"Aye, aye Sir," I said, leaving him and walking out to talk with the yeoman.

"This will be your office Senior Chief," the young yeoman's name was Fuller, he showed me to an empty room.

"Looks like no one has used this in ages," I said, looking around the stark bare office.

"Don't worry Senior Chief," Fuller grinned, "I'll have this place cleaned up and furniture hauled in. It'll look brand new when you come in Monday morning."

"Meantime, what else do I need to know about?" I asked.

"All I know is I was told to give you anything you needed," Fuller replied, opening the window to a nice breeze coming in off the Bay.

"I guess then I'll go take a look around the boat pool," I said. "You have my home number if the Commander needs to get hold of me. I guess I'll see you Monday mornin'."

"Aye, Senior Chief!" Fuller said, walking back to his desk. "I think you'll like it here; Commander Bilts is a hellava nice boss."

"I know," I said matter-of-factly. "We served together on a destroyer in the fifties."

"No kidding?" Fuller said, sounding impressed.

I left the building and strolled down the way to the piers. It was like coming back to your boyhood home and seeing the old familiar trees you used to play on; I knew every boat hoist and paint shed. I sat on a bollard and watched the water gently splash against the pilings, alone with my thoughts.

Suddenly there was a huge splash and I realized I'd disturbed a sleeping Sea Lion. He surfaced about twenty yards out and turned to stare at me with a look that said: "What the fuck did you come down here and wake me up for?"

I smiled, and then he woofed once, took a breath and disappeared under the water.

I started thinking about Barb; maybe I better pop the question. I'll do it the next time she brings it up. Meantime, I needed to get squared away with this new job, and try and make myself useful to Commander Carter Bilts. Carter Bilts I thought, you just never knew in this Navy when you'd cross paths with old friends and shipmates.

I spent the remainder of the morning recalling the *Warhol* and our trip back from Korea, through the Middle East and Europe.

The sites we'd seen, the memories we'd brought home with us. The fun and excitement of the foreign port calls.

I wonder how that English woman in Portsmouth is doing. God, I can't even remember her name!

Chapter Forty

"Come on honey," Barb shook me awake, "you don't want to be late your first day!"

"Shit!" I yelled, holding my arm where Barb had grabbed me. "Don't be so rough! You didn't get enough last night?" I laughed.

"You smart-ass!" Barb said, pulling the blankets off me. "You better get up and I don't mean that thing!" she pointed at my erection.

"All right, all right!" I replied, jumping up and heading for the shower, lifting her nightdress as I passed and poking her in the rear with my hard-on.

The meeting with Commander Bilts that Monday morning went well. All we did was talk about old times and Fuller, as promised, had the office ready and waiting.

"I'll start bringing in the files on the personnel assigned to the boat pool," Fuller said, all business. "You'll need to know who's who out there. And one of the things the CO has you down for is to coordinate with incoming ships any small boat repair or replacements."

My ears picked up at that; this was of interest to me. "What else am I doing?" I asked, watching Fuller as he placed a large pile of file folders on my desk.

"That's all I have so far," he answered. "The Commander said to make you comfortable, give you the personnel files, and then start bringing you ship requisitions as they come in."

I could feel Sully's hand in all of this; probably his memo included a "soft duty" note. Coming from a Rear Admiral that meant, "leave him the fuck alone!"

I just hoped he didn't make things too easy for me. I needed to be working, the harder the better. I'd get bored without responsibility; I had to have something to get my hands dirty on.

I got tired of looking through personnel files by mid-afternoon, they only told you so much about a man. I preferred to get to know someone by working alongside him.

I told Fuller I was going to check things out at the docks and strolled out.

I went down to the boat dock and sat on my favorite bollard, and to my surprise a Sea Lion splashed into the water, surfaced a short distance away and looked back at me, and then he dove again. If it was the same one he'd have to get used to it, I was here for a good long haul; maybe do the next four years here and then retire with a fat and sassy pension. Maybe even buy a house in Sausalito near John and Dory. Life could be good for the next twenty years or so with Barb.

The remainder of the year flew by; the job at the boat pool was a "gold-bricker's" dream. The only time I got off my ass at the office was to go sit my ass back down again on the bollard.

The Sea Lion, I'd named him Gus, and I were on friendly terms. He didn't bother diving into the water any more when I woke him up. Ol' Gus simply opened his eyes, woofed a greeting, and then went back to sleep.

Christmas at Dory's was coming up, Roy would be home on leave, and Barb and I had settled down to a slow, simple life. She hadn't brought up the issue of marriage and I wondered whether she'd decided to leave things as they were.

"Hi, come on in, Merry Christmas!" Dory said, smiling as she took our coats. "Oh Jake, Roy just got in this morning; he's out with Dale but they'll be home any minute."

"That's great!" I said. "I'll be looking forward to seeing him."

"Hey, Merry Christmas!" John hollered, yelling from the kitchen. "I'm a little behind. I burnt the damn gravy I'd spent all afternoon on, and then had to start again!"

"Anything I can do?" Barb yelled back.

"Nah, you guys get a drink," John answered. "I'll be out in a minute."

We had just toasted one and all with festive greetings when the front door opened and Dale and Roy burst through laughing and tickling each other.

"Hi everybody!" Dale shouted as she ran upstairs to change.

"Merry Christmas Uncle Jake," Roy came over and shook my hand. "Merry Christmas Aunt Barb!" Roy said, hugging Barb and lifting her off her feet.

"Put me down, you fresh sailor!" Barb squealed with delight.

"Put her down Roy!" Dory commanded. "She's not one of your floozies!"

"Oh, lighten up Dory!" John said, coming out of the kitchen.

It was obvious Roy and Dory were still not reconciled over this whole Navy business.

"You're looking good Roy," I said, jumping in to get the conversation turned around. "James River must be good duty."

"It's a bore Uncle Jake," Roy replied, making himself a drink. "One thing for sure, when my hitch is up in two years I want out!" he added.

Dory gave him the eye but didn't say anything about the drink.

"You haven't said anything about this to me," she seemed to perk up.

"Well, that's a decision you've made that will make everybody happy!" John said.

"I figure I'll go to college," Roy continued, sitting down beside me. "Dale has me convinced to apply to Berkeley; says there's lots of guys going there on the GI Bill."

"Well, it's about time you came to your senses!" Dory said, surprised and relieved all at the same time. "Is there any chance he could go back to Vietnam Jake?" Dory asked, looking anxiously over at me.

"I don't think so," I replied, surprised at Roy's announcement myself. "With Nixon talking about ending the war, it's not likely."

Just then Dale came bouncing down the stairs. She had grown into a beautiful young woman and was no longer the radical she'd been in her freshman year. Still strong-willed and opinionated, but with more maturity, still a bit anti-military for me but I had to respect that.

"Merry Christmas Uncle Jake," Dale kissed me on the cheek, "And to you, too, Aunt Barb," Dale said, hugging Barb. "Did I miss anything? Or has Roy already told you he's going to go to Berkeley when he gets out?" she added.

"He's told us, but not what he's going to take at Berkeley," John said, getting up to go back in the kitchen.

"One thing James River has done is get me interested in water, rivers, tides, oceans, currents; I think I want to study oceanography," Roy said, sipping his drink.

"That's wonderful Roy," Barb said, squeezing his arm.

"I thought so too," Roy said, looking down slightly embarrassed. "I was hoping everyone wouldn't think I was nuts."

Dory still hadn't said much, but I could tell by her expression that a tremendous load had been lifted off her shoulders.

"So, Dale will graduate in 1970," I said, "and Roy will start his freshman year that fall. I think your folks should be mighty proud of both of you," I added, putting my hand on Roy's shoulder.

"Come and get it!" John shouted from the dinning room.

Barb and I said our good-byes and got into our car for the trip back to Oakland. It had been a wonderful Christmas dinner. John kept putting bigger and more elaborate dinners on every year, and the clincher was Roy was coming home to the life Dory always wanted for him.

Things were working out; we'd go into this New Year more positive than the last one.

It was damn cold the remainder of that winter. I spent all my time holed up in the office with Fuller bringing me hot cups of "Joe" every hour or so.

With the spring, ol' Gus came back to his favorite sleeping spot. Occasionally I'd bring him down some fish and lay them by my bollard. I'd stare out across the Bay and pretend I wasn't watching him; soon he would bounce over with his comical locomotion and gobble up the free lunch. He must have been the only one lazier than me on the whole base.

Nixon was determined to end the hostilities in Vietnam and the papers now were full of the negotiations going on at high levels.

The word must have spread through the fleet that ol' Jake was at Alameda in a cushy job. Soon old friends passing through on ships would drop by the office to chew the fat.

Ernie Nuefeld, whom I'd shared quarters with in Little Creek, came through on a carrier and we'd managed to get shit-faced in one of the local bars one night. Another time Billy Rogers and "Ringo" Bertram from the *Pocatello* came through on a cruiser. They'd both made Boatswain's Mate Petty Officer Second and we all got shit-faced at the same local bar.

By this time Barb expected at least twice a month someone would come through, and she didn't mind too much, although I noticed my breakfasts were rather skimpy and cold the morning after any of these visits and trips to the local bar. Talking over old times and drinking with shipmates made me yearn for the sea again. But I'd promised Barb, and myself, that I'd do my time here in the Bay area and bow out gracefully.

That fall Tom Schumacher from my days on the *Oak* came through after a tour in Japan. He was on a destroyer and was heading around to Norfolk. Instead of getting shit-faced this time, I invited Tom home for supper, which was more his style. Tom was never the rowdy type, more like a college professor in a sailor's suit with his pipe and horn-rimmed glasses.

Barb was delighted and we both enjoyed Tom's company very much. Apart from the incessant pipe smoke, the evening was a treat. Tom even slept over on the couch.

"I can't remember when I've enjoyed a night ashore more," Tom said, eating breakfast the next morning. "As Jake can tell you, I'd just as soon stay aboard and read a good book."

"Yeah, I remember you always seemed to be the one helping someone back on board after they'd boozed too much on liberty," I said, sitting back and enjoying the bright morning.

"Well we enjoyed having you," Barb said. She had taken a liking to Tom; he was truly a gentleman and Barb hadn't met too many of those lately.

"Any chance you getting another sea billet Jake?" Tom asked.

"Don't even bring that up around here," I replied, watching Barb's smile turn into a frown.

"That's right," Barb said, waving a spatula at me from the stove. "This sailor is land-locked and beached…for good!"

"Oops! Looks like I brought up a touchy subject," Tom laughed.

We all burst out laughing, for no good reason other than to be with friends having breakfast together doesn't need a reason to laugh, or cry!

Barb came down to the base with Tom and I. His ship was sailing that afternoon and she wanted to see him off.

The ship Tom was on was one of the newer Forrest Sherman Class destroyers, the *USS MacGilray*. She cut a fine figure tied alongside the pier. Her flush deck had a slight banana shape to it, rising at the bow then curving back towards the stern. Destroyers had always been my first love. If it was possible for a man to have deep affection for an object, then I had one for a cleaned-lined, sleek, fast destroyer.

"Bye Tom," I said, holding on to Tom's hand firmly, "See you next time through."

"Good bye Tom," Barb sobbed, hugging Tom, "You'll always be welcome at our house."

"Good bye Barb, and thank you so much for your hospitality," Tom said, choking back his emotions. "I'll be heading for the Mediterranean next, but I'll be back this way before you know it, I promise you that."

Tom let go of Barb, slapped me on the back, then quickly trotted up the gangplank.

"Bye Tom," we both called after him, waving as the *MacGilray* slipped her lines and slowly inched away from the pier. We could still see Tom waving from the stern half the way to the Golden Gate Bridge; Barb sighed and held tightly on to me.

"Want to meet Gus?" I asked, lifting her chin up to look at me.

"Who the hell is Gus?" Barb replied, still teary.

"Come on down to my quiet retreat," I said, taking her hand.

We walked down to the spot where two small wharves met and spotted Gus laying beside my bollard; he was waiting impatiently for his lunch.

"Hey Gus," I yelled to wake him up, "I want you to meet my lady. Barb, this is Gus," I said, pointing at the huge Sea Lion, "Gus, this is Barbara-Jean." Gus opened his eyes wider than he normally did, woofed twice, then wobbled over to see if I had brought him anything. Barb threw her head back and roared with laughter.

"What's with the seal for God's sake?" she laughed, almost bending over double with mirth.

Gus did a double take and started woofing up a storm, he looked as if he was enjoying this too.

"Barb," I said, holding her to me, "will...will you marry me?"

"Oh Jake...oh Jake," Barb couldn't get her answer out. "Oh Jake, oh Jake," she repeated over and over. "Yes! Yes! Goddamn it!" she finally got it out.

Chapter Forty-One

"I just got a call from Akima," Barb said, when I came in that evening from the base. "She said she and Charlie would be delighted to stand up for us at the wedding."

"That's great honey," I replied, throwing my briefcase down and kissing Barb smack on the mouth.

"Only thing is they can't come out until Charlie gets things set up to operate without him for a week," Barb squealed, continuing to chatter as she struggled out of my grip.

"And guess what? They just had a baby boy three months ago and she's done a damn good job of keeping that from us."

"You know Charlie," I said, "Likes to keep his business to himself."

"I think maybe spring next year," Barb said, taking a breath. "That will give Charlie and Akima time to organize their calendar and it won't take the spotlight away from Dale's graduation in the summer."

"What ever you say sweetie," I said, kicking my shoes off and peeling a banana in the kitchen.

"They called their little boy Otis Washington Charles Sparks!" Barb said, picking up my shoes and placing them in the hallway. "That's a mighty big handle for a little guy. Wonder where they got that name from?"

My mind flashed back to that morning in Vietnam when Charlie experienced stomach cramps and had reported to sickbay. I guess the guilt Charlie felt over Otis' death was deeper than I'd thought. Maybe he felt naming his son after young Otis would help heal the wounds.

I didn't say anything to Barb about the name. She hadn't stopped talking long enough for me to get a word in even if I'd wanted to.

"I think we should just keep it simple," Barb continued, fussing with the pots and pans she needed to cook dinner. "Just John, Dory and the kids, Charlie and Akima of course, the girls from the office…what about the base…who do you want? Do you think Commander Bilts would like to attend?"

"Yeah, the Commander will come, also Fuller and his wife," I said, throwing the banana peel absent-mindedly into the sink. "The guys from the Chief's mess are going to want to have an honor guard at the church, complete with swords."

"That would be nice for you Jake," Barb picked the peel out of the sink and took it over to the trashcan.

That was the way it was for months before Barb finally got over her school-girlish excitement and we could get back to normal.

The talk of the wedding went right through the Christmas holidays. Roy said he wouldn't be able to get off, but he'd be home for good that fall anyway. Dale wanted to be a bridesmaid; the wedding kept growing in leaps and bounds.

Withdrawal of troops continued as the war in Vietnam wound down. Men were still being killed down there and everyone was still wondering when it would finally stop.

"Morning Jake," Commander Bilts said when I came in one morning. "What do you think of this claim by Nixon that he'll have all the troops out of Vietnam by the end of the year?"

"They just started the withdrawals last year. I don't think the President is thinking realistically," I replied.

"Do you think we can trust the North Vietnamese to stay north of the 17th parallel if we ever do sign a deal?" he asked, looking up from the newspaper.

"No, Sir! No, Sir I don't!" I replied without hesitation. "Every one of those gooks I met over there was either trying to rip us off or trying to get us killed!"

"Strong words Jake," Bilts said, looking surprised at my statement. "Anyway, we've got to get out. This business is tearing the country apart. Look at this!" he exclaimed, holding the front page up for me to read.

"President Nixon's invasion of Cambodia causing massive unrest on university campuses across the country…"

"I agree, Sir," I said, reading the headline. "Instead of having everyone out by the end of 1970, it looks like it's likely to escalate again."

"On a lighter subject," Bilts put the paper aside, "your wedding Saturday. Would it be all right if I bring a lady friend I met at my Church a short time ago?"

"No problem at all, Sir." I had wondered whether the Commander was queer. He'd never spoken of a wife or lady friends; I guess I now knew he was straight.

I walked down for a quiet hour with Gus the afternoon before the big event. I sat on my bollard and munched on a bag of peanuts. "Gus ol' buddy, tomorrow I'll be a happily married man."

Gus yawned looking up at me, he smacked his chops a couple of times and then went back to dozing.

"I'd invite you, but I don't think the other guests would appreciate your presence as much as I would," I said, looking down at him.

He yawned once more and plopped his head back down closing his eyes.

I looked out across the Bay and saw a large LHA coming in to dock. I could clearly see a full complement of helicopters parked on her deck, and the water reflected off her hull and seemed to sparkle with thousands of reflective beams in the sunshine.

Saturday went off without a hitch, except the small quiet affair we'd planned had turned into an event with a hundred people jamming the small hall we'd rented for the reception.

An honor guard with raised swords had stood outside the church doors; all the girls from Barb's bank had brought boyfriends and husbands. Fuller and his wife, Bilts and his very attractive widow from his church, the Bakstroms, and it seemed the honor guard had invited themselves and spouses as well.

Then to top it off, half way through the evening, with everyone dancing and enjoying the ample refreshments, two familiar figures came through the door.

"Hey Jake, ya old bastard!" it was Bullet-head. "So you got fuckin' married eh?" He hadn't changed; the image of the foul-mouthed sailor was in evidence wherever Bullet-head made an appearance.

"Excuse me!" Barb said, sounding shocked. "Keep that language for the cable locker, sailor!"

"Sorry ma'am!" Bullet-head laughed, "Just came in from a long haul at sea; ya know how it is."

"Well, keep it to yourself!" Dory added, looking at Dale as if a bee had stung her.

"Hey Jake, ya know my best buddy," Bullet-head continued, not listening to the women, "My bestest buddy Tyler Dicks!"

I hadn't said a word from the moment the two had walked in. I was in shock when I saw Bullet-head, but then went into paralysis when I'd recognized the guy with him as Rabbit!

"Hi Jake, long time no see," Rabbit said. He'd never gotten the message that I hated his guts, and had hated him ever since that episode in the Philippines years ago.

"Oh what the hell!" I thought. "It's my wedding day; let it rest for the evening. No point in spoiling it for Barb."

I shook Rabbit's hand and had to endure the bear hug Bullet-head put on me. "Where's the fuckin' beer Jake?" he yelled, looking around as he released me.

Barb couldn't help laughing as Bullet-head went towards the bar; he was oblivious to the red faces he left in his wake. It was the same wherever he went in public.

"The fuckin' *USS Medford*," drooled Bullet-head, "She's a fuckin' good ship Jake," Bullet-head rambled on drunkenly. He and Rabbit were amongst the last still in the hall, "And hey…ya remember Ocha?…that fuckin' Mexican son-of-a-bitch?…well, he's on board too."

I remembered Ocha; he was a nice kid. He'd gone with me on that CIA extraction up the river in North Vietnam. That was the same trip I'd taken Bullet-head along because of his talents with diesel engines.

"Jake, I think you better get your friends on their way," Barb said, yawning. "We best get out of here and let them clean up."

"Yeah, you're right," I said. "Come on Bullet-head, I'll get you and Rabbit a cab." Thankfully, Rabbit had been passed out for the last hour and I didn't have to put up with him dribbling all over Barb and me with that buck-toothed smirk of his. He'd told me twenty times over the course of the night what a lucky bastard I was to have married Barb.

I managed to lift them up and get them staggering towards the door. It only took another ten minutes to wave down a cab and send them on their way.

"Well, Mrs. Rickmeyer," I said to Barb when I went back into the hall. "Would you like to have me escort you home?"

"That would be nice," she said smiling, "And carry me over the threshold, I want you to do that!"

"That, and I'll undress and put you to bed as well," I said, suddenly horny despite the long day and hectic evening.

"Mmmmmmm," was all Barb said as we got in the car.

Monday morning was busy at work. Two ships needed boat replacements and I was writing up requisitions and making calls all day long.

I had hoped to get down to see Bullet-head and young Ocha before the *Medford* sailed that afternoon, but I missed her. She'd left before I got a chance to get free of the office.

"Wonderful ceremony on Saturday," Bilts said. Then he'd kept me talking about his lady friend and that had taken up more of my time. "What did you think of Betty?' he'd finally asked.

"I thought she was lovely," I told him.

"Do you think she thinks I'm suitable?" he asked me.

"Yes, I do Sir," I answered him. I was glad when that first day back after the wedding was over. Barb had kept me in bed all day Sunday; she'd been saving something all these years because she'd been insatiable.

"Fuller," I yelled through the door, "get me the shore-line for that destroyer that needed a whaleboat. I need to talk to the Chief Boatswain."

"Aye, Senior Chief!" Fuller yelled back.

Chapter Forty-Two

The death of four students at Kent State University in Ohio that year had shaken the country to its roots. I was glad Dale had graduated that year and was now teaching first graders in a small elementary school in San Francisco. I was never happy with Berkeley as a university; too many Goddamn long haired, pot-smoking commies.

Roy had come home in September and immediately started classes at the University of California at San Diego. That college was more suited to his studies and had a few less radical assholes than Berkeley I thought.

Dory and John were sitting back enjoying their together-again family, and Barb and I were looking at houses.

"This one Jake," Barb said, looking through the list the realtor had given us. "It has two bedrooms, one and a half baths, and look at the kitchen and living room!"

Barb had taken the fact that Charlie and Akima had backed out of the wedding at the last minute in her stride. In fact, she'd never mentioned it since we'd had to quickly ask John and Dory to fill in. Now she was anxious to invite them over for Christmas once we had our new house.

"You know it wasn't their fault darlin'," she said, still flipping through the list. "I can understand how they must have felt when the baby got sick."

"Yeah, Charlie was really sorry the last time I talked to him on the phone," I said, thinking back over old times with Charlie. Now that they were coming this Christmas, it would be great to see him again.

"Remember when you and Charlie came up from Pendelton that time and he and Akima fell in love on the spot?" Barb said, stopping on one particular page of the listings. "This one Jake! Let's go look at this one!"

"Okay!" I said.

I'd be glad when this house hunting was over. I'd be happy with anything that didn't have a leaky roof, and had a porch were I could sit and watch the sunsets.

"This is it," the realtor said. He was a skinny middle-aged man with long sideburns and a moustache. "Look at that view across the Bay, and you can just glimpse the south end of the Golden Gate Bridge from this corner of the porch," he added, striding over to the corner and flinging his arms wide encompassing the view.

"We'll take it!" I laughed. "You check out the rest of the house honey. I'm satisfied," I said, sitting down on the porch swing and sighing.

We busted our butts for a week but we got moved from Barb's old apartment, where she'd lived for ten years, into our new home. Barb and I would have to commute across the Bay every morning, but the trip on the ferry was a pleasant one, and we could catch up on the local gossip while relaxing over our morning coffee.

"Oh, Akima!" Barb exclaimed, taking the small boy from Akima's arms at the airport. "He's just gorgeous!" The two women were cooing and coring over the child.

"Hiya Jake!" Charlie said, gripping my hand in the vice that was his giant mitt. "It's good to see you!"

"You look great Charlie," I smiled, blinking to hold back the tears of pain I felt from my crushed hand. Charlie had put on about fifty pounds and didn't look all that good really. I was just being diplomatic.

"I'm still upset we couldn't make the wedding," Charlie said apologetically. "These things happen; we just thank the good Lord Otis got over his illness."

"This is going to be a better visit," I said. "Dory and John have made the biggest Christmas dinner yet and Barb just reminded me that's where you two guys met."

"Oh, that's right Charlie," Akima said, laughing. "It is, isn't it!"

"Let's get you guys home and settled, then we can all go on over to Dory's," Barb said, holding tightly to Otis. Akima would have a hard time getting him back when they left to go home to Tennessee.

"I can't believe it!" Dory said excitedly. She threw her arms around Akima and then kissed and hugged Charlie, "Merry…Merry Christmas!"

For once John was at the door to greet everyone and not in the kitchen. He kissed Akima on the cheek and shook Charlie's hand, quickly releasing it before Charlie could get a good grip.

"Merry Christmas! And to you too Jake," he added, as he peered over Charlie's huge shoulders at me.

"Merry Christmas!" Dale and Roy chimed in; they were standing farther back in the hall.

I'd never seen so many happy people; it was good to see Charlie again. I only now realized just how much I'd missed the big lug.

The dinner was excellent, Charlie ate enough for two and John was beaming with all the compliments he was receiving.

"I tell you John," Charlie said, "you could open a restaurant in Memphis and they'd have to beat people off with sticks! Mmmmm!"

"Don't give him ideas now Charlie," Dory said, clearing away the dishes.

"To tell you the truth," John said, getting up to help, "I've been running over some figures and I may just try that one of these days."

We all laughed as Dory gave him a playful kick in the butt. "Get in the kitchen and start the dishes Monsieur Le Chef!" she added.

The evening passed all too quickly, and Charlie and Akima's entire visit went by in a flash. The week was over before it had begun.

"Listen Jake," Charlie said, "I could use you in Memphis; you'd be skippering your own tugboat."

"I appreciate it Charlie," I replied, relaxing over dessert the night before they were to leave. "With the new house, though, and the opportunities with the Harbor Board; they're looking for ferry captains all the time. I'll probably wrap it up in a couple years and stay put. Barb likes the place and so do I."

"Anyway," Charlie added, "any time Jake, any time."

"Thanks Charlie," I said, feeling a deep attachment for this man.

"We have to get on!" Akima was taking Otis from Barb's clutch, and trying to pry Charlie and me loose from each other's arms, all the time trying to juggle the bags she needed to take on board with her.

"Bye Charlie," I said, "take care of yourself and look out for Otis. He's going to be a handful in a year or two."

"Goodbye Jake," Charlie said, letting his tears flow.

"Come on you big sentimental slob," Akima said, pushing Charlie down the ramp. "Bye you two, thanks for a wonderful time!" she called back as she herded the big lug onto the plane.

"Bye," Barb said, almost whispering, "I'll miss you guys!"

The trip home from the airport was silent, neither Barb nor me saying anything, both lost in our own thoughts. Tomorrow I had to get back to the base and do some work. Barb had used up her Christmas vacation with the Sparkes' visit, so tomorrow morning we'd be on the ferry together enjoying the usual San Francisco Bay fog.

"Jake!" Bilts called out one morning. "Come in a moment will you?"

"Yes, Commander?" I asked, going into his office, "Anything wrong?"

"On the contrary Jake," he began, "you've just been promoted to Master Chief. Congratulations!"

"Well…I'll be darned!" I didn't say damn out of consideration for Bilts' deep religious beliefs.

"It looks like they may be planning on giving you early retirement," Bilts continued. "I heard through back channels I'll make Captain next year; that'll be just before my retirement."

"I'd always planned on doing my thirty years, Sir," I said, puzzling over his words.

"They'll probably give you the option next year of going after twenty-eight," Bilts grinned. "Leave you in grade a year, that way you won't lose any benefits. I think we've both done our duty Jake." Bilts nodded his head up and down and added, "I've asked Betty to marry me. She said yes, by the way. We'll retire to Florida, enjoy the good life."

"Congratulations on your wedding plans," I said. "To tell you the truth, I haven't thought about my own retirement though."

My head was spinning. "I wasn't going to think about it until my anniversary in November 1974."

"My advice would be to start thinking about November 1972," he smiled. "Barb is going to be overjoyed; now you can do some traveling together. You'll have over a year to get used to the idea."

"I need time to absorb all this," I said. "Master Chief, and now looking down the barrel of retirement all in one morning, wow!"

"Take the day off Jake." Bilts came around his desk and shook my hand, "Congratulations on your promotion. What about having dinner with Betty and I one night next week?"

"Yes, fine…thank you, Commander," I accepted Bilts' congratulations and invitation to dinner.

"Congratulations Senior…I mean Master Chief!" Fuller said, also grinning. "I'll get your rank patches for you if you like."

"Yeah, thanks Fuller," I said. "Oh, and will you pull my sheet and see what awards I'm entitled to? Then get me a brand new set of ribbons!"

"Aye, aye Master Chief." Fuller went straight to his filing cabinet.

I put my hat and coat on and strolled down to watch the boat traffic on the Bay, and to try and clear my head.

I knew Barb would be delighted; she had been talking of quitting her job lately. We didn't need for her to work; it was just something to occupy her time while I was away all day. Now with the new house she wanted the free time to fix things up the way she wanted them.

"Jake, that's wonderful!" Barb yipped when I gave her the news about my promotion.

"I'll call Dory and John, we'll go out somewhere and celebrate!"

"Commander Bilts also mentioned I'd probably get the option to retire next year," I added.

"What! That's even better," Barb said, now really excited. "Maybe you should think about Charlie's offer of that tug job."

"I thought you liked it here," I questioned her. "I was thinking more along the lines of a Sausalito ferry captain."

"That'll work," Barb cried, putting her arms around me. "Whatever you want, you know that's fine with me baby."

"Mmmmmmmmmm…maybe we better stay home and celebrate?" I said, feeling the stirring in my belly.

"I said," Barb moaned, her voice husky, "whatever you want is fine with me baby…"

I wore my blues with the bullion Master Chief patch sewn on, plus the new set of ribbons Fuller had gotten for me. Barb had fussed over my jacket and fiddled with my tie that morning, I knew how proud she was of me and I knew how much I loved her.

"Hey Fuller!" I called out when I'd hung up my hat and sat down at my desk.

"Yeah, Master Chief?" Fuller replied, poking his head in the door.

"I notice a second Navy Commendation on this bar," I said, pointing at the ribbon. "I didn't know about it, what did the citation say?"

"I remember that one," Fuller said. "Some covert operation behind enemy lines in North Vietnam…classified…that's all it said."

"Damn Ding!" I said aloud.

"Pardon, Master Chief?" Fuller said, looking at me in surprise.

"Nothing Fuller, carry on," I said.

So Ding had recommended decorations for that extraction job upriver. His precious Gook colonel must have been valuable. A Navy Commendation for me; I hope he didn't forget Bullet-head, Ocha, Randolph and Williams while he was at it.

The rest of that year proved to be as routine as the Navy could make it. Ships came and went, the peace talks in Paris were on again, off again; old shipmates passed through. Even Gus made his visits, although less frequently these days. He seemed to have a couple of lady friends hanging around and paid less attention to me.

The summer was hot and the fall was smoggy. I was looking forward to the end of the year and some extra time at home with Barb. She had me working every day off on a complete re-paint job inside and out.

"Master Chief Rickmeyer!" I said, answering my ringing telephone.

"Hello Jake, Tom here!" Tom Schumacher's voice was easily recognizable.

"Hi Tom," I said, "Where are you?"

"Just berthed," Tom answered, "the *MacGilray* is on her way out to Vietnam. We're here for a few days, the usual supply, fuel and personnel requirements."

"I can't believe it!" I said, happy to hear Tom's voice. "Can you get away? Barb will be delighted to see ya."

"Yeah, not much for me to do," Tom answered. "I'll stay over with you guys if you like. I'm really only a passenger on the trip down. I'll be transferred to an LHA when we join up with the Task Force down there."

"I'll come get ya," I said. "Where are you berthed?"

"The old carrier pier number-3," Tom answered. "We're outboard of a second destroyer, the *USS Pepperdine*.

"How about 1600?" I asked. "Meantime I'll call Barb and tell her to get the spare bedroom ready."

"I'll be ready with a change of underwear," Tom laughed. "See you at 1600."

"Tom," Barb said, hugging Tom as we got out of the car. "It is so good to see you! You look really well."

"Seeing you has lifted me up," Tom said, kissing Barb on the cheek. "I've been saving this bottle of French wine ever since Cannes."

"You were in Cannes?" Barb laughed, taking the bottle. "Let's chill it and have it with supper!"

"Here's your room Tom," I said, showing him into the spare bedroom. "You won't have to use the couch this time; the bathroom's over there if you want to clean up."

Barb had put on a prime rib as soon as I'd told her I was bringing Tom home. The dinner was delicious and we all sat back in the living room after the meal, hardly able to move. Tom's French wine had added that little something extra to the occasion, now the coffee we were drinking set the mood for some good conversation.

"What was the French Riviera like Tom?" Barb asked, fascinated with Tom's visit to Cannes. "Did you see any of those topless French starlets?"

"To tell you truth, I wasn't impressed at all," Tom replied, starting to fill his pipe from his tobacco pouch. "The only thing I liked about it was the wine. I had three bottles but drank the other two!" he added, grinning.

"What's with the transfer onto an LHA when you get to 'Nam?" I asked Tom.

"What's this 'Nam business?" Barb asked, suddenly looking across at me.

"I didn't tell you, honey, but Tom's on his way to Vietnam," I said, getting up to re-fill the coffees.

"No, you didn't tell me," Barb said, looking concerned. "Will you be all right Tom?"

"Oh yeah, I'll be on the flagship," Tom said. "I'll be lifted with the Christmas turkeys when they join up with the *Medford*."

"The *USS Medford*?" I said, remembering her visit. "I know a couple of hands aboard her, old friends; they were at our wedding."

"Oh, not your friend Bullet-brain?" Barb laughed. "He was such a character!"

"Bullet-head!" I said, correcting Barb. "And another Chief on board who will claim he's a friend of mine. But let's just say he's a long-time acquaintance and leave it at that."

"The *Medford* is flagship to the Task Force Vice Admiral Rooks is commanding," Tom said, lighting off his pipe and filling the room with a sweet, rich aroma.

"Sully Rooks!" I said, shaking my head. "He's back down there? And a Vice Admiral now eh?"

"Yeah, the old gang from the *Oak Island*," Tom said, puffing away. "The *Medford* has all the latest telecommunications equipment on board. I guess they're worried the North Vietnamese will push south across the 17th parallel and bust through the DMZ."

"I thought the pullout was proceeding on schedule and two-thirds of our troops would be out by the end of next year," I said.

"Let's face it Jake," Tom replied, looking thoughtfully into the bowl of his pipe, "the Gooks will take the South the moment we're out of there. This is just a Goddamn joke about the South Vietnamese Army taking care of themselves. That's why we had to go in there in the first Goddamn place!"

"Let's change the subject," Barb interrupted. "Tomorrow I'm taking you in to San Francisco, Tom, and you can help me pick out the new curtain material for the bedrooms."

"I'll not be much use to you, but I'll keep you company!" Tom laughed.

Tom and Barb spent the next four days shopping and just relaxing around the house. I took off early every day and we went out to dinner a couple of times. It was just good to take some time off and talk about everything from turtles to turnips.

The day Tom left, Barb came down to see him off. Together we delivered a happier, fatter sailor to the *MacGilray*. Tom claimed he had put on five pounds in the four days he was with us.

"Goodbye Tom," Barb sobbed, her eyes tearing up, "I'll miss you!" She hugged Tom tightly for a full minute, and then kissed him on the cheek.

"Goodbye Barb," Tom said, gently putting his arm around her. "You always make me feel part of the family when I'm here."

"Take it easy Jake!" he said to me grabbing my hand in both of his. "I'll take a month the next time I come through and we'll go try out the wines in the Napa Valley vineyards."

"It's a date!" I replied. "Oh, I almost forgot, there's a young Boatswain on the *Medford*, name of Ocha. Look him up and say I said hello will ya?" I added.

Tom walked across the gangway and within five minutes the *MacGilray* was slipping her lines. We had crossed over on the inboard ship and she was now preparing to follow the *MacGilray* out. We quickly crossed back over and hurried down the gangway to the pier.

We watched Tom's ship nose out and start to pick up speed and the *Pepperdine* soon followed her. The two destroyers and an all-purpose supply vessel were sailing together as far as the Philippines.

"I'm glad I'm not standing here waving goodbye to you any more Jake," Barb was reflective. "I've said my last goodbye to you!"

Chapter Forty-Three

It had been bitterly cold all November and on through December. January was crisp and clear with some of the chill of the previous months missing. It was just such a crisp, but sunny day that Commander Bilts called me into his office.

"Jake," Bilts said, looking at me as I came through the door, "I believe you know Mr. Carlos Campssini."

"I'll be darned…Ding…how are ya?" I said, disbelieving what I was seeing. Ding rose from his chair and took my outstretched hand.

"I'm fine Jake, good to see you!" Ding replied, looking more like the CIA agent I knew him to be. He was dressed in a blue suit, button-down white shirt, and a conservative tie.

"What brings you to this neck of the woods?" I asked, thinking Ding was just passing through.

"I came to see you Jake," Ding said, looking serious. "Would you excuse us Commander?" he said, turning towards Bilts.

"Err…yes…certainly," Bilts stammered, looking unsure of himself. Being asked to leave his own office came as a surprise to him. He got up looking slightly embarrassed and left, closing the door behind him.

"Jake," Ding began, "I need you to do a job for me. It's classified and until you agree to do it, I won't be able to give you too many specifics. I will tell you up front it involves another asset extraction from a North Vietnamese river."

"A river trip, there must be a hundred good boat drivers down there you can use!" I said.

"There is," Ding replied quickly, "but there's only one who has the complete confidence and trust of Vice Admiral Rooks, Senator Ed Morrow, and myself."

"That's very flattering, but I'm shore-bound now and looking at a short time to retirement. Narr…get someone else," I said, not wanting to go back down there again.

"I know you've put in your time Jake," Ding said, persisting, "but there are two other reasons apart from those I've already given you. True, there are others who we could trust and are competent to do the job. But you're the only one who has made an extraction from this particular river before." Ding paused, "And you're the only one who knows the asset personally."

"Personally!" I exclaimed. "I don't know any North Vietnamese CIA assets personally!"

"Yes you do," Ding continued. "That's all I can tell you until you're in. If you agree, I'll give you a complete briefing on the plane trip over."

"I promised my wife I was done with Vietnam," I said, knowing Barb would go nuts, plus I wasn't all that thrilled about this deal myself. This CIA bullshit always gave me the creeps. "Can you give me any more details?" I asked.

"It's very sensitive. With the peace talks going on, we don't want to give the North any reason to poke fingers at us," Ding said, running his hand over his hair as if straightening imaginary tuffs. "I can tell you it will only take three weeks of your time, and after that we'll fly you home and you can take your promotion and retire."

"Promotion?" I questioned. "I've already gotten it!"

"That one sure," Ding always knew every detail of your life. "I'm talking about promotion to Master Chief of the Navy, the highest rank you can obtain as an enlisted man Jake."

"Three weeks, extraction upriver, specifics to follow, fat promotion at the end of it," I groaned, glancing up at the ceiling. "I'm tempted, but I'll never get Barb to agree to it."

"Your country needs you Jake," Ding said, walking over to the window and looking out. "You're the only one who can do this Jake. If we don't send in a man who's personally known to the asset, we'll lose him. There are still Marines in Quang Tri Province and they'll take the main blow if the North cross the DMZ."

"I'm a little rusty on the boats these days," I interjected.

"We have reason to believe there may be a push coming within the next three months," Ding continued, not listening to me. "This asset can give us details of it, and perhaps other valuable information about the North Vietnamese Army's plans; hundreds, perhaps thousands of American lives could be at stake."

"You really are pressuring me Ding," I said, torn between agreeing to go, and getting up and running out of the room.

"I've already told you more than I should have," Ding said, walking back to his chair. I noticed he limped slightly; that broken ankle must have been worse than I thought.

"How long before I need to give you my answer?" I asked, being pulled into the net, but I couldn't help myself. It would gnaw at me for the rest of my life if I thought I'd not done my part, especially if it could have saved lives.

"Come into work tomorrow as usual," Ding said, looking intently at me. "Be standing outside the main entrance at 1015. Transportation will take you to the aircraft."

"What do I tell my wife?" I was already on the plane and I knew it, so did Ding.

"I'd prefer it if you told her nothing," Ding said, turning in his chair. "Tell her you're going to Pearl for three weeks to assist the Admiral with a fleet inspection. I'll have those orders cut and in Bilts' hands this afternoon."

"Anything else?" I asked, annoyed at how Ding had manipulated me so easily.

"Nothing Jake," Ding answered. "Pack a bag as if you were going on a three-week trip. You won't need anything really; everything you require will be supplied."

"I hate to lie to Barb," I said, only half-trying to change Ding's mind. It would be easier on me to stick to the Pearl Harbor story; maybe it was kinder than telling her the truth.

"The less she knows the better," Ding replied. "Deniability is the keyword. If she doesn't know anything, it's better for all concerned."

Chapter Forty-Four

The plane had no markings, just painted a dull gray color. I had been outside the door at 1015 just like Ding knew I'd be. Bilts had cracked a joke about three weeks in Hawaii in January and who did I know to get selected for that kind of soft duty. Fuller even added that a yeoman would probably be a good thing to have along on the trip. I'd just smiled and pretended to enjoy the ribbing.

I'd been seated in the second row of eight rows of spacious seats with lots of leg room. The plane looked like a Boeing 707 that had been modified for the CIA's use.

The eight rows of seats only took up a small area of the plane. Beyond the seats was a door, behind which I had no doubt there were things that only God, or the Devil, should know about.

I settled back in my seat and went over my last night with Barb. I'd done what Ding had suggested and told her about the Pearl Harbor inspection assignment. She didn't say anything, but I knew she wasn't buying it.

Halfway through the night I'd woken to find her crying. "What's wrong honey?" I'd said, taking her in my arms.

"Nothing," she'd said through her tears, "Go back to sleep baby."

She seemed overly quiet when I'd left this morning. I had acted like a jerk, trying to pretend everything was honky-dory and how I was looking forward to the three weeks in Hawaii. I hated lying to Barb, but knew no good would come from telling her the truth.

I dozed after the aircraft was airborne. I hadn't seen Ding; he was back there somewhere with the secrets. It must have been a half-hour or so, then I awoke to a tap on my shoulder.

"You awake Jake?" Ding asked, sitting down in the seat beside me.

"I'm okay!" I answered, sitting up holding back a yawn. "Now I guess you tell me who we're going to grab."

"I knew that would be your first question," Ding said, looking pleased with himself. "Remember Vung Tau? Bubba Slats and his Vietnamese counterpart Tran?"

"The black marketeers, sure I do," I said, my interest aroused.

"Well, the asset we're extracting is Tran!" Ding continued, "Nguyen Tran Vin! He was a double agent, supposedly a Vietcong cell member. Once we broke up the black market ring, he escaped to the North. His credentials were perfect. He made himself invaluable to the intelligence section and was soon promoted to a high ranking position."

"All the time working for the CIA?" I said, hardly believing it. So that's how Tran had escaped the net, the net that'd closed so tightly around poor old Bubba and the others.

"Now you know why you were the only one we could send in to get him," Ding said, pressing the overhead button. "Like some coffee?" he continued casually. "We need to go over some details. Anything you need, I can send a coded message to the *Medford* and have it ready."

"The *Medford*!" I said, my mouth dropping open. "Are we operating off the *Medford*?"

"Yes, Vice Admiral Rooks is aboard her," Ding replied. "He's responsible overall for this operation, under our watchful eye, of course." Ding asked the arriving flight attendant for two coffees.

"It's a small world, Ding," I said. "I seen a good friend off a couple of months ago who was on his way to join the *Medford*."

"What's his name?" Ding asked, taking the coffees when they arrived.

"Schumacher, Chief Tom Schumacher," I answered, taking my cup from Ding.

"He's in communications," Ding replied. Ding had a million bits of information in his head and he could pull them out effortlessly. "The Chief is the code decipherer. He'll be busy on this operation. Washington will be second-guessing every move we make. They'll have one eye on the diplomatic shenanigans going on in Paris and one eye on us."

"Do I get to pick my own boat crew?" I asked, between sips of my scolding hot coffee.

"Jake, you get to have any damn thing you want," Ding said, smiling, "And as I remember, you don't want our up-to-date aerial photos either; you go by ripples and sailor's gut instinct!"

With that we both broke up laughing. This might be fun after all!

Da Nang looked little changed from the last time I saw it as we came in for a gentle landing. We would be overnighting on the base, and then helicopter transport from the *Medford* would pick us up in the morning and take us out to join the ship.

"The jeep will be outside at 0645 Jake," Ding said, checking us into the transit barracks. "The chopper lifts off at 0700 and we should be on board by 0930."

"I'll see you then," I said, dragging my ass to the room. I was totally beat, the jet lag had kicked in.

I went to sleep fully dressed, laid out prone on the bed. I woke up at one in the morning and lay there fully awake; jet lag was a son-of-a-bitch. Making that long haul across the Pacific with only a refueling stop on Guam could really screw you up.

I couldn't go back to sleep, so I dug my pistol and shoulder holster out of the bag. It was the only thing I'd kept as a souvenir from my two previous tours. The 45 had been with me on all the other boat trips and I considered it my good luck piece.

I carefully cleaned the gun, loaded three magazines with shells, and then placed everything beside the bed. From now on I'd keep the pistol handy at all times.

"You get breakfast?" Ding asked, climbing into the jeep beside me.

"Just some toast and coffee," I replied, throwing my bag in the back. "Damn jet lag had me hungry at all the wrong times!"

Another CIA type joined us this morning; he was dressed in Army fatigues just like Ding. These guys liked to play the part of the warrior when they were in-country.

The big Marine CH-46 Sea Knight had the rotors turning over before we had completely cleared the rear ramp. It was slam-bang down in the seat, the cargo master checked your safety harness, and we were off.

The huge chopper clattered its way out to sea, and then turned northeast by my reckoning. All of a sudden I couldn't keep my eyes open any longer and I must have sunk into a deep sleep.

I felt the chopper lose altitude and change directions sharply. I blinked my eyes several times to wake myself up and saw the deck of the *Medford* directly below us.

I'd slept the entire trip out to the ship; I'd needed it. The next couple of weeks would be demanding.

Chapter Forty-Five

The first briefing took place the afternoon we arrived. Sully and the *Medford*'s captain were present; the landing craft commander, Bullet-head who was in charge of the small boat division, also a Marine Corps colonel and a lieutenant, along with Ding and myself.

"Good afternoon, Gentlemen," Sully said, opening the meeting. "This is Mr. Carlos Campssini and Master Chief Jake Rickmeyer," he continued, nodding at Ding and me. "They have just arrived from the States and will be undertaking a mission to extract a North Vietnamese officer from enemy territory. I'll let Mr. Campssini take it from here."

"Gentlemen," Ding said, standing up and unfolding the map he'd hung up on the board. "One LCM, with Master Chief Rickmeyer in command, will go up this river," he continued, pointing out the winding line of the waterway on the map, "to a pre-arranged pickup point at this old Pagoda, and then return to the *Medford*."

There was a slight scraping of chairs, which always signaled you had gotten the attention of everyone in the room.

"Most of us in this room have done this type of thing before; it just requires careful planning and preparation," Ding droned on. "Master Chief Rickmeyer not only has been up this river, but he knows the Pagoda and area where the asset will be waiting. That, and other reasons are why we flew him out here especially for this operation."

Ding paused, looking around the room and then fixed his gaze on the boat commander. "Master Chief Rickmeyer will need your complete cooperation as to selection of boat and crew."

"He has it!" the boat commander replied immediately.

"And the Master Chief will have command over the Marine detachment that will be going along!" Ding said, looking at the Marine officers, who in turn glanced at the Admiral and got a slight nod back from Sully.

"Aye, aye," the colonel replied. He was obviously not happy about the arrangement and Ding noticed the swapped glances between the two Marines.

"This is not a seek and destroy mission," Ding's voice got louder, "so the Marines won't leave the boat except to set a defensive perimeter, in which case, command of the detachment will revert back to the Lieutenant. Your main objective, however, is to protect the LCM and its extracted asset and Master Chief Rickmeyer is in command. Is that clear?"

"Perfectly clear, Sir," the Marine colonel replied.

"Any questions?" Ding asked, folding his map and sitting down.

No one had anything to say.

"Good," Sully said, taking over again. "We have a couple of days to prepare, the Marine detachment will be briefed has to what equipment and other needs they'll have. Lieutenant Terkle, a Gunny Sergeant and an eight-man squad will go with the LCM. Master Chief Rickmeyer will organize and brief his boat crew with the complete assistance of the boat commander and anyone else he needs to get things done."

Sully looked around the room, focusing on each person just as Ding had done.

"If there are no questions at this time, we will start getting the details attended to," Sully said, wrapping up the meeting. "We'll be notified when the asset is in place and we have a green light to go. That is all for the moment Gentlemen. Anything I can help with, my door is open at all times."

We all rose to leave.

"Just a minute Jake!" Sully said. "How are you?" he asked, taking my hand.

"I'm fine, Admiral. I didn't think I'd be seeing you down here again," I said, grinning. It was always nice of Sully to take the time to say hello.

"Sorry to pull you in on this," Sully said, apologetically. "I'm sure Carlos explained why it was we needed you."

"He did, Sir," I replied, standing a little straighter, "and I'm proud to have been asked."

"I knew I could count on you Jake," Sully said, slapping me on the back. "By the way, this is Captain Bakeworth; he's commanding the *Medford*."

"Glad to meet you, Sir," I said, shaking hands with the Captain.

"I've heard a lot about you from the Admiral, Master Chief," Bakeworth said. "If I can help in any way let me know."

"Thank you Captain," I said, releasing his hand.

"Now, if you'll excuse us Jake," Sully said, clearing his throat, "we best get on with this!"

"Aye, aye Admiral," I said, standing smartly to attention for a brief moment, and then I left the room hell-bent on catching up to Bullet-head.

"Wait up Bullet-head!" I called as I spotted him disappearing down a hatch.

"Hi ya Jake!" Bullet-head said, his voice gruff and strained. "I saw ya talkin' to the fuckin' brass, so figured I'd catch up when ya finished fuckin' brown nosin'!"

"Fuck you!" I laughed, "How have ya been?"

"Fuckin' good Jake," Bullet-head replied, grabbing my hand. "How's that fuckin' nice lookin' broad of yours?"

"Barb is great!" I said. I couldn't help liking this guy, despite his foul-mouthed, irreverent character. "Will you volunteer to make the trip upriver with me?" I asked.

"I would in a fuckin' minute Jake, you know that," he replied, "but I got a young motor-mac that fuckin' builds diesel engines."

"He's got to be good!" I said.

"He is," Bullet-head said, responding with enthusiasm. "Lud Pizzer is his name, we call him Pissy for short."

"Can we get together with him tomorrow?" I said, suddenly feeling the jet lag kick back in. "There are a couple of modifications I'll need to make to the boat."

"Ya got it Jake ol' buddy," Bullet-head said, smiling and wiping his face with that ever-present oil rag of his. "The Boat Commander and I will be in the deck well first thing in the fuckin' mornin'."

"See ya then," I said, leaving Bullet-head and making my way to "Officer's Country." I had been given the use of an officer's cabin to use during my stay aboard. I guess there were perks to being the man-of-the-moment on board ship.

There was a message from the switchboard waiting for me; it was from Tom wanting to get together. I left a reply for him to meet me for supper in the Chief's mess that evening. I took my sweaty shirt and pants off after struggling out of my shoes; and I was asleep before my head hit the pillow.

"Jake!" a voice said. It was Tom. I'd been sitting in a lounge chair with my nose stuck in the Navy News.

"Tom!" I yelled, leaping to my feet, "Good to see ya. I bet you never thought we'd be sailin' together again in the South China Sea?"

"Not in my wildest dreams," he replied, a grin from ear to ear. "I knew you were coming, though, and the circumstances concerning your visit."

"Of course," I said, laughing, "everything goes through your hands to be decoded right?"

"Most of the classified stuff, yes!" Tom said, digging out his pipe and blowing through the stem.

"Ya want to eat first?" I asked. "I'm starving, and then we can catch up on how life's been treating you."

"Okay, let's eat first. The chow on this scow is excellent," Tom said, sticking his pipe back in his top pocket. "How's Barb doing? She get the curtains hung all right?"

The next morning I was up early, showered, shaved, and had eaten a half-dozen-egg omelet. I was in the well deck looking around when Bullet-head arrived with the Boat Commander.

"Good morning Master Chief," the Boat Commander greeted me.

"Morning, Sir," I smiled. "How are you Chief?" I added, grinning at Bullet-head, who looked like he'd slept in the bilge all night.

"My usual fuckin' bright self," he responded, his voice rasping. "Pissy will be along in a minute and we can get fuckin' started…here he is now," Bullet-head added, looking up at the approach of a nice-looking young man.

Lud Pizzy was in his early twenties with the knowledge of a mechanical engineer, which is what he was planning to be when he got out of the service and went back to school.

"What I need, Pissy, is an extra fuel tank welded down on the deck, with internal piping going directly to the engines' fuel supply," I explained. "Carrying extra fuel on deck in oil drums is too damn dangerous; then we need to test run everything twice."

"I know exactly what you want," Pissy said, scratching his ear. "The LCM has a good range, but being caught short of a gallon of gas upriver wouldn't be too smart." I'd told Pissy about me going upriver, but not about what we were going to do up there.

"I'll leave you to it," I said, knowing Bullet-head was right about Pissy; he was the man for the job. Now I had to get hold of Ocha, talk him into going with me, and sign up another deckape.

I had Ocha summoned over the P.A. to report to my cabin, I wanted somewhere I could explain the mission to him in private. Within ten minutes there was a knock on my door.

"Enter!" I yelled. The door opened and there stood Ocha, looking older, but just as serious as I'd remembered him. "Come in Ocha, how are ya?"

"Good, Master Chief," he said, standing with his cap in hand.

"I won't beat around the bush," I began. "We have another extraction mission. Matter of fact, it's to the same spot we went before." I felt Ocha was responsible enough to give most of the details to, even before he'd signed on. "Would you go with me? It's strictly voluntary."

"I'd be glad to," he said, raising his eyebrows. "It's been a little dull around here lately."

"Good! It will be as deck crew; I'll be driving myself," I said, making that clear. Ocha was now a Boatswain's Mate Second and he may have gotten the wrong idea why I'd asked him. "I need one more man. You know the guys on board and you know I want the best."

"Sounds fine with me," Ocha replied. "I know just the guy; he's on my boat crew, name's "Tiny" Polanski."

"Don't tell him too much, okay?" I cautioned. "Just that it's behind the lines and may be dangerous. I want him to know that much before he volunteers for the mission."

"I understand Master Chief," he said.

"Call me Jake," I said. "We've been through enough together to drop the formalities." I continued, handing him a sheet of paper, "This is a list of gear we need from the armory. Get the Boat Commander to sign it, and then take it to Chief Gunner's Mate Dicks. Tell him it's for me."

I didn't want to have Rabbit nosing around, but he was a good Gunner's Mate and he'd make sure we got the best rifles and other gear, and anything else we needed.

"Okay Jake, I'm on it," Ocha said, smiling.

"When you draw the M-16s and ammo, and anything you think of to add to the list, report to the well deck. If I'm not there, start helping the motor-mac on the boat, his name is Lud Pizzy."

"I know Pissy, he's a nice guy. Will I bring Tiny down?" he asked, one foot out the door.

"Yeah, I'll see ya there!" I replied. Things were moving fast. I wanted the work completed on the boat and at least two test runs with the extra fuel tanks before we got the word to go.

Nothing happened for the next four days except keeping busy with preparations. Ocha had introduced me to "Tiny" Polanski, who stood 6 feet 5 inches and weighed close to 300 lbs. He was a good choice and dug in to help wherever I asked.

The young Marine lieutenant and his gunnery sergeant came down every day trying to be useful. I knew Lieutenant Terkle was nervous, and his Gunny was not as old and wise as I'd hoped. He too was young and apprehensive about the mission. The Captain had given his permission for us to test run the boat, so I invited the Marines along to get a feel for the LCM and the way I would handle it.

The LHA slowed and lowered her stern gates and we were out in a dress rehearsal for the actual night. When the time came the *Medford* would slow, but not stop completely, to launch us.

I ran the boat at about half-speed until we were well clear of the larger ship, then I opened her up. The engine sounded like a purring tiger, pulsating with perfect timing; damn that Pissy was good!

Both Ocha and Tiny were first class hands to have on a boat; "knew which way to coil a rope," as the saying went. Even the Marines looked like they were happy at last to be doing something. They pointed their rifles over the side and practiced loading and unloading while the LCM was plowing through the water like a sperm whale.

I had Pissy switch the spare fuel tank back and forth a half-dozen times, each time the engine never knew the difference and didn't miss a beat.

"Let's go back!" I yelled over the engine noise. "Ocha, radio the *Medford* we're done with the test run and coming home to roost!"

"Aye, aye Jake!" Ocha called back, giving a closed-fisted sign in case I hadn't heard him.

"Jake, that was a morale booster for the men," Lieutenant Terkle said, smiling after we'd got back aboard and secured.

Terkle was now calling me Jake; I liked that. And I was starting to think he wasn't the stuck-up little asshole I'd first thought. He'd be okay once we got going.

"And to be truthful, it was good for me too," he added. "I think this is a unit that's now ready for the mission."

"That's great Lieutenant," I replied, feeling satisfied with all our hard work. "Now we wait for the green light!"

It was two more days before the Boat Commander came down to the well deck where the crew and me were sitting on the gunwales chewing the fat.

"Briefing room in twenty minutes, Jake!" he said, excitedly.

"Aye, aye!" I replied, looking at the boys as I got up. "This is probably it, so get any last minute checking done now!" I ordered, starting up the ladder to the walkway.

The briefing room was buzzing with chatter as we entered. The Captain and the XO were seated at the top table; the Marine colonel, Terkle and the Gunny were off to the side; Bullet-head, the Boat Commander and I sat together at the other end. Just then Sully and Ding entered from the opposite hatchway.

"Gentlemen!" Sully said, addressing the room which had suddenly grown dead quiet. Everyone had risen when the Admiral entered.

"Please be seated," he continued. "We just got the word; the green light is on for tonight. The asset is in place and the pickup password was sent thirty minutes ago." The Admiral paused, looking around the room with a look of satisfaction on his face. "I know everyone is ready, and I'm confident this will be a complete success."

He looked at Ding, who nodded his agreement.

"Are there any questions about the extraction, about the part you have in it, or anything concerning this mission?" Sully asked. "Now is the time to ask." The room remained silent; everyone knew the details inside and out and what was expected of each of them.

"Good," Sully continued, looking at his watch. "The *Medford* will change course north; in fact, she already has!"

There was some polite laughter at the Admiral's attempt at humor.

"The ship will be off station at 2100, we'll launch the LCM and then stand off to avoid discovery. The password for a successful extraction is "The egg's in the nest", and when you clear the river the message is "Pick up the chick". Apart from those two signals, you are to maintain complete radio silence."

The Admiral paused for all that to sink in, then added, "That is all Gentlemen, let's get on with it." He concluded, looking at me directly, "Good luck, Jake, and to your crew." Then glancing at the Lieutenant, "Good luck to you and your squad Lieutenant. I'm sure you're anxious to get saddled up!"

"Aye, Admiral," Terkle said proudly. "We're ready!"

The meeting broke up and I returned to the well deck and told everybody to go and get as much rest as they could, and then to get a good hot meal and to standby at 2030. There was no use having people stand around for hours getting uptight if they didn't need to. I left Bullet-head to take care of the fueling and stowing of all the gear; 2100 would come around soon enough.

Everybody was accounted for. The Marines were loaded down with enough firepower for a battalion and the boat crew looked rested, although they looked odd in their helmets with M-16s strapped across their shoulders. I looked at the watch I'd just synchronized with Terkle; it was 2055. The ship shuddered slightly as power was taken off her engines and the stern gate made a clanging noise as it was lowering. "Fuck!" I thought out loud, "we'll wake up the whole countryside."

The LCM slipped out into the darkness. There would be a quarter moon later that night; once we got in the river it should provide us with just enough light to see the features on the banks.

"Ocha!" I half-whispered.

"Yeah, Jake?" Ocha replied, coming back to the wheelhouse.

"Pass the word, everyone check their weapons and lock and load, then absolute silence after that," I ordered in a low voice. "Tell the Marines if I as much as hear a fart from them, they'll be dumped over the side!"

"Aye, aye Jake," Ocha nodded, "I'll pass the word!"

The river was as narrow as I'd remembered it. We had no problem with sandbars as we ran upstream; they shimmered like silver ribbons wherever they broke the surface and the ripples made by the submerged ones were easy to spot to the trained eye.

I bobbed and weaved and made good time to where I thought the old temple ruins were. As soon as Ocha saw it he was to give a long whistle, the same signal we'd used before.

Finally Ocha gave the signal with a low whistle. I slowed the boat around the bend and drifted, gently nudging the boat against the old stone wharf.

I could just see the shadowy figure of Ocha as he leapt off the boat with the bowline and held us fast. I checked over my shoulder and saw Tiny standing by with the stern line loosely thrown over a crumbling stone bollard.

I expected Tran to appear and we'd be on our way. He surely had been told we'd be there and would be waiting for us, ready to go.

I checked my watch; it was two minutes to midnight. We could remain for two hours, but 0200 was the deadline for heading back. The idling boat made a popping noise as we sat waiting. I didn't like this.

"Terkle!" I said, keeping my voice down as much as I could.

"What's up Jake?" Terkle said, whispering as he came back aft.

"I don't like this," I said, squinting into the shadows thrown around by the ruins. "Can you send two men ashore and have them check out the temple?"

"I'll go myself," he replied.

"No!" I quickly ordered. "Send the Gunny and another man; you'll be needed here if we get into trouble!"

"All right Jake," Terkle said, starting back. "How long should they search?"

"Just one thorough pass through the area, then we'll back off and wait under the trees!" I whispered after him.

I watched the two dark figures climb onto the wharf and make a crouching run into the ruins. We waited another five minutes, each minute an eternity. I was getting jumpy and I could sense the tension building in the boat.

Suddenly a football sized object arced over from the direction of the temple and landed with a thud in the well deck.

"Jesus!" a Marine screamed, "It's Gunny's head!"

Yellow bursts from gun muzzles opened up immediately from the ruins; the Marines in a reflective action returned fire, opening up with everything they had.

"Slip the lines! Slip the lines!" I yelled, screaming at Ocha and Tiny.

I gunned the engine and started reversing away from the wharf. The Marines kept up their return fire, and they ran to the other side of the boat as I swung the craft around to head downriver.

One stupid asshole kept his finger on the trigger of his M-16, and as the boat swung around he raked the bow section with automatic fire. I saw Ocha slam against the ramp with the force of the burst.

"Fuck!" I yelled at the top of my voice. "Tiny get forward, Ocha's been hit!"

Tiny jumped into the well and was at Ocha side in three steps. Then as I straightened the wheel and pushed the throttle to the maximum, I heard the mortars.

"Wump! Wump!" at this close range they could practically throw the projectiles. Two bursts blew geysers of water in the air close astern and then I felt the steering go. I fought desperately to gain control; we were headed at top speed towards the opposite side of the river. We hit the bank with a grinding thud, driving the bow up on the muddy shore and into the trees.

"Get off!" I ordered over the gunfire. "They'll blow us to pieces here!"

There was a mad scramble to clear the boat as another barrage of mortar rounds hit, one of them right in the center of the well deck.

The LCM lifted out of the water for a brief moment, then crashed back, the bow section sticking on the bank and the stern section rolling over and sinking.

I was flung into the water and swam to shore, yelling out to anyone who might still be alive as I crawled up the muddy bank. All around me I saw pieces of cloth, metal, smoking debris; it was now strangely quiet.

"Over here Jake," it was Tiny. I made my way to the sound of his voice and found him lying under a tree with Ocha's lifeless body in his arms.

"Jesus! No!" I cried. "Where's Pissy?" I was looking desperately around for anyone else alive.

Tiny nodded towards the bow section.

"Not Pissy too!" I moaned. I knew he was dead the moment I crawled over the ramp and saw him. I also saw two other bodies hanging half in the water from the torn mid-section.

"Lieutenant Terkle, you anywhere?" I shouted, crawling back over to Tiny.

"Here, here," someone cried out from farther down the bank.

Working my way over the tree roots towards the voice, I saw Terkle struggling to get to shore. He was dragging another Marine with him. I helped them both up onto the bank and pointed out Tiny under the tree.

"We'll meet there…I heard someone down this way…I'll go after him and bring him back to the tree. Stay there!" I ordered.

I passed another dead Marine along the way, or what was left of him.

The voice I'd heard had come from a kid who looked fourteen. He had Tab Hunter good looks with short, blond hair, and he was badly wounded; he still had the radio strapped to his back and I hoped it was working.

"Can you walk or crawl?" I asked him, unhooking the straps of the radio.

"No, my legs were chewed up pretty bad," he said, his arms swinging widely to emphasize his words. Then he suddenly went silent, slumped back, and was dead!

I struggled with the radio trying to get an open channel. It didn't make any difference about the radio silence; the Gooks knew we were here now.

"Navy ship...Navy ship...this is Jake...we are down...we are down....need immediate assistance!" I sent the message in plain language and hoped any ship or aircraft hearing us would get the word out.

I listened for a few minutes, then made my way back to the tree. Tiny was still nursing Ocha's dead body. Terkle was trying to wrap a bandage around the other Marine's chest and a third man had made his way out of the water. He was lying on his back, trying to catch his breath.

"I can confirm two of your people dead down the bank, with the two on the boat that's six, counting the Gunny and the other Marine who went ashore at the temple," I said, trying to catch my breath.

"Burns here said his buddy didn't make it to shore, so that makes seven Marines KIA," Terkle said, tears running down his face.

"With Ocha and Pissy gone, that makes only the five of us left," I said, looking at Tiny. "Ocha's dead, Tiny; put him down. I want you to gather up everything you can find for defense; rifles, pistols, knives, anything. Bring everything back here."

"Lieutenant, I need you to look for any C-rations, water containers, anything we can use. They know they got us; they'll probably wait until dawn to come across," I said, propping the radio against the tree.

"Okay Jake," Terkle replied.

"Whatever your name is, Burns is it?" I asked the Marine lying on the ground. "Go out about fifty meters and make a wide circling reconnoiter. See if you can see anything."

"Aye, Master Chief," he managed to croak out. He lifted himself up and checked the M-16 he'd managed to hang onto, and then disappeared into the night. Tiny had put Ocha's body down and was picking through the bow section of the boat. He was behaving like a zombie; his actions were slow and machine-like. I knew he was in deep shock, but there was nothing I could do about that now. Damn Tran! That motherfucker would get us all killed.

I tried the radio again, "Navy ship...any Navy ship...this is Jake with extraction mission...we are down...we need immediate assistance...enemy has us boxed in…any Navy ship!" I don't know why I just didn't broadcast the *Medford*'s name. I guess I was still trying to maintain some kind of secrecy for the mission. I knew if my name was mentioned, the *Medford* would know where the message was coming from.

"This is all I could find," Terkle said, coming back with some water bottles; he had scoured the bank in both directions. "I'll go out and see if I can make contact with Burns."

"Be careful," I said. "If they've already crossed over, they'll be waiting. I don't think they'll risk an assault until it gets light."

"Okay!" Terkle said. "I'll take that pouch of hand grenades Tiny found; I'll use them if I see anything."

He disappeared into the shadows. Terkle was a good Marine. He came through when things got hot and he took care of his men.

I looked at my watch it was 0330. They should have been here by now. What the fuck is going on?

Tiny was still searching the bow section, I could hear him grunting as he tore off pieces of broken decking. The next thing I knew there was an enormous splash and I jumped up to see Tiny swimming across to the other side.

"Here I am you motherfuckers! You hear me…you motherfuckers?" Tiny had stopped halfway across and was yelling out. "Come get me, you motherfucking assholes!" he shouted, starting to swim again.

"Tiny!" I yelled. "Get back here! You hear me? Get back here!"

He kept swimming to the other side and climbed up on the stone wharf. Tiny stood there and raised his arms like some giant Greek God, "Here I am…here I am…here I am…here I am motherfuckers!" he started chanting rhythmically.

A burst of gunfire erupted from the temple area and Tiny flopped around like a broken puppet before he fell back into the water. I stared in disbelief; the gentle giant was gone.

"What the fuck happened?" Terkle asked, crawling out of the undergrowth, with Burns right behind him. "We heard gunfire."

"They got Tiny," I said, adding quickly, "Terkle, you face out along the upstream bank; Burns you face the downstream. I'll keep trying the radio."

"It's almost 0400, they should have picked up the first broadcast just after midnight. They must have heard us Jake!" Terkle said, settling in behind a stump and looking intently upstream.

"Either way, when we don't show up, they'll know we're in trouble," I said, knowing help must come soon. "It'll be light around 0630, we'll have to make a decision whether to start making our way downstream before then. No point in sitting here for them to pick us off one at a time."

I tried the radio one more time; then checked my forty-five and the M-16 Tiny had found under the two dead Marines on the boat.

0515, it's too quiet…where the fuck are they? Wait, is that the muffled sound of an engine? It died away…No, there it is again.

"If that's not an LCM-8 I hear, I'll eat my shorts!" I yelled to Terkle.

"I hear it too!" Burns hollered. "Holy Mother of Christ, they heard you Master Chief!"

"Keep your head down!" I ordered, hearing the excitement in his voice.

"It's a boat all right!" Terkle agreed. "They'll see the wreckage once they come round the bend."

With a roar, a boat appeared in the pre-dawn darkness coming around the bend at high speed. It was an LCM all right; they spotted our wrecked boat and immediately started to throttle back.

I stood up to shout a warning about the Gooks on the other side in the temple, when the mortars started. They ringed the boat with a well-patterned salvo; the second salvo blew the LCM out of the water. I saw the bodies of two men flying high into the air, and then come down in the river well astern.

"Jesus H. Christ!" I said in disbelief. "Stay here, I'll go see if they're still alive."

Working my way down the bank, I saw one of the men dragging himself out onto the bank.

"What the fuck!" I yelled, not believing my eyes. "Rabbit, what are you doing here?"

"Bullet-head and me came for ya Jake…they was gonna leave ya hangin' out to dry!" Rabbit said, gasping.

"What are you talking about? That was Bullet-head with you?" I asked, looking at the other body drifting face down in the water.

"Yeah, me and Bullet-head…we…we took a boat and came for ya Jake!" he said, wincing from the pain. He was badly injured from the mortar blast.

"What are you saying Rabbit?" I said, trying to make him comfortable. I dragged him farther out of the mud and held him in my arms.

"Tom…Tom Schumacher told us…he read…he read the message…the mission was called off from Washington…" he gasped, struggling for breath. "That fucker Ed Morrow called to abort the mission…said to cover it up…" Rabbit kept talking through his pain, "Remember that asshole Ed Morrow…always playing it safe when we went ashore…remember Jake? Remember all those times…those times on the ol' *USS Roe*?"

"Take it easy Rabbit," I said, cradling his head in my arms. "The Admiral will get us out, Sully will send help!"

"Jake…ya don't get it!" Rabbit winced, doubling up with the pain in his belly. "The Admiral…the fuckin' Admiral…he was the one who ordered no rescue attempts be made!"

I couldn't believe what Rabbit was telling me, what was he talking about? Yet here he was, and that was poor Bullet-head in the water face down out there.

"I don't get it Rabbit, why?" I pleaded.

"Fuckin' politics Jake, they done sold ya out…Jesus Jake! I'm hurtin' bad!" he whimpered, crying out.

"Take it easy old friend; what the fuck did you and Bullet-head think you were doing?" I said, laughing at the irony of it all.

Gunshots suddenly erupted from the area where the others were. I could distinguish the sound of M-16s in the firefight for a while, and then all went silent. I started to hear Vietnamese voices coming through the brush. I cocked my pistol and held Rabbit tightly to me.

My fingers went numb and I couldn't hold onto the gun any more. I hadn't heard anything and I didn't feel anything.

It was getting lighter and the voices were getting closer. I could understand them now, were they speaking English? Then I recognized my Grandfather's voice among them.

"Jake, where you been all mornin'?" Grandpa said, walking towards me, "Hot diggaty, them fish been up since before dawn!"

"The worms, Grandpa, I had to get the can of worms from the barn!" I replied.

"Well come on Jake my boy, them big-uns ain't gonna wait all day!" he said, still walking towards me.

"The can of worms is heavy, Grandpa. Can you help me?" I pleaded, feeling my body going numb with the weight of the full can of worms.

"Sure Jake my boy, here give 'em to me…"

* * * * * * * * *

Dateline Saigon: 16 Americans reported missing, presumed dead. US Navy sources today reported two landing craft, with 16 Americans on board, were lost in bad weather following exercises close to the DMZ. The exercises were being carried out from amphibious ships patrolling north of the city of Hue. All contact with the craft was lost following heavy seas and high winds. Further attempts to find the missing men, or recover their remains, has been called off due to continued inclement weather.

Printed in the United States
26821LVS00003B/130

9 781588 514899